The Twin Worlds Saga
The Faded Dragon

by
Cameron Michaels

979-8-9874092-0-6
1st edition 2023 – Paperback

Published by Cameron Michaels
Book Cover by Felix Ortiz
Edited by Robin Larin

Prologue

From Eternal came Light.
From Light came existence.
From existence came Shade.
From Shade came war.
From war was reality split in two.

S UCH WERE THE Words of Beginnings. Why they had come to his mind among the swirl of voices was a mystery. Perhaps the beginning of the end reminded him of times long past, like the fragments of a parasite still clinging to its host. Or maybe it was his name. It had been so long since he could utter it. Since anyone could. At first, many feared it, but now it was practically forgotten. He only knew himself as the Keeper now, and even that was barely true. He tried brushing it all away, focusing on the task at hand.

The Keeper knew he was in Deerium, the old world of the elves. Far southward, hidden away in the Waters of the Righteous. In the dimly lit cave-like prison, he was watching something, though none could see him. He couldn't even see himself, scarcely existing in a spiritual sense. But he was there somehow, and it was time to make the first move.

The figure chained to the wall could hardly move, the experiments of the Righteous Ones finally taking their toll. This poor soul was once a dragon of the Drake, but he had fallen low too many times. The figure had lost the Great Dragon War on his world and did not share in the victory of his people when they came to Deerium. He was forsaken, and the last hope of the self-serving elvish cult.

The Keeper felt the voices from the deep cascade to him like a river once more. *The Righteous Ones have failed*, they said. *We have failed. They could not control the Devil's Flame, and their work has made us lose sight of him.* In a way, they were right. All their planning was at risk. His mind flashed back again.

The first period in Deerium was known as the Age of the Elves, pure beings that came into existence through the power of the Eternal, the Creator of the Twin Worlds. From the very oceans, the elves were formed and emerged onto the land with knowledge and abilities all but unimaginable. They were granted great magic, and through this, Deerium grew into a land of green and plenty.

Thousands of years passed underneath their rule, and slowly they began to forget where they came from. The name of their Maker was lost to legends and myths, one of the Keeper's finest achievements. None were stronger or wiser until a new species of creature appeared—the dragon. These huge beasts walked on four legs with razor-sharp claws, hardened skin, and massive wings that shot from their backs. Yet despite their animalistic features, they retained intelligence on par with the elves.

From another world separate from Deerium, simply called the Drake, they came in search of a new home. The elves feared they would lose all they had made and would not dare share it with the likes of these strange beings.

So began the great conflict that would conclude the first age. For despite all the magic the elves possessed, there was one thing the dragons had that they could simply not fight against.

From the mouths of the creatures came a fire that consumed everything it touched. However, this was unlike any fire the elves had ever seen in Deerium. It would be known as the Devil's Flame.

The war that followed was given no name. Many sought to coin titles for it, but none ever remained in the pages of history, only in the mutterings of drunken men. Shame was one of the Keeper's favorite tools, and it had worked splendidly.

After much struggle, the elves retreated into the mountains of the Claw. Unfortunately for them, living away from their natural source of magic in the green plains of Deerium and festering in the hatred of their failure cost them much. Their descendants lacked any semblance of magical abilities yet still retained intelligence. These descendants were an entirely new species of being and became known as mortals, or humans. They were weak and easily manipulated, just as they should be.

Thus began the second age: the Age of the Dragons, a reign that also lasted thousands of years, but in the world of Deerium, the dragons could not breed properly. Away from their world, their offspring lacked the intelligence of their ancestors and were nothing more than animals—they were named the Second Dragons.

In a desperate attempt to save their race, the original dragons used their magic to take on forms like that of the elves and went into the mountains to breed with those that remained.

But these offspring were neither elf nor dragon, but rather some mix of the two. These beings were called the Takahrn: elvish in body with sparing draconic features. But as they belonged with neither, they were eventually denied by both elf and dragon alike. They were the Keeper's final piece on the board. However, he had overstretched his reach.

Filled with guilt and regret, in a final and decisive battle, the dragons chose to leave Deerium forever, returning to the Drake. Having sealed themselves in their destroyed homeland, leaving their descendants behind, the dragons vanished.

The elves near extinction, the voices said. *The Takahrn bore fruit, and we lost him. They* lost him!

Peace, my children, the Keeper replied, keeping his gaze intent on the chained figure. *All is not lost. The wandering beast still roams upon Phoenix Peak, and this forsaken one will soon bend to us.*

The wandering beast cannot be controlled. And this one has been trapped in his weaker form. He cannot summon the Devil's Flame until he is free.

The Keeper smiled. *He will never summon the Devil's Flame again, not after he calls for us. But he will still accomplish what is needed. Alone, he will fall short, but we can use that. The humans will spread across Deerium. They will rebuild, and the Takahrn will not be accepted. They will be enslaved, and this one will stand over it all. He will bring the beast to his will, and his resolve shall fall to mine. Then we will ascend.*

The voices grew quiet. He knew they were contemplating his thoughts.

Footsteps could be heard down the tunnel. Six elves in white cloaks grew visible, purple Anamoris marks painted on the fronts. The chained figure on the wall raised his head with a grunt, staring at them in defiance. The Keeper watched him with glee as his mouth opened, and strange words came forth: the Calling Words. The six elves halted their stride when the sound reached their ears.

Do you see, my children? the Keeper said. *He calls us. He will be our sword. My sword.*

Chanting echoed in his mind. The voices were satisfied, and as the Calling Words were complete, the Keeper gave the figure what he desired. Dark mist swirled around the prisoner. The lights of the cave flickered and snuffed out, the snapping of chains ringing through the walls.

The Faded Dragon awakens.

Part One
For the Crown

Chapter 1

G AHLAIA LOOKED THROUGH the bars of the small opening on the steel door above her underground prison. The sky gave off a pinkish glow that slowly began to illuminate her hard, square living quarters. The sun was beginning to rise.

Gahlaia sat up, groaning. Her wings were bothering her again. They were stuck to her back by a thick chain that wrapped her chest and stomach three times over, giving them no room to breathe. She strained to scratch them before resorting to rubbing against the concrete wall.

She began to stand up and almost immediately sat back down. Her tail was cramping. It was wrapped around her left leg, strapped in place by a thin chain. It ensured that she wouldn't make any attempts at running. Gahlaia winced at the pain. There was nothing to be done but wait until it stopped.

As the feeling slowed to a crawl, she tried once more to stand, but slower this time. Her horns were inches from touching the roof as she straightened up. They had grown quite a bit since yesterday and now had pointed ends instead of the round nubs she knew so well. As she reached up to feel them, she nearly pricked her finger.

She looked up again at the sunrise and noticed the pink sky slowly change color to an unusual dark red that matched her eyes. This day was special. She knew that. This day came only once a year. It was her birthday: the Day of Great Divide.

Five hundred years old, she thought. An especially important year. It marked her transition into a full-grown Takahrn. It marked the start of her adulthood. Her horns would stop growing today, but that wasn't what excited her.

Gahlaia looked down at her hands only to be disappointed. At the ends of her fingers, her nails stuck out like talons. At first glance, they looked fully grown in, but through the rising sunlight, she still see through them like fogged-up glass. They hadn't completely hardened yet. *Patience, Gahlaia. They'll be ready by the end of the day.*

She slowly sat back down and closed her eyes, trying to rest as long as she could. There was no reason to be anxious. She'd waited this long. She could wait a little longer.

Exhaustion began to take its toll on her again.

An hour later, Gahlaia woke to the sound of metal on metal. She squinted and looked up.

A man stood above her cell, banging a steel bar on her roof. It was the owner. She had never come to know his name, and she hardly cared. "Come on, slave!" he shouted. "Everybody else has already started. Get up!"

Gahlaia stood up silently.

The man reached into his back pocket and fished out a key, which he inserted into a slot on the other side of the roof. He pulled it open like a trap door.

He stood back as she climbed out of the underground cell. It felt good to be out of the cramped metal box, and she inhaled the morning air with relief. The usual landscape lay before her. Trees were scarce, swaying as if the slightest breeze could knock them over, the dust from the ground causing her to blink as it brushed onto her face. The heat was uncomfortable but not quite unbearable today.

The Dirtlands were never pleasant to behold, but living there was cheap, and to the simple folk, that was enough. Trade with Pordika was steady, and many found that satisfactory.

Two men appeared from behind her and began to inspect the chains on her body to ensure everything remained secure. Her hands, feet, tail, and lastly her wings. It was nothing new. The same routine as every other morning. When they were satisfied, they moved away to examine the other slaves.

"What's the matter?" said the owner, still holding the metal bar in his hands. "I've come to enjoy your insults. Where's the kicking and screaming, swearing you'll leave one day? Don't tell me you're getting civil on me. Please . . ."

He moved forward and yanked on Gahlaia's blond hair as if to try and evoke a reaction. "Civility never suited your kind . . . Divider."

She flinched slightly at the sharp pain but remained silent. Normally, that phrase would get her reeling quickly, but not now. Today would be the last day she would have to put up with this. *Give me all the bruises you want, old man. After today, it won't matter.*

She gave a slight smile, but he just ignored it. He backed up a bit. "Oh, I'm sorry! I completely forgot," he continued. "Today is the Day of Great Divide, after all, and from the look of your horns, I'd say today is the day you've finally come of age among your species. If that's the case, being the daughter of the Dragon King and all, wouldn't that make you some kind of royalty?" He chuckled as the idea crossed his mind. "Well, Your Majesty, excuse me if I don't bow to your approval."

He gave an awkward sort of curtsey after speaking.

Still, Gahlaia preferred to remain silent, keeping the slight grin on her face. She could tell he was annoyed, and it pleased her a little.

He walked toward her and shoved her forward into a long row of wooden stools that the other slaves were standing on. When they came to the one that remained empty, she quietly stood upon it.

"Maybe today will be my lucky day," he said. "Perhaps I'll finally get you sold for a reasonable price."

He leaned forward, close to her ear. "But it matters little. I'd get just as much from one of those horns of yours."

Gahlaia had been with many slave traders throughout her lifetime, but she had been with this specific one for about forty years since he was a young man. Ever since she'd come here, she had done nothing but fight against her enslavement, and due to her unruly behavior, most wouldn't even place a bid on her. Those that did were quickly convinced otherwise. She would jump at them before being subdued. By now, everyone in town knew her, and her reputation kept her from being sold.

But so long as the owner could sell her regrowing horns, she gave him profit. Many medicines and concoctions for ailments were devised from Takahrn talons and horns, and it was the one reason she had not been starved. In that aspect, she counted herself lucky. For her species, horns and wings were not consistent parts to have, and her growing strength was altogether unique. Draconic traits appeared to pass to Takahrn at random, and those without were either given more labor than the rest or killed.

She looked around at the other slaves. She knew most of them well. They were all Takahrn, and many of them had been here almost as long as she had, especially the older ones. Even though none of them looked it, they were all hundreds of years old, though their specific ages varied. A few might be executed within days if they weren't sold soon.

Gahlaia doubted she was in any real danger. The owner seemed to get a sort of sick entertainment from her attempts to struggle and fight against it all. Today was probably the only time she didn't do something reckless.

One of the other slaves looked over at her. Gahlaia didn't recognize him. He appeared young at first glance, but most of them did. His tail was chained, and he had no wings or horns. His talons were long like hers but not as thick.

On his right shoulder, she noticed a mark that looked like it was part of his skin. She recognized it immediately. It was a word from the elvish tongue: old symbols, each with its own meaning. The mark on the slave's shoulder translated to the word "wind." He was imbued with Terrkoris magic. One of the few.

In ancient times, the elves would be blessed by the Eternal with a mark that would grant them the ability to use one of the two forms of magic. Terrkoris affected the physical world and Anamoris the spiritual. Terrkoris was a broad form and thus had many different marks. Any elf with access to this ability would only be able to use a small piece of it. However, Anamoris had *one* mark. A being with this form of magic could access all its power—the capacity to manipulate the very soul within themselves and other people, so long as the soul was willing. It was a rare and deadly gift to receive.

He looked down at her hands, and excitement rushed over his face. "Is today the day?" he asked in a lowered tone.

She nodded.

His excitement was quickly transformed into relief and gratitude, and he said nothing more.

Ten minutes passed before a small crowd began to surround them. Not too long after, the owner walked out in front of the row of slaves, the metal bar still in his hand.

Gahlaia looked around at the gathering people. *Excellent.* There was no one new in the crowd. Everyone had been there before, which meant her reputation preceded her. There was very little chance she would get sold today.

"Alright, it seems everyone is ready to begin," the owner shouted above the murmurings. "Let's start with this fine young lad."

THE DAY HAD passed into evening, and the crowd had completely vanished. The sun was starting to set, and the dark red sky that plagued the day turned to pink and orange.

The entire selling process had blurred in Gahlaia's head. It seemed to drag on forever. Not many were sold today. Most people had come merely to observe as if the Takahrn were some sort of exhibit, relics of the past that refused to die. Other than the low sales, much went as usual.

When the final biddings drew to a close, Gahlaia looked down at her hands again. She could tell her talons were already getting harder, but they still weren't completely done growing. *Just a little bit longer.*

All the slaves stepped off their wooden stools, and the two hired men began to go from slave to slave, inspecting the chains one last time before sending them back to their underground cells. Gahlaia made no struggle during her inspection and watched the men move to the slave she had briefly spoken to earlier.

As she began to walk to her cell, the owner stepped in front of her. "You're never sold," he said in a calm voice. "Why do you think that is?"

Gahlaia said nothing.

Without another word, he swung his metal bar, striking hard into her gut. The wind knocked clean out of her, and she went down on one knee, her lungs gasping for air.

"I asked you a question."

She looked up at him and coughed. "Bad luck, I guess," she responded.

"Or perhaps you've given them a reason to despise you."

"Many of us weren't sold today. Besides, I—"

Her sentence was cut off by a kick to the stomach. She lurched forward, holding in the urge to vomit.

"You're right," he said, raising his voice for the rest to hear. "Not enough of you were sold. I'm beginning to grow impatient."

The owner stood up and motioned to one of his men, who swiftly handed him a sword. He dropped the metal bar onto the dirt, grasped the sword with both hands, and placed the blade an inch from her left horn. She closed her eyes, preparing for the inevitable, only to be pushed back by a strong gust of wind.

The owner was immediately thrown off his feet, and his sword fell to the ground near his face. The wind suddenly changed directions, rushing straight down like lightning from the sky, and pinned him to the ground. No matter how hard he tried, he could not move. He screamed in pain, as the wind pushed down on him, putting increasing pressure on his body.

Gahlaia blinked, looking around to see what was happening. She turned to her left to see one of the slaves, knees slightly bent and arms outstretched toward the owner. It was the male she had spoken briefly with earlier in the day. The mark on his left shoulder was glowing a bright white. He spoke no words, instead keeping his focus on the task at hand.

"Shoot him!" the owner shrieked. "Shoot him now!"

Several of his men quickly drew back their bows, and arrows flew straight toward the slave from all directions. He made a quick motion with his hands, raising them upward. As he did, the wind moved from the owner, catching most of the shafts midair, flinging them away. However, he couldn't stop them all. One shot into his right shoulder blade while a second pierced his left leg. The Takahrn fell to one knee.

The owner regained his footing, grasping his sword once again, and rushed at the man.

Gahlaia tried to get up to stop him despite the pain in her stomach, but her tail, still chained to her leg, began to cramp up again. She fell back down, the ache too much for her to handle.

Within moments, the owner was upon the slave, thrusting the blade through his chest.

Time moved in slow motion in Gahlaia's head. Tears welled in her eyes as she looked into the face of the slave who had saved her from disgrace and he looked back at her. He gave a brief smile before falling to the dirt, the blade still in his chest. He was dead.

The owner wiped his forehead and leaned over the motionless body. "Truly a pity," he said, nudging the corpse with his index finger. "Given another day, I could have made a silver coin or two off this thing."

"Stay away from him!" Gahlaia screamed. "Have you no honor? Leave the dead in peace!"

The owner smirked, pulled the sword from the body, and strode toward her. "Hold her down!" he shouted to three of his guards.

The men grabbed her by the arms, bracing her back forward.

"Honor," the owner said, staring at his blade, transfixed by the bloodstains. "From what I've heard of the ancient dragon culture, not all of them were born with horns. It was considered a sign of superiority, strength, leadership . . . and honor."

The owner moved to her left side, eyes still on his sword. "To be gifted with such a symbol of power was a blessing to the bearer. Perhaps that honor transcends your ancestors and remains with your kind. If I was so unlucky to be born without such honor . . ."

His gaze moved to Gahlaia, and grasping the sword with both hands, he swung in one swift motion, cutting clean through her left horn. ". . . then perhaps I can borrow some of yours."

Her mind went black. All she could think about was the pain. She shrieked in agony and her head slumped down. It wasn't the first time her horn had been removed, but that did little to numb the sting of a blade.

The owner picked up the piece of her horn and turned away, his face returning to its bitter expression. "Get them in their cells! I don't have all night."

BACK INSIDE HER cage, Gahlaia awoke with a start. The moon beamed down upon her, serving as the only source of light in the pitch darkness of the cramped cell.

Touching the end of her severed horn, she felt no pain at all. It had already begun to heal, but it would take days before the tip would grow back. As her head started to clear, realization flooded over her. She looked down at her hands and smiled. Her talons were no longer see-through. She could feel it.

Gahlaia pressed them against the metal wall, and the steel dented under pressure. The nails, however, remained unharmed, harder than stone. *Finally.*

She put her hands to the chains that held her wings in place, and with almost no resistance, her talons cut right through. She proceeded to do the same to the shackles binding her hands and finally her tail. Gahlaia stood up and stretched her wings as far as they could go in her tight quarters. It had been so long since she was able to move them, but they still felt strong. Strong enough perhaps to finally free her.

For once, she was thankful for the slave camp she was imprisoned in. Out of all the owners she had been with, this one cared the least about keeping the Takahrn from escaping. He held enough confidence in his underground prisons. Too much. There were no walls around the camp, just flat plains of dirt. The main town was half a mile away. No one could hear her escape. All the men who took orders from the owner lived in the village and were not paid enough to stay overnight.

The only thing keeping the slaves from leaving, aside from the prison cells, was the owner himself. He had built a small house right next to the cages in case he needed to check on them during the night. No ordinary Takahrn could break through the metal bars. But Gahlaia wasn't ordinary. Though she did not possess the magic of the elves, she had inherited her father's strength, a trait her family line had long borne.

She reached for the roof of her prison and tore at the lock. With a loud screech, the latch came free. She flung open the roof and pulled herself out of her hole. Gahlaia spread her wings out and felt the night breeze flow past them once again. Freedom was hers at last.

"No!"

The door to the owner's house swung open and smacked the wooden wall on the other side. Within seconds a sword slashed down toward her. She jumped back as the moonlight flickered off the blade, inches from her face. Her focus came back to her, and she growled under her breath. In her moment of joy, she had forgotten all about him. It almost cost her life.

The owner swung at her again. Throughout her years, Gahlaia had come across many skilled sword fighters. This man was no master, and he was tired. Her reflexes, her strength, and now her claws. She had the advantage.

The owner came at her with diagonal cuts, slashing recklessly. She dodged and spun away from the attacks as if they were nothing. It was mere child's play to avoid the sword in the hands of the angry old man.

He breathed heavily, hunched over yet still burning with hatred. He swung his sword downward again, and Gahlaia brought her right hand up to meet the assault.

The owner stood in shock as her claw cut through the blade like butter, and giving one last battle cry, she thrust her left hand toward his throat. His scream was silenced as her draconic fingers pierced his windpipe. She stared at the man she had hated for so long, nails still in his throat, as he struggled and failed to take one last breath. His body grew limp, his weight pulling the claw from his gullet, and fell to the ground as a lifeless husk.

In that single moment, Gahlaia almost felt pity for him, if pity was the right word. There were no words for one so pathetic and disgusting as him. No friends to mourn his demise. No one to comfort him but the dirt that now covered his corpse. She gave out a long sigh, but her anger was still there.

Looking out across the camp, she glanced at the other prison cells. The Takahrn were awake, hands grasping the roof doors in silence, trying to make out what had taken place. Gahlaia let a smile slip out. This wasn't just her freedom, but theirs too. They had all suffered at the hands of mortals. They were her family. The only family of recent memory anyway.

Walking to the other underground boxes, she sought to free her kin.

Chapter 2

Day one of the third month.

BORHIIM AWOKE TO the sun glazing his face. He squinted at the light and groaned. As his vision adjusted, he could see Gwendall pulling back the red drapes, her golden hair glistening in the sunrise. If it was anyone else waking him up, he might have made a fuss. But he had grown used to her enjoyment of the morning, even if he didn't understand how someone could enjoy it over a little more sleep.

He opened his mouth to make a snarky comment but paused when he noticed the sun's unusual color. It gave off a dark red hue that covered the entire sky. It marked a very specific day that he knew all too well: the Day of Great Divide. He had seen this day come and go every year, and every time it stirred something inside him. Something that he did not quite recognize. A feeling, perhaps, that clawed at the back of his memory. Every time this feeling came over him, he hoped it would reveal its meaning, but to no avail. *Perhaps this day holds meaning for my life*, he thought, but he quickly shrugged those feelings away. His past had always been a mystery to him, one that would likely never be solved. Today was just another day.

"I knew you would like it," Gwendall remarked. "It's amazing, right? And it marks the start of a special day."

Borhiim chuckled, putting his hand in front of his face to block the sunlight. "What's so special about it?" he said, sitting up in his bed. "So the sun looks darker. Doesn't mean much."

"It's the Day of Great Divide! The day the old war ended, and the day the first human king established the Deerium kingdom. Doesn't that interest you?" Gwendall beamed in his direction. She was always very enthusiastic about old history. She was still young, in her early twenties, yet she knew more about history than anyone else Borhiim had ever met.

He frowned. "You don't need to tell me what it means. Besides, if it's so important, maybe the king should parade himself across the Dirtlands to add to my excitement," he said.

"Like the king would come anywhere near here. And besides, he isn't even the king yet. His coronation is still days away."

"I don't know. A day titled with the words 'Great Divide' doesn't seem like a day worth celebrating to me."

"But who knows?" she continued, ignoring his grumblings. "In a few weeks, we may end up meeting him if you get out of bed."

That's right. Today we start our journey to Deeria.

"I can't wait to see Valia," Gwendall said. "I'm ready to leave this place and live the life of luxury in the capital."

Valia was the capital city of Deeria, one of the four sectors that made up the whole of Deerium. Norvad occupied the northwestern sector. Cleptyn resided in the eastern sector. Verish was south. And Deeria, the grand sector, united and led the other three. From Valia, the king would command the three rulers of the other sectors and maintain the peace that Deerium held for so many years. Even in the Dirtlands and to the edge of Verish his rule was felt. Or at least it would be once the new king was coronated.

"Are you always so enthusiastic, or is today just more than usual?" Borhiim remarked with a half smile.

Gwendall punched him in the shoulder, and he slumped back under the covers. "Come on," she said, walking out of the room.

"Get up. I want to get a few more things for our journey before Doryan arrives."

Borhiim had met Gwendall's brother only a few times, and just from those meetings, he could feel his commanding presence and authority. Doryan was the grand general of the Verish army that protected the Southern Border, a massive wall that separated that sector from Deeria to the northwest and Cleptyn to the northeast. It was built in the first age before the old war, and now often used to control trade across areas.

Initially, Doryan was suspicious of Borhiim and leery of letting him stay in their home, but every month he had to travel to Deeria and join the three rulers to give the king their analysis and input on the state of the people. After hearing of all the help Borhiim had given Gwendall in his absence, Doryan chose to allow him to remain.

Beholding the Southern Border would already be an amazing sight, but more than anything, Borhiim wanted the chance to see Doryan once again. He wanted to hear his stories of how he rose into such a position despite his lack of a noble birth. Going from a low life in the Dirtlands to the grand general of all Verish—Borhiim found it inspiring.

Quickly, he pulled himself out of bed, clothed himself, and entered the main room of the house. Gwendall had already prepared a stew, which was placed in front of his seat at the table, and headed into town to buy supplies for the journey to come.

The square stone house was not much different from the others in town. Other than the main room, which took up most of the space, and his own, there was only one other: Gwendall's. Rarely did he go in her room. He always thought it a breach of privacy even if Gwendall did not care as much as he did about such matters.

Borhiim ate his meal in silence, reflecting. It had been exactly three years today since Gwendall had found him wandering in the outskirts of the Dirtlands and taken him in, but it felt as though no time had passed at all. For him, it felt like yesterday, and yet the same questions still hung in his mind. *Why did I come to Verish? How did I end up stranded in the desert? What events led me to this place?* Normally he could just put such thoughts behind him, but not on this day. Today posed the greatest question of all. *Why does my memory not go past the Day of Great Divide three years ago?*

Having finished his stew, Borhiim exited the small house in search of Gwendall. The red hue of the sky became even more radiant, but he did his best to ignore it. The town was busy as usual. People were up and about, the small marketplace was bustling, and children ran through the dirt playing as they always did, chasing one another with sticks or flipping bronze coins in huddles in order to win pretend prizes from one another. Stone houses hunched together closely, forming lines on each side of the dirt road. The marketplace, however, was built completely from wood, with a row of five carts offering assortments of food, clothing, and trinkets. People flocked around the food cart filled with piles of fresh bread, cheese, and dried rabbit meat displayed over its surface.

Whatever strangeness the day might bring, the town and its people were one thing Borhiim could always count on for consistency.

As he moved toward the market, he could see Gwendall bargaining with an elderly man over the price of some rabbit meat. He chuckled for a moment, then noticed something in the background past the marketplace.

About half a mile from town, he could see a group of people forming in front of an old wooden house. Borhiim knew what it was—the slave market. It seemed like every week the man who lived out there would find more Dividers to sell. Personally, he didn't care much for the slave trade. Gwendall never considered buying a slave for herself while Borhiim was around, but she also didn't think fondly of them. Her parents were killed by a Takahrn attack when she was very young. Now, most of her support came from the income of her brother's efforts on the Southern Border.

Borhiim had laid eyes on Takahrn only a few times, but for the most part, slaves worked the ground further north. Any use for them in town was done once all the houses were completed. Now, most people who came to the daily market would be from parts of the Dirtlands outside of town or even from other parts of Verish. This was the only place to buy slaves for miles, and it had built quite the reputation. Purchasing Takahrn like they were fresh meat always disgusted Borhiim, but today his curiosity was higher than usual.

Walking past the market, Borhiim made his way toward the group. He pushed his way through the small crowd until he reached the front. He just wanted to see the Takahrn, then he could leave. He had always been driven away from the selling for one reason or another, and his interest had finally bested him. However, what he saw shook him to his very core.

A group of about twenty different Takahrn stood in a long line, all of them on wooden stools. Their body structure was that of a human's, but they had long tails—some of them even had horns and wings. Each of them was chained at the shoulders and their feet to keep them from escaping. Most looked downcast as if their whole world had been shattered right in front of them. As Borhiim stared, the man who ran the biddings called out the names for each Takahrn, and people gave their bids based on copper or silver pieces. His stomach began to turn, and he swallowed hard. This whole process was inhuman.

He had seen enough. He turned to head back, but before he could so much as take another step toward town, he heard the owner call out a name.

"Gahlaia."

Borhiim stopped. He had heard that name in town before. She had built herself a bit of a reputation in the Dirtlands. She had been a victim of the slave trade longer than anyone—yet never sold. He turned around and looked upon the face of the Takahrn the owner had named. She had pointed horns coming out of her long, blonde hair, with dark red eyes that matched the sky, and a beautiful face not even the grime and filth could cover. Her wings were chained to her back and her tail wrapped around her leg in another chain used to restrain her.

When her name was called, all grew completely silent. No one would give a bid. The discontentment on the owner's face became clear in an instant, but he did not linger. He moved on to the next slave, but Borhiim's gaze stayed on Gahlaia.

Of course, her beauty was obvious, but there was also something about her that reminded him of . . . he wasn't sure what. She appeared almost familiar to him, but at the same time, she was a blank slate. As if reaching for a word on the tip of his tongue, he couldn't seem to place her.

As he stared, her face turned and her eyes met his. Her expression was blank, and yet that single gaze moved him. Something was wrong, but he wasn't certain what. Slowly, the feeling at the back of his memory grew stronger than ever, tugging at his mind until it snapped. His vision blurred and flashed.

Stumbling through the crowd of people, he lurched back toward town.

Not even halfway there, Borhiim fell to the ground. His head grew dizzy. Images began to race before him, and words blared in his mind. *The Claw. An elf. A dragon. Mother. Father . . . The Righteous Ones.* None of his thoughts made sense. It was all coming too fast.

His brain felt ready to explode.

Clutching his head, he opened his mouth to scream, but just as quickly as it had come, it was gone. His vision returned like nothing had happened, but his head still ached slightly.

Standing back up, he walked back to town, gasping for breath. *I can't wait to get out of here.*

GWENDALL SLAMMED HER hands on the food cart in a huff, the townsfolk behind her standing in awkward silence. "This is a scandal!" she exclaimed, preparing to throw the sliced rabbit meat back in the old man's face. "It's not even been a week since you raised the price, and you think you can get away with it again?"

The man put his hands up in defense, stumbling over his words. "But hunting has grown harder this year. Rabbits are the only animals around to prey upon, and they offer little in substance. Even the slaves are struggling to catch them now. They're too scarce for the price I had."

She threw her hand down again, and he jumped in surprise. "Then why don't you deal with the tradesmen from Pordika? Most other towns do. We wouldn't have this problem if you weren't so traditional!"

"Their prices are too high," he whined. "We wouldn't gain much in profit if we traded with them. Now, please. There are others behind you."

Shaking her head and suddenly becoming aware of the scene she was making, Gwendall fished into her pocket and tossed twelve copper pieces onto the wood. "You're lucky my brother's not here," she grumbled.

Stepping out of the line, she expected to see Borhiim standing in the doorframe of the house, but he wasn't there. She turned left and right, trying to spot him among the small groups or perhaps playing with the children, but he was nowhere to be seen. *Of all the times to vanish*, she thought. *And after I had finally gathered up the courage . . .*

Gwendall let a sigh slip out. Today was supposed to be a special day. It had been three years to the day, and only now did she feel even remotely prepared to tell him. All this time they had bantered like siblings, and mostly she told herself that was fine, but recently she wasn't so certain. Borhiim took care of her, was kind to her. He had worked the fields, dug in the mines further north, even opened a market stand a few times. How could she not start to feel . . .

"Gwendall?"

Borhiim's voiced instantly snapped her out of her trance, leaving her heart pounding. "Borhiim!" she exclaimed, pointing to the food in her basket. "You will not believe what I had to go through to get all this. The old man—"

She paused when she noticed Borhiim's expression. He looked pale, ready to fall from a light breeze. "Are you alright?"

"What?" he answered. "Yeah, I'm fine. I just have a headache."

"Well," she said, "we had better get back home. We need to sort all this food out and be ready to leave before my brother gets here."

He nodded, and shuffled toward their house, apparently unaware of the frustration on her face. *Maybe later.*

GWENDALL AND BORHIIM spent the next few hours in silence. They gathered their things and placed them in packs. There wasn't much that Borhiim owned other than clothing. To be honest, the journey to Valia didn't hold much excitement for him. Sure, he didn't care for the heat and filth of the Dirtlands, but a life in the capital city was something that would take awhile to get used to. He had always imagined one day living in the Northern Forests up in Norvad. The only real reason he had agreed to leave for Valia was because that was where Gwendall had always dreamed of living. She always talked about how amazing it would be to sing and dance in the courts of the king. It was her dream, and since she was the closest thing Borhiim had to family, there was no way he was going to leave her now.

A throb of pain shot through his left shoulder. He inhaled sharply through his teeth. It intensified like a forest fire. He grunted and Gwendall turned at the sound.

He straightened when he saw her looking in his direction with concern. "I'm . . . fine," he said. "I think I slept on my shoulder last night, that's all."

Gwendall shot him another look of concern, but when he returned her gaze, she let it be.

As Gwendall returned to her task, Borhiim walked out of the main room into his chamber and closed the door, locking it. He turned to the right to see his reflection in the mirror that hung from the wall.

He reached to pull up his left sleeve only to reel back from the searing pain. Steadying himself, he slowly rolled the sleeve again.

Borhiim stood there in shock. On his left shoulder, a large patch of skin had become twisted and almost deformed like a scar. It curled into the shape of something, still too rough and misshapen to become clear. *What is this? What's happening to me?*

Without warning, his head began to pulsate. The pain in his arm rose once again to match his increasing headache. The images and names returned to his mind. He fell to the ground, shaking violently, and let out a yell, gasping for air like a man drowning at sea.

A banging came at his door.

"Borhiim!" Gwendall shouted from the other side, pulling hard at the handle. "Borhiim, what's happening in there? *Borhiim!*"

Another volley of loud bangs battered the door.

Names and words flashed before him in a similar pattern as earlier. *The Claw. An elf. A dragon. Mother. Father. The Righteous Ones. The Claw. An elf. A dragon. Mother. Father. The Righteous Ones. The Claw. An elf. A dragon. Mother. Father. The Righteous Ones . . . Never forget, my son.*

Then, in an instant, they vanished. Air returned to his lungs, and he breathed hard. The headache softened a bit, but his shoulder still ached. Shakily, Borhiim crawled to the door and unlocked it. Gwendall rushed in immediately and crouched down to look him in the eyes.

"What is going on?" she demanded as she embraced him. "You need to tell me!"

Borhiim took a moment to catch his breath before responding. "I don't know what's happening, Gwendall. That . . . that's the truth. I don't know what's happening to me."

She shook her head, a small tear falling down her face. "I can't lose you," she said. "I can't. You've been here for so long. If you left, I don't know what I would do. You mean too much to me. I—"

Borhiim raised a hand. "No more. I'm fine. You don't need to worry."

Gwendall nodded, sniffled, and helped him stand. "Get some sleep. Rest. Doryan will be here soon. I'll wake you when he gets here."

There was no point in arguing. She was right. He could feel his body trembling with exhaustion, so he dragged himself to bed as Gwendall left the room. Immediately, his head resting on the pillow, he was overtaken by sleep's pull. Yet even in slumber, he found no rest. His dreams turned to vivid nightmares as his lost memories took shape.

The Claw. An elf. A dragon. Mother. Father. The Righteous Ones . . . Never forget, my son . . . Never forget who you are.

Chapter 3

T HE UNDERGROUND PRISON bars squealed as Gahlaia clawed at them. Giving way to the pressure, the metal door offered one final scream as it swung open and the prisoner within climbed out. Gahlaia released him from his chains, and the freed Takahrn spread his long, dark wings and tail, lifting his face upward to the moonlight.

"May the Eternal bless your days, sister," he said, grasping her hand in a firm grip.

It had been a long time since she had been addressed in the old ways. She nodded to him in return. *That's the last one*, she thought. There were twenty-two Takahrn in total who circled Gahlaia, waiting for her to announce what they should do next.

She faced the newly freed Takahrn. He had no horns, but his pointed claws and strong build gave him a powerful presence. His face was wise but youthful, complemented by his long, curly black hair. Gahlaia had seen his face across the slave lines more days than she could count, but never had he spoken to her.

"You know who I am, yes?" she asked. "Do you stand with me?"

"We stand with you," he returned, stamping his foot into the dirt.

She smiled warmly. "Tell me your name, brother."

"Craden. Son of Cradous, King of the Skies, and Avorah, elf of the Hallowed Forest."

Gahlaia was familiar with both names. Cradous was a dragon

many of their kind had respected greatly. He had been one of her father's closest advisors. Avorah was an elf who had watched over the Hallowed Forest with great wisdom, at least before it became what it was now. Before the end of the war. Before it grew dark. Few ever referred to it by its true name anymore. Since the third age, many had called it the Forest of Shadows, and it deserved that title.

This Takahrn truly came from great descent.

"Well, Craden," she began. "We have no army. I plan to make a move all the same, but as far as numbers go, we stand little chance."

"We don't need an army," another Takahrn remarked.

Gahlaia spun around to face her. She didn't recognize her. She had brown hair and white wings, and her horns had not completely grown in yet.

"Deeria is vulnerable," the Takahrn said. "The king is on his death bed, and his son will take the throne not long from now."

"We could take the new king hostage on his coronation day," Craden chimed in. "Perhaps barter for his release."

Gahlaia nodded. She had thought of the same idea some time ago and was happy to see the others were thinking similarly. If they could get across the Southern Border without being seen and take the king when he revealed himself, they could demand freedom for the Takahrn without having to wage what would likely be a deadly war for all.

"What is your name, sister?" she asked. "How do you know all this?"

"Anahka. Daughter of Zerthon, elf from the Green Hills of Cleptyn. My mother left without so much as a name, so forgive me if I can't give you her title."

She straightened her back, showing no remorse in her speech. She continued. "I was a slave in the courts of Valia but was transferred here due to unruly behavior. My head was worth more in the

Dirtlands than rolling on the floor of the king's prison cell."

"If you had a calendar," Gahlaia said, "could you point out the day of the king's coronation?"

Anahka thought for a moment, then nodded. "The day has already been chosen. The old man is at death's door, and his subjects know it."

Assurance flooded Gahlaia and she sped out of the circle, running into the wooden house behind them. The owner's limp body still lay in the dirt near the doorway. She opened cabinets in search of what she so desperately hoped was there. She knew he had them but wasn't sure where to look. Entering the main bedroom, she found her targets. On the wall, to the left of the door, a calendar hung by a nail. Under the bed lay a rolled-up map of Deerium.

Gahlaia hurried back to the group, knelt, and spread out the map. She placed the calendar in the right-hand corner as the Takahrn gathered around and watched.

Anahka's eyes darted over the dates. "Here," she said, pointing to the calendar. "Day fifteen of the third month."

"That would give us fourteen days to reach Valia," Craden responded.

Gahlaia remained silent, shifting her gaze to the map. Though she had been enslaved for many years, her knowledge of the landscape of Deerium was still vivid. Her memories of her father teaching her about the ways of the land flashed back to her.

She pointed to the Dirtlands on south on the map. "We're here," she began. "If we are heading for Valia, then we have two options. We could go around Dragorish Canyon and pass through Pordika, the Verish capital . . ."

"Won't it be dangerous going straight through the capital?" Anahka asked. "Couldn't we just go around?"

"That could take too long," Craden replied. "We need to reach

Deeria before the coronation. But if we get spotted in Pordika, we could have the Verish army crashing down on us."

"What about the sea?" one of the Takahrn asked from behind. "Couldn't we pass along the Great Sea's edge?"

Craden shook his head. "Not enough time. Besides, we can't all fly. Would any of you really want to risk swimming with the Sirens?"

They fell silent. Not much was known of the Sirens other than that they devoured anything that crossed the Great Sea. They were vicious people, numbering more than any could count.

Gahlaia moved her finger westward. "We could also cut directly through Dragorish Canyon," she said. "It would save us a lot of time, but it could be extremely dangerous."

Craden cocked his head. "Are the stories really true? Do you honestly believe that one of the Second Dragons lives in the canyon? I thought the humans hunted most of them down."

"I don't know," Gahlaia responded.

The beast from folklore had scared most from going near the canyon. They called him Dragorish—it was his stories that inspired the name of his home—but few believed he existed. He was a story for bartenders to tell their customers, and to most people he was nothing more. Whether or not he actually existed was a question none had chosen to answer.

"Not all of us have wings," Anahka said. "Not all of us would be able to fly over the canyon."

Gahlaia looked up at their group. Three out of twenty-two Takahrn before her bore no wings.

She turned back to Anahka. "We could carry them across. We have the strength to do it. I say we take the path through the canyon, then we can find a way over the Southern Border." She knew a trip over Dragorish Canyon would be risky, but compared to facing a potential army or the Sirens, she was willing to take a chance on a fable.

Craden and Anahka looked at each other and then back to Gahlaia. They nodded in unison.

"Like I said," Craden remarked. "We stand with you."

Gahlaia stood up and took a deep breath. "Brothers and sisters . . . none of you have any reason to stay. I freed you to give you back your lives. They are yours to do with as you will. They don't belong to me. You owe me no allegiance."

She pointed ahead, past the town in the north. "If you come with me to Valia, we could end this conflict between humans and Takahrn without the need for war, but there's no guarantee. If any of you wish to leave, now is the time. I won't have anyone join the company only to turn tail and run when times get hard. You stay and risk death for something worth fighting for, or you leave and keep your freedom."

She paused and awaited an answer.

Craden was the first to respond. He put a clenched right hand on his lips and then placed his knuckles on his chest. The rest of the group followed the gesture.

Gahlaia was speechless. It was the elvish salute: a sign of undying loyalty. Her mother had taught it to her when she was just a child, but it had been generations since she had seen it done for anyone.

She returned the motion and looked up into the sky. The night was still young.

She gazed back at Craden and Anahka. "We need horses," she said. "We can't fly all the way to Valia, and those who can't fly need a way to keep up with the group."

As the words left her lips, a series of lights in the distance caught her eye. It came from the edge of town.

Torches.

"Craden, come with me," she commanded. "Anahka, lead the

rest around the western side of town."

The two nodded and the group split up, moving toward the lights from opposite sides.

BORHIIM WOKE WITH a start. He had hoped that sleep would free his mind from what had happened earlier, but it had only succeeded in moving his pain from reality to his dreams. His head still ached from his previous outburst, and now the pain had spread. He could still feel the burning in his left shoulder. However, now he could feel a similar sensation in the tips of his fingers and tailbone.

He pressed his hands to his head. *Why is this happening?*

He grumbled his way out of bed and entered the main room. Everything was dark. The sun had gone down. Gwendall stood in the doorway of the house, looking out.

"How long was I asleep?" Borhiim asked.

Gwendall turned around with a start. "Don't scare me like that!" she said. "You've been asleep all through the main portion of the day, tossing and turning more times than I could count."

She turned her worried gaze outward again. "He's late. He said he would be here by midday on the Day of Great Divide. I know he did."

"It's a long journey from the Southern Border," Borhiim said. "They'll be here soon. He's probably just behind schedule is all." He put a hand on her shoulder. "He'll be alright. I know he will."

Moments later, torchlights came into view. As they approached the town, figures emerged from the darkness. Ten men mounted on horses, all clad in white armor.

The man at the front of the company stood out from the others. His armor was outlined with gold, distinct from the pale coloring of the others. His breastplate looked as though it were made of dragon scales, painted in white Verish tradition. Strapped to his back was a large ax with a blade longer than its handle, which looked more like an elongated sword hilt than a handle. His hair was dirty blonde and braided down past his chest. On his left shoulder, a symbol was carved into the plating: an X with an arrow straight down the middle. The mark of a sector's grand general.

"Doryan!" Gwendall exclaimed. "You made it!"

She rushed out to meet them. Borhiim stepped out of the house to observe the group's arrival, eyes fixed on their leader. The horses finally came to a stop, and after the grand general dismounted, Gwendall embraced him excitedly.

He smiled as he returned the gesture. "Of course I made it," he said. His voice was strong and deeper than Borhiim remembered.

Doryan lifted his gaze to him. "I hope my sister hasn't given you too much trouble in my absence."

Gwendall gave him an outraged look, but he shrugged it off.

"Not in the slightest," Borhiim replied, "save for a few early morning wake-up calls."

Gwendall's angry gaze spun toward him, and Doryan laughed.

The other nine men dismounted, and with a wave from their leader, grabbed some bread from their satchels and began to gnaw on it.

"That's new," Gwendall remarked, pointing to the ax on Doryan's back.

"It's elvish," he said. "The king recovered more ancient weapons spread out across Deerium, likely used in the war at the end of the first age. They're imbued with Terrkoris magic, enhancing the physical strength of both the user and the weapon itself."

Borhiim's jaw dropped. They had been recovering elvish metals for years, but he had never seen such a weapon. To find the magical weapons from the first war was truly a historic find, let alone a great honor to wield one.

"We can't travel tonight, I'm afraid," Doryan said, changing the subject. "With Takahrn raids more frequent, we didn't take the roads, and my men are tired. If we start by early morning, we can still make it back before the coronation." He turned to Gwendall and smiled. "Arinay has spoken with the king. They have a place prepared for you in Valia, in the palace."

She beamed. Her dream would finally become a reality. "How did she manage to convince him?" Gwendall asked.

"She didn't do it alone," he replied. "Rorgan helped persuade him. Without him, you might not have had a chance."

Rorgan. Borhiim had heard that name before. He was the ruler of Norvad, the northern sector, and one of the king's most trusted tacticians. He was young and intellectually brilliant, arguably the greatest mind in all Deerium. When Rorgan had traveled to Verish four years ago, he had met Doryan and Gwendall. Since then, they had become good friends, despite the distance between their kingdoms. Borhiim had never met him, but he had heard good things about him from Gwendall. They were always sending letters to one another.

Normally the name would give him no reaction, but now something was different. The pain in his head, shoulder, fingers, and tailbone all seemed to flare up at the mention of it. He winced and inhaled quickly through clenched teeth.

"Are you alright?" Doryan asked.

He nodded but couldn't make out the words to reply.

"It's happening again, isn't it?" Gwendall asked, worry returning to her face.

Borhiim couldn't respond. His movements grew stiff. He could feel the attack coming again, but this time he was ready. He made every effort to resist, but it felt like pushing against a current. The more he tried to fight the onslaught, the more his head felt like it might burst. The noise around him began to fade. He could see Doryan and Gwendall moving their lips in a concerned fashion, but he couldn't piece together what they were saying.

The memories started to fill his mind once again, with names and words repeating in the same pattern. *The Claw. An elf. A dragon. Mother. Father. The Righteous Ones... Never forget, my son... Never forget who you are.* The last two sentences repeated themselves over and over until they rang out like a war cry.

Reality melted away from Borhiim's vision, replaced with a new setting. He was no longer in the Dirtlands but in a massive cave. Before him stood a tall, familiar figure. The man had dark brown hair that matched Borhiim's and pale skin. On his left hand was a mark—an elvish mark. It translated as "stone." *This man... He's an elf.*

A loud crash like thunder came from outside the cave. The figure turned to Borhiim and put his hands on his shoulders.

"I love you, son," he said, tears welling up in his eyes. "Go find your mother. She'll take care of you."

He moved to face the back wall of the cave. As he thrust his left hand forward, the mark upon it began to glow. In an instant, a tunnel carved its way through the mountain. Borhiim had no control over his body, forced to play his part in the memory. He walked to the tunnel and crouched his way in.

Boom! Another crash from outside.

The elf backed away from the passageway and faced the entrance to the cavern, the sky outside shaded dark red. Massive claws gripped the edge of the cave, and the deep blue face of a dragon came into view, its wide mouth and nostrils giving off a scarlet hue. Within seconds, out of the beast burst the Devil's Flame, a dark and unnatural fire.

The elf clasped his hands together, the mark on his hand glowing once again. Rapidly, the walls of the large entrance closed in front of him, blocking the assault. Sweat poured down his face as he held his hands together, trying to hold back the destructive blaze. But despite his efforts, cracks began to appear in the stone, and flames trickled in little by little.

He looked back at Borhiim, still in the entryway to the tunnel.

"Go!" he cried. "Leave before it's too late!"

Borhiim slowly backed away, keeping the man in view.

"Never forget, my son!" the elf shouted to him, tears rolling down his face. "Never forget who you are! You are Takahrn, and we are proud of who you have become!"

The wall finally gave way to the flames, and the dragon reappeared, roaring in fury. The elf turned toward the tunnel and clenched his hand into a fist. With that final motion, the entrance to the passageway sealed itself closed, and Borhiim was alone.

His vision blurred again.

Before he knew what was happening, he was on the ground, looking up at Doryan and Gwendall. The nine men behind them all had their swords drawn. The pain Borhiim had felt had lessened and only remained in his head.

But something felt different. His tailbone was sitting on something solid. He lifted his left hand and gasped. It wasn't human. He held his fingers before his face. They were talons. Borhiim twisted to look at his left shoulder. The deformed skin had changed into a mark that was some form of elvish, but it wasn't a mark he had ever seen before. He turned his head to the right and felt something move underneath him. Out from beneath his back slid the tip of a tail, with hair pointed like an arrow on its end.

Panic began to swell up inside him. He looked to Gwendall and

Doryan for assurance, but they remained speechless.

One of the men behind them slowly pointed his blade toward Borhiim, hands shaking. "What . . . What are you?"

Chapter 4

GAHLAIA PEERED FROM around the side of a house, watching the scene with confusion, Craden standing next to her. None of it made sense to her. She played the situation back over in her head. They had followed the torchlight to the near edge of town. It had been a small group of Verish soldiers and what looked like a general who had stopped at a small house where two people greeted them: a man and a woman.

Abruptly, the man collapsed. At first, Gahlaia thought the general might have struck him down, but no assault came. The stranger lay in the dirt, shaking like a leaf, muttering words that she couldn't make out. He swung his arms nonsensically, ripping and tearing at his left shirt sleeve.

As they watched, the man's form started to change. His entire body twisted and billowed like smoke until it melted away, replaced with something new. His hands changed to claws, and a tail grew and twitched from behind. The general and the woman knelt over the form in a state of panic, and the other nine soldiers drew their blades.

"This doesn't make sense," Craden whispered.

Gahlaia remained silent. She had seen this person before. She remembered spotting him momentarily at the slave trade earlier today, but she had a strange feeling that she had seen him somewhere else. Somewhere far from here, in an age long past. Inching closer to the edge of the wall, she squinted to focus on his face. The man shifted unconsciously to the right, giving her a brief look at the mark on his left shoulder.

Suddenly it clicked.

Gahlaia had seen that mark only once before. It was an elvish symbol—a unique one. "I ... I think I know him," Gahlaia said slowly.

"What?" Craden asked, surprised but keeping his voice at a whisper. "Who is ... ?" His voice trailed off as he focused his gaze. "By the Eternal, it's him."

"Borhiim ..." Gahlaia couldn't pull her eyes away. He was her childhood friend before the dragons were driven from Deerium, when they lived in the mountains of the Claw. One of the first Takahrn. Her ... *How did I not see it before?* "He's one of us."

"But how is that possible? How did he take the form of a human?"

Gahlaia couldn't answer. She wasn't focused on Craden.

Borhiim awoke, and one of the soldiers pointed his blade at him.

Gahlaia looked past the soldiers to the nearby houses. Anahka stood at the ready, looking confused and upset. Behind her, the rest of the Takahrn were trying to look over her shoulders to catch a glimpse of the scene.

Gahlaia motioned her to stay put. "You and I are going to take out the general," she said, darting her gaze toward Craden. "Anahka will take the other soldiers from behind."

"Should we risk revealing ourselves in hopes that this stranger might be a Takahrn?" he asked.

Gahlaia didn't like the idea of being exposed. But if this man was the person she had once known, then he might be the most powerful being in the entire kingdom. They needed him. "He is a Takahrn, Craden," she responded. "He deserves his freedom, just like the rest of us."

That was the end of the debate. That was all that needed to be said. He was her friend, the one who had once been closest to her, and she wouldn't leave him to die.

BORHIIM'S PANIC ESCALATED. He kept turning his hands over, hoping it was all a nightmare. His tail twitched, and his shoulder burned.

Gwendall and Doryan stood up, their faces still looking shocked.

He looked at his feet. His boots were destroyed, sharp talons shooting from the ends of the leather. He yanked off the boots, revealing the pointed nails underneath.

As he stood up, the soldiers all pointed their swords toward him, the moonlight reflecting off their clean blades.

Borhiim stepped forward and tried to find the words to explain. "Gwendall, I..." he searched for a reason, but even he didn't understand what was happening. "I don't know what's going on."

Gwendall took a step back.

Doryan began to slowly lift his right hand toward his left shoulder, reaching for the handle of his ax. "You're one of them, aren't you?" Doryan asked flatly. "You're a Divider."

He shook his clawed hands in front of him. "No, I'm not. I'm human!"

"Don't lie!" one of the soldiers yelled from behind. "We can clearly see what you are, monster."

"I'm not a monster!" Borhiim responded. "I've lived here for years under Gwendall's roof." He looked her in the eyes, but she struggled to keep his gaze. "Gwendall, tell them."

She paused. "Doryan... it's true," she said slowly, looking up at her brother. "He's been living here in the Dirtlands for three years. He's never hurt anyone."

Doryan looked back at her, keeping his right hand in position. "Have you forgotten what the Dividers did to us?" he asked. "It was because of their attacks on the Dirtlands that we lost our family. Without Rorgan, we wouldn't have survived!"

His hand inched closer to his weapon. "Every day, we lose more soldiers protecting civilians from their attacks on smaller towns across Deerium, not just Verish. For all we know, he has been waiting for an opportunity to strike at me, or Pordika for that matter! He could be gathering information for an assault on Arinay, and I won't lose her. Not after . . ."

The general dropped his gaze, mumbling so Borhiim couldn't hear. Something was on his mind, that much was clear, but it was kept too close to the chest to be clearly understood.

"I'm not gathering information," Borhiim reassured him. "I'm not an assassin!"

"And how can you prove that?" Doryan asked, finger outstretched. "Look at you."

Gwendall put her hand on his extended arm and lowered it. "Please, Doryan," she said. "He isn't one of them. He isn't a threat."

Doryan hesitated as Gwendall's imploring eyes began to break through his rough exterior. Slowly, he lowered his right hand.

Borhiim let out a sigh in the moment of silence, but it didn't last long.

Out of the skies to his right, Borhiim caught the glimpse of two winged figures swooping down toward Doryan, claws outstretched for the kill. Doryan caught his horrified expression and turned. With a split second to react, he jumped aside, a talon digging its way into his shoulder. He faced his attackers, blood trickling down his left arm. They were both Takahrn, sharp horns emerging from their heads and wings from their backs. One, a man with pitch-black hair and a tail that twitched in anticipation. The other, a woman with blonde hair, her right index finger red with Doryan's blood.

Borhiim watched in horror as Doryan reached for his ax, but the woman charged him with blitzing speed, right hand extended toward his throat. The general dashed sideways and jabbed his left knee into her gut, the air quickly escaping her body. He grabbed the handle of his elvish weapon, his muscles tightening in response to the Terrkoris magic as veins popped down his neck and legs. Doryan swung hard with one hand as though the ax weighed nothing at all.

The attacker quickly retreated from its reach, extending her wings and taking to the air. A soldier from behind swung at her leg, but the male Takahrn knocked the blade away with his left claw and slashed across the soldier's neck with his right. His silver breastplate immediately stained red with blood, the man fell to the ground.

Seven other soldiers advanced, one hunched down over the lifeless body.

"Now, Anahka!" the female yelled.

From behind, a group of Takahrn rushed out from the shadows. The soldiers turned to face them but were too slow. They were caught in a pincer attack. Doryan swung his ax as if it were made of wood, keeping the onslaught at a distance, but his focus clearly was protecting Gwendall. She stood motionless, racked with shock.

Borhiim also stood frozen. It was the Takahrn from the slave trade, but how they had escaped was beyond him. In that moment, it was too much of a blur for him to process. But the female who had initiated the attack stood out to him. *Gahlaia.* The name pounded in his head like a drum as he tried to shake the pain away.

He watched in silence as Doryan swung his ax upward at a winged Takahrn swooping down toward him. The blow connected, and the figure spun backward, hitting the dirt in an unnatural position. Another Takharn claw sliced across the back of Doryan's leg and he fell to his knees, his weapon dropping in front of him.

They were surrounded. A talon stopped inches from the general's throat.

Borhiim had hoped the townsfolk would come to their aid, but those he saw peek out of their houses at the sound of the battle swiftly slammed their doors. The town had seen far too many raids for courage to present itself this time. Attacks from the Takahrn were inevitable—from where, they cared not.

Twelve dead bodies lay in the dirt, nine of them human.

Borhiim looked to Gwendall, on her knees and shaking in disbelief, then back at Gahlaia. His head began to hurt again, the pain slowly increasing. *No. Not now!* All these events were becoming too much for him to handle.

"Borhiim . . ." Gahlaia said giving a brief smile. "That's your name, isn't it? Please tell me it's you."

Borhiim didn't respond but kept his gaze on her. Visions started playing over in his mind. Visions of two children playing together. Laughing together. He clutched his head. *This isn't real. This isn't real! THIS ISN'T REAL!*

"You remember me, don't you?" she continued. "You remember me from years ago."

"You know her?" Doryan screamed. "We trusted you!"

The visions grew stronger in Borhiim's head. "*No!*" he replied. "I don't know her, Doryan! I don't know any of them!"

He turned to Gwendall. Tears ran down her face. "Gwendall, please. I don't know them."

She wouldn't return his gaze.

"Borhiim, you do know me," Gahlaia said, outstretching her hand. "We can help you. We can protect you."

As the hand touched his shoulder, he looked into her eyes again. *Those eyes.* How could he have forgotten them? A smile began to form at the corners of his mouth. "Gahlaia . . . My—"

That was all he could take.

Before he could think anymore, Borhiim felt something crack like a twig in the recesses of his mind, and he fell to the ground, shaking and twitching.

DORYAN WATCHED, IMMOBILIZED and infuriated, as the Divider called Gahlaia picked Borhiim up and hoisted him over her right shoulder.

"What do we do with him?" a female Divider asked, waving a hand toward Doryan.

"We could use him as a hostage to get through the Southern Border if it comes to that," Gahlaia responded. "Take his weapon, tie him up, and put him on a horse." Gahlaia raised Borhiim's still-shaking body onto a horse and climbed on.

The Divider grabbed a coil of rope hanging from one of the horse's saddles and walked to Doryan's back. Keeping his right hand on Doryan's throat, he reached for the ax.

"You should leave," Doryan said to Gwendall.

She said nothing, remaining still as a statue.

When the hand came to take the weapon from his grasp, he squeezed the handle tighter, focusing his mind. The Terrkoris magic surged through his body again stronger than ever before, his skin turning pale. The Divider in front of him had no time to think. Doryan's arms ripped through the rope like it was paper, swinging his ax with surprising speed.

Before the Divider knew it, his hands were gone. He dropped and screamed in pain.

Doryan turned and struck down the enemy whose hands still clasped the rope. Once the deed was done, he spun around and finished off the Divider in front of him.

"We need to leave!" Gahlaia commanded. "We need to leave now!"

Eight winged Dividers took to the skies. The nine others, three of them wingless, had already mounted the other horses. With a kick to the animals' sides, they were off.

Doryan trailed behind them on foot, running at a pace faster than if he had mounted a steed. Behind him he heard Gwendall let out a gut-wrenching scream.

"Doryan! Don't leave me!"

But his attention was directed to one target, all other thoughts drowned out as the Terrkoris flooded his body.

I'll kill them. I'll kill them!

GAHLAIA AND HER comrades rode into the dead of night, Anahka riding at her left side, Craden in the skies. She turned to look behind them. Doryan was still bolting, keeping at a near equal pace with them.

There were eighteen Takahrn left, including herself and Borhiim, his twitching body behind her. They had lost five of their brothers and sisters in the attempt to save one. Gahlaia couldn't even remember their names, even though they were the only faces she had seen for years.

"Gahlaia," Anahka said over the sound of the galloping horses. "We need to head for Dragorish Canyon. We might be able to lose him there."

"That's still two days' journey away," she responded, "and the horses are already tired from their trek to the Dirtlands."

"Then what are we supposed to do?"

Gahlaia grunted. There wasn't much choice in the matter. She had hoped to go around, but it was in their direct path. "There's a small group of mountains a few hours from here. At its center is a pond called the Waters of the Righteous. We can run the horses until we reach it. Just follow my lead."

THE MINUTES PASSED into hours before the mountains came into view. There were two in front and two behind. Together the four crags formed a square with a flat plain at its center.

As they approached, Anahka turned to get a view of their pursuer. He was keeping pace, but his strides grew slower, and the gap between him and the Takahrn had at least tripled. He was almost a speck in the distance.

"How is he doing that?" she said. "How is he still running?"

"That weapon he carries," Gahlaia answered. "I think it's elvish. However, he's only human. He can only use a limited amount of its power before it starts taking a toll on him."

"Then why can he still use its power?"

"Didn't you see what happened earlier? The weapon is taking a toll, which is why he's slowed down. He just doesn't care anymore. The man's a maniac."

Before long, the mountains were upon them, and they headed straight for the center. The horses huffed and snorted. They didn't have much left to give.

Gahlaia spun back toward Borhiim, who was still hunched over the saddle. He hadn't woken up yet. She turned back to face the path ahead of her, frustrated. If he never roused, it was all pointless.

They stopped. They were now surrounded by a large, grassy plain. At its center was a pond of water, clearer than any of them had ever seen, just wide enough for three people to fully stretch in its depths. The air felt strangely fresh, with a smell that left an oddly sweet taste on their tongues, overpowering their senses. It was magic—there was no doubt about it.

Still, they remained wary. Even the mortals, who knew less than they did, feared this place. The stories of what had been done here and the unnatural feeling left behind were enough to put anyone on edge, despite the beauty around them.

Gahlaia and the others dismounted, and the Takahrn in the sky swooped down to the ground. They led the horses to the pond and let them have their fill. Pulling flasks of water from the saddles, they passed them around until everyone had been satisfied.

Gahlaia placed Borhiim's now limp body on the ground near the water. He looked almost peaceful in the grass, save for his pounding chest and erratic breathing. She heard murmuring in the group. Questions like "Is that him?" ran around the circle. They had all seen his face somewhere, in a life long ago.

"Everyone," Gahlaia said as they placed the flasks into the water to refill them. "Follow me back to the mountains. That general is on his way here, and it won't take him long to find us. Craden, lead twelve of those with wings up the mountain."

He nodded.

She glanced toward Anahka. "You and I will stay with the three on the ground. He must come through the pass between the two mountains. When he does, you and I will face him. With his attention on us, Craden can bring an attack from above."

All gave the elvish salute, a knot swelling up in Gahlaia's throat. She returned the sign, and everyone moved into position.

Anahka and Gahlaia stood at the entrance of the plain with three other Takahrn standing behind them. Gahlaia wished to say something but struggled to find the words. The knot in her throat still clung like an aftertaste. Had her judgment fallen short? It hadn't been a day and already they had lost their kin. "I'm . . . sorry, Anahka," she said. "None of this would have happened if I had just killed the general earlier. Maybe we shouldn't have gone back for Borhiim. I—"

"It's fine," Anahka said abruptly. "We followed you because we wanted to save our brothers and sisters. We knew there were risks." She paused, staring her comrade dead in the eyes. "For the first time, we live among our own as free people. For the first time, I feel like I live among family. If we die . . . we don't die alone."

Anahka's words rang true in Gahlaia's mind. Now she could focus on the task at hand. The speck in the distance grew closer and closer.

Gahlaia breathed hard with anticipation. "May the Eternal give us strength . . ."

Chapter 5

ALL WAS DARKNESS. No visions. No repeating words. Just the simple yet haunting quiet of nothing.

Borhiim's recollection of how he had come to such a place eluded him. He couldn't remember anything past falling to the ground after a surprise attack from the Takahrn and his strange transformation.

He sat in the shadows of wherever he was for what felt like an eternity before he began to feel something. A pulsating sensation slowly began to build in his head like an exhilarated heartbeat. As it grew stronger, the darkness around him began to respond in turn with brief flickers of dim light. Every pulse grew louder, and the world grew brighter until it all clicked into place.

A flash of white dazzled his eyes, and he blinked at the all-consuming brilliance.

When the light faded, he was no longer in the shadows of the void but rather watching a grand rewinding of time racing before him all at once. It was like he was standing on the outside looking in as major events from history streamed past him with such speed that he could barely take it all in.

It kept going back further and further until it finally stopped abruptly. Borhiim floated above the skies, staring, as confusion and adrenaline consumed him.

A major battle was taking place. Borhiim recognized the place immediately as the Green Hills in northeastern Cleptyn. Many elves from ancient times called it home.

Before him spread range after range of smooth mounts covered with thin grass, some scorched with dark red fire. It was the Devil's Flame, moving furiously and melting everything around in its path into oblivion.

Thousands of elves and dragons collided in a fierce clash that transformed the very area into a vast crater, the battlefield a mass of magic and devastation. It was unlike anything Borhiim had ever seen before.

Massive beasts the size of fortresses, with wings that towered over the ground, cast great shadows. They swooped down, burning through skin and soil in an instant, then swinging themselves back into the skies with a crack that sounded like thunder.

They all looked different. Black, white, blue, red, silver, gold, green, yellow, and many more various colors that passed over too quickly for Borhiim to process. Some had long horns that curled into sharp tips. Others had huge spikes that looked more like steel than skin riding from their backs to the tips of their pointed tails, with tufts of hair on the ends. Some still appeared as smooth as silk, with scales that shone in the setting sun.

The elves all wore thin silver armor and helmets that curved into a spike at the back. They carried longswords and large axes that hung from their backs, most remaining sheathed or unused. They all bore elvish marks somewhere on their bodies, determining what form of magic they could summon for retaliation.

They moved their arms and hands in specific motions to strike back at the creatures that flew in from above. Control over water, stone, trees, wind—even enhancement of the physical body—all forms of Terrkoris magic were on display.

Borhiim scanned the army, trying to find an Anamoris user. It was an extremely rare type of magic but very potent when in use.

Before long, he found one.

An elf on the front lines of battle dodged from side to side with incredible agility to avoid the shadowy blaze from the clouds. He was tall, far past six feet, and wore a helmet with three long silver horns—two on the side and one in the back. A curved broadsword hung sheathed on his back. He had golden hair that flowed down to his ribs, which reminded Borhiim almost immediately of Gwendall's. An elvish mark lay on his right wrist: the mark of the Anamoris, giving him full access to the magic of the soul.

A long stream of Devil's Flame blasted its way down toward him and the remaining front lines. He leaped backward with a flourish, but the shockwave of the attack sent him off balance, knocking him flat on his back.

Scores of elves burned to nothingness. Not even their ashes remained. A large, gaping hole was left in the ground through the middle of the grassy hill where the assault took place. Out of the clouds, a large yellow dragon crashed into the mud, soldiers cracking under its immense weight. It roared at the golden-haired elf as he quickly retook a fighting stance. It opened its large mouth, and the dark fire came toward him.

He outstretched his right arm toward the beast as the blaze grew closer, and just as fast as it had appeared, the fire died out. The dragon stood motionless. The elf pulled his hand back as though he meant to rip the very soul out of it, and the dragon's skin began to harden and crack. He clenched his hand tight, and a sort of energy shot its way out of the beast's body. It collapsed on the ground, a lifeless and hollow shell.

The elf gasped for breath as he released his grip on the magic.

Borhiim's vision zoomed in and focused on the elf as a soldier ran up to him, also gasping for breath. The elf looked at the messenger expectantly, with a glint of hope in his eyes.

The soldier, however, hung his shoulders low, as if defeat were already upon them. He gave the elvish salute, then spoke above the crackling sound of wings and flame. "High Elf Tarkuv," he said, "the Righteous Ones sent a falcon carrying a letter addressed to you . . . They regret to inform you that they won't be joining us."

Shock covered the High Elf's face, and he stepped back at the news, gritting his teeth. "Traitors!" he bellowed. "Cowards! All of them! Without them . . ." He collapsed to his knees and put his hands to his face. "We're doomed. Every last one of us. We can't survive this without that senseless cult!"

Tarkuv paused for a moment, breathed, and regained his composure. He stood up, gave the elvish salute to the messenger, and turned to face the destruction before him. He ran ahead of the rest of his army and stood tall atop one of the mounts to face his people. Pulling out his broadsword, he raised it high into the air and bellowed a great war cry. The rest matched his scream resoundingly.

"We must stand our ground!" he yelled. "If we are to die, then let us die here among our brothers and sisters! Among our family! Among our comrades!"

He turned and looked to the many scores of dragons that had gathered in the sky. They swooped down low to the ground in unison.

The High Elf gave another war cry and charged, his army following behind. "*For glory!*"

As the armies clashed, Borhiim's vision began to shift away from the elves and move eastward, toward the skies. The dragons flew across the air in formations and swooped down to strike the ground with the Devil's Flame. In a large group, they fell atop the massive forces of elves, starting at the front and moving to the back. The world shook and reverberated with their landing.

Terrkoris magic flew into the air in full force. It seemed as though the whole world would burst from the sheer output of magic and spiritual energy swirling around the battlefield.

Borhiim's view finally refocused and zoomed in on one of the creatures. She was silver with deep blue eyes that matched his own and long ears that drooped down next to her neck. She had no horns or spikes, giving her whole exterior a polished look. She was in the back of the formation, diving toward the ground along with the others. Her nostrils and mouth glowed dark red as she prepared to attack.

Suddenly, a large cluster of stone rose from the ground and struck her in the left wing. It fractured under the impact, an audible crack sounding even above the noise of war. It drooped to her side, and she fell out of the group, moving to her left. The dragon struggled to lift the wing back up, directing her descent away from the main portion of the battle before crashing and rolling through grass and mud.

She lay motionless on the ground for several minutes while the battle boomed to her far right. Her ear perked up, seemingly at the sound of muddy footsteps coming toward her over the thundering of magic and fire. She struggled to turn her head to see who approached her.

It was an elf, clad in the usual silver armor. In his right hand was a long, clean sword that reflected the sunset from its gleaming blade. He had dark brown hair and a mark on his left hand that translated to "stone." Borhiim recognized him almost instantly as the elf from his previous vision in the cave, the one who had called him his son.

The dragon tried to stand to defend herself but quickly fell back down. She groaned in pain, struggling over and over to pull her body from the ground, failing each time. The elf walked cautiously toward her large face and raised his weapon high above his head. The dragon's eyes moved out toward the large cluster that formed the mountains of the Claw in the distance. She breathed in deeply, as if preparing for the end.

She waited for nearly a minute for the elf to finish it, but no attack came.

She looked up, and he still stood above her, sword frozen in his hands. "What are you waiting for?" she said in a booming and scratchy tone. "I am defenseless. End me."

The elf stumbled back and slowly lowered his blade. "I can't," he replied. "Throwing our lives away in this war makes little sense to me. Few of us cling to the old ways, and where wisdom once made its home, foolishness and arrogance have taken its place."

She rolled her eyes. "Pretty words for a soldier, but then again, what else should I expect from an elf? You can talk about wisdom and arrogance all you want, but they mean little when you're the one holding the blade in your hand." She squinted at the man. "It was you and your people who started this war, and it is you who carries out your ruler's command to slaughter us for the sake of glory."

"Perhaps." The elf stared at the shining sword in his hand before letting it drop it into the mud. "I have watched and run with my brethren, but I have never killed any of your kind. My blade is clean. I do not wish to kill you, dragon."

She snuffed out a sharp breath through her nostrils. "So, you're a coward then."

He shrugged his shoulders and chuckled. "I suppose I am. I never had the courage before to stand against my superiors when the call to war was made. But . . . I think I have the courage now." He paused before continuing. "I swear by the Eternal, I will not raise a hand against your people."

"The Eternal?" she said in curiosity. "I thought the elves forsook the name of the Eternal. I've seen your temples. You worship nature and the long-forgotten souls of the dead."

"As I said," he responded, "few remain that hold to the old ways. It isn't looked highly upon."

The dragon let out another breath of air and looked away. "Then at least our people have that in common," she said. "We squandered the gifts the Eternal had given us and fought among ourselves for power. We destroyed our world, and now we'll destroy yours."

"Is there not still a chance for us to live in peace?"

She laughed at the thought. "It seems like a foolish hope to cling to at this point. Just look."

The elf turned to gaze at the battle that still raged. The elves were on the brink of defeat but still held their ground against the fierce onslaught of dark fire. "This may be the end of our rule," he said, "but under your people's rule, perhaps peace can be found between us. It'll take an age to accomplish, but with the Eternal's guidance, perhaps the impossible is still attainable."

The dragon laughed again. "You talk much, even for one of your kind. If there were more like you . . . then perhaps this peace you desire would not be so far off." Her large eyes met his. "Tell me your name, elf."

He straightened his back and gave her the elvish salute. "My name is Zaruf. I hail from the World's Edge, in the southwestern corner of Deerium."

As he finished speaking, the dragon's form began to change. Her beastly figure melted away, and in its place was a person not that different looking from an elf. Her hair was silver. It was short on the right side, barely past her chin, and long past her shoulder on the left. She wore a thin grey robe. Her eyes remained the same deep blue that matched her dragon form, glistening with a tint of dark red.

The elf stared in shock at her immense beauty as she slowly limped toward him, barely able to stand.

"My name is Boria," she said in a more soothing and quiet voice than before, "a dragon from the Western Spikes of the Drake."

Borhiim looked at the woman in confusion. He recognized her somehow. At the very least, he knew he had heard stories and legends about her. He remembered the name from one of Gwendall's stories. Boria would later be called the Elvish Dragon, the first of her kind to take an elf as her husband.

He didn't have much time to take it all in as everything began to speed up again, but this time he shot forward. Events flashed before him in seconds until it he stopped once more, still hundreds and hundreds of years in the past. He looked from the clouds at a large cluster of tall mountains. Taller than any he had ever seen. His vision turned to focus on one mountain in particular and zoomed into a cave that drove deep within. Inside were the same two figures from before.

Boria sat on the floor, a blanket covering her legs. Sweat gleamed on her face. In her arms, partly wrapped in a blue cloth, was a newborn child with brown hair and blue eyes. Male from the looks of it. He cried as Boria rocked him back and forth, outstretching his left hand toward her. On the tips of his fingers were tiny, pointed nails. A little tail poked its way out of the cloth. Borhiim could tell the child was a Takahrn—helpless and innocent.

Zaruf sat next to Boria, beaming at the child. He was a father.

"He's beautiful, Zaruf," Boria said. "He's perfect."

"Isn't he?" Zaruf said. "I can hardly believe that he's here."

He turned to look at his wife. She returned his gaze and kissed him.

"What do we call him?" she asked. "Something elvish?"

"No," he responded. "We should name him after his mother." He stopped to think before answering.

"Borhiim."

Time froze. He didn't know what to do with this new revelation. Borhiim clenched his eyes shut and squeezed his head with his hands. *No! No, no, no! This isn't who I am!* His head began to hurt again, but the pain slowly faded to the back of his mind. Deep down, he knew this was coming. A revelation that had already occurred, but he had rejected it. He just wanted things to go back to the way they were.

Borhiim opened his eyes again only to see that he had moved forward in time again. His vision swirled and stopped in a familiar place. It was the same vision from before of Zaruf in the cave. He was no longer a spectator. Like before, he viewed things from the perspective of his younger self, forced to play his role in history. The same scene played before him once more until Zaruf closed the entrance to the tunnel, forcing Borhiim to go forward.

An hour passed before he reached its end, the sound of the battle behind him fading into nothing. As he peeked his head out, he recognized the place as where he had been born. It was Boria and Zaruf's home. He stepped out of the tunnel and stood up, looking for his mother, but stopped when he noticed a group of five elves standing to his right. They wore bright white cloaks and hoods, the Anamoris mark painted in purple on the front, the same mark etched in various places on their bodies—a cheek, an arm, a leg.

They looked at the boy with silent expectation, and as Borhiim raised his voice to speak, he was quickly silenced by a blow to the head from behind. He didn't feel the pain of the attack but fell to the ground anyway.

When his sight returned, he was on the floor, vision blurred and dazed.

The hooded figures, now six, stood in a circle around him. They glanced at him before turning to each other to discuss what they would do next.

"Our assumptions were correct," one on the right said. "He bears the mark. No other Takahrn that we've seen carries one like his."

"The foolish mother," another said. "Did she think she could hide him forever?"

"What do we do with him? We can't kill him. He's too valuable to us. With his power, we could turn the tides of battle. The dragons' reign would end, and the elves could regain control. For too long the mortals have been given leave to do as they please. We could wipe them clean and start again."

"He must be our weapon," replied a third elf near Borhiim's feet, more commanding than the others. "Together we can bring him to obey our every command."

"What do you suggest?" a tall one on the left asked. "We cannot bend his will. His soul is too strong for that."

"We cast a spell on him," the third elf said. "Block out his memories of the past. Make him believe he's mortal."

"We can change his form and block his memories," chimed in the first, "but his long life can't be altered. He'll realize who he is after he watches those around him grow old."

They remained silent for a few seconds.

Then the tall elf spoke up. "We can have his memory reset," he said. "Every ten years, he'll forget who he is. He'll have no time to question where he came from before he starts back at the beginning."

"Very well," responded the first one. "Are we in agreement then?"

They all nodded slowly in unison. Stretching their hands outward over Borhiim's body, they closed their eyes.

He inhaled air quickly and sharply as a deep pain shot throughout his entire body. It felt as though his very essence was being toyed with. The elves started chanting phrases that stuck in his mind before his vision went black again—words that would cement themselves in history.

"We rise as the pure . . . As one we hold to perfection . . . We stand as the Righteous Ones."

The scene faded, and Borhiim was once again in darkness. However, before him stood a figure that shone like a light amidst the shadow. It was his mother, her silver hair flashing in the brightness.

Boria stood with her arms crossed, glaring at him. "Borhiim," she said, "why do you not accept your past?"

"That isn't my past," he answered. "I'm human. I'm not a monster."

The light grew brighter, and Borhiim squinted as it increased.

"You've never been a monster," she said, her voice softer. "You are a Takahrn, and you are my son." She pointed to his left shoulder. "The mark you bear—do you know what it means?"

"No," he replied. "I can't translate it."

"You can," she returned. "I ask again: do you know what it means?"

Borhiim looked at the curved marking etched into his skin. Slowly, it started to come to him. It was an ancient word. A word that he had learned long ago when he was just a boy, it's meaning lost on him until now.

"Devil's Flame."

"You are the only one not of the dragon race who can wield its power," she said. "To summon the Devil's Flame, one must have access to both Terrkoris and Anamoris magic. That is what makes it so dangerous. It burns through all—body and soul. You have that power, Borhiim. Only you."

With that, the spell broke loose from his mind. The headaches ceased, and all his memories returned to him. Memories of wandering across the land. Memories of Gahlaia, his childhood friend. He had traveled for so long. Hungry, alone, afraid, unsure. How had he forgotten it all? And yet, he was left conflicted. *Those days were so long.*

Borhiim glanced back up at his mother as she began to fade from view. "Wait!" he yelled. "Don't leave me. Please!"

"She needs your help, my son," she responded, her voice growing faint. "Gahlaia needs you if you are to change the course of history . . . Save the kingdom. Save Deerium. Save the Twin Worlds."

BORHIIM AWOKE FROM his slumber with a start. He lay on his back, grass rustling around him. To his right was a still pond of water. He looked to his left to see Gahlaia and the other Takahrn locked in battle. It took him a second to understand all that had happened to him before it all came back.

Realization and assurance flooded him, and as he rose to his feet, he glanced at his reflection in the pond. A dark red glow flashed in his blue eyes. The mortal who had once dwelt in him was gone, replaced by someone else, holding at his fingertips a power he could scarcely hope to contain.

Chapter 6

THE CRESCENT MOON still hung high in the sky as Gahlaia held her position against the incoming danger.

Doryan's features became clearer as he grew closer, barreling down toward them with extreme fury. The blood on his left arm had dried and crusted to a dark shade, the wound completely sealed—closed like a scar. His skin was tight and thin under the strain of his weapon's magic. Gahlaia could see that his life was forfeit before the battle even began. He had been using Terrkoris magic that his mortal body was not meant to wield for so long. Even if he killed them all, his form would decay before he could ever return to the Dirtlands.

She looked up toward the mountains that sprawled before her. Craden and his followers were in position above a small cliff atop the mountain to her right. Anahka's tail twitched in anticipation, and the three other Takahrn behind them bowed low in ready positions.

"This is it," Gahlaia whispered to herself. She stretched her wings outward in a wide span and Anahka followed suit.

Doryan grew closer and closer, his war cries becoming more and more audible.

She raised her left hand and held it in position, waiting for her opportunity. "Now!" Gahlaia yelled, as Doryan sprinted through the mountain pass.

Anahka followed her as the two of them shook their wings forward and flew low to the ground toward the general, the three others following close behind on the ground. They halted as Doryan prepared for his first swing, their feet dragging across the dirt. The ax sliced sideways toward Gahlaia's and Anahka's chests. They let their sliding feet skim forward as their bodies swung back to dodge the attack, using their wings to cushion their descent to the ground.

As the large blade whizzed past them, the gust smacking their faces, the three Takahrn behind jumped over them, talons reaching out for the enemy's throat. Doryan leaped back, but his immense speed had slowed since the last encounter. The two strikes on his left and right nicked the ends of his once braided hair, but the middle attacker's claw slashed into his left cheek. He stumbled as he landed off balance, but the Takahrn didn't hesitate to resume the offensive. They sprinted forward, their hands ready to slice through his rough skin, Gahlaia and Anahka close behind.

Doryan jumped again, flipping over the three in front. In midair, he swung his ax downward toward the one who had struck him. The weapon made contact, digging deep into the Takahrn's spine with a crack. As he landed firmly in the dirt, the corpse remained stuck on the blade, and he threw it off harshly in Gahlaia and Anahka's direction. The limp form spun, crashing into their knees. They fell hard, Anahka's face striking the rough soil.

Gahlaia put her arms out and caught herself before she hit the dirt. She looked up to see Doryan above her, his ax raised high to finish her. The two wingless Takahrn rushed in from behind to assist, but he anticipated the assault. He spun around and charged straight for them. They jumped over his low swing, their arms outstretched in one final attempt to finish the battle quickly, only to be met with a clenched right fist. It splintered into the first one's jaw, slamming his head into the other's. They crashed to the ground and lay motionless.

Doryan turned back toward Gahlaia, who had regained her

stance. Anahka rose slowly, dazed, her nose bleeding and bruised from the prior impact. They breathed hard as they prepared for the general's next move.

"You kill my men," he said, his voice scratchy and rough, "and then you run like cowards. You Dividers are all the same."

"You started this when you put us in chains, human," Anahka said, gasping for air between words. "We're ending this before you enslave us all."

Doryan spread his arms outward. "What do you hope to achieve?" he asked. "You expect us to accept you after what you've done to our people? To our families? To our kingdom?"

"Enough talk," Gahlaia said. "You're a soldier. Talking isn't your strong suit. If you're going to kill us, then shut up and get on with it already!"

His face grew red with rage, and he bolted at them.

Gahlaia raised her right hand upward and swung it down. With the signal given, Craden and the others swooped down from the cliff.

Doryan looked up just before the collision and dove away, several claws slicing down his back, leaving dents in his plating. He grunted at the pain but managed to narrowly escape the initial surprise attack. He rose to his feet. They had him surrounded. Gahlaia and Anahka on his left, Craden and his followers on his right, and the two mountains in front and behind. There was nowhere to go. The wounds on his cheek had nearly healed, but little droplets of warm blood still trickled down. He spat as it rolled toward the edge of his mouth.

"This is your last chance, general," Gahlaia said. "Drop your ax and surrender, and you may live."

Doryan laughed and wiped the right side of his face, the back of his hand stained red. "I'd be a hostage," he said, grinning. "I'm not the one who deserves to be put in a cage."

That was the last straw.

The Takahrn charged. Doryan closed his eyes and tightened his grip on the ax. In those few seconds, Gahlaia watched a final flourish of Terrkoris magic shoot through his body, his face growing thin and skeletal. The wound on his cheek healed instantly, and he opened his eyes moments before his attackers made contact. He threw the blade side of his weapon hard into the dirt. It cracked and created a shockwave that knocked them all onto their backs.

Before Gahlaia could pull herself up, Doryan was upon her, throwing his ax downward toward her face. She brought her hands up to meet the strike, her strong, sharp claws digging into the blade of the ax, catching it an inch from her face. They held for a moment. It was a battle of strength now, and Doryan had the overhead advantage. Her arms began to tremble under the immense pressure.

Gahlaia twitched her tail, wrapping it around his right leg, and then pulled, trying to knock him off balance. Instead, Doryan lifted his leg, slammed it hard into her tail, and dragged it across the ground. She screamed in agony but held her arms in position, her strength waning fast.

Craden and the others regained their balance and charged to save their leader.

"Move any closer," Doryan threatened, "and she dies."

He tugged harder at her tail, and she screamed louder. The elvish metal nicked Gahlaia's chin, and the other Takahrn froze.

"Just . . . do it already," Gahlaia said in an uneven voice. "You'll kill me anyway." She turned to Anahka, who was still frozen in place. "Dying . . . among family."

The pressure increased, the ax pressing lightly against her face.

"Enough, Doryan."

Gahlaia felt the pressure lighten, and she darted her eyes to her side. A figure strode across the grassy plain toward the group. It was Borhiim, his blue eyes now showing clear outlines of dark red. He had ripped the sleeves off his tattered shirt, fully revealing the elvish mark on his left shoulder.

The other Takahrn backed up toward the mountains, gazing at the mark on his shoulder. Murmurs rose from their ranks. Borhiim's name passed from their lips, and Doryan darted his eyes to and fro in bewilderment.

Borhiim outstretched his left claw toward the general. "Just walk away," he pleaded. "There doesn't need to be any more bloodshed."

"Tell that to my dead men," Doryan said with a grimace. "Tell that to my mother. My father. Tell it to any of the other people who lie nameless in the dirt because of you and your kind!"

"Don't do this. Please. This is a battle you can't win. Surrender . . . Gwendall wouldn't want this."

"*Shut up!*" Doryan shrieked. "You have no right to speak her name. You destroyed all she could ever want. You betrayed us all."

He turned back to Gahlaia, who still persisted in trying to push his ax away from her face. She was once again focused on staying alive, arms groaning in protest and her tail growing numb with the pain.

A battle cry rang through the mountains, and before she could grasp what was happening, the Devil's Flame blasted from Borhiim toward Doryan's upper body. He looked up in shock, released his grip on his ax, and tumbled to his left to avoid the flames.

Gahlaia lay motionless as the shadowy blaze passed overhead, the shockwave of heat nearly unbearable. When the flames had faded away, she held merely the blade of the weapon in her claws. The handle was completely burned away as if it had never existed.

Doryan stared at Borhiim in disbelief, and the other Takahrn remained still as statues.

Gahlaia seized the opportunity and rushed the general, holding the ax blade in her left hand. Doryan hooked his right fist toward her jaw, but his speed was gone. He no longer had his weapon to keep fueling his magic, and his mortal state was all that remained, shriveled and weak. She easily knocked away the blow with her right hand and thrust the blade into his stomach, her face inches from his.

The air shot sharply out of him, and he stared at her blankly, heaving and groaning.

She clasped his throat and opened her mouth, revealing her fangs underneath. "For the lives you've taken," she whispered, "and for the innocent who have lived under the feet of your people . . . may the Eternal leave you nameless in the dirt."

She pulled the broken blade from his stomach, and he staggered back before falling to the ground. He was dead.

Gahlaia tossed the red-stained metal next to the body before turning to gaze at Borhiim, his eyes returned to their natural shade of blue. They all remained motionless, staring at him with a mix of shock and terror.

He ignored their gazes and strode toward the two wingless Takahrn that remained motionless in the dirt and filth. He felt for their pulses as the rest of the group surrounded him.

"They're alright," he said. "They're still alive, but this one has a broken jaw, and the other one probably has a concussion." He turned to the dead Takahrn splayed behind him in an unnatural form. "I can't say the same for him, though."

Gahlaia sighed. "That makes seventeen of us. We keep this up and we'll all be dead before we get anywhere near Valia."

Borhiim turned his gaze to Doryan's corpse, and a worried look passed over his face. Finally, he closed his eyes, shook his head, and stared up at Gahlaia. "Eighteen, actually," he said. "I'm with you, Gahlaia."

She turned to match his gaze, eyebrows raised. "Ah," she said, relieved, "so you remember me then?"

He nodded. "It was hundreds of years ago, but I've had a bit of an awakening as of late. I remember everything quite clearly now."

"So, you really are *that* Borhiim?" Anahka asked, "The son of Boria and Zaruf?"

He nodded again.

"That's quite the stroke of luck," Anahka responded. "And you and Gahlaia—"

"When we were just children," Gahlaia interrupted. "It was long before the dragons were driven back to their homeland. What I don't understand is what happened back in the Dirtlands."

"First, help me carry these two back to the pond," he said. "Then I'll explain everything."

CRADEN AND BORHIIM carried the two unconscious Takahrn back to the flat, grassy plain, and Gahlaia carried the dead body of her fallen comrade to the foot of the mountain, leaving the general's where it lay. The others assisted in digging a proper grave, placing him inside.

Gahalaia murmured a quick prayer to the Eternal, and the rest bowed their heads low in reverence. "Rest in peace, brother."

When they all returned to the pond, the two had awoken, the first one's jaw already starting to heal. That was one saving grace of not being human. They mended faster than any mortal. The thought reminded Gahlaia of her own wound that she had suffered earlier. She lifted her hand and felt for the end of her left horn. It still was a nub, but it had started its healing process. It would be pointed and sharp within a day or two.

Borhiim sat down with the rest of the Takahrn and retold everything in great detail, from his parents' first meeting to his unfortunate encounter with the Righteous Ones. When he had finished, they stared at him in skepticism, save for Gahlaia.

She cocked her head and looked down in thought. "You say you saw visions of the past," she said. "Visions of a great battle at the end of the first age and a vision of your birth."

Borhiim nodded.

"My guess is what you saw was the Battle of Fate," Gahlaia continued, tracing a claw in the dirt. "It was the deciding battle in the war between elves and dragons. The High Elf Tarkuv was struck down by my father, Gahlorm. Those who survived fled into the mountains of the Claw where they lived out the rest of their lives during the second age."

"That was my assumption," Borhiim responded.

Gahlaia squinted, still toying with the soil. "There's one thing I don't get, though. How could you have seen these visions in the first place? They aren't your memories."

Borhiim sat in silence, thinking of an answer. "To summon the Devil's Flame, I possess a small portion of both Terrkoris and Anamoris. In turn, since the dragons also had this power, they too had a connection to both."

He spread his hands over the plains. "History lies in the soil of the world around us and in the souls of those forgotten. Anamoris and Terrkoris are tangible in their nature. Attuning with both of them, one could look briefly through times gone by."

"You're telling me that you did all of that in your sleep?" Craden questioned.

"I suppose." Borhiim shrugged. "There have been elves who have done it before."

"Not like that," Anahka said. "Not to that extent. But wait. What about your mother? You said she spoke to you. Even fully powered

Anamoris elves were never able to speak with the dead directly. How were you able to?"

"I'm not sure," he responded. "I'd tell you if I could."

Silence once again covered the plain. Weariness from their journey was beginning to set in, and the night still fell young over the land.

"Well," Gahlaia said with a yawn, "we all need to get some sleep. We head for Dragorish Canyon at sunrise." She looked to Borhiim. "You know what it is we're going to do. Are you still with us?"

He gave the elvish salute. "People have died for this," he said. "If this is how we can change things for our people, then of course we should. I don't like the idea of going to war with the humans, but something needs to change. If we take the king hostage, perhaps we can get him to see our perspective. I don't see another way."

She nodded at his response and slumped down into the grass, the rest following her example. The horses stood near the pond, their reins firmly tied to some long, heavy stones lying near the water's edge.

Sleep took them all in seconds.

BORHIIM OPENED HIS eyes and looked around. It was still dark. All slept soundly. He had hoped he would sleep through the night until the sunrise, but he had a lot on his mind as of late. So much had happened in such a short time. It had only been a single day, but to him, it felt as if it had been weeks. He couldn't stop thinking about Gwendall. They had left her in the Dirtlands, and the look on her face, hands to her mouth, had not left him. His dreams were haunted by it. What would she think of him now? He had helped in the death of her brother. Was there truly nothing else he could have done?

Maybe he could have persuaded Doryan further, but thinking of what he could have done only made him feel worse.

He sighed and decided it would do him good to take a quick walk before returning to his slumber. Slowly, he rose to his feet, the grass rustling slightly. He walked away from the group, being careful to not step on anyone. He passed Gahlaia, sleeping on her right side. Her blonde hair almost glowed in the moonlight, her beauty showing through despite the dirt covering her face and body. Borhiim stood for a moment before catching himself in a daze. He shook his head, and the grass rustled louder in turn.

He froze. Gahlaia's slumbering figure shifted and groaned but remained in position. Satisfied, he continued his exit from the group.

He came to Doryan's body. It had decayed at an incredible rate, likely due to the magic he had pushed himself to use. There was hardly anything left that could be buried. Guilt reaching its peak, Borhiim turned and looked upon the body no more.

He circled the outskirts of the plain along the sides of the mountains surrounding them. As he walked, he noticed many unusual things about their resting grounds. The grass in the center of the plain formed a perfect square, and past it, the land returned to dirt and rock, as if something or someone kept the place in constant care.

Borhiim assumed it to be the work of the elves. Many places marked as holy in their culture were shaped in specific ways using Terrkoris magic. Even after they were long gone, the spell still held to the world. Magic may not exist within most of the living as it once did, but nature still radiated with the same potential that it did in ancient times.

Borhiim ran a claw over a mountain wall in curiosity. With the light of the moon still hanging in the sky, he could see carvings molded into the rock. They were ancient elvish inscriptions, written in a sort of pattern. However, feeling the indents in the rock, he concluded that these writings were not the work of Terrkoris magic. The shapes were rough and showed signs of wear, as opposed to the perfect precision and lasting effect of the grassy plain.

Walking around the outskirts several times, he noticed that the carvings would stop and then repeat every twenty feet, directly at eye level. Every cluster of markings made up a total of three sentences each, stopped, and then continued in the next batch. Borhiim recognized the words.

"We rise as the pure. As one we hold to perfection. We stand as the Righteous Ones."

He shuddered as the phrases left his whispering lips. They disgusted him. So much of the Righteous Ones' work was done in secrecy, but he knew much of this place. They became religious leaders after the rejection of the Eternal, and the Waters of the Righteous was where they conducted many of their practices. The pond was kept clean for baptisms, initiating the believing as pure. But only the six kept the name Righteous Ones. It was a position of power, and they held it until their disappearance from the world.

He turned his gaze away, but as he did, he caught something in the corner of his eye and focused on it. On the side of the northwestern mountain was a dark crack. Moving toward it, he realized that it was a form of door that slid into the mountain. A small metal handle stuck out of it, a keyhole at its bottom. It was only slightly open, allowing some moonlight to seep in. He grasped the handle and pulled to the side, but it held fast. It was old, and the weariness of its long years without use was taking its toll. He put his left hand on the open side of it and, clutching the handle with his right, shoved as hard as he could to the right to get it to budge. Finally, with a loud scrape across the ground, it gave way and slid open.

Borhiim looked back toward the Takahrn to see if any were

awoken by the sound. Seeing them still in their same spots, he walked into the dark opening.

He couldn't see anything. The moon went only so far into the deep cavern, and he was running out of light. Holding his left hand outward, Borhiim focused his senses. He felt the mark on his shoulder burn, and his eyes twitched. He snapped his fingers, and a sudden burst of shadowy flames erupted from them. He bent his head back abruptly from the shock. The flame shrank until it floated lightly above his palm, spreading light through the cavern. He could feel the Devil's Flame tug at him, resisting slightly, but nothing substantial enough to matter.

He continued his walk through the cave, which slowly shaped itself into a long hallway. He looked across the walls for markings of some sort only to be left disappointed. There was no trace of the writings anywhere, and the rocky walls were rough and unpolished. If this was the Righteous Ones' work, then whatever was at its end was not cared for in the slightest.

Borhiim squinted. In the distance, he could see the dead end of the hall, with pieces of metal hanging from the wall. As he moved closer, an unnerving feeling came over him. It trembled and pulsated deep in his core, and the closer he got to the end, the more powerful it felt.

Suddenly, he heard footsteps coming from behind him. He turned, listening to the sound getting louder until an individual appeared before him.

It was Gahlaia, rubbing her tired eyes and groaning to herself.

"Good grief!" Borhiim said, letting out a breath of relief. "Don't scare me like that. What in the world are you doing here?"

"I could ask you the same thing," she replied. "You're supposed to be sleeping. We have a long journey ahead of us."

"I had a lot on my mind. I was just taking a short walk." He looked at her intently before gesturing at the dead end. "Gahlaia, do you know where we are? You traveled all across Deerium with your father when you were young. Surely you have an idea?"

She shook her head. "I had no clue that a cavern like this existed," she said.

"But why the Waters of the Righteous?" Borhiim asked. "Of all places, why bring us here?"

"I didn't want to come here," she responded. "Originally, we were going to go around, but that general had other plans."

Borhiim turned, his flame directed toward the end of the hall. He walked forward, Gahlaia following behind.

"Do you feel that?" he asked.

"I feel it," she said. "It feels like someone's pulling at my insides."

Borhiim had felt this sensation before when he had his memories wiped. It wasn't a pleasant thing to recall. "This place . . . It's filled with Anamoris magic."

Reaching the end, they stood in silence at the scene before them. Connected to the wall were four links of chains, two at chest level and two outstretched on the ground. At their ends, the shackles had been cut loose or ripped off. Whatever was there before had broken free.

In the corner of the room was a cluster of bones. Six skeletons lay motionless in the dirt, several on top of each other.

"These are elvish bones," Gahlaia said. "Any other skeletons this old would have decayed by now."

Borhiim nodded in agreement. He stepped closer to them, the feeling in his core gripping him harder than ever. It was coming from the skeletons. "I think . . . I think it's them. The Righteous Ones."

"How do you know?"

"I'm not certain, but who else would know this place exists, and there were six of them in total, so it's very possible."

Cocking his head, Borhiim spotted words written in the dirt, barely noticeable under the skeletal carcasses. It wasn't elvish but rather draconic, but he couldn't make it out. The feeling grew too unbearable, and he stepped back from the scene. He spun and faced Gahlaia.

"They had someone or something chained up in here. Something very powerful. Whatever it was used Anamoris to do this, and yet . . ."

Borhiim shook his head to gather his thoughts.

It was Anamoris magic at its core, but it felt twisted. Twisted in a way that left an almost deathly stench to it, and it was starting to cloud his thinking. It was spiritual energy, but there was also something more. Something defiled. There was a story here, but one he couldn't fully piece together.

Chapter 7

Day two of the third month.

PRINCE TIREHN STOOD on the large balcony of his father's palace and stared out into the streets of Valia. His coronation was not too far off, and the thought of ruling all Deerium made him fear for himself and his people.

As a whole, the land of Deerium relied on strength and intellect in its leaders. Deerium's royal primogenitor, King Graan, was not chosen for his bloodline but because the people wanted him to rule. That was why the rulers of Cleptyn, Verish, and Norvad did not come from that royal bloodline; they were instead tested into their positions. But the rulers of the central kingdom of Deeria, and therefore all of Deerium, still traced their ancestry to Deerium's first king, and the people of Deeria desired no interlude of testing between kings.

So Tirehn's coronation was planned before his father's demise. He went untested—but his coronation implied a standard Tirehn was meant to meet. His father and he had never reached a mutual understanding when it came to ruling. There were things Tirehn wished to change. He only hoped the people would follow him.

He breathed slowly. He was born for this. It was this coronation that his father had raised him for. Tirehn lifted his chin and closed his eyes, feeling the chill breeze blow softly across his face.

"My lord," came a voice from behind.

Tirehn broke from his daze and turned to face the speaker.

It was Raggorin, the king's closest advisor and a teacher of the sword. He and Tirehn had always been on good terms, but the prince had grown closer to him in recent weeks, seeing as Raggorin would be Tirehn's consultant when he would take the throne.

Raggorin wore unusual clothing for a servant of the palace, but it was customary for his people who lived in the Gorrobin Mountains of Cleptyn. His shirt was a leather cloth that strapped to his right shoulder and crossed diagonally down to his waist, revealing most of his bare chest. His right arm was covered by a lone sleeve, and his left kept unadorned. His pants were baggy, a dagger remained sheathed and strapped to his right leg, and a large elvish broadsword hung from his back, an old gift from the king.

He bowed toward the prince. "I pray you slept well?" he asked, his voice low.

"I did, Raggorin," Tirehn responded. "Thank you. It's a fine morning, is it not?"

"It is indeed, my lord." Raggorin walked to the balcony's edge and joined the prince in watching the sunrise.

"Your people have always intrigued me," Tirehn said, glancing over the man's clothing. "Some of the few with any semblance of magic. I would expect at least some of you to buckle against the snow and freezing temperatures of the Gorrobin Mountains."

Raggorin gave a half smile, shrugging his shoulders. "We may have lost the Terrkoris marks of our ancestors, but atop the Cleptyn mountains, we retained some semblance of their strength. The Eternal's final gift to a dying people."

The prince nodded. It was an explanation he had heard numerous times. Most elves had been driven to the mountains of the Claw in the old war, but Gorrobin, elvish commander of the east, had surrendered peacefully along with those serving under him, so the dragons left them to their lands. Pleased with their decision, the

Eternal blessed their human descendants with a semblance of the Terrkoris their ancestors once possessed, and thus the Gorrobin tribes were formed, some of the greatest warriors known in all the sectors.

"It's a comfort knowing that some magic still presents itself to some of us," Tirehn said.

"Magic is fickle," Raggorin returned, "yet it remains a constant part of life. Remove it from one group, and it simply takes root elsewhere."

"You know," the prince said, facing the doorway, "I could get used to your words of wisdom. I never tire of them."

Raggorin let a chuckle slip, following the prince to the door and through the long corridor of the palace.

The interior of the palace was covered with smooth wooden flooring and tapestries hanging from the walls that told stories of days gone by—great battles from the old war, the founding of the four sectors, and one that always caught Tirehn's attention: King Graan, the first king, and his decisive battle that drove back the Takahrn. They had tried to lay siege to Valia during a peace treaty, but he managed to rally his forces and drive them to submission. So went the story, one that his father had drilled into his head early on.

They walked through the hall, and took a right toward two large, silver doors. A soldier stood on each side, spears in hand. As Tirehn approached, they stamped their feet together and turned sideways before the door.

He looked to the man on the left. "Is she awake?" Tirehn asked.

"Yes, my lord," the soldier replied. "She awoke about an hour ago."

The prince turned to Raggorin and motioned for him to stay put, and with that, the prince pulled the doors open and closed them behind him. He looked across the room and stared at the figure standing on the other side.

Ahmeras turned to look at him and smiled. She wore a white silk shirt and grey pants. In both of her hands, she held thin swords, still sheathed. On her left cheek was an elvish Terrkoris mark that translated to "shape" in the ancient tongue. He nodded at her, and she tossed a blade in his direction. They unsheathed their weapons and took fighting stances.

Ahmeras came at him with a diagonal cut, but he blocked it with the blunt end of the blade. She pushed hard, and the swords screeched as she closed the distance, their faces inches from each other.

Spinning his blade down, Tirehn released the pressure from their clash, the swords swishing to their sides with a flourish. He moved to the offensive, crashing the blade down to force her back.

Ahmeras held her ground but was slowly giving in to the prince's strength. Raggorin had trained him well over the years.

He raised his sword and brought it down hard. She met his attack with equal force, her knees nearly buckling as metal met metal. The thinly fashioned weapons rang upon impact.

She grunted as he pressed harder, using his weight to push her to the ground. Slowly, Ahmeras dropped her left knee.

"Yield," Tirehn said. He pushed further down, her own blade touching her right shoulder.

Ahmeras twisted her blade diagonally, letting the prince's weight slide his sword away from her, giving her the chance to regain her footing. Spinning herself to the right, she cut toward his side. He recovered quickly and parried the assault but retreated to prepare for the next move.

Ahmeras advanced swiftly, bringing with her a volley of cuts and quick strikes. Tirehn stepped back as the onslaught continued, driving him to the closed doors behind him. Putting her strength into a final swing, she slashed her sword toward his chest.

Tirehn blocked the strike, twisting his body sideways, allowing his blade to drag across hers until it reached the hilt. Grabbing her wrist with his left, he bent his weapon downward, ripping her weapon from his grip. As it hit the floor, the prince stamped his right foot on top of it. She was defenseless and defeated.

"That's one for me," Tirehn said with a chuckle.

Ahmeras shrugged. "Don't get too cocky," she said. "I won yesterday, so this just evens out the score."

The prince leaned down and picked the sword up off the ground, walking across the room to retrieve its sheath. "I could do without the use of actual swords though. Since we started doing this, I've gained my fair share of scars, especially the one on my left leg."

She waved a dismissive hand behind her. "Oh please, I barely scratched you."

"It still hurts, actually," he muttered. "I'm not sure it's healed completely."

Tirehn sheathed the blades and set them on the bed. "You're lucky. We don't all heal as quickly as you do."

"It isn't my fault you're mortal," Ahmeras said with a laugh, tucking her hair behind her pointed ears.

The prince walked up behind her and put a hand on her shoulder. "You look beautiful today."

She lifted her head and faced him, rolling her eyes. "I'm an elf, Tirehn," she replied, pointing to her mark, "and a shapeshifter at that. I can make myself as beautiful as I want."

She closed her eyes. The mark on her cheek glowed a bright white and vanished from her face, her form changing completely. She was now taller and thinner, her hair changing from black to blonde. It grew from its original shoulder length down to her waist. Her clothes also transformed into a red dress that covered her feet as her eyes shifted from brown to green.

Ahmeras curtseyed, flashing a smile. "Better?" she asked, her voice a higher pitch that starkly contrasted her previous tone.

Tirehn's expression stayed unflinching. "No," he said dryly, "because it isn't you."

Ahmeras leaned forward and embraced him. Her façade melted away, returning to normal. "And that's why I love you, Tirehn. You always say the most ridiculous things with a straight face."

"I love you too," he answered with a laugh, wrapping his arms around her in return. "I guess I'm just lucky you didn't use that to try and impress my father when I introduced you."

"Why would I?" she said as they released each other. "I have a Terrkoris symbol on my face. Of course he would want his son to marry someone with a connection to the old magic."

"That's not why he allowed our betrothal," Tirehn responded. "As far as we know, you're the last of your kind. He wants to preserve your race."

She shook her head. "He wants a trophy. He wants a queen who will strengthen his line. He's not looking out for me nor the elvish bloodline." Her face flushed as her old frustrations resurfaced.

"I agree that he hasn't been the perfect ruler," he said, "maybe not even a good one, but you can't honestly blame him for the extinction of your kind."

"He only protects those he sees as being worthy of his protection, Tirehn," she exclaimed, "while the rest pick up the table scraps."

"Deerium has lived in peace under my father and his father's rule and all the other kings that came before them. That can't be dismissed so easily." He spoke the words confidently, but they were practiced. In truth, not even he was sure he believed them. Peace meant different things to different people.

"Only the humans live in peace!" she insisted.

Tirehn looked up toward the ceiling in frustration and put his hands on his waist. "Not this again . . ." he mumbled.

"The Takahrn live in slavery," she continued, ignoring his previous remark. "Those who don't, live in fear of the king's rule."

"They struck first, Ahmeras," the prince replied. "They attacked us when we first established a kingdom away from the mountains of your ancestors. You know that."

"So, an entire race is to be held accountable for a single action in history? That was hundreds of years ago!"

"You know that wasn't the only action. We could be on the brink of war. Dividers—"

"Don't call them that," she interrupted.

"*Takahrn* raid villages throughout Deerium, calling themselves the Grey Wings. They burn and destroy everything, plastering their banner to walls."

"And frankly, I can scarcely blame them for it," Ahmeras returned. "We aren't on the brink of war—it's already here. It's just that no one will admit it."

"If we release the slaves," Tirehn argued, "they could join together and attack Valia or any of the capital cities of the other sectors. It would be a slaughter."

"And they would do so because they have been hunted or imprisoned by your father and his ancestors for hundreds of years!"

Tirehn let out a long sigh. "What do you expect me to do, Ahmeras?"

"You'll be king," she said. "Show the people how to live. Be their example. Make peace with the Takahrn."

"And how would I do that? The rulers of the other sectors wouldn't stand for it. We'd have a civil war on our hands."

Ahmeras turned her back to the prince, clenching her fists. She looked as if she were ready to burst fire from her skull. Finally, she let out a breath and relaxed. "Sometimes making the right choice means walking the hardest path," was all she could say.

Tirehn stepped forward to reply only for a knock to come loudly at the silver doors behind them. They swung open, and Raggorin strode in.

"Come quickly, my lord," the advisor said. "It's your father."

TIREHN ENTERED THE dimly lit room, with Raggorin stopping at the door. On a big wooden bed at the far end, covered with sheets and blankets, lay his father, King Hyrehn.

Two soldiers stood straight, one at each side, swords drawn and held in front of them. Nodding to them, the prince knelt and gazed at the king. His head was all that stuck out of the covers, his unkempt grey beard flowing out, eyes shut.

"Father?" Tirehn said, lightly shaking him by the shoulders. No response came.

"King Hyrehn!" Raggorin called from across the room. "Your son has come to see you."

A loud cough followed, and the king opened his eyes slightly. He turned his head toward the prince. He was extremely pale, his features almost skeletal. Whether it was illness or old age that had led him to his death bed Tirehn could not say, nor could anyone else. It was true that he was old, but his decline had come so suddenly.

However, these were not things that Tirehn gave much thought to. His mother had died in childbirth, and since that day, many noticed a change in the king's disposition. He grew rougher and blunter, but the worst of it was directed upon his son. He showed the boy little anger in his youth, but neither did he give him care.

Instead, Hyrehn gave him to many tutors and trainers to learn how the world worked and how to properly rule, but the king himself remained emotionally aloof. Tirehn had grown used to it in his young adulthood, but it came with a price. He had hoped that for once, on his death bed, at his end, his father would show him some emotion. But the king simply squinted at him, wearing the same expression he always had, and Tirehn felt nothing.

A hint of disappointment stung in the back of his mind.

Several moments of silence passed as the king stared at his son, occasionally coughing through his scruffy beard. Eventually, he pulled his left hand out from under the bedsheets and motioned Tirehn to come closer. He leaned in, and his father lifted his face close, speaking softly through cracked lips.

"Truth . . ." said Hyrehn. "Truth is folly . . . You will be king. Find an idea to stand upon . . . and the people will follow. Proclaim sins to be acts of holiness . . . and they will stand by you."

Tirehn pulled back. *What does he mean?*

But before he could respond or question him, Hyrehn leaned further in, his lips nearly touching his son's ear. He trembled slightly, and his voice shook, taking the prince by surprise. "Help me," he whispered. "His voice . . . I hear his voice. He's always in my head . . . repeating his name to me . . . over and over and over and over . . ."

He continued to repeat the words, and Tirehn's heart sank deep in his chest as they slithered in his mind. *What is this? Has he gone completely insane?*

Then sluggishly, the king struggled to mutter out one final word. A name.

"Tarubas . . ."

A final exhale later, King Hyrehn's head slumped back down onto the bed, his eyes now blank.

Letting out a long breath, Tirehn lifted himself to his feet and turned to Raggorin. "The king is dead."

THE REST OF the day passed swiftly, and soon sunset was upon them.

Tirehn and Raggorin watched as the soldiers placed the king's body into an iron coffin, the mark of a crown etched onto its lid. Before closing it, Raggorin pulled out a long and wrinkled scroll, held shut by a seal, and placed it in the corpse's hands.

When the advisor took his place back at the prince's side, Tirehn nudged him in the arm. "What's that?" he asked. "Why did you put that with the body?"

"It was his final request," Raggorin responded in a whisper. "He asked that he be put to rest with it in his hands."

The prince stared at the parchment with curiosity until the coffin was shut tight. "What was so important that he kept the scroll sealed?" he wondered.

"None can say," Raggorin said. "Only the king has read it."

They sat in the quiet as they watched the men carry the coffin into the tomb, pulling the heavy metal door closed. Even after the soldiers left their posts, the two remained, standing in the stillness until the sun had set and the skies darkened.

"Tell me, Raggorin," Tirehn said. "Was my father any different around you? Did he speak of anything important? Anything at all?"

Raggorin kept his head low, pondering. "I became his advisor and protector when you were just a boy," he said. "If there was truly a good and kind man underneath, he never showed it. He spoke little to me and even less so in his later years."

Tirehn breathed out harshly. "Quite blunt of you to talk of the dead in such a way." But when the advisor started to bow in apology, he put up a hand. "It's fine. You're not wrong in stating the obvious."

The prince drooped his head down, his father's final words echoing in his brain as he tried and failed to decipher their meaning.

"Something on your mind?" Raggorin asked, noticing the prince's clouded expression.

"He said some things to me that I can't piece together," he replied. "They make me wonder if he really had lost his sanity in the end."

"If you don't mind me asking, what did he say?"

"That truth is folly. That the people would follow me regardless of any idea's supposed merit."

Raggorin put a hand to his chin. "That doesn't make sense. Why would he tell you a thing like that? And on his death bed no less."

"There's more," Tirehn said, his heart sinking again. "Before he died, he whispered something to me. It almost sounded like he was begging for his life. Like he wasn't in control of himself."

"What's that supposed to mean?"

"He said a voice was speaking in his head." He paused. "And he gave me a name: Tarubas."

Raggorin squinted and shook his head. "I've never heard that name," he said.

"Nor have I," Tirehn returned. "It's been frustrating me to no end. It's been years, and only at the end does he say something that leaves a lasting impression." He clenched his fists until his knuckles turned white.

Raggorin squeezed his temples between his thumb and index finger, trying to muster an explanation. "Well," he thought aloud, "either the king truly had gone mad, or someone . . . this Tarubas . . . could have had a hand in the death of your father."

Chapter 8

Day three of the third month.

THE EVENING HAD set in. They had covered a lot of ground for one day. Borhiim glanced behind him. They had left the Dirtlands far behind them and had entered into rockier terrain. They would be crossing the Dragorish Canyon soon, a massive gorge that stretched from Pordika to the Bay of Beginnings, where the elves first washed onto Deerium soil.

It was an understatement to say that it would be difficult to cross the canyon. It would already be a bit of a strain for the Takahrn to fly across, but what was worse was there were three of them that were wingless, Borhiim included. To safely cross without taking too much time, they would have to be carried over. Thankfully, three Takahrn had already volunteered to take on the task: Gahlaia, Craden, and Anahka. Not surprising. Craden and Anahka had really risen to the occasion among the group.

With their three chosen, they remained on mounts, saving their strength for the crossing. Borhiim slapped the reins on his horse to keep pace with the rest as his mind kept racing. Everything had been planned but with the assumption that everything would go smoothly.

There was also the issue of Borhiim's control—or lack thereof—over the Devil's Flame. It hadn't done anything yet, but he could feel it: a resistance steadily increasing within him, and it left him uneasy.

He shook his head, trying to clear away his concerns about the upcoming situation.

"Hey," Gahlaia said, riding on his left. "You're going to drift from the group if you're not looking ahead."

"Right," Borhiim replied. "Sorry. I guess I'm a little unsure about crossing the canyon."

"Well, it's too late to rethink it now," she returned. "We're almost there, and we need all the time we can get."

THE SUN WAS beginning to set in the west, leaving the cloudy sky orange. They had finally reached Dragorish Canyon. The Takahrn removed their supplies from their horses' saddles and released them to the wild of the World's Edge. The rest of the journey would be taken on foot.

The wind began to pick up as Borhiim stood near the cliffside looking into the gorge. Something didn't feel right to him. He knelt down and placed his hands to the ground. He closed his eyes and focused the Terrkoris magic into his fingertips and spread it into the bottom of the canyon. His mind dispersed with it, searching for signs of life.

Sure enough, somewhere deep below, there was movement. Something crawled beneath his line of sight and began to frantically grasp at the walls of the cliffs, climbing them. Borhiim was unsure of its size, but it felt large. He struggled to follow its quick movement upward, unable to track it with Anamoris. Whatever it was, it bore no soul.

Then to his surprise, he began to feel a response. The creature could somehow feel itself being watched and sent out a reply. Borhiim could sense a swell of magic reverberate back into his fingers, his hands trembling with a sting of pain.

It was angry, and it was hungry.

"Do you feel anything?" Gahlaia asked, kneeling beside him.

Borhiim released his grip on the magic but could still feel the invisible bite in his fingers. He lifted his head, peering out toward the other side of the gorge. "He's down there," he said, "and he knows we're here. If we're going to cross, now is the only time."

"Get into position!" ordered Gahalaia. "Go!"

The group sprinted toward the cliffside and took to the skies. Craden and Anahka held the first two wingless Takahrn in their arms, and Gahlaia carried Borhiim, his feet dangling across the drop. The wind pressed hard on their faces, pushing against their wings.

As they neared the other side, the tingling feeling returned to Borhiim's fingers. The beast was close. He looked at both sides of the cliffs, but he saw no sign of the creature. He clenched his fists and focused himself, preparing for an attack.

The Takahrn in the front landed safely, and the first two wingless ones were released onto the rocky ground. Gahlaia and Borhiim followed close behind, but as they approached, a great screech rose from the canyon, bouncing from wall to wall and into the skies.

It took a few seconds for Borhiim to realize what was happening. Near the top of the cliffside, a huge animal emerged out of the rocky wall, leaving a gaping hole in its wake. It was wingless, at least ten times the size of any adult human. A large spike shot down its neck and stopped short of the main portion of its back, which was covered with dark brown fur. The skin on its chin stretched down raggedly below its pointed snout.

It was Dragorish.

Grabbing the walls of the canyon, it pulled itself up the side on all fours, heading straight for the two Takahrn as they neared the edge. Borhiim's mark on his shoulder burned as he prepared to fire the Devil's Flame. But before he could fully release the attack, the beast leaped at Borhiim, its claw smacking across his body, releasing him from Gahlaia's hold.

Both creature and Takahrn dropped into the chasm, free falling through the air.

"Borhiim!" Gahlaia yelled as she swooped down after them, her wings folding in the wind.

Craden and Anahka flew down to support them, the other Takahrn following close behind, but Borhiim and Dragorish were already too deep into the canyon. The beast swung another claw at Borhiim as they plummeted down, grazing the top of his head. Borhiim refocused and shot out a blast of dark fire toward his enemy, landing a hit across its left shoulder and blazing a large scar into the side of the cliff. Dragorish was flung toward the wall, screeching in pain as its charred wound met with rock.

The attack blasted Borhiim back, keeping him out of his foe's reach. He looked up and outstretched his hand as Gahlaia dove toward him, his body struggling not to spin with the airstream. She grabbed him by the arms and spread her wings to stop their plunge. She shouted as her wings flailed, and as they slowly began to fly back up, Borhiim looked down. The creature below them clawed the cliffside, and with its left arm dangling, it struggled to climb back up. Still, it moved faster than he would have liked.

"Why is it so interested in just us?" Gahlaia shouted over the howling wind.

"It's me," he responded. "He senses the Devil's Flame. He's drawn to it."

As they continued upward, they met Craden and Anahka on the way, their faces filled with distress.

Returning to the surface, Gahlaia released Borhiim and bent down, gasping for breath. "That thing is right on our tail," she said. "We need to get out of here before it reaches—"

But before she could finish her sentence, Dragorish leaped out from the canyon and sprawled before them, its wounded arm dragging on the ground. It shrieked, leaving the Takahrn to cover their ears at the immense sound.

"Stand back!" Borhiim shouted, and he gathered himself once again.

The beast charged toward him but halted when the Takahrn stretched his hands outward. The shadowy flames burst forth again and formed a wall between them. The creature growled and twitched as the Devil's Flame flashed and swirled before it.

Borhiim reached deep into its mind with the Anamoris, looking for any sign of a soul. Nothing of the sort remained in the animal's core, but there was something there. Something deep within, though very slight. Emotions and memories long buried that had now resurfaced.

"You're afraid," Borhiim said, keeping the wall of flames between them. He pushed the blaze farther and Dragorish stepped back. "You know what this is, don't you? You're . . . envious."

Sweat slid down his face. He was losing control of the Devil's Flame. It pulsed sporadically before him as it spread beyond his grasp. Finally, he pushed the magic forward, and the fire blasted straight ahead.

Pushing off his hind legs, the creature jumped over the wall of dark flames, its feet scorched by the assault. It gave another roar as he fell toward Borhiim, who leaped away as the beast collapsed. Gahlaia rushed past him and charged at its neck, digging her talons deep into the thick flesh. The other Takahrn, seeing the Devil's Flame vanish, followed in their attack. Dragorish shrieked and shook violently to get them off its back, but to no avail. Before long, it stopped moving, lying dead on the rocks.

Borhiim breathed out hard as he examined the scene. It was a bittersweet sight for him. A creature that had been cast out by its own because it lacked a will of its own. It was soulless, but there were still emotions buried underneath. Emotions of an abandoned animal.

"So ends the life of yet another one of the Second Dragons," he said, staring at the large carcass. "It might very well have been the last of its kind."

"May he find peace," Craden chimed in, putting a hand on Borhiim's shoulder.

"The Southern Border is five days' travel away," Gahlaia said, still regaining her breath. "We need to cover as much ground in that direction as we can before nightfall."

And with their orders given, they resumed their travel northward.

GAHLAIA SAT UP and stretched her wings wide, letting out a long yawn. The moon glistened high in the sky, bringing with it a fresh chill.

She felt for the tip of her left horn. It was sharp and pointed once more, healed completely. She sat in silence, thinking of the days to come. Sighing to herself, she gazed at her surroundings. Nothing but rock-filled terrain as far as the eye could see. Some Takahrn slept soundly, their wings curled around them like blankets; those without tossed and turned on the stony floor.

She looked at the empty space where Borhiim had lain. *Where is he off to this time?* Rising from her resting place, she decided to go look for him.

Past the group, in a place where the ground dipped, she found Borhiim sitting alone on a large rock, his face directed toward the moon. He turned when he heard her footsteps on the rocks behind him, and now aware of her presence, he resumed his gazing at the sky.

"You can't keep doing this," she whispered. "It's no wonder you hate the mornings."

"As bossy as ever," he returned. "You haven't changed a bit."

Gahlaia gave a low chuckle as she stood to his right, and they enjoyed a moment's silence as the moonbeams blessed them with a gentle glow.

"What is it you intend to do?" Borhiim asked, finally breaking the quiet.

Gahlaia squinted at the question. "What's that supposed to mean? You know what we're going to do."

He waved his hands in correction. "No, I mean after. After you've captured the newly crowned king, what then? Do you expect the humans to just release the remaining Takahrn from slavery?"

"I expect them to obey the command of their leader. If we can take him hostage, then the rest won't have a choice."

Borhiim shook his head. "There are other rulers. The king may be their leader, but the rulers of the other three sectors may be provoked to act independently. This might lead to full-scale war."

Gahlaia held back a sarcastic laugh. "War is already upon us," she said. "Takahrn and mortals have been in a struggle since the end of the second age."

She focused her view upon Borhiim, who still marveled at the moon above. It surprised her how little he had changed. *Always distracted.*

She continued. "No path is without bloodshed. Not now. War is here whether we attack the king or not. If we don't do what we set out to do, then those who hide away across Deerium will. But with a surprise attack, we may yet turn things to our favor."

Borhiim stared into Gahlaia's red eyes. "And what of the humans?" he asked. "Will they be enslaved like we were?"

She shrugged. "Does it matter? They started this battle. We're just finishing what they began."

"Funny. That's exactly what the dragons said when they drove the elves into the mountains all those years ago, and we all know how that story ends."

"Don't lecture me about dragons and elves," Gahlaia said, her voice rising slightly. "My father was prepared to let the elves return to their homes as a sign of peace, but they murdered my mother in cold blood and blamed it on the dragons."

He rose to his feet. "I'm with you, Gahlaia. I've told you as much already, but I want us to think about what comes after we accomplish our task."

Gahlaia let a laugh slip. "No human would agree to make peace with us."

"You say that as if there are no humans who want to change."

"That's because there aren't, Borhiim! I've seen how far humans will go to change," Gahlaia exclaimed, wrapping a hand around her left wrist. "I spent a lifetime in chains, under the feet of lesser people. Those who wanted no part of it simply looked away and ignored it."

"Lesser people? I've spent a lifetime as one of those lesser people, and there are many who desire something different, but those who wish it were so stay silent out of fear. If they speak up, they're banned as traitors."

Gahlaia threw her arms up in protest. "Traitors? That's quite the sacrifice for those who live their lives imprisoned! What's being called a traitor compared to slavery?"

"You have no right to judge an entire race by its worst parts!" Borhiim accused, pointing a finger toward her. "You think the Takahrn are so perfect? What about the Grey Wings, that sick group of our people that strikes at defenseless villages across the kingdom? We may have been wrongly treated, but don't go around saying we are completely innocent either. You're overzealous!"

"And you're a coward who rejects that which is necessary in the face of war!"

Borhiim turned his back and stepped away, growling under his breath and rubbing his palms over his face. Then, letting out a long sigh, he faced her again. "Just . . . think about it, Gahlaia," he said slowly, his voice back to a whisper. "I'm not saying it will happen, but if the opportunity presents itself, we need to make peace with them. If we don't, the conflict between our ancestors will just repeat itself."

Gahlaia bent her head and remained quiet. They stood stiffly as the moonlight poured down upon them.

"Those days . . ." she said, matching his tone. "Those days in the mountains when we were children . . . Do you miss them?"

Borhiim gave another sigh. "Very much so," he responded. He stared at his talons, flipping his hands over. "For years, I couldn't even remember where I came from. I had no memory of my childhood, and now that I have them back . . . a part of me wishes I could forget them again."

She gave him a faint smile. "As I recall, we argued then too."

He returned her smile with a chuckle. "And yet, we were the best of friends. It's hard to remember a day when we were apart. Our parents always seemed to like that."

At his response, her shoulders dropped. She felt as though she were a child again—alone, afraid. "We lived in momentary bliss. Looking back, it feels like it was over too quickly."

"You may sound like your old self," he said, "but I was wrong. You have changed, haven't you?"

"Life tends to do that. We've both changed, for better or worse."

Borhiim sat back down in his spot, gazing once again at the splendor of the moon. Outstretching his hand, he offered her the stone to his right. "Care to join me?"

Gahlaia smiled briefly and seated herself next to him, recalling days gone by. The smiles he gave her released much of the tension, but even so, she couldn't help but think of the words he had spoken to her.

It had been hardly any time at all, and already she had left two men dead in the dirt. One of them was the brother of Borhiim's closest friend, and yet she had acted on instinct, letting vengeance do its job. Part of her felt justified in her actions, yet the conversation that night had stirred up conflicting feelings she had tried so hard to suppress. For the first time in a long while, she was uncertain. Her convictions were strong, but Borhiim had known her better than any other Takahrn, and even now she valued that. She valued him.

I don't know. The Eternal save me, I don't know.

Chapter 9

Day six of the third month. Nine days until the coronation.

T IREHN EXITED HIS chambers and strode down the corridor. Today, the three rulers of the other sectors had arrived for a meeting with the prince, and he was running late. He had overslept, his mind filled with dreams of a mysterious being reaching for him in the night. His father's words still hung in the air around him, and the more he tried to ignore them, the more they penetrated his thoughts. If someone was responsible for the king's death, there was no way of finding out at the moment. There were no known records of anyone named Tarubas in the main library, and any efforts to find such a name anywhere had been fruitless.

Tirehn came to the end of the corridor and stood before two golden doors, the guards nodding as he approached.

Raggorin was already waiting. "You're late."

"Don't lecture me right now," Tirehn said, his voice still scratchy from his slumber. He cleared his throat. "Let's just go."

The guards pushed on the long, golden handles, and the doors swung open. The room was big, its walls silver. In its center stood a square table with a chair on each side, the one farthest away still vacant. At the far end of the room sat a throne that gleamed with gold and bronze, with bright red cushions on the seat and back.

The three people sitting at the table—two women and one man—turned to look at the prince.

Tirehn took his place in silence, Raggorin standing at his left with his arms behind his back. He nodded to the three sitting before him, and they placed their folded hands upon the wooden table, directing their attention to a map spread out in the middle.

The woman to the prince's right was Arinay, ruler of Verish. She was a few years older than him, in her midtwenties. She was average in height but held herself straight with pride. Her hair was light blonde, covering the left side of her face. Her white dress bore a plate of silver armor on the right shoulder and a pointed sleeve on the left.

The woman to Tirehn's left was Zinnyah, ruler of Cleptyn, and despite being in her forties, appeared much younger. She was the tallest of the four and had long, ginger hair braided down her back. She was layered from shoulder to foot in silver armor save for the mail, fashioned completely of green dragon scales that slid under her breastplate, covering her stomach. A sheathed shortsword hung at her waist, dangling under the table. To her left stood a short man wearing a long cloak, keeping his head down. The prince had never seen him before.

Finally, facing Tirehn sat a young male of similar height and strength. He was Rorgan, ruler of Norvad, and the former king's highly valued strategist. He was dressed more casually, wearing a grey leather jacket, the hood pulled back. Sewn into the left shoulder of his clothing were three stripes of black signifying the third sector, as Norvad was often called.

To his right stood his grand general, Naggyn. His face remained hooded, and his shoulders were plated with bronze, three spikes protruding from each. A shortsword hung from his right hip and a broadsword was strapped to his back. In his right hand was a strangely designed elvish spear that reached from his feet to his head, with three pointed tips—two to the sides and one upward.

If Tirehn wished, he could have chosen to select new rulers, but he saw little reason to do so. King Hyrehn had handpicked these three during his rule, and while he resented following in his father's footsteps, there was no reason to remove them from office when they were still capable.

"Apologies for being late," he said. "Arinay, where is Doryan? Wasn't he coming as well?"

"My grand general requested leave to the Dirtlands," she replied. "Your father gave him permission to bring his sister Gwendall here to live in Valia, as you may recall."

The prince nodded. He gestured toward the cloaked figure next to Zinnyah. "And who is this?"

"His name is Nokdin," Zinnyah answered. "He is my new advisor and one of Deerium's greatest scholars."

The man bowed toward Tirehn but said nothing. He appeared almost sheepish, clearly not used to being in such company.

"Before we begin," said Rorgan, "I wanted to express my condolences to you, my prince. Your father was a good king and a great man."

Tirehn doubted the truth behind that last statement but decided to let it slide.

"Likewise, my lord," Zinnyah agreed. "We are all stricken by his departure."

"Thank you," Tirehn responded. "I appreciate the sentiment, but the time for mourning will have to wait. What of the Grey Wings? Have we tracked their location?"

"They attacked a village west of Shayna," Zinnyah said, pointing on the map. "They moved down the edge of the Gorrobin Mountains, and we lost them in the snow."

"They could be heading for Deeria," Arinay said. "Perhaps they intend to attack Valia during the coronation."

"It's definitely possible," Rorgan said, "but their numbers are too large to get through unnoticed. They would risk exposure and be completely outmatched in a full-scale battle."

"All the same," said the prince, "they could send a smaller force to attack us here. I'll call for more soldiers to defend the borders of the city."

They all nodded in agreement.

"What of the Gorrobin tribes?" asked Arinay. "You said the Dividers crossed the edges of their territory. Is it possible that they are aligned with the Grey Wings? If so, they could strike Valia with a much larger force."

"If I may," Raggorin stated, "my people have remained neutral and isolated from the rest of Deerium. They desire no feud with either side. But if they were to discover the Grey Wings among them, they would drive them out."

"Besides," added Rorgan, "they would still fail to match the strength of Deeria. The main sector holds the strongest army of the four. It would be suicidal. They would need Gorrobin and Cleptyn to strike together to even stand a chance."

"That aside," Tirehn continued, "our main focus should be the distribution of our forces across the sectors. The people need to know that they can be protected."

He paused for a moment as the others gave their agreements. *Should I tell them what my father said?* he thought. *And what of Ahmeras? Should I discuss peace with the Takahrn?*

Thinking it over, he decided to wait to gather his thoughts about the latter but figured it wouldn't hurt to speak sparingly about the possibility of the king's murder. At this point, he was desperate and overly curious. "There is one more thing I wish to bring up," he said. "Tarubas . . . Does that name mean anything to any of you?"

Looks of confusion flashed around the table. They shook their heads.

"I don't think I've ever heard it before," Zinnyah replied. "Why?"

"I . . . happened to come across it," he said. "I found it a bit unusual, so I thought I might ask if any of you knew what it meant."

"Strange," Rorgan said. "Was it a name written in the history books without a given context? As far as I know, no one in Norvad goes by that name."

"Nor in Verish," Arinay said.

"Please," Nokdin interrupted, his voice low and shaky, "may I speak for a moment?"

Tirehn waved a hand toward him.

"I believe I have heard that name before," the scholar said. "I traveled much in my youth and came across many ancient manuscripts that even the library has never seen. Tarubas was an ancient name from a time long past, given to a person long forgotten."

The prince leaned forward in his chair. "Who was he?"

Nokdin shrugged. "Not much is known about him, but I remember coming across the name in an old elvish book. Any other reference to him within the text calls him 'the Forsaken.' That's all I can remember at the moment."

The prince let out a small sigh of relief before leaning back again. "Thank you, Nokdin. By any chance, did you bring this book with you?"

"I bring most of my rare findings with me everywhere. I'll search my quarters for it tonight."

TIREHN WALKED TOWARD a narrow spiraling stairway, holding the light in front of him. He limped slightly, still hurting from his duel with Ahmeras earlier that day. They hadn't spoken of the heated conversation they had several days ago. Rather, it hung in the air like an overwhelming stench, but neither of them wished to address it. Tirehn tried his best to push such thoughts out of his head and focus on the task at hand.

He quickly strode down the steps until he reached a small marble door, its black form stainless and smooth. He pulled out a key and inserted it into the keyhole below the handle. It clicked, and the door opened with a screech. Stepping into the cramped room, the prince moved his candle to the right, revealing a small shelf that was filled with books and scrolls. He set his light aside, pulled a book out at random, and began to read.

Tirehn had known of this room's existence for quite some time but was never able to get in. Only the king possessed a key to the entrance, and despite asking his father numerous times in his youth, he was denied every time. Now he understood why. In a sense, it was a forbidden library. Within contained the works of spells and secrets that were either better forgotten or simply for the king's eyes only. Such were the politics of the kingdom.

When King Hyrehn was on his death bed, he had given the key to Raggorin, who then gave it to Tirehn. With the events of the past few days, his curiosity had been postponed momentarily, but now he had a reason to go poking around. Tirehn wanted to find the meaning behind his father's last words. However, his desire to see what lay within the secret room went deeper than that. More than just wanting to find some clarity, he was drawn to the concept of someone pulling the strings that led to the king's death. He needed to learn more about Tarubas, and if he was going to find answers, this was the only place left. Nokdin wouldn't have any new information until tomorrow, and he was tired of waiting.

Hours flew by as Tirehn flipped through pages in search of a lead, skimming as fast as he could before moving on to the next book. Eventually, he came across something of interest—a manuscript on the practices of Anamoris, the magic used to manipulate souls and spiritual energy. This was something that intrigued the prince. His father said he heard voices in his head, which could connect back to Anamoris magic. He dug deep into the text, learning about the complexities and dangers around the mysterious power. Spell after spell followed with their dangers described shortly after.

One specifically stood out to him: an incantation that allowed someone to change the identity of a soul. He read the words carefully.

> *The soul controls the mind, and the mind controls the body. Bestowing a strong false identity upon the soul can breach the mind. Anamoris counteracts Terrkoris, and the subject assumes a new form. This can be done both voluntarily and involuntarily, and depending on the willingness of the host, memories can remain or be repressed. This is both a weapon and a tool. Beware . . . This requires immense strength to complete successfully. Failure will always be fatal to the user.*

Tirehn decided to stop there. It was getting very late, and his desire for sleep was starting to overwhelm him. He closed the book and placed it back on the shelf. But as he raised himself from the floor, his eye caught the scrolls on the end of the rack. There were four in total, all dusty and wrinkled. He looked them over briefly, each of them sealed, and upon each seal was a name. They were the names of the kings who ruled over Deerium after the humans spread across the land during the start of the third age.

The scroll furthest to the right had the name "Hyrehn" written on it. His father.

Tirehn stared for a second before realizing that something was amiss. There was a missing parchment. *There were five human kings,* he thought. *King Graan: the first king. He doesn't have a scroll.*

Then it hit him. *Father . . . The scroll he took to his grave.*

NOKDIN LOOKED OUT his window. The sun had set, and he had only now noticed. He had been scrounging around his quarters for hours, searching for the manuscript that the prince had requested.

"I know I put it somewhere..." he murmured to himself, pushing aside stacks of papers that lay on his bed and starting through another pile of books. He was lucky that Zinnyah had allowed him to travel to Valia with so many of them. He never liked the idea of his works and findings leaving his side. He always feared losing them, but bringing most of them with him had created a similar effect to misplacing them.

The scholar looked at each cover and opened them briefly before moving on to the next, panic beginning to grow in his chest. Then, seeing a familiar sight among the pile, he pulled out the book he sought for so long. It was completely white, save for the purple Anamoris mark in the center of its front cover. Written on its first page was a single line of text.

"We rise as the pure. As one we hold to perfection. We stand as the Righteous Ones."

Nokdin spent the remaining night in silence, searching for the name the prince was so interested in. His memories of the contents came back to him. It was some sort of elvish volume that documented the life and rituals of an ancient religious group. Most of it described their teachings on how to worship nature and the souls of the dead, as was customary after the rejection of the Eternal in the middle of the second age.

However, in the last quarter of the book, the tone shifted. The pages described a prisoner they had captured and brought to their home to study. What the being was the text didn't say, but a name was written once among the constant babblings: "Tarubas."

Nokdin continued his search through the volume. Throughout the rest of it, the author did not refer to him by name, but rather opted to call him "the Forsaken." The passage spoke of a prison they held him in within the mountains, using him as a sort of experiment for their Anamoris spells. Skimming through the text at a quicker pace, Nokdin looked for any signs of the identification of a species. *Was he elvish or human... or perhaps...* His finger stopped on three words that composed a title. Shock overtook him.

"The Faded Dragon."

He placed the book down, a smile of victory and triumph on his face, but it did not last long.

All the candles in the room went dark in unison, and he froze as he heard footsteps on the floor behind him.

Nokdin whirled around with a start only for a hand to grasp his face. He opened his mouth to scream, but nothing came out. His head began to ache, and he started to feel a strong tugging sensation deep within his core. The room around him began to pulsate in his vision, the dark figure looming over him like a beast upon its prey. A voice began to seep into his mind, severe and terrifying. It felt like blades scraping against his skull, rupturing it, until the voice was all he could think of.

You have never heard of him. You know nothing of him. Forget all of it. It means nothing to you . . .

A hand reached out in the darkness and retrieved the white book lying on the bed. The figure released its grip on the scholar and exited the room, slowly closing the door behind it.

Nokdin dropped to the ground, his body twitching and shaking uncontrollably. His thoughts melted away as he began to fall into unconsciousness, a single name fading into the darkness.

Tarubas. Tarubas. Tarubas. Tarubas . . .

Chapter 10

Day eight of the third month.

GAHLAIA PULLED THE hood of her cloak further over her head, water droplets falling from the ends of thick fabric. The rain came down hard, mixing dirt and rock into mud. She kept her wings folded tightly to her back to protect her from the chill that pressed the downpour sideways. She would have almost looked human under the clothing were it not for the horns sticking out of the hood. It was amazing what a couple of silver coins could buy. Borhiim had payed an old man who was selling the latest fashions in the northern section of Verish, acquiring their new cloaks along with his silence.

Gahlaia squinted her way forward, the heavy fog almost completely blocking her vision. In a way, it was a blessing in disguise. As the Takahrn neared the Southern Border, none of the soldiers would see them from the top of the wall. They had traveled slightly more east, staying clear of the West Gate. With Borhiim's abilities at their disposal, there was no need to enter and risk exposure, and with the rain and fog, there was no reason to look for a blind spot in the wall.

Things were finally starting to look up, as if the Eternal had set His gaze upon them.

Finally, Gahlaia caught the large shape beginning to manifest itself in front of them. It stretched both left and right, far past her line of sight. Staring up at the border wall, she found the top was nowhere to be seen. *Good.* She looked behind her. The group of Takahrn still followed, with Borhiim, Craden, and Anahka trudging along at the front. Gahlaia sent them a half smile. They had reached the Southern Border at last.

Borhiim nodded to her knowingly and moved past, placing his left hand on the stone surface. His mark glowed red through the fog, and the wall began to simmer and weaken. Clouds of steam rose from his hand as he pressed it into the melting stone. He moved his arm back a bit, and the Devil's Flame blasted to life. More steam covered the area, decreasing everyone's view in the thick blackness. When it cleared, a rough hole was visible in the wall, appearing as a doorway they could walk through without touching the burnt edges. Though the wall was thick, stretching further than thirty feet, the magic had melted it like rain washing away filth.

Gahlaia's smile grew. They were so close now. She turned toward Borhiim, who was panting uncontrollably. "You alright?" she asked.

He met her gaze, sweat visible on his face inside his hood. "I'm fine," he said between breaths. "But it's getting harder to control. The Devil's Flame. It's like trying to push against a river, and I think it's getting worse."

"Well, don't overexert," she said, trying to offer comfort in her words. "We might need you in the coming days."

He flashed a smirk in her direction. "Don't you worry about me. You're not the only stubborn one here."

Gahlaia stepped through the hole, the rest following close behind.

TWO DAYS PASSED uneventfully. The rain had stalled the day prior, only to return with almost equal force. No longer were they in the rock and filth of Verish. They were now in Deeria territory, surrounded by grassy plains and flatlands. Still, none of it made much difference. The weather made sure of that. There might have been beauty to behold in those lands, but the downpour provided quite the distraction.

Gahlaia wasn't quite sure where they were. She had glanced at the map briefly, but the mist and wind had washed away nearly all traces of their location. She stopped, glanced around, and grunted. The rain had betrayed them. While it proved great protection to get past the Southern Border, it now kept them from moving forward.

As Borhiim came to her side, she faced him. "At this rate," she said, barely audible over the pounding rain, "we could pass Valia and not even know it."

Borhiim had no words of comfort. There was nothing they could do but press onward and hope they reached their destination. They were still at least two days away, so their only solace was the hope that this unusual weather would let up before then.

She felt him put a hand on her shoulder, but she was no longer looking at him. A short distance away, emerging from the fog, lay a vast lake, its edge straying near their right side and continuing northeast.

Relief had never felt so freeing.

Gahlaia rushed ahead, nearly slipping on the wet grass underneath, and placed a hand on the lake's surface. It was completely solid. Her smile stretched across her face until her fangs shone through. "The Lake of Ice," she said. "I've been here before."

She pressed a talon on the ice and ran it hard across the surface. *Not even a scratch.* Her powerful claws left no marks on it, and it seemed unaffected by the rain. Any drops that landed upon its slippery exterior were merely absorbed until they vanished completely.

Borhiim approached the lake cautiously, appearing uneasy. Touching the ice with his palm, he recoiled almost immediately.

"You feel it then?" Gahlaia asked. "You feel what's underneath?"

"Yeah . . ." he responded slowly, transfixed by the frozen area before them. "It's like no Terrkoris magic I've ever felt before. Like it's holding something below . . . So, the ancient scriptures are true."

Gahlaia had been taught many things about the land of Deerium when she went traveling with her father in her youth. This place especially was one she could never forget. Gahlorm had told her the story that had been passed down for thousands of years, and she had read it many times in ancient scrolls. She played the old tale over in her head.

Before the elves and dragons, the Eternal locked Himself in a great battle with Soluhtar, known as the Wrath Reaper, and keeper of the Shade. The end result led to the creation of the Twin Worlds: Deerium and the Drake. Using the powers of the Light, the Eternal brought low the influence of darkness, cleansing reality of its hold. But pieces of the dark survived, some taking form within the hatred of the living while others took physical shape, hoping to one day return to the skies. The Eternal found grotesque forms among his creation and sealed them deep underground, surrounded by ice and magic. Weakened, the creatures succumbed to the power of the Light once more, and there they remained forever trapped in their frozen prison of ice.

She shuddered. Few knew the name of the Wrath Reaper, and those who did dared not speak it lest his reign resume. Such was the old story, and to most humans, it was but a folktale. To the Takahrn, it was as true as the ground beneath their feet.

"When are the stories ever wrong?" Gahlaia asked. "This is no lake. It's a cage."

She looked up. The rain had slowed a bit, and the fog had begun to give way. She gazed out and to her surprise saw more shapes to her left. West of the lake's edge, tents could be seen faintly. There were about twenty, each one fit to hold at least five people. Gahlaia took a step forward, then stopped. Over the howling wind, her ears had caught the faint sound of feet on the mud and grass. She turned to her fellow Takahrn in warning, but it was too late.

Out of the shadows, a large band of figures pounced at them. It was all too quick. Before long, they were on their knees with talons at their necks.

Gahlaia stared up into the face of a horned Takahrn standing above her. Sure enough, looking around at their captors, she saw that they were all Takahrn. They wore thin grey clothing with the mark of a wing and a claw upon the shirt, drawn in black ink.

Borhiim recognized the symbol. "You're the Grey Wings!" he shouted.

"We're Takahrn!" Anahka said from the outskirts of the group. "We're on the same side!"

Their attackers hesitated, pulling their claws back for a moment. "Pull back their hoods!" one of them yelled to the others.

In unison, they all grabbed at the group's cloaks and tugged them back. Gahlaia's horns stuck to the material and ripped it as the hood fell to her side, the drops of rain streaming down her face. The Takahrn above bent closer to make out the shape of her horns in the fog. He came too close.

Gahlaia sneered. "You get any closer," she said, "and I'll rip your gullet out."

He backed away, the rest of the attackers doing the same, lowering their hands.

"Take them to Vytorr," one of them shouted from the back. "He'll want to see them."

WHEN THEY ARRIVED at the cluster of shelters, they were directed to the center. Gahlaia counted twenty-two tents circling a larger one in the middle. Takahrn peeked out from behind flaps of cloth to look at the new group entering their sanctuary. Reaching the big tent, the Takahrn holding them parted and bowed, pointing toward the entrance. Gahlaia's group entered slowly.

Within the shelter, a single Takahrn sat at the far end. His wings, hair, and tail were all light blonde. He waited until Gahlaia and all her comrades had entered, barely fitting inside the tent. He cocked his head and spoke calmly to his subordinate in the back. "Who are they?"

"We found them wandering near the Lake of Ice," came the reply.

The man turned his head to look at them, his eyes darting immediately to Gahlaia. He rose to his feet and outstretched his arms in a welcoming manner. "My brothers and sisters," he said, "I bid you welcome. I am Vytorr, son of Vius." He bowed slowly.

Gahlaia recognized the name Vius. He was once a general among the dragon ranks. She found it strange, however, that this stranger did not mention who his elvish mother was, as it was tradition to name both.

"You're the leader of the Grey Wings?" Borhiim asked.

Vytorr straightened himself and glanced at the mark on his left shoulder. "You know of our cause?" he questioned.

Borhiim glared. "Oh yes. I know what you've done to villages all around Deerium. I know of the innocent lives you've taken."

Vytorr moved through the Takahrn to stand before Borhiim. He was extremely tall, almost seven feet. He bore no shirt, revealing his tough musculature. Etched down the left side of his collarbone was an elvish symbol that translated as "armor."

He sighed as he towered over Borhiim. "Exaggerations, perhaps, but I don't blame you. The true meaning of our cause can be so easily misunderstood."

Borhiim didn't recoil. He stood his ground, staring up into the bright green eyes. "I've seen it," he responded. "You raided the Dirtlands not two months ago. If the Verish army hadn't shown up, you would have killed everyone there."

"Ah, then I was right in my assumption. You were exaggerating." Vytorr leaned in and whispered, "Because no human life is *innocent*."

"What is it you seek to do?" Anahka asked.

"I wish to cleanse this world and start anew," the tall Takahrn replied. "Rid it of its most unforgivable sin."

"The humans?" Borhiim asked. "You wish to wipe them out without remorse?"

"They would do the same to us. Kill or be killed. Only one of us will remain when the dust clears. That is the way of things."

"But there's another way," said Craden. "We were on our way to Valia before we were jumped by your lackeys. We can still end this without it coming to war."

Vytorr smiled and lifted his arms. "That's perfect," he said. "We also had a plan for getting into Valia."

Gahlaia had remained silent during all this, gathering her thoughts. Finally, she made her decision. "How?" she asked.

"I'll show you," Vytorr answered, outstretching his hand toward her. "Shall we discuss terms?"

Hesitantly, she took his hand, but Borhiim put a hand on her shoulder with a concerned expression. He shook his head firmly.

"I'll be okay," she said, shrugging off his hand. "Trust me."

The agreement made, the rest of the Takahrn left the tent one by one, Borhiim the last to exit.

Alone, Vytorr directed Gahlaia to where he once sat. On the floor, a map nearly identical to the one they had in their possession was spread open.

He knelt and pointed to their location. "We stand upon the western edge of the Lake of Ice," he began, "with Valia to the northwest." He traced his finger to the left. "Perfectly westward from us is a small village, and these last few days, Deeria has stretched its army across the sector. If we attack in a singular point, we can draw them to a specific location, giving us the opportunity to strike the capital when it's vulnerable."

"You're going to attack a village?" she asked.

"Of course. There are Takahrn enslaved there who could be freed and added to the cause. Plus it gives us a chance to bring the king's army to one location."

Gahlaia was bewildered. "But if you did draw them to that location, you would be slaughtered. You can't match their strength. You said it yourself that Deeria had moved its army across the sector. With the forces already there, you'll likely be outmatched."

Vytorr nodded in agreement, stood up, and walked to the exit. "Come with me," he said, motioning outside. "You'll understand better."

Without hesitating, he spread his wings and took to the skies, the storm above smacking against his body defiantly.

Gahlaia removed her cloak, threw it back into the tent, and followed, embracing the rain once more.

UPON SEEING GAHLAIA vanish from sight, Borhiim trudged away

from the tents. He didn't feel the slightest tinge of safety among the Grey Wings. It was true that they were Takahrn, but that was the only comforting thought. Nothing else screamed trustworthy, that much was obvious.

Sitting in the wet grass, giving the rain leave to trickle down his bare arms, he stared east. He watched the Lake of Ice as it remained unchanged by the storm around it, and in that moment, he thought he could hear a voice. It was faint at first, like a weakened echo from across a canyon. Then, steadily it grew, itching at his skull.

He grimaced, trying to focus on what the words were saying, but they were too muddled. It was several voices, all saying the same thing yet overlapping each other. The dialect contained sharp sounds, reminding him of the old language the dragons spoke in their infancy, but little did he know of that tongue. The words crawled inside Borhiim's head without meaning, giving him a headache.

He may not have known their intentions, but as they grew louder, Borhiim found himself feeling his own body react. Not physically, but rather his soul drew toward the source. It was an exchange difficult to describe in words, and as his vision began to blur, he felt the sensation call out.

The lake . . . What are they saying?

"Borhiim? Are you alright?"

The trance vanished as soon as the question hit his ears. He felt a hand rest on his shoulder, and sure enough, Craden stood above him with a worried expression.

Borhiim let out a sigh, shrugging his shoulders. "Yeah. I just would prefer not to be around the Grey Wings. Not at the moment anyway."

Craden sat down, brushing his dark hair behind his ears. "Understandable, but if they can add to our cause, would it not be worth trying to ally with them?"

"Perhaps," Borhiim responded, "if they would indeed do so, which I doubt. You and the rest were slaves, so maybe I don't understand as you do, but I know what the Grey Wings have done and the families they devastated for the sake of a 'righteous' cause."

"One might argue that's what we're doing as well. Capture a king to force an entire kingdom to see things another way. Maybe only death can end things at this point."

Borhiim shook his head. "But the king can still be persuaded. He isn't even the king yet. What if the only reason change hasn't occurred is because those with the voice to do so are too afraid to speak up? If so, should we not give them the opportunity instead of cutting it short?"

It was Craden's turn to sigh. "It's possible, but what happens if they don't? Whether we like it or not, we are walking toward an inevitability. Even if this the prince does agree with our goals, what then? There are three other rulers with control over their own armies. One of them is bound to disagree, which would lead to a civil war."

"You don't know that."

Craden shrugged. "The world did not become this way without disdain. If the rulers don't fight back, then the people will. There will be death no matter the outcome. Are you prepared for that, Borhiim?"

Before Borhiim could reply, two talons grabbed Craden from behind, wrapping firmly around his neck and pulling him flat on his back. He was given almost no time to react, the air wrenched from his windpipe in an instant.

Borhiim turned in shock only for two more claws to outstretch toward his face. He dropped to the ground and rolled away as the tips nicked his cheekbones. But just as he escaped the snares of one attack, another fell quickly upon him. A foot jabbed hard into his right rib, then the left, then the right again.

The world a haze, he turned on his back, flailing and slashing at anything he could, but it was of little consequence. His arms were grasped firmly as someone pulled him up by the nape. Borhiim stared at his foes, struggling for breath. They were Takahrn—seven of them. They stood before him with stern faces. To their side, Craden lay in the grass, beaten to unconsciousness.

"We should kill him now," one in the back said. "He wields the Devil's Flame."

The Takahrn holding Borhiim turned at that. "You heard our orders. We need him. We need them both."

With a few reluctant grunts, they dragged the two back toward the tents. Borhiim felt the Takahrn squeeze tighter around his windpipe, and with his last ounce of strength, reached for the magic. No response. It refused him. He pressed harder, and still it held back. It slipped through his mental fingers, and in deep frustration, he felt it evade him at every attempt. The Devil's Flame had, for the first time, gone beyond his control.

Soon enough, he had no strength left and was dragged helplessly against his will.

LANDING WITHIN A small patch of trees, Gahlaia and Vytorr stared out toward the small town before them. Gahlaia tried to focus through the patches of fog that still permeated the air. She made out masses of soldiers surrounding the exterior. Far too many to count. She faced Vytorr for confirmation, but his expression remained confident.

"Don't you see?" she asked. "If you attack this village, you'll fail to overtake it completely. Even in a surprise attack, you'll lose far too many Takahrn."

He laughed. "You underestimate our strength," he replied. "The soldiers will stand down if we take hostages. Then we catch them in a pincer attack."

Gahlaia was utterly confused. The plan made no sense. "You'll still have too many casualties. Besides, you would kill villagers to get to the soldiers. They're defenseless. Innocent." She was startled at her own words. Why did she care? They were human. Mortal. What had they done to deserve such mercy?

And yet . . . She hadn't seen much of the humans' good side. Few of her kind had, save for Borhiim. He had lived as one for most of his life. For hundreds of years he lived like that, and he pleaded for her to understand his point of view. He had seen the other side. The side none of them were willing to accept. His words rang in her ears, and once again she felt conflicted.

"Does it matter?" Vytorr asked, breaking her from her trance. "As I said, no human life is innocent. They started this generations ago. We can finish it right here."

"But there are too many deaths on both sides for it to be worth the risk. How can you truly believe—"

Gahlaia stopped herself. It became all too clear in her head. She stared at the Takahrn, but he remained motionless, unflinching as the rain fell down his bare skin. She shook her head. At once her conflict fell away. *Overzealous indeed. This is what we could become.*

"You don't plan on taking this village back, do you?" she asked. "It's a distraction so you can draw out the rest of the army. It's a suicide mission."

A smile stretched across Vytorr's face. "Well done," he said. "You're not the daughter of the Dragon King for nothing. Yes, it's a distraction. While a smaller force strikes this village, we move to

Valia and attack the prince directly."

"You'll sacrifice both humans and Takahrn pointlessly!" she shouted.

"Not pointlessly. We'll end the war, and no path in war is without bloodshed."

Gahlaia's stomach turned. These were her words, and only now was their meaning clear. Only now did she understand. "The war has not yet begun," she replied. "Would it not be better to end it before it begins—rather than start it?"

Vytorr scrunched his face as if he might vomit. "You mean make peace with them? As if the humans would agree to such a thing."

"But is it not in our best interest to try? Shouldn't we try to avoid death when it is our choice to do so?" She could scarcely believe what she was saying. For so long she had hated the humans. Part of her still did, and maybe always would. Yet here she was defending them. *Borhiim is one of us. If anyone can see a way through, it's him.*

Vytorr walked forward, closing the distance between them. He put both hands on her shoulders. "This is happening," he said, "with or without you."

Gahlaia shook him off. "Is that a threat? Against one of your own?"

He paused for a moment, but only a moment. "Those who don't stand with us stand with the enemy. There is no middle ground. No grey area. Those spawn of the elves never deserved this world. We are the future, Gahlaia. We are the greatest parts of both dragon and elf. These mortals are nothing more than a shadow of a dying past. Surely you understand that."

Silence stretched between them.

Gahlaia thought back. "The elves . . ." she began. "Why do you hate them? What did they do to you?"

Vytorr stumbled over his words for a second before giving his reply. "What they did to all of us. They started the war back in the first age. They were arrogant enough to challenge the dragons, and now we pay the same price with the humans. They hungered for war, just as the humans did."

"Your mother," she said, ignoring his remarks. "Who was she?"

He didn't move. He looked like a wounded child trying desperately to cling to some semblance of tranquility. Gahlaia could see the pieces coming together. Not all elves or dragons were proud of the Takahrn, not even if they were their own kin. She pressed further.

"Your mother abandoned you, didn't she?"

With that, Vytorr's calm exterior broke. "*Shut up!*" he shouted, lunging for her. "You know nothing!"

Gahlaia spread her wings and jumped back. "You're blind, Vytorr," she called over her shoulder. "Blind to what you're doing."

She turned on her heels and launched herself to fly back toward camp, her pursuer close behind. She had to warn Borhiim and the others.

BORHIIM LOOKED AROUND. All of his comrades had been brought to their knees, split into two groups of hostages. Borhiim and Anahka knelt among nine, Craden among eight, all with talons waiting at their necks. As he winced at the heavy drops of rain, Borhiim reached out once more for the Devil's Flame. The mark on his shoulder flickered but ultimately grew cold as he felt the power slip out of reach. He grunted at his failure, struggling to come to grips with it.

His focus was interrupted at the sound of wings descending from above, and Gahlaia landed in front of them. She was trembling, and a few seconds after, Vytorr came crashing down behind her. His foot cracked into her spine, the sound audible over the downpour as she was flung to the ground at Borhiim's feet.

"Gahlaia!" Borhiim cried.

Heaving with evident pain, her arms shook as she struggled to lift herself, her gaze meeting his. "I'm sorry," she said. "This is my fault."

Borhiim had no words. He was too angry to reply. Angry at himself. He pushed even harder to grab the magic at his core and felt only a slight response before it vanished once more. "The Devil's Flame," he said through clenched teeth. "I can't—"

"As I said," Vytorr interrupted, "we do this my way, with or without you." He strode toward them slowly, the elvish mark on his collarbone glowing a bright white, his skin changing texture. He now looked more like a stone giant than anything.

Gahlaia hoisted herself up and faced him. "You wouldn't kill your own," she responded, her back hunched.

He raised his right hand. "Wouldn't I?"

Borhiim looked to his left, toward the eight Takahrn kneeling there. The talons held at their throats pulled closer to the skin at Vytorr's gesture. In a panic, he tried one final time to bring the dark fire to life, but the failed effort only sank his heart farther.

Craden, amidst those ready to fall, darted his eyes among Gahlaia, Anahka, and Borhiim. "This is my family," he uttered, his neck bleeding as he spoke. "Dying among family."

"Dying among family!" repeated the other seven beside him just before Vytorr threw his hand down. There was no hesitation. All Takahrn kneeling to his right dropped to the ground, throats slit open.

Borhiim's tears melded with the rain on his cheeks as he stared wide-eyed at the corpses. He heard several shrieks of terror next to him, one possibly Anahka's, but he couldn't tell. Then silence. No sight. No thought. Everything faded.

And in that single moment, he thought he could hear voices. They called in words he could scarcely understand, but their meaning was not lost on him.

The lake . . . The Shade . . . They want a soul.

Gahlaia gazed in horror at Craden's lifeless face looking out blankly. She screamed, rushing toward Vytorr, claws outstretched. He stood his ground at the attack, his mark still glowing white. Her nails met his neck but did not rip through, brushing off like a fist against stone.

Vytorr took the opportunity, grasped her by the neck, and slammed her into the mud. "You won't penetrate my skin," he yelled over her cries of pain.

Borhiim's rage was almost overwhelming. He felt it fuel him like wood given to flame. The voices never stopped chanting, only growing louder until they were practically screaming at him. His anger now had a target, and he stood just over Gahlaia's body. The mark on his shoulder lit up in the fog. Without so much as calling for it or even pressing for its presence, he felt the Devil's Flame rise inside him.

"*Vytorr!*"

A shockwave of heat and magic shot outward, knocking every-one surrounding Borhiim off their feet. Anahka and the other Takahrn saw their chance and flew up toward the dark rain clouds. The fiery blast came crashing directly into Vytorr's upper body, and all he could do was lift his arms for protection. His stone shield of Terrkoris began to crack and crumble under the Devil's Flame, and he was steadily pressed back. Before long, the dark fire had licked itself completely around Vytorr's entire body, burning his barrier away bit by bit. It didn't take long for it to succumb, and soon his Terrkoris mark went black.

If he screamed any final words, no one heard them. He was dead, the burned grass where he once stood serving as the only proof that he had been there at all.

Borhiim tried releasing his hold on the shadowy blaze, but it continued its rampage. He shook his arms around the surrounding area, the fire following with him. Tents erupted with smoke and fire, and the Grey Wings ran in terror, some caught up in the flames. Grunting to control the magic, he raised his hands to the clouds. The Devil's Flames formed a hole in a rain cloud above, quickly replaced with massive amounts of steam, then subsiding.

Borhiim panted hard, turning his gaze to Gahlaia. She lifted herself again, grabbed him by the shoulders, and flew to the sky. He heard her moan in pain at the ache that continued to press on her back.

The Grey Wings, realizing what had happened, followed the group into the rain.

As they flew onward, Gahlaia and Borhiim joined up with Anahka and the rest, their faces full of terror and panic.

"The Lake of Ice!" Borhiim yelled. "Take me to the lake!" They looked at him in confusion, but he insisted, "It's the only way."

They glided east until they reached the frozen surface, the Grey Wings following high to the west. As they hit the ice, Gahlaia dropped Borhiim suddenly, the pain in her spine clearly overwhelming her.

Borhiim stared into the sky. Nearly one hundred Takahrn were swooping down toward them.

"What now?" Anahka asked.

"Stand back!" Borhiim shouted. He placed his hands on the cold surface, trying to bring back the fire. He felt his eyes flicker back and forth between blue and red, struggling to grasp the magic. The voices were screaming at him now as if they would rip his skull in two.

They want a soul.

The ice under his palms began to melt, and he felt an uneasiness below. As the surface began to thaw, black smoke rose from within the lake. A sick feeling came over Borhiim. Something had awakened in the depths.

He jumped back, casting the dark fire in front of him like a wall. Murky smoke billowed out of the lake and slithered on the ground westward. The Grey Wings, having landed upon the surface ahead, stepped back as the darkness swelled up before them. The smoke thickened, and from its unclear shape, Borhiim thought he saw claws reach out from it. Shadowy hands that spread out in a misty formation. *The Shade wants a soul.*

It billowed over the front lines of the Grey Wings, and soon, their expressions changed. Never had Borhiim seen anyone look so afraid. So terrified. Most tried to run, scrambling away from the lake, but the first that the darkness fell upon were not so lucky. Their bodies turned to ash before becoming one with the shadow. The rest of the Grey Wings flew into the fog southward. The Shade followed them until it reached the edge of the lake. Once there, it froze, leaving its prey fleeing and screeching in the distance. Instead, the fog reared toward Borhiim and the other Takahrn.

Borhiim held the wall of Devil's Flame, but the Shade simply crawled through it, completely unaffected. It reached out with its tendrils, and his mind began to crack under the pressure. His arms started to shake violently, and he lost hold of the flames before him. The others could only watch in fear.

But just as he started to succumb, the shadow pulled away. In his mind, he thought he heard a shriek. *The Light . . .* he heard. *The cursed Light!*

Then the cries were abruptly silenced. Something was pulling the Shade away, back toward the melted ice it had come from. The shadow slithered into its hole, and the ice froze above it, sealing the prison once more.

Only the rain remained, and all of them looked blankly at each other. None of them understood what had taken place, not even Borhiim.

"What did you do?" Gahlaia asked, staring at him.

Eyes wide and breath heavy, he shook his head. The voices were gone. "I'm not sure."

"Craden . . ." Anahka said, barely heard over the sound of the wind. "All of them. We lost so many . . ."

A tear rolled down Gahlaia's face, drowned in the rain. "We'll make it worth it," she said as she stood up. "We have to reach Valia, or it meant nothing."

Looking out toward the clumps of empty tents, she could spot several lifeless bodies in the mud. "Dying among family . . ." she repeated, and soon the others joined in, heads bowed low.

Chapter 11

Day twelve of the third month. Three days until the coronation.

TIREHN SWUNG SIDEWAYS toward Ahmeras' hip. It was reckless and sloppy. She easily blocked the silver blade, bringing her left elbow into the prince's chest. He let out a gasp as he fell to his knees. His mind went blurry for a moment before he regained his focus. Looking up, he saw Ahmeras standing over him, sword at his neck, and her right foot on his hand. He sighed, releasing his grip on the blade, and she relented.

"You've gotten slow," she said, picking up a scabbard and sheathing her blade. "That's the third time in a row I've beaten you. You're head's not in it."

"I know, I know," Tirehn replied. He sat up and caught the sheath tossed toward him. "I've had a lot to think about recently with the coronation and all coming up soon."

She cocked her head in concern. "And why haven't you told me about it?"

"Because you already know what's bothering me, Ahmeras."

The words from their last argument still hung in the air. Neither had brought it up again in the last few days, and neither really wanted to.

"I know we've had our differences," Ahmeras said, breaking the awkward silence. "I know we don't always agree, but—"

He put a hand up and shook his head, still sitting on the smooth wooden floor. "Please don't," he said. "You have no reason to justify your feelings toward the Takahrn. You never have. If anything, I've just needed time to consider what you said to me. I'm just . . . I was afraid."

Ahmeras threw her sword onto the bed behind her and joined the prince on the floor, leaning her head on his shoulder. "I understand being afraid," she replied softly. "But sometimes there are things that must be done. Do we truly have the right to keep the Takahrn's freedom from them because of our fear?"

Tirehn gave a half smile. Despite being the same age as him, Ahmeras had wisdom far beyond her years. Perhaps it was the elvish insight her ancestors had passed down to her.

"You were right," he responded. "It's like you said: Sometimes making the right choice means walking the hardest path. I think I'm ready. When I'm crowned king, I'll make the order. The Takahrn will be set free."

Ahmeras smiled at him, but it quickly faded. "But why the sudden change?" she asked. "What brought all this on?"

The prince sat in the quiet for another moment. "I've realized that there may be an enemy more dangerous than any troubles we might have with the Takahrn." He shifted himself to face her before continuing. "Ahmeras, my father said some things to me before he died, and I'm not sure how to deal with them. He said that truth is folly, that no matter what I did, the people would follow."

"Why would he say that?"

"I'm not sure. I've spent the last few nights in his secret library, reading all the books and manuscripts I could find. Inside were four scrolls, each documenting important moments in every king's life. I read my father's, but there was nothing there that spoke of what he said."

Ahmeras shut her eyes and put her hands up in confusion.

"Wait . . . There were five mortal kings. Why only four scrolls?"

"The first ruler, King Graan—his scroll is missing."

Ahmeras was silent a moment. "Your father's grave!" she said in realization. "Didn't he ask for a scroll to be taken with him into his tomb?"

"Yes, he did. Whatever answers I need are in there, but it's forbidden to enter the tombs. There will be guards patrolling them day and night."

The Tombs of the Kings. Since the early days, the tombs were meant to remain untouched. It was King Varn, the second mortal ruler, who started the tradition after his father died. His thinking was that those who had kept the peace should be given one final show of respect, and while some thought it strange, the tradition stuck.

Ahmeras shrugged. "That's never stopped you before. You're the prince. What can they do?"

"There's more though," Tirehn continued. "Before the king died, he said some other things too. He said there was someone named Tarubas talking to him in his head."

"Tarubas? Strange name."

"Exactly. When I asked the other rulers about it, Zinnyah's new advisor said he knew something about the name. But when I approached him about it the next day, he acted like he had had never heard it before, like he had forgotten everything we talked about."

"Forgotten? That's a bit—"

"Coincidental is what it is!" Tirehn exclaimed. "The king dies mysteriously, and when we look too deeply into it, the only possible lead suddenly turns cold out of nowhere?" Tirehn shook his head, gritting his teeth. "No . . . No. Something isn't right. None of it is. If this Tarubas person can control people like this, then it means he's using a power that hasn't been seen for hundreds of years."

Ahmeras put a hand on his chest. "Be careful, Tirehn," she warned. "This could go deeper than either of us realizes. We can't tell anyone about this. Not even Raggorin."

Before either could continue the conversation, a knock came at the door and Raggorin entered. Tirehn turned to see his friend's stern face. "My lord," he said with a bow, "the three rulers have gathered in the throne room. There's something you should see."

THE GOLDEN DOORS to the large room slowly opened, and Tirehn strode toward the table in the center, the three rulers standing in front of their respective chairs. As the prince regained his place among them, he noticed a new person in the room: a young woman, almost as young as him. She was of medium height and had long, golden hair that flowed to her waist. She wore simple clothes, making it clear to him that she wasn't from Valia. From her appearance, Tirehn assumed she was from Verish, most likely the Dirtlands. Her demeanor was shy and uncertain, her head drooping down and gaze directed toward the floor. She stood next to Arinay.

"Who might this be?" Tirehn asked, gesturing toward the woman.

Arinay gave a slight smile, but her shoulders drooped. Her eyes were red as if she had been crying. She placed a hand on the woman's shoulder. "This is Gwendall. She's my grand general's sister. The late king had given her permission to live here in Valia as an act of appreciation for my subordinate's accomplishments. However . . ." She lowered her head.

"What?" Tirehn asked. "What's happened?"

Gwendall rose to look at the prince and curtseyed, revealing the tears streaming down her face. "Doryan," she whispered. "My brother . . . is dead."

The whole room grew deadly silent.

"Who . . . ? Where . . . ?" was all Tirehn could muster.

Gwendall slammed her palms upon the wooden table, the sound ringing in his ears. "*He's dead!*" she cried. "The Dividers murdered him!"

The others leaned in to the conversation. Arinay motioned to a soldier at the back of the room, and the man placed an item before them on the wood. It looked like part of a large ax blade, severed or burned from its handle. It was covered in dry, crusted blood.

"When Doryan failed to return to Pordika," said Arinay, "my soldiers went looking for him. After picking up Gwendall and searching for his whereabouts, they were eventually led to the Waters of the Righteous, where they found this lying next to his body."

"That's his ax," Rorgan replied, eyes wide. "I gave it to him myself. It was one of the elvish weapons we had recently found. But how did you find him? He could have been anywhere in the Dirtlands."

Gwendall furrowed her brow. "I led them there. I'm . . . not sure how. I just knew he was there."

Tirehn saw Rorgan fidget for a moment, but he chose to ignore it, directing his attention back to the conversation.

"Who made the attack?" Zinnyah asked. "Was it the Grey Wings?"

Arinay shook her head. "It was a group of slaves that had been held in the Dirtlands, along with a spy who had been posing as a mortal."

"A spy?" Tirehn was confused. A Takahrn, living as a human? It was unheard of. Impossible even.

"Borhiim," Gwendall responded, wiping the tears from her

cheek. "His name is Borhiim. Three years ago, I found him wandering across the desert, his memory unclear. He was hungry and had nowhere to go, so I took him in. He helped me around the house while Doryan was away. He was no different from anyone else who lived there, but on the Day of Great Divide, he started acting strangely. He would black out for no reason, which led to his transformation during one of his episodes. Soon after, we were attacked by the Dividers."

The prince sat back in his chair, reviewing the events placed before him. None of it made sense. The idea of a Takahrn living in human form was already far-fetched, but at the same time, it may not have been as impossible as he originally believed. He had spent the past nights cooped up in his father's secret library, learning all he could about the magic that had long been lost to the mortal world: Terrkoris and Anamoris. There was still so much he didn't understand, but he knew enough to see what was happening.

The memory altering spell. The one in the Anamoris manuscript. This Borhiim could have been subjected to it somehow.

Tirehn placed a hand to his chin in contemplation. "Is it possible," he pondered, "that Borhiim's transformation and the attack of the slaves were merely coincidental? You said it yourself that he was acting strangely. That he was blacking out in strange instances. Does that not suggest that he might not have had control of himself?"

"That is quite the coincidence," Rorgan responded. "He may have been posing as a distraction while the other Dividers completed preparations to strike."

Tirehn rose from his chair, leaning past the edge of the table. "Then tell me this. Did he attack along with the slaves? Surely that would give us a surer way of approaching the situation."

"No," Gwendall said. "He blacked out again soon after they showed up. After my brother retaliated, they took Borhiim and fled."

"That may suggest a possible coincidence, my prince," said Rorgan, "but at the same time, if he didn't plan the attack with them, then why would they take him? He wouldn't be much of a hostage." He lifted a hand, directing a look toward Arinay. "Besides, why are we ruling out the possibility that these slaves were working with the Grey Wings? By all accounts, this resembles one of their previous attacks."

"A mark wasn't left on the town," Arinay replied. "If it was the Grey Wings, they would have attacked with more force. Besides . . . I received word from the Southern Border this morning. The Grey Wings have been captured."

"Wait—captured?" Tirehn exclaimed. "All of them? How?"

"I'm . . . not entirely certain. They were wandering aimlessly north of the West Gate. According to the message I received, they looked scared out of their minds. When we ambushed them, they hardly put up a fight."

"Did you execute them?" Zinnyah asked.

"Not yet." She turned toward Tirehn. "I was actually waiting for your order, my lord. You will be the next king. These decisions fall to you."

With that, the room grew quiet once more.

The prince paused in thought. There was a lot to consider. He had told Ahmeras that he would choose to make peace with the Takahrn if possible—but at the same time, the world could be better off without this group. They were a cult of the overzealous, masquerading their cause under the pretense of amity. The other Takahrn didn't necessarily reflect their views. But if any of them chose to make peace, should he throw that chance away in the name of justice?

"Keep them imprisoned," he replied. "We can decide their fate at a later date, but when the time comes, I will speak with them myself."

Surprise filled the others' faces.

Raggorin placed a firm hand upon his shoulder. "My lord!" he exclaimed. "Is that wise? Should we not dispose of them now?"

"My decision is final."

"But they're dangerous," Arinay chimed in. "More than dangerous, in fact. They are responsible for countless deaths across Deerium. Shouldn't we—"

"I said my decision is final!" Tirehn's sudden outburst hushed all voices immediately. "You asked for my order, and I have given it!"

Soldiers murmured from the back, and Tirehn shot them a glare. They stuttered before returning to silence. He shrugged the hand off his shoulder and walked toward the exit, Raggorin following close behind.

"This meeting is over," he commanded. "I need time to think about our next move. The coronation is almost upon us, and I have a lot to process. For now, direct Gwendall to her chambers. She's surely had a rough time as it is with us discussing her brother's death right in front of her."

Rorgan moved around the table toward Gwendall and outstretched a hand to her. "Very well," he said. "May I show you to your room, my lady?"

She took the hand, and they followed Tirehn out the doors until they diverted down a hallway to the right.

The prince continued straight through the corridor in silence, trying to contain the events swirling in his mind. He strode toward his room and pulled the door open, ignoring the soldiers near the entrance.

"My lord," Raggorin said at his back. "If I may—"

"Don't," Tirehn replied. "Just don't. I need time, Raggorin. Give me some time. Please."

The door slammed behind him.

Tirehn stared blankly at his room and walked toward the glass door leading to his balcony. Outside, he stood at its edge and breathed in a light breeze as it brushed across his face, closing his eyes in momentary bliss. He needed to forget what had transpired, at least for now. There were more pressing matters that needed attending. *My father's grave,* he thought. *Tonight, my father's grave.*

He opened his eyes and gazed into the sky. Dark clouds rolled in from the distance. It looked like rain would soon make its way to Valia. Heavy rain.

THE SUN HAD set.

Tirehn approached the large tombs in front of him. They were lined up in a row like massive square stones, twenty feet apart from each other, sliding metal doors on their faces. There were at least ten of them, but only the first five had been filled. They had golden signs nailed above the doors, naming the kings that rested within. Each one was guarded by a single soldier standing directly in front of the entrances.

Tirehn looked through the mist and rain, making out the names. At last, his gaze came to "King Hyrehn." His father. He strode toward the tomb, mud splashing his boots.

As he approached, the soldier stationed there took a fighting stance, pointing his spear. "Who goes there?" he shouted. The prince removed his hood, showing his face to the man. He hesitated. "Prince Tirehn? My lord, what are you doing here?"

"I wish to enter my father's grave," he replied. "Step aside, sir."

The soldier stumbled a bit but didn't turn his spear away. "I'm sorry, my lord. I can't do that. It's treason to enter the Tombs of the

Kings. They must be left to rest. It's tradition."

"I'm aware of the tradition. I wish to pay my respects to the late King Hyrehn. Will you not let his own son see him one last time?"

The prince took a step closer, and the soldier's resistance slowly melted away. He lowered his spear. "As you command, my lord."

Tirehn nodded to him, and the man turned to pull at the door. It took a moment before it gave way, screeching open. The prince entered, closing the door behind him. He pulled a small match from his back pocket, struck it against the wall, and lit the torch hanging there. Tirehn pulled the torch from the wall and walked toward his father's casket. A foul smell began to swell in his nostrils. With his right hand, he undid the latches and lifted the lid. The disgusting smell became unbearable. Tirehn gasped and coughed, trying to endure it.

As the lid halted at an open position, he peered into the casket. There King Hyrehn remained, decay slowly beginning to take him. He wore a grim expression, the only expression Tirehn had ever seen him wear. His hands held a scroll. On the middle of it was a seal that kept it closed, upon which was written a name: "King Graan." *The missing scroll.*

Tirehn pulled the parchment from his father's lifeless grasp and closed the casket, blocking some of the smell. He knelt on the stone floor, leaned the torch against the casket, and removed the seal from the scroll. He noticed that it was a slightly different shade from the other scrolls. The seal had less wear, and the color had not faded quite as much. Tirehn assumed his father had opened the scroll prior and resealed it when his death drew near.

Picking up the torch again, he rolled out the parchment, search-ing for something that might catch his eye. It didn't take him long. He stopped near the beginning and read:

Day 7 of the third month, Year 3267 of the second age: the Age of Dragons.

It has been several years since the dragons released us from the mountains, deeming us harmless to their cause. Harmless, they say? They have grown arrogant in their old age. We are the descendants of elves. We are the descendants of the Eternal's first children. We are the future! But it matters not. They cast us out into the world, expecting us to die off on our own. But little do they know.

Today we split Deerium's land into four sectors: Norvad, Cleptyn, Verish, and Deeria. They chose me as their king, and I appointed three rulers to manage the first three sectors while I lead from Deeria. This is only the start. Soon, we'll create a kingdom greater than even the elves could hope to achieve.

Day 14 of the third month. Year 3270 of the second age: the Age of Dragons.

Thirteen days ago: the Day of Great Divide. Fire and smoke could be seen from the mountains of the Claw, even from this distance. However, now it grows silent. Some say the dragons have finally left Deerium, returning to their old world. But it matters little. The old ways are finished. The elves are extinct, and the magic of the ancients has grown cold to us. Tomorrow, I plan to speak to the people. The year will be changed. A new age will begin. Our age.

Day 23 of the third month. Year 1 of the third age: the Age of Mortals.

Something has appeared before us. Something I thought was extinct along with the old ones. The offspring of the elves and dragons have revealed themselves. The shadows of the past.

The abominations of the ancient ways. The destroyers of everything we've built—the Takahrn.

Their leaders were brought before me today. They speak of peace and unity, but I know such a thing will never be possible. Deep down, I know they see it too. They possess strength and abilities far beyond our own. They possess long life, and some even wield the magic of old.

Why? Why must the Eternal gaze upon them with such kindness? What have they done? Did they restore the ruined world? Did they build this great kingdom? They're nothing but old mistakes, born with gifts they don't deserve. They'll divide us. They'll be the schism that breaks apart what we've spent so long creating.

Or perhaps the Eternal does not gaze upon them. Perhaps the Shade favors them. Yes, that must be it. It must be. The Takahrn may feign ignorance, but I understand. In time, they will increase and go beyond us. They do not wish to unite with us, they wish to replace us. We will lose all we have worked so hard to attain.

Very well. I know what they seek to do. I know, and I will not let them win. I have offered a banquet with their leaders. Just me, my advisors, and the Takahrn leaders. When the time is right, my forces will strike them. Kill them all. The leaders, my advisors, all of them. When I leave the dinner as the sole survivor, the people will see my dead followers with claw marks upon their necks. They will fight back against the Takahrn. Enslave them.

But I will not mourn for my advisors. They will die for the future. Our future. A future that they paved the way for. The Age of Mortals will become the greatest period known throughout history. I have no regrets. I do this for my people. They will be given the truth they need to survive. My truth.

Tirehn dropped the scroll and stood up. He couldn't believe what he had read. His mind began to whirl. This was too much. Too much for him to handle. "The enslavement of the Takahrn," he said aloud. "It was all a lie? A selfish ploy to remain in power?"

He put a hand to his face. He wanted to scream. He was sick of all of it. The coronation. The secrets. The lies. All of it.

As he reached down to pick up the scroll, his gaze darted to the very end, and he moved the torch closer. There were words written on the right edge, but they carried no date. There was no sign of a year or month. The writing was sloppy compared to the rest as if it had been jotted down quickly without the proper care.

I see his shadow everywhere I go. He creeps behind the curtains and sleeps within my nightmares. But when I look again, he's already moved on, as if he seeks a new victim for his games in the dark.

I hear his voice in my head. He speaks his name to me when no one is there to interrupt his presence. Has he only now shown his true nature, here at my end, or has he always been there? I cannot tell.

I feel him. He approaches like Death coming to greet its next plaything. I can feel his hands on my soul, pulling it away, squeezing its last breath.

There he is. I see him.

His name. I hear his name once again. Perhaps it has never been our world. Only now do I understand. It's his. Only his.

His name. Again.

Tarubas has com—

The last scribbled word of the text was almost unreadable. Tirehn's anger swelled up inside his chest. He turned in rage to glare at his father's casket, throwing his torch toward it. It bounced off and landed on the stone ground, sparks bursting from it.

"Coward! You filthy coward!" he cried, falling to his knees. "A line of kings and cowards. If you had just told me. If you had just said something. Anything! Why didn't any of you say anything?"

The words of his father rang in his head over and over.

Truth is folly.

Find an idea to stand upon and the people will follow.

Proclaim sins to be acts of holiness and they will stand by you.

Truth is folly.

Truth is folly . . .

"All of you are cowards!"

Chapter 12

Day thirteen of the third month. Two days until the coronation.

THE RAIN HAD come and gone the past few days with varying degrees of force. Today offered a slim amount compared to the previous days. Clouds still covered the sky, but the fog had completely given way, the sun's rays glistening through the heavens. It was refreshing to see the path before them, especially when they were so close to their goal.

Gahlaia moved ahead of the group and stood at the top of the slight hill that had formed in their path of mud and grass. She looked down and let out a sigh. The long, circling wall of Valia stood only a few miles in front of them. They had made it. She raised her fist and the other nine Takahrn halted.

"We've done it," Borhiim said, standing at her side. "We've finally arrived at the capital."

"Don't celebrate yet," Anahka said from behind. "We still have the king to worry about. Until the coronation, he'll be hiding away in the palace."

Gahlaia stared at the wall surrounding Valia with a mixture of amazement and disgust. It wrapped around in a perfect circle. While it wasn't as tall as the Southern Border, it was just as thick, with fully formed battlements atop its crown. It had also been built completely by Takahrn slaves shortly after King Graan brought them low. In truth, the entire city had only begun its first stages of fortification when the enslavement began. It was a testament to what the mortals had done and was as much of an insult as the word "Divider."

Borhiim faced Gahlaia, her gaze fixed upon the great city. "I assume you have a plan?"

"Of sorts," she replied. "You're our only way in. You're the only wingless Takahrn left among us, and with your cloak, you could pass as a human if you stayed hidden. Scout out the walls for a blind spot. When night falls, we'll follow you in."

Borhiim nodded, gave the elvish salute, and turned toward the capital. But once he had moved past, he stopped and turned back toward her. "Remember what we discussed. Please, when the time comes, give the king his moment to speak. If we can end this without starting a war, then we should."

Gahlaia didn't reply but instead returned the elvish salute.

Assured, Borhiim departed.

GWENDALL SAT IN her chambers quietly, all lights snuffed out. She stared down at her silver and golden dress, toying with the smooth fabric. A dim light came through the drapes that covered her glass door in the back. She stood up from her bed, walked to the end of the room, and stood before her mirror, trying to find satisfaction in her appearance. But even amid the new brilliance of Valia and all the hospitality it had brought her, she felt nothing. No drive to do what she had hoped above all else to do.

Since she was little, all Gwendall had dreamed about was the life she could live in the great palace of Valia, or even Pordika, or any of the other capitals. She wanted to be among royalty, live in a place where she could feel free. Where her brother could live free. Where she could find happiness with the man she cared for.

But then... had Borhiim ever cared for her? All the happy memories they had shared had been lies. He was no human. He was a Divider. A ploy to lead his comrades to her brother. It was because of them that Doryan was now dead, and nothing could bring him back. She may have made it to the city of her dreams—but at what cost? What were dreams without those she wished to share them with?

Tears ran down her face. They tickled her cheeks until they dropped to her feet. She clutched the fabric in her hands and pressed it against her legs, her teeth clenched. She wanted to yell, break something, anything to make the pain go away.

A knock came at her door, startling her. A familiar voice rang out from the other side.

"Gwendall?" Rorgan said from outside the door. "May I come in?"

She straightened herself, wiped the tears from her face, and opened the drapes. A grey light came through the glass, revealing the cloud and rain beyond. "Yes, of course," she responded, turning toward the entrance as Rorgan stepped inside.

Gwendall had known Rorgan for quite some time now. They were not so different in age, which helped them get along nicely. He had been the ruler of Norvad for the last four years, but they had met before that. He had always enjoyed travel, and when he arrived in the Dirtlands some time ago, he met with Doryan and Gwendall. Soon after, he volunteered himself to be tested for leader of Norvad, and the king awarded him the title once his capabilities were clear. He then recommended Doryan to be Arinay's grand general to protect the Southern Border. Since then, he had pushed Gwendall to ask the Verish ruler for a chance to live in Valia. It was thanks to him that she had made it here, and it was because of him her brother continued to be held in such high regard, even after his death.

"You look beautiful," he said with a bow. "I presume that's the dress you'll be wearing for the coronation?"

"Yes," she returned. "I was given plenty to choose from, but I think this one suits me best."

Rorgan looked more closely upon the sparkling clothing and nodded in agreement. "The gold matches your hair, yet the silver contrasts it. A wonderful combination."

Gwendall chuckled, turned toward the glass door, and opened it. A strong breeze brushed across her as it swung wide. She stepped out onto her balcony, making sure to stay under the roof to keep from the rain's fury.

"Since when did you become so attuned to fashion?" she asked.

Rorgan joined her outside, watching the lightning flash in the sky. "You forget, my lady. As ruler of Norvad, I often have to tolerate all the fanciful outfits of grand occasions. It's not exactly a choice I made." He gave an exaggerated sigh and put the back of his hand to his forehead. "It is the burden I must bear. I curse the day I grew accustomed to the sight of fabulous gowns."

Gwendall elbowed him hard in the side, and he let out a laugh. "Stop that!" she said with a half smile. "I happen to be one of those people in fabulous gowns, thank you very much."

"Sorry. You looked like you could use some cheer. You seemed more down than usual."

She shrugged. "Well, given the circumstances, what did you expect? This isn't exactly a time for euphoria."

"No, I suppose it isn't. Still, you could use some bliss after everything that's happened."

Though she didn't feel much better, she forced a smile upon her face. It was the least she could do. "Thank you, Rorgan. I appreciate the thought."

For several minutes, the two of them stood in silence with nothing to break it but the patter of the rain and the crack of thunder.

Gwendall turned to Rorgan, who stood staring at the skies with a look that perplexed her. It was one of deep sorrow and longing.

"I wonder what it would be like to live among the clouds," he said. "The dragons could fly freely through the heavens, and the elves could control the world around them like a painter filling a canvas. They lived life without care. Without boundaries. And us... We live by them. Not a day goes by that I don't envy them at least a little." He dropped his gaze. "Sorry. I can get a bit philosophical sometimes."

"No, no. It's fine, Rorgan. In a way, I agree with you." She looked up as a great streak of lightning flashed above them. "We need a roof over our heads to hide away from the weather. Those before us laughed at such things. They thrived in any situation."

She bent her head. If she were like the dragons or elves, perhaps she could have saved her brother. *Perhaps Doryan would still be alive if I weren't so helpless. So weak . . .*

"Tell me," she began again. "If those closest to you were taken away . . . if you lost the only family you knew, what would you do? How would you even begin to deal with something like that?"

Rorgan stood in thought, squinting. "I'm not sure I'm the best person to answer that question, to be honest," he replied. "I lost any semblance of a family when I was just a child. My own brother hated me from the day I was born, and it took us years before we found any common ground. When we finally did, he was taken from me, along with everything else I loved. I was left alone, and no one came back for me. It wasn't until I met King Hyrehn, the other rulers, your brother, and you that I finally felt a sense of purpose." He put a hand on her shoulder. "My only reason for hope is here with me."

"I'm sorry," she murmured. "I didn't know."

He removed his hand and stared once more into the clouds. "I guess that's how I made it through. I found something I could put my hope in. Something that drove me to be the greatest and strongest I could ever be, as ridiculous as that sounds."

"What is it that you put your hope in?"

He paused, as another flash of lightning split the sky. "A chance. A chance to live."

TIREHN MOVED INTO the long hallway. He wanted answers, and he was running out of places to look. He had already patronized Nokdin enough times that he was sure the scholar was afraid to look him in the eye, that much he was certain. It was too coincidental. *It has to be Anamoris*, he thought. *It has to be.*

As he paced through the corridor, he looked up at a large sky-light above him. The clouds were beginning to dissipate, leaving more room for the sun to shine through. It was still midday. Normally he would wait until sundown to enter his father's library, but he had grown impatient. Perhaps he had missed something. Some clue that could lead him to his mysterious enemy. If anything, it would give him a chance to finish reading the Anamoris book held within. If Tarubas did use that form of magic, it would do him well to be aware of its capabilities.

Tirehn reached the spiraling stairway he had grown accustomed to and began his descent but paused when he heard a footstep slip across the floor just behind him. The prince spun around, but there was no one there. He squinted, darting his gaze around before returning to the staircase. His hand rested on his sword as he descended. Something was amiss.

Arriving at the marble door, he unlocked it and slowly pushed it open.

He cocked his head slightly toward his shoulder. From the corner of his eye, he spotted a shadow in the stairway. His suspicions were correct. He had been followed, and now he was trapped between the small room and the figure looming above. He grasped his blade on his right hip and unsheathed it, taking a ready stance.

The man leaped down to the bottom step and in one swift motion lunged his entire body toward Tirehn. In his right hand was a long and unnatural looking spear. In his left hand was a shortsword. His face was hooded, and his shoulders were plated with spikes.

The prince pressed forward to meet his foe. With the tip of his sword, Tirehn knocked the spear away and thrust toward the man's chest. The figure turned sideways, the sword point ripping through his shirt and scratching at armor plating underneath. He brought his shortsword up toward Tirehn's arm, but the prince pulled it back just in time, weapons clashing.

The man took a swing at Tirehn's head with the spear, its tips pointing three ways. The two on the sides were horizontal, the one middle vertical. The prince outstretched his right arm and caught it inches before it reached his skull. It took him a split second to recognize the weapon. It was elvish, one of the few given to the grand generals.

The man grasped the spear tighter, and the prince saw his muscles tighten. *Terrkoris!* He threw Tirehn hard against the wall, the spear inching closer to his head. The man's shortsword swung toward the prince's chest, but Tirehn pressed the small blade against the wall next to him, trying to keep it in position. He grunted, trying to keep both weapons away from him. The figure was slowly beginning to overpower him, and he couldn't hold him in place much longer.

With a deep breath, he prepared to make his move.

Tirehn ducked swiftly, releasing his hold on the shortsword but keeping a hand on the spear. The man fell forward, his own weight used against him. The prince jumped to the side and brought his blade toward the figure's stomach and sliced across flesh. The man screamed and fell to his knees.

Tirehn kicked him away, pulling the spear from his hand. With his flow of magic gone, the attacker was just another man, weakened from his onslaught. He rose, still holding his shortsword and keeping one hand on his wound. Tirehn threw the spear behind him, and grasping his sword with two hands, swung with all his might at the opposing blade. It tore from his foe's hand and scraped across the wall before falling to the ground.

The prince grabbed the torn shirt and pressed the man against the wall, steel at his neck. He grasped the figure's hood in his hand and pulled it back, revealing the face. It was Naggyn, Rorgan's grand general.

"Who sent you?" Tirehn yelled. "Is Rorgan behind this? Speak!"

Naggyn laughed, wincing. "Rorgan?" he responded. "You can't be serious. The Norvad ruler is nothing compared to my master."

"Your master? Tarubas?" There was no response, and the prince was losing patience. "Speak! Speak or lose your tongue!"

Naggyn gave a deathly grin. "Then why don't you go ahead and do it, my high and mighty prince? What you do is inconsequential. You are nothing but a pawn. All of you! Pawns in his game."

"I won't play his game. I know what he is, how he manipulates people."

The grand general let out a guttural laugh. "You know nothing! You think you know what he can do? You've seen but a taste. He's ruled these lands for centuries. Your father and his father before . . . all a means to an end. His end."

"Then why did he send you to kill me?"

Naggyn's expression began to change from one of sadistic enjoyment to complete terror. His voice shifted into a whine. "Kill me," he said. "Just kill me. *Kill me!*"

"Not until you answer my question," Tirehn said, shaking him.

"If he finds out I failed . . . I can't go back to him now. He'll torture me. Please just end me."

"Not until you answer my question!" Tirehn shook him harder.

Naggyn grunted in defiance but relented nonetheless. "Your soul. It's stronger than your father's. He can't reach it like he did the others. You had to be disposed of. Replaced."

Tirehn thought for a second. Based on all he had read in the secret library, along with the scroll of King Graan, it was all starting to add up.

He sighed in frustration and pushed Naggyn toward the staircase. "I'm taking you to the dungeons. You're going to answer for what you've done."

At that, the general struggled to pull away. "*No!*" he cried. "No, no, no! You have to kill me! He'll find me!"

Naggyn scrambled back and tried to press the prince's blade into his chest, but the prince moved it upward, bringing the blunt end down on his skull. His unconscious body fell limp onto the ground, and Tirehn dragged it up the stairs, calling for a guard to come assist him.

THE MOON BROKE through the thin clouds. Borhiim stood against the wall, the other Takahrn standing next to him.

Gahlaia looked at him with concern. "You sure this will work?"

"For the last time, yes," he whispered back. "The guards never come to this side of the wall. They only scout from above."

He pointed to a large hole in the mud. He had spent the last hour burning the small tunnel, going directly under the wall. It was wide enough to fit one person at a time. "It's now or never," he said.

She shot him one more doubtful glance before crawling down into the hole, the other Takahrn following behind her. It only took them a few minutes before they reached the other side. Gahlaia wriggled out and looked around. She pulled her cloak closer to her skin as the breeze chilled her. It was a cold night, even without the rain.

Borhiim emerged next, followed by Anahka and the others.

Gahlaia faced him, and he smiled with confidence. "All of you need to stay out of sight," he explained. "Stay near the wall's edge if you have to. When the time comes, I'll give you the signal."

With that, Gahlaia turned toward the other Takahrn and gave the elvish salute, which they returned. "This is it," she said. "For our brother and sisters. We can end a war before it even begins, right here and now." She looked back at Borhiim. "Dying among family."

He nodded. "Dying among family."

WHEN NAGGYN WOKE up, he was in a prison cell. Panicked, he looked around. He was surrounded on three sides by stone walls, with a small, barred window at his back near the ceiling. Two soldiers stood guard at the cell door, long spears in their hands and swords hanging at their sides. He leaped toward his bars, terror striking throughout his body. He had to get out before his master found him. He had been told in great detail what happened to those who failed to impress. Throughout his years of servitude, he had never left any stone his master desired unturned. Only now did he feel truly in peril.

He had always felt confident in his ability to survive. It had gotten him to where he was. For years, he felt he lived to serve a greater purpose: to stand at his lord's right hand. But now he understood. He was nothing more than a puppet, and all puppets eventually lose their value. When that time comes, their strings are severed, and they are tossed aside.

If he couldn't find a way of escape, he would be more than tossed aside.

He turned as he heard the clang of armor. The guards had straightened themselves as a man walked down the stone steps leading to the prison. Naggyn's heart pounded in his chest but then slowed as he recognized the figure. It was Rorgan, an expression of alarm upon his face.

He bowed toward his ruler. "My Lord Rorgan," Naggyn said. "Have you come to see your lowly general in his lowly prison cell?"

"Prince Tirehn told me what you did," he replied. "How could you betray Norvad like this? How could you betray Deerium?"

Naggyn snickered. "Please. I'm not betraying anything. I'm serving a greater purpose than you could possibly understand."

Rorgan breathed out his nostrils and clenched his jaw tight. He shook his head and turned to one of the soldiers. "Leave us," he said. "I need a word with my subordinate."

The men looked at each other with uncertainty. "I'm afraid we cannot do that," one soldier replied. "Prince Tirehn has given us strict orders to remain on guard."

"And I'm telling you to leave us. Now."

There was no hesitation in their response. They clanged their feet, holding their posts. "Forgive us, my lord. We have our orders."

Rorgan slowly cocked his head toward the soldier who had spoken. He kept his gaze on the man, but the soldier did not move. Finally, he rolled his eyes and lifted his hands, palms up.

The torches dimmed. Naggyn watched in uncertainty that swiftly changed to fear. When Prince Tirehn had asked him about Rorgan earlier, he believed he was telling the truth, but now he saw.

The soldiers dropped their spears and clutched their chests. They opened their mouths as if to scream, but nothing came out. It was as though all sound had been sucked out of the room. A flowing energy formed in Rorgan's open hands, drawn from the two men before him. He lifted the swirls of magic to his head and smiled, his eyes flashing purple.

"The weak-minded . . ." he said, turning his gaze toward Naggyn. His voice was deeper and grittier, completely different from what it was before. It was a voice the general knew well. "The weak-minded are so easily manipulated."

He closed his hands and the energy dissipated, the two soldiers collapsing to the stone floor. Their bodies turned to ash and then vanished completely. Nothing was left but their armor.

The candlelight flickered out.

Rorgan walked toward the cell door, his body slowly changing in the darkness. He made a motion with his hand, and the cell door opened. His body was mostly invisible in the shadows, but Naggyn could make out the figure of a taller, much older man, with two glowing eyes piercing the darkness.

Naggyn fell to the ground and crawled to the far corner. He knew this man. He knew him well. *Master . . .*

Tarubas walked toward his prey and leaned down, placing the long nail of his index finger on his puppet's chin.

"R-Rorgan?" Naggyn whimpered.

His master shook his head. "No . . . What's my name?"

"Tarubas!" he finally squealed. "You?"

"Yes, Naggyn," he replied, white fangs glistening in the moonlight. "But no need to worry about that now. You have betrayed Deerium. You have betrayed me, my kingdom, everything."

Naggyn choked as a sudden burning sensation filled his throat. It made its way to his chest, his head, his arms, until it spread everywhere. Invisible knives cut their way into his soul, his mind growing numb as the pain consumed him. His body twitched and shook on the floor as Tarubas stood over him in amusement. No cry for help reached his lips. He just flailed on the stone floor, helpless.

"Please . . ." he let out. "M-Master . . ."

And as his body disintegrated, he felt his soul vanish into darkness.

Chapter 13

Day fifteen of the third month. Coronation Day.

BORHIIM WALKED THROUGH the crowds that had begun to huddle together within the streets of the great city. Even a capital that large was having trouble holding everyone inside, and more were pouring in by the hour. News of the crowning of the new king had spread far and wide across Deerium. Falcons bearing messages of the sudden death of King Hyrehn and the presentation of the new leader had been sent to every village of every sector, and now the masses were arriving in droves to see what would become of their kingdom. It was one of the few occasions that would ever draw so much attention.

But the day was not only the coronation of the new king; it also promised a grand wedding. Borhiim had heard stories of the prince's betrothed. Some even said she was elvish, the last of her kind. However, he preferred to hold such expectations in check. After all, he was there for an entirely different reason. In a way, he almost regretted what he and the other Takahrn had come to do, but such thoughts were brief. The people around him all wore expressions of joy and celebration, but what of his people? The Takahrn were refused such luxury, and today that would be rectified. Both sides deserved the joy they desired, but only one received it. *That's going to change*, he thought. *It has to.*

He slowly shuffled his way through the crowds, trying not to get on anyone's bad side. He left his hood back but kept his hands hidden under the sleeves of his cloak. His tail remained coiled around his left leg to keep away suspicion. He wanted to blend in, and luckily for him, the crowds were far larger than he expected. He would have no trouble making it to the palace so long as he didn't anger any locals or drunkards.

He lifted his nose above the sweat of bodies surrounding him and smelled the morning air. The fragrance of rain still hung in the air, but all harsh weather had subsided the previous night. The clouds had worn themselves thin, becoming nothing but scattered brushstrokes as the sun's orange rays glinted off them with dazzling beauty.

Borhiim turned to look at the buildings that lined the edges of the cramped roads. Every structure was connected to the last, all of nearly equal height. They only spaced out when the path on the ground forked to the left or right. Several bore signs with names of markets, taverns, and inns. Others were simple square houses, filled with bustling and happy people exiting through their doorways to join the commotion.

Borhiim couldn't help but smile. Despite the chaos, this was a cheerful place. A fairly stark contrast from the villages of the Dirtlands. Most people there kept to themselves, engaging in conversation only if something needed to be bought or sold, or if a new string of gossip had made its way south. Nonetheless, Borhiim was starting to tire of the constant shoving from all directions and the growing humidity from the bodies crowded around him. He would make it to the palace before the new king made his appearance, but it would definitely take some time.

As he slowly moved forward, Borhiim focused inward, reaching for the magic within. It felt weak and reluctant to show itself, increasingly unpredictable, as if the Devil's Flame were the vessel and he were the magic. Some days it would be bursting from his fingers without a second thought, challenging to reel back in. Other times, like today, it would refuse to show itself. It was a fickle thing, a powerful yet frustrating combination of the two magics that made up the world around him.

He reached deeper inside himself and eventually began to feel its fiery pull. It was there; it just needed some persuading. When the time came, he would need it. Without it, he wasn't sure he or his comrades would survive the day.

Borhiim continued to pace himself until he had finally pushed his way closer to the gates, giving him a clearer view of the palace's middle balcony. He was in position. Now all he had to do was wait. Lowering his head, he offered a solemn prayer to the Eternal, trying to calm his nerves. The world was about to change, unbeknownst to everyone around him. The crowds continued in joyous celebration, many circling in rows of dancing and singing, completely unaware of what was to come.

TIREHN YAWNED AS he pulled open his drapes. His mind cleared as he recalled the events of the past days. Just thinking about it all frustrated him. How could he be so careless? He had done nothing but make mistakes at every turn, and his unseen enemy had foreseen them all.

The secret library his father had left him was gone, burned to ash. Focused on his assassination attempt, he had forgotten to lock the door, and it had been destroyed in that small window of time. No doubt it was yet another attack from his dark adversary.

But while he kept that situation quiet, the state of the prison was not something that went unknown.

When he had entered the dungeon where he had left Naggyn two days ago, he was gone, along with the soldiers he had stationed to guard the general. It had certainly prompted commotion among the other three rulers. It was perplexing and frustrating. People didn't just disappear without leaving behind some sort of trail to follow.

Tirehn was certain Tarubas was behind Naggyn's disappearance, or at least someone serving under him. There was no doubt in his mind now that his foe wielded Anamoris magic. The soul controlled the mind, and the mind controlled the body, so long as the soul was willing or weak-minded. With the possession of such power, Tarubas could have done whatever he wanted with the bodies. It was a weapon that the prince was not sure how to combat.

He groaned and tried to push the thoughts out of his mind. *This is a happy day. I need to focus on the here and now.*

Tirehn turned and looked to a large table placed in the center of the room. Upon it was his ceremonial clothing for the occasion. A white shirt and pants, with gold armor plated on the shoulders and elbows. He was never one for theatrics, but Ahmeras had chosen the fabric herself. For her, he would relent. It was a day for her as well, possibly even more special than it was for him.

With a sigh, Tirehn made one last attempt to push aside his frustrations and began to put on his coronation garments. When he was prepared, he stepped out of his room, Raggorin waiting for him with his hands held behind his back. He nodded to the prince, and they walked down the corridor. The advisor remained dressed in his usual clothing, the garments of his people who lived in the Gorrobin Mountains, and he wore them with pride.

"Raggorin," Tirehn began as they walked onward, "what is your opinion of the Takahrn?"

Raggorin hesitated for a moment. "I'm a bit uncertain, to be honest. Like us, they hold potential for both good and evil. I can't say I have seen anything other than their bad side, but that doesn't mean the good doesn't exist. The many should never be judged based on the misguided few. Perhaps it's the same with the Takahrn."

Tirehn stopped and turned to his friend. "And what if I told you I was planning to free them from their enslavement. What then?"

Another pause.

"You are my prince," Raggorin answered, "and soon you will be my king. I will follow you wherever your leadership takes us. But you must know that it won't be an easy task to accomplish. I'm not sure what the reaction will be."

"Sometimes making the right choice means walking the hardest path," Tirehn mused quietly. "If it isn't done eventually, then people will only continue to be afraid."

Raggorin nodded. "Very well, my lord. If this is the path you wish to take, I will serve you to the end."

They soon arrived before Ahmeras' door. The two soldiers standing on each side clanged their feet together as the prince and his advisor approached.

Tirehn walked forward and knocked on the door.

"Come in," came a voice from inside, and he opened the door and stepped in.

Ahmeras stood before him, still in her casual attire, looking into a large mirror. A long white dress was sprawled out on the bed, dazzling with hints of golden streaks along the sides. She had made it herself. Maids ran to and fro across the room, preparing to put the dress on their mistress.

"I assume we won't be dueling today?" Tirehn said.

"Oh, hush," she responded, turning toward him. Her pointed ears stood out from her curly black hair that tumbled over her shoulders. She outstretched her hands, and Tirehn took them in his.

He felt like he needed to say something. Something meaningful before the momentous occasion. "Ahmeras," he said, "I know you don't like talking about your past, but when I met you three years ago, wandering near the Southern Border, I thought you were the most beautiful woman I had ever seen."

Ahmeras rolled her eyes, blushing slightly, but he continued anyway. "I was just a boy, but even then, I could tell you had many memories you wished to forget. People you wished you never knew. You were always so distant, even when we took you back to the palace."

Ahmeras smile faded, as if the mere mention of old times left her downcast.

"I know my father allowed me to call you my betrothed only because you were among the last of your kind, but I never saw you like that. You were broken. With everything that had happened with your brother—"

"Don't say his name," she said abruptly.

He put his hands up in apology. "I just . . . I wanted to put a smile back on your face. You deserved that much at least." He caressed her cheek with his thumb. "I love you, Ahmeras."

She placed her own hand over his and her smile returned. "I love you too, Tirehn."

GAHLAIA STARED INTO the distance. She was getting tired of sitting around. They had been clinging to the edges of the capital wall for a full day, and her bones were growing stiff.

They had huddled together in a cluster of cloaks, folding their wings underneath and keeping their heads low. Any soldier who happened to walk past would easily mistake them for a group of citizens down on their luck. Such a thing wasn't uncommon, especially in such a large city. Still, the long hours were growing more boring than the last, with no access to food.

Gahlaia's stomach growled. None of them had eaten anything for nearly a week. Their bodies could handle it, but the desire remained all the same. She repressed the urge to imagine anything revolving around food, but with the waiting going so slowly, it was getting harder to keep her mind on track.

She turned her head and stared out past several structures. She could barely see the tips of the palace, the ruckus of the crowds ringing out loudly even from their distance. *Just wait for the signal*, she thought.

"Anahka," she said, turning her gaze back to the group still huddled in a rough circle, "tell me where you're from. What was your upbringing?"

Anahka looked confused by the question, and the other Takahrn cocked their heads in curiosity. "Why the sudden interest?" she returned.

Gahlaia looked in both directions and then back to her. "We aren't exactly going anywhere anytime soon. Perhaps some history can help pass the time."

Anahka shuffled on the stone floor uncomfortably. Clearly, her past was not something she cared much for. "Zerthon, my father, was one of the few elves who fought on the front lines during the Battle of Fate and lived to tell the tale. When they lost the battle, he was forced into the mountains of the Claw along with the rest. They say he was dragged from the Green Hills, away from the only home he had ever known. Yet even in the mountains, he was strong. As the years went by, he slowly began to return to the old ways. He started giving thanks to the Eternal instead of following whatever religion they had previously."

"What about your mother?" Gahlaia pressed.

Anahka shuffled once more. "I never knew her. When the dragons gave birth to the Second Dragons, they soon realized that their offspring were not intelligent. Without a connection to their old world, the creatures bore no soul. They were animals.

"Soon the order came down that dragons and elves would be allowed to mate. My mother, whoever she was, mated with my father and gave birth to me. When she saw what I was, she left us. Where she went is beyond me, and I doubt even the Dragon King knew."

Anahka pointed a talon out toward the city. "Unlike Borhiim, not all of our parents were keen on having Takahrn children. To some, we were no better than the Second Dragons that came before us."

Gahlaia nodded. She had no words for such a story. Most tales the Takahrn had to tell were not much different. They had all suffered loss on some level.

"What about you?" Anahka asked "What's your story?"

Gahlaia shrugged. "There's not much to tell."

"You are the daughter of Gahlorm the Dragon King. There has to be a story there."

Gahlaia sighed. "I remember traveling across Deerium with my father. He explained the ways of the world and how the elves had once roamed the lands. When we weren't traveling, I stayed in the Claw with Meriss, my mother. They mated soon after news of Borhiim's parents got out. Gahlorm called her the Queen of the New World, and many thought it scandalous."

Several of the Takahrn nodded along with the story. Many of them knew it well.

"What about the Battle of Extinction?" Anahka asked. "That was the final conflict that led to the dragons' departure. Where was your mother in all of that?"

Gahlaia lowered her head, cutting and tracing through the stone floor with her claws. "She was murdered. Assassinated by the

Righteous Ones. They disapproved of the union, and it was her death that drove the dragons to attack in the first place."

"I'm sorry," Anahka said.

Gahlaia turned once more toward the city, staring at the tips of the palace, trying to keep her mind focused. *Just wait for the signal.*

Tirehn took a deep breath. His heart pounded in his chest. He stood at the top of wide, long staircase that led to the lower level of the palace, breathing hard. He had prepared for this moment for years, yet even with all the time spent, he still couldn't help but feel nervous.

Raggorin let a slight chuckle slip. "Calm yourself, my lord," he said. "The last thing your people wish to see is a king flailing about like a fish."

"Blunt as ever, I see. . ." Tirehn grumbled under his breath.

A trumpet sounded from below the stairs, and the two men began walking down the steps at its call. The prince kept his eyes forward, his mind going completely blank.

The stairs led them to a hallway ending at wide, golden doors like those at the entrance to the throne room above. A soldier stood on each side, dressed in armor that mixed gold and white, the ceremonial colors for the grander events in Valia.

As the men approached the big doors, the soldiers pulled them back, leading into a massive ballroom. The whole area was circular, the wall laced with smooth stone. Soldiers stood on the outside, forming a ring around the hundreds of people within. Harps and flutes were playing, the people in the middle forming lines of dance to the melodic music. However, when the prince and his advisor stepped into the room, all went silent, eyes fixed upon them.

Two trumpets sounded to the left, and all immediately bowed toward Tirehn. He looked into the crowd and recognized some of the faces. Arinay, Zinnyah, and their subordinates were spread thin in the mass. Gwendall stood in the corner next to Rorgan, dressed in beautiful garments.

When Tirehn bowed back toward the crowd, all spread to the edges of the room, taking their seats at round white tables. The three rulers stepped away from the festivities and took their positions. Once the rest had seated themselves, Raggorin nodded to his lord and took a step back.

The prince now stood alone, all eyes on him.

He looked straight ahead to the far side of the room. Before him stood Korophis, the palace elder, robed completely in white. He had a thin grey beard that hung down his chest, a golden circlet held in his left palm and a silver one in his right. The three rulers stood directly behind him, hands behind their backs.

Tirehn strode slowly toward them, keeping his gaze in front of him. He had never felt so many eyes on him at once. His heart began to pound again. He tried to think of things to calm himself, but any such thoughts escaped him now.

He stopped directly in front of the elder, knelt, and bent his head low.

Quiet hung in the air for a brief moment before the trumpets sounded again. None spoke as the music filled the room.

The doors Tirehn had come through opened once more. The harps and flutes began to play in beautiful harmony a low and sweet tune.

He turned his head, and in stepped the most beautiful sight the new king had ever seen. It was Ahmeras, outfitted in her white wedding dress, gold streaks lining the sides. Her hair was pulled back behind her pointed ears, the elvish mark quite clear on her left cheek.

Murmurs rose from each side of the room. Many of the guests had heard rumors, but few had seen Ahmeras for themselves. An elf, alive and beautiful, strode slowly toward her betrothed.

She smiled as she approached, and Tirehn felt a knot in his throat. This was real. She was real, and it was perfect.

He couldn't help but smile back. There were no words for what he beheld, what he felt. It wasn't something he could express in words, nor did he wish to. The music and a smile were all he needed to convey his emotions.

"Hi," she whispered to him, kneeling at his side.

He couldn't respond. He just nodded and took her hand in his. They turned back toward the elder, bowing their heads.

The music fell silent.

Korophis raised both his hands, displaying the crowns. "Today," he said in a gruff voice, "we find ourselves standing before a new kingdom. A new legacy. A new beginning. A king and queen who will lead us into the future. Leaders who will drive out the darkness of the old world and forge a new path for the people to cross."

Tirehn recited the words in his head as they were spoken. He had read them over in old textbooks. They were the words his father was coronated with and his ancestors before him.

"My lord," Korophis began. Tirehn raised his head. "You have accepted the responsibilities of this world and its people upon your shoulders. You have allowed the burdens of Deerium to fall upon you. But this woman has offered herself to you, to stand at your side in times of happiness, and in your times of pain. Do you accept her as your wife and as your queen?"

"I do," Tirehn replied.

"My lady," the elder continued. Ahmeras raised her head. "You kneel here today, prepared to share in the joy and heartbreak that will follow, ready to gaze upon the bright and difficult future ahead. But this man has offered himself to you. To stand at your side in times of great cheer and in times of great sorrow. Do you accept him as your husband and as your king?"

"I do," Ahmeras replied.

"If you would speak wisdom to your people," Korophis stated, "speak it now."

"We have none to say," Tirehn and Ahmeras said in unison, following the words the previous kings and queens had once said. "For true wisdom does not come from words but the willingness to do what is necessary."

The elder lowered the circlets and placed them upon their heads. The two rose as he spread out his arms toward the ceiling once again, speaking his final words. "I hereby pronounce you husband and wife. May the Eternal bless your reign . . . king and queen of Deerium!"

The cheering and applause reached its peak as Tirehn and Ahmeras embraced in a kiss. They released and gazed briefly at the mass of people before striding through the crowd, which parted as the two left the ballroom.

The doors shut behind them, and the music and dancing recommenced, still audible behind the walls. They ran up the steps and stopped when they reached the second floor of the palace, standing in the middle of the long, empty corridor. Any bustling that once filled the regular days of the higher level had all moved to the celebration below.

The two stood frozen, staring at each other.

"What now?" Tirehn asked with a half smile.

Ahmeras squeezed his hand. She leaned in and kissed him.

He returned the kiss, putting a hand to her cheek, but they quickly pulled away from each other when a loud "Ahem" came from behind.

Raggorin bowed straight and unflinching, his arms crossed in front of him. "Forgive me, my lord and lady," he said, "but I believe it is time for you to present yourselves before your people."

He gestured forward, toward the far end of the corridor. Glass doors lay at the end, leading to the main balcony. "While the royals celebrate in the ballroom, the citizens of Deerium await your arrival outside. Will you not address them?"

Tirehn sighed and turned to his bride. "I suppose if we must . . ." he said.

Ahmeras shook her head, rolling her eyes. "Lead the way, Raggorin."

BORHIIM KNELT DOWN, giving his legs a small break from the strain of standing for so long.

The people murmured across the city. It had been several hours since they had first gathered. He had heard the music from deep inside the palace, but aside from that, he assumed it would still be awhile before the new king decided to show himself.

His thoughts were quickly silenced when two soldiers appeared upon the large balcony above, blowing trumpets.

Borhiim's heart skipped a beat, and he frantically reached deep inside for the Devil's Flame, preparing to give the signal. It still felt weak and unwilling, but it was there all the same. *We're so close. We can't fail now.*

A hush filled the air, all eyes on the balcony.

Then the crowds quickly began to shout with words of praise. The new king and queen appeared at the railing, smiling at those below.

Borhiim tried to steady himself with all the pushing and shoving around him. He couldn't believe his eyes. From where he was standing, he could see the pointed ears and Terrkoris mark. The queen . . . She was elvish! The rumors were true.

He breathed in, gathering the magic inside. It resisted his pull. He grunted, trying to find focus as another elbow jammed into his back. His fists clenched, talons digging into his palms until they drew blood. *I need you now!*

With one more push, the energy inside finally began to rise. It grew and grew. He felt the heat inside him, and his breathing became more rapid.

He raised a bloodied hand into the sky, and the dark flames emerged in streaks of murky red. A massive shockwave knocked the crowds back, leaving him standing alone, Devil's Flame spewing from his hand.

Instantly, chaos ensued. People ran and shrieked in terror.

Borhiim stared up at the balcony, releasing his hold on the magic with a grunt. The newly crowned king and queen stood there in shock and disbelief, looking unsure of what had just taken place.

Soldiers left their posts in front of the palace and charged toward Borhiim. Only two men came within a few feet of their target before they were quickly subdued by figures swooping from the sky. Winged Takahrn flew down, kicking the soldiers unconscious.

Borhiim looked up in the chaos and saw Gahlaia make a beeline for the balcony.

The king and queen were being escorted into the palace by a tall man. He wore strange garb that only partly covered his muscular chest. From his appearance, he looked like one of the people from the Gorrobin tribes.

Anahka flew down, grabbed Borhiim under the shoulders, and hoisted him toward the second level of the palace.

"STAND BACK, MY lords!" Raggorin yelled over the shrieking crowds below.

Tirehn was hardly able to process what was going on before he was pushed toward the glass door along with Ahmeras.

"Raggorin, let me—" the king began, but before he could finish, a female Takahrn came flying toward them, her claws outstretched.

Raggorin pulled out the elvish broadsword resting on his back, the wide blade glinting in the sunlight overhead. He swung it with a heave toward the flying attacker, but folding her wings in a swift motion, she dropped to the balcony floor.

She fell hard to the ground and slid toward Raggorin's feet. He didn't hesitate for a second, bringing the blade downward with incredible speed.

The Takahrn rolled and pushed off the floor with her wings, regaining her footing. The broadsword crashed into the tile, cracking the surface.

Raggorin pulled it out with a heave and readied himself again. The two stood a few feet apart, each waiting for the other to make the next move.

Several other foes flew up to the balcony, one carrying the wingless Takahrn from below.

Raggorin backed up, holding his blade out in front of him, pushing Tirehn and Ahmeras further toward the glass doors.

Tirehn took a step forward, but his advisor placed an arm to the side, blocking his path. "My king," he said, "I need you to leave."

The king shook his head. "Move aside, Raggorin," he ordered, gazing at the group of Takahrn in front of him.

"Step back, Tirehn!" The advisor pressed his arm harder against the king and held him in place, despite his best efforts to push through.

"Takahrn!" Tirehn yelled. "I understand your anger and your pain, but—"

"Do you?" the female attacker interrupted, pointing a finger in his direction. "Do you truly understand? Our kin across your lands suffer under the feet of your people. They sit in chains! From where I'm standing, it looks like you have it pretty easy."

Tirehn sighed. He pushed against Raggorin. "Let me through," he commanded.

"Tirehn," Ahmeras said from behind, "what are you doing?"

He glanced back at her. "I'm walking the hardest path. Now let me through."

Raggorin slowly lowered his arm, letting the king stand before the Takahrn.

The glass doors behind swung open, and the three rulers came through, shock upon their faces. Tirehn eyed clusters of soldiers beginning to form below and behind the doors, placing arrows to bowstrings.

Gwendall appeared next to Rorgan, and she put a hand to her mouth. "That's them," she whispered. "Those are the slaves that murdered my brother."

At the sight of her, the wingless Takahrn's eyes widened. He recognized her.

"My king," Arinay said, "I must ask that you back away from them."

Tirehn ignored their pleas and gestured toward the attackers. "Please," he said, "tell me your names."

The female and wingless Takahrn both approached, and the soldiers raised their bows. Raggorin raised a hand to keep them from firing.

"My name is Gahlaia," the attacker replied, "daughter of Gahlorm, Dragon King of the Drake, and Meriss, Queen of the New World."

"My name is Borhiim," the wingless one said, "Son of Boria, the Elvish Dragon, and Zaruf, elf from the World's Edge."

Tirehn had heard those titles before. They were names known from the old stories of the second age, Gahlorm especially. If this was the Dragon King's descendant, she would have been considered royalty among the Takahrn. Now it made sense why they followed her.

"Borhiim," Tirehn said, pointing to Gwendall, "do you know this woman?"

He nodded. "She took me in all those years ago. Helped me get by in the Dirtlands before my memories came back."

Tirehn smiled. *So, it was an Anamoris spell.* "Anamoris magic?" he posed.

"You know about the old magic?" Gahlaia asked.

"Of course."

Tirehn then turned toward the people behind him. They looked very disoriented. "All of you have to listen to me!" he began. "We are being used. My father was murdered by an unseen enemy. The same enemy who used Naggyn to try to assassinate me. He has been using my ancestors to rule Deerium from behind the scenes for centuries."

"Who?" Rorgan asked, stepping forward. "Who is this enemy?"

"His name is Tarubas. He has used Anamoris magic to control the minds of my forefathers and could very well be the reason Borhiim lost his memories."

Borhiim shook his head. "Tarubas wasn't the reason. I was placed under an Anamoris spell by a cult of elves called the Righteous Ones. But . . ."

The Takahrn murmured among themselves. Eventually, Gahlaia

raised her voice. "We know the name Tarubas."

Tirehn exhaled in relief. *Finally, a lead.* "Who was he?"

"He was my father's older brother," she answered. "In the Drake, he was called the Faded Dragon. He and my father waged war against each other long before the dragons came to Deerium, but when they joined forces against the elves it was believed that Tarubas was killed in battle, felled by the Righteous Ones. If he's somehow still alive . . ."

"Gahlaia," Borhiim said, "the prison. Remember? The Waters of the Righteous?"

"What is he talking about?" one of the Takahrn asked from behind.

Gahlaia addressed the king. "In the mountains past the Dirtlands, we found a prison in the Waters of the Righteous. Whoever was held there used Anamoris to escape. We also found the corpses of the Righteous Ones within. It could be Tarubas if he still lives."

"My lord," Arinay said. Tirehn turned back toward her as she spoke. "Can you honestly believe the words of these Dividers? They attacked and killed Doryan, along with his men."

"And how many more will die if we leave things as they are?" Tirehn responded.

"How can you believe that?" Gwendall exclaimed. "All they have proved is that they are murderers. They struck down my brother in cold blood!" She looked directly at Borhiim, anger in her eyes, and he lowered his gaze.

"We may have killed his soldiers," Gahlaia defended, "but we gave Doryan the chance to stand down. Multiple times! He would have killed us all!"

"Which you would have fully deserved!"

Tirehn threw his arms upward and shouted above the commotion. "*Silence!*"

All grew quiet.

The king walked toward the Takahrn, glancing back at the others on the balcony. "The kings before us were wrong. This is not our world alone. It belongs to the Takahrn just as much as it does to us. If we are to fight against Tarubas, then we need to stand together."

"And what proof do you have that this Tarubas exists?" Zinnyah asked. "You're asking us to believe that a dragon still lives in Deerium and has been controlling everything from behind the scenes. I can't be the only one who calls that far-fetched."

Tirehn motioned to Raggorin, and the advisor pulled a long scroll from the back of his belt, handing it to the king. He unrolled it and raised his voice. "This was written by King Graan, the first mortal king of Deerium."

For the next several minutes, the king read portions from the scroll. He recounted how Graan assassinated the old Takahrn and finished by reading his last words.

"Tarubas has come," Tirehn concluded, lowering the scroll. "We have all been blind. None of this is worth starting a war over. So as your king, I declare that the Takahrn be released from their en-slavement."

The three rulers stared at each other in uncertainty. They had no words. Not a single one of them.

Eventually, Arinay shook her head. "No," she said. "I will not stand for this. These Dividers tried to kill you, and now you'll side with them over your own people? All because of a single scroll that none of us were told about prior?"

"I'm not siding against you," Tirehn said. "We all need to stand together. Besides, I wasn't sure who I could trust. Tarubas was getting his information from somewhere. I'm just not sure where."

"You couldn't trust us?" Rorgan exclaimed. "We are your com-rades. We've helped you and your father keep peace between the sectors."

"You call this peace?" Borhiim questioned. "The Takahrn sit under your feet, hunted and enslaved like animals!"

His gaze turned to Gwendall, and he outstretched his hand toward her. "Gwendall . . . Please."

She took a step back, rejecting his offer.

Arinay continued to shake her head. "As far as I'm concerned, Verish will not stand with you, Tirehn. Not with this."

"Nor will Norvad," Rorgan added.

Tirehn looked to the third ruler, but she remained silent. "Zinnyah? Will you stand with me?"

The ruler growled to herself in frustration. "I'm sorry, my king," she replied, "but Cleptyn will not stand with you."

She paused and gestured toward the other two rulers. "But neither will we stand with you. We will not be a part of another war. I refuse to take either side."

With that, Zinnyah pushed her way past the soldiers and departed before anyone could object. The other rulers hesitated before leaving their king where he stood. Raggorin began to move forward to stop them, but Tirehn placed a hand on his shoulder.

Gwendall looked briefly at Borhiim, a tear trickling down her face. He kept his hand outstretched, but she ignored it. Turning away, she joined Rorgan to the exit.

Tirehn raised his hand, and all soldiers lowered their bows, returning to their posts. Before long, the Takahrn, the king and queen, and Raggorin were left alone on the balcony. Their gazes were directed below where the crowds had once again gathered. But there were no cheers. They had heard the declarations of their new ruler, and Tirehn could see each and every one of them processing his words in various ways. He too was unsure how to feel. He wasn't certain how this moment would play out, but Tirehn hadn't expected this.

The gates of the palace opened, and groups of horses departed the city, diverting back toward their respective sectors. Tirehn and Ahmeras looked out as the gates shut, their burdens already heavy. Gahlaia and Borhiim stood among their kin, unsure of what to do.

"Raggorin," Tirehn said, "spread the word. The Deeria sector must release all Takahrn from enslavement immediately."

Raggorin bowed at the command and rushed out through the glass doors.

Borhiim turned to his comrade. "We did all of this so we could avoid war," he muttered. "But now . . . it's upon us all the same. Craden was right. I wasn't prepared for this."

"We were never sure of what would happen," Gahlaia responded. "There's nothing more we could have done."

"There still may be a way to negotiate with the other sectors," Tirehn said over his shoulder. "But as you say, for the time being, there's nothing more to be done."

He lowered his head, staring into his terrified city. He repeated the words Ahmeras had once said to him over and over in his head.

Sometimes making the right choice means walking the hardest path . . .

THE SUN BEGAN to set over the horizon.

Rorgan stared south, smiling to himself. Everything was going better than he had hoped. His eyes flashed a deep purple before the color vanished quickly. Sharp teeth began to form behind his smile.

Almost a mile away, Gwendall and the others were preparing for camp before they continued their journey back to Norvad. Rorgan stood alone.

As the sun finally fell into a slumber and the night chill settled in, a hooded figure strode up from behind. The man was cloaked in black with a long scythe strapped to his back.

He bowed to the Norvad ruler. "My Lord Tarubas," he whispered, "you summoned me?"

"Yes, Draag," Rorgan responded. "Naggyn has failed me. I pray you will not do the same."

"My will is yours to command, my liege."

"I want you to watch the king very carefully. Stay out of sight and report all his dealings back to me, down to the last detail."

The man lifted his head, revealing a small Terrkoris mark under his chin. It translated as "shadow." He smirked, giving a nod to his master. "As you command," Draag responded. "But . . . may I ask . . . ?"

Rorgan sighed. "Speak your mind if you must."

"Why leave him alive? Why not kill them all now?"

"Their deaths will grant me nothing. War is coming whether they realize it or not. Verish just needs to be pushed, and we will follow suit. Besides . . ." Rorgan looked back in the direction of the camp, his keen eyes fixed upon Gwendall. ". . . I have the girl. Within her lies the power to destroy any obstacle, and when she gives in to me, everything else will be of little consequence. I will finally have all that I need."

Curiosity satiated, Draag bowed once more, vanishing into the darkness of the night.

Part Two

For War

Chapter 14

Day seven of the fifth month. Almost two months since the coronation.

BORHIIM AND GAHLAIA strode toward the wooden house east of the village. Gahlaia sighed and mumbled her thanks to the Eternal under her breath. This was the last slave trade in Deeria that had yet to release their captives, and she was growing tired of their journey across the sector.

Since the order had come down to release the Takahrn, many had refused to do so. The king had expected as much and appointed Gahlaia and Borhiim as the overseers of the process. With a group of twenty soldiers handpicked from the palace, they journeyed across Deeria to ensure the slaves were released in a timely fashion. Ultimately, the people conceded to the idea, and the Takahrn were set free one village at a time. However, on the journey back to Valia, a messenger falcon had arrived with word of a slave trader who refused to release his captives. Throughout the process, the man had feigned ignorance, and despite sending word that he had freed the Takahrn, he kept them under chain all the same. Thankfully, his village was on their way back.

Gahlaia raised her fist, and the men behind her halted their horses. She dismounted, along with several others, and stood before the entryway.

Borhiim glanced at the rusty old house and looked back at Gahlaia. "It reminds you, doesn't it," he said, "of the owner's house in the Dirtlands?"

She shrugged, keeping her gaze forward. "Let's just get this over with," she mumbled, taking a few steps toward the wooden door.

But before she could knock, it swung open, almost smacking her in the face. The bolts creaked loudly under pressure, and a sword stabbed out of the opening toward her chest. She turned sideways and jumped back.

Out of the opening, an old man rushed for Gahlaia, swinging the blade back and forth wildly. His faded white beard brushed to his side as he charged forward. "Die, you animal!" he screamed in her face.

The soldiers behind Borhiim drew their weapons, but he motioned for them to hold.

Gahlaia kicked back on her right heel and swung her right hand across the sword as it came toward her left cheek. Her talons met the steel and sliced right through, leaving nothing but a blunted end. The old man staggered back in horror, and Borhiim grabbed him from behind, his sharp index finger pointed toward his prey's neck. The man froze as he heard a whisper in his ear.

"Do that again, and I cut your throat," Borhiim said.

The man gulped as he slowly raised his hands in surrender.

"Take us to where you're keeping the Takahrn," Gahlaia demanded. "Then you can come with us back to Valia. I'm sure the king would like to have some words with you."

The man spat at her feet. "How dare you speak to me, Divider!" he yelled. "That is all any of you are! This doesn't change—"

His words were quickly cut short when Borhiim pressed his finger to the man's skin. Relenting, he nodded in defeat. Borhiim lowered his hand, and the man walked silently toward the back of his home, head drooped down low. The soldiers followed closely behind, swords still drawn.

They were led to a large rectangular cage that stood nine feet tall and at least twenty by ten feet in length and width. Within the barred cage were seven wingless Takahrn, two males and five females. They wore the same grey cloth over their sickly skinny bodies, hunched in a circle. They seemed oblivious to the onlookers.

Gahlaia looked closer, and her stomach began to feel sick. Within the caged area, the grass had grown long, but several patches were missing as if they had been pulled from their roots. In the center of the circle of Takahrn lay a pile of greenery. They shoved it into their mouths hungrily, desperate to satisfy the gnawing in their stomachs.

Borhiim shifted his feet uncomfortably at the sight, and a few of the soldiers looked away. For a Takahrn to go hungry to such a point of desperation . . . *They must have been starving them for months*, Gahlaia thought.

Three muscular men stood in front of the cage door, looking at the group of soldiers with confusion. Borhiim stepped toward them, his left hand firmly grasping the old man's arm, putting his right on Gahlaia's shoulder. She kept her gaze on the slaves. One of them noticed the group outside and looked her dead in the eyes. He bore no expression, the edges of his mouth stained dark green. A knot swelled in her throat, and she looked away.

"It's alright," Borhiim whispered to her, hand still on her shoulder. "I'll take care of it."

She put her hand on his and nodded, taking a step back.

He released his firm grip on the old man and approached the three guards in front of the cage, pointing a clawed finger toward the door behind them. "All slave trading has been outlawed," he said, two fangs briefly showing underneath his upper lip. "Open the door."

They looked back at him with gruff expressions and stuck out their chests, holding to their silence.

Borhiim waited another moment before bolting at all three of them. They raised their hands to throw fists only to be thrust backward, their heads slamming into the metal cage behind them. The Takahrn's strength was unnatural by human standards.

They shook their dazed skulls to regain focus, but Borhiim held two of the men by the chest, glaring over the one in the center. "I won't ask again," he said.

One of them slowly reached for a knife at his hip, but the soldiers moved forward in support, pointing their blades toward his hand. Borhiim released his grip, and the men slumped to their knees. One pulled a key from his pocket and held it up. Borhiim took it and placed it into the rusted metal door. The captives stood to their feet and rushed to the closed entrance. He continued to fiddle around with the key until it finally started to turn. With a click and a squeal, the door swung open, and the Takahrn ran out.

Gahlaia looked at them and managed a smile. She gazed at each of them in silence, unsure of what to do next. One Takahrn in particular caught her eye. She was tall, wingless like the rest, and had brown hair that barely passed her ears. Unlike her brethren, she had horns, and her tail was shorter. On her left shin, she bore an elvish Terrkoris mark that translated "tree." Her hands were chained to her sides unlike those of the other slaves, who were allowed to move freely. *Likely to keep her from using her magic.*

She stepped forward to the Takahrn and put her talons to the chains, cutting them away. Without a second thought, the slave immediately darted toward the old man, knocking him to the ground. She put her hands to his throat, throttling him and shaking his body up and down violently.

Gahlaia rushed to her side and grabbed her arms. "Stop!"

"Yeah?" the Takahrn snarled. "And why should I? Do you have any idea what he's done to us? He needs to pay!"

"Yes, he does," Gahlaia replied, "but not like this."

The Takahrn hesitated for a moment and then released the old man, who lay gasping and coughing for air. She rose to her feet and stared at the ground.

"Tell me your name, sister," Gahlaia said.

"Rista, daughter of who knows and who cares," she replied bluntly.

"You don't know your lineage?" Borhiim asked.

Rista shrugged and motioned to the other six. "None of us do. We were all part of arranged mating between the elves and dragons, and they never much cared to elaborate who they were before leaving us to take care of ourselves."

Gahlaia wasn't surprised. She and Borhiim were rare cases when it came to the union between the two races. Most mated for the sake of prolonging their family line only to be disappointed with the result. It was a sick and cruel time for most, but such was the reality for many Takahrn.

"A new king has been crowned," Gahlaia continued, "and he hopes to change things for Deerium. This whole sector has been ordered to free all Takahrn. You may join us back to Valia if you wish, but so long as you don't attack the villages, you're free to leave. We can provide you with food before you depart, but all I ask is that you not kill anyone along the way."

Rista nodded, and the others muttered their agreements. "We have nowhere else to go," she said. "If you allow us, we'll go with you, assuming this king is who you say he is."

With that, the soldiers bound the hands of the old man and the three guards, and they all returned to the west side of the village. Among the horses, other Takahrn stood waiting for them, remnants of other freed slave groups who chose to join them. When they had all eaten, they took their leave back to Valia.

Gahlaia looked back toward the village and recalled a time not long past. Replace the grassy plains with dust and rocky terrain, and it didn't look too different from the town she had left behind in the Dirtlands.

"It's odd to think about, right?" Borhiim said next to her, clearly thinking the same thing she was. "So much has changed, and for once it looks like it's changing for the better."

She turned her gaze toward him and gave a brief smile. "I suppose it is," she replied. "With a little time, maybe it will get even better still."

In the Verish capital, Arinay's dreams swirled like a whirlwind. Old memories that she had tried so hard to forget now pushed themselves to the surface without resistance. All she could do was observe as she relived them.

In the vision she was in her chambers in Pordika, watching as the young ruler of Norvad rode into her capital city, several other soldiers riding by his side, along with a man she did not recognize. He wore old clothing she assumed was from the Dirtlands. He had dark blonde hair that was braided and hung down his back. Arinay moved from her window and went down to the doorway to meet them.

Rorgan bowed to her as he dismounted, and the others did the same. "Ruler Arinay," he said, "there is someone I would like you to meet. I happened upon him and his sister when I traveled down to the Dirtlands a few years back."

"Did you now?" she replied. "And what is your name, sir?"

The man stepped forward, keeping his back as straight as a board. He was even taller than she had thought. "Doryan, my lady," he responded in a deep voice. He gave a slight bow toward her, appearing uncomfortable with the gesture.

She chuckled at his awkwardness. "Well, Doryan, why has Rorgan brought you here?"

"I wish to enlist as a soldier and join the guard on the Southern Border."

Arinay was taken aback by the comment. She hadn't met many who willingly enlisted in the Verish army, let alone as a guard of the border. It was their job to keep out any potential raids or invaders, and with the Grey Wings attacking villages across Deerium, their job had just gotten a lot harder.

"Why the Southern Border?" she asked.

"Work is scarce in the Dirtlands," he replied. "I have my sister who needs to be provided for, and I hear the Southern Border patrol pays well."

"Well, you certainly have your priorities straight. And what makes you so sure you're up to the task, Doryan? Have you ever used a sword?"

"Yes, my lady, but personally I prefer an ax."

"Have you ever had to kill another person?"

"Yes, my lady."

She thought for a moment before Rorgan chimed in once again. "I can vouch for his capabilities, Arinay. He bested each one of my men in single combat."

"Did he?" she said with raised eyebrows. She took a step forward and looked up at the man's tall figure. "Very well. You'll be trained by one of my generals, and if they see that you have potential, then I'll see what I can do."

Doryan gave another bow. "Thank you, my lady. I will prove myself. I swear it."

The dream moved and swirled once again, pressing forward

several years.

Doryan grew into quite the soldier, and he quickly flew up the ranks. When her old grand general fell in battle during a raid by the Grey Wings, Doryan eagerly took his place. His command over his subordinates was astonishing, and his capabilities were truly incredible. But more than that, Arinay had built a strong friendship with both him and his sister, Gwendall. Soon, he became someone very dear to her.

The dream moved forward again.

Doryan approached her about asking the king for permission to let Gwendall live in Valia, the capital of Deeria. With the help of Rorgan, she and Doryan convinced him to allow it. Back in Pordika, Doryan and Arinay prepared to go their separate ways. She needed to travel to Valia for the prince's coronation, and Doryan was leaving for the Dirtlands to pick up his sister along with a friend she had been taking care of for the past few years.

"What's his name again?" Arinay asked, folding clothes into a grey sack.

"Borhiim," Doryan replied. "Gwendall has been keeping him under her roof while he helps her at home and around town."

Arinay smiled. "And you're sure there's nothing going on there? I mean, almost three years of living in the same house . . . There's bound to be some kind of relationship brewing."

Doryan shrugged, pulling his clothes out of his bag frantically before going through some drawers. "I wouldn't know," he said. "I haven't seen her in months. He's respectable enough and clueless as ever." He grinned, closing one drawer and moving to the next. "I doubt he would catch on if she said it to his face if she did have those kinds of intentions."

Arinay looked at him curiously, watching him scramble through her room. "What in the world are you doing? Those are my drawers."

"I think I misplaced something is all," he said over his shoulder.

"And you expect to find it by looking through my drawers? You have your own room."

"Just give me a second."

"Well, what is it you lost?" No answer. "You're seriously not going to tell me?"

"It doesn't matter what it is," Doryan mumbled.

"Oh, so this doesn't matter?" she said, holding a necklace outstretched in her hand. Hanging at its bottom was a ring—a betrothal ring.

Doryan turned around and stared at the necklace in shock. He was completely frozen. "Where did you get that?"

Arinay's heart pounded hard in her chest. "It fell out of your bag earlier today."

There was a long pause between them.

Doryan took a few steps toward her. "I was going to tell you about it," he said in a deeper voice than usual. "I just wasn't sure when to bring it up."

"Why? I'm always here."

"It's just . . ." He was stumbling over his words, something very uncharacteristic of him. He was always very direct, but now he actually sounded nervous. "I'm not of royal blood. I'm not much for fanciful things, or ballroom dancing, or anything of the sort. I've never been much of a gentleman. I'm a soldier, and I'm not—"

Arinay put a hand up and shook her head. "There is no royal blood. I'm a ruler. I got here by my own merits, as you have. Besides, I know exactly who you are, Doryan. You're my grand general, and royal blood has nothing to do with being a gentleman. You're as much a gentleman as any other man in the fancy ballrooms. The only difference is you know how to swing a sword . . . or an ax."

Another long pause as she took a step closer, looking up at his face, waiting. "Well . . . ? Are you going to ask me?"

He smiled. "Not yet. I need to do it properly."

"And when would that be?"

"When I get back. I'll meet you at Valia for the coronation. Seems like a better time than any."

"You should probably have this back then," she said, pressing the necklace toward his chest.

He looked down at it and pushed her hand back, wrapping her fingers around the thin chain. "Keep it. Then maybe you won't forget to remind me when I get back."

Arinay threw herself into his arms, and he held her, placing his chin on the top of her head. "Please come back to me," she whispered.

"I will. I promise."

The dream spun in her head, those final words repeating themselves over and over.

Slowly, a figure grew visible in the distance. A dead body in the dirt. A gash laid open the corpse's stomach, a broken and blood-stained ax blade lying to its left. The dead face of Doryan stared blankly into the distance.

Please . . . come back to me.

ARINAY ROSE FROM her bed in a cold sweat, a fading yet vivid nightmare twisting its way through her head.

A knock rang out at her door. She shook herself and regained hold of reality. The dream had been devastating, but part of her wished she could go back to it.

Another knock.

"Yes?" she replied.

The door cracked open, and a soldier's head peeked through. "All preparations have been completed, my lady. The Grey Wings have been brought from the Southern Border."

She cleared her throat. "Very well. I'll be down shortly."

"Also, a messenger falcon from Deeria addressed to you arrived this morning."

She sighed and nodded. "Alright. Just set it on the dresser."

The soldier quickly entered the room, placed the parchment in the correct place, bowed, and closed the door behind him.

Alone with her thoughts once again, she got out of bed and dressed herself.

She took the paper on her dresser, read the message, then quickly crumpled it up and tossed it across the room. It was another of King Tirehn's requests for negotiation. If anything, he was stubborn, but time and time again she had refused to speak with him. She would not set the Dividers free. They were too dangerous. Too unpredictable. She had seen firsthand what they were capable of.

Visions from her nightmare flashed back into her head. She tried to brush them away, but they continued to prod at her mind. She looked down and pulled open one of her drawers. It was empty save for a single necklace bearing a ring. It was spread out neatly, the ring glistening with a blue sapphire.

Arinay gently pulled the necklace out and stared at it with longing. Her lower lip began to quiver, and she clutched it to her chest, falling to her knees. She couldn't hold back the tears any longer. For so long she had kept herself from mourning as if her mind refused to believe he was gone. After all, he had promised. During her days in Valia, part of her still waited for him to come through those golden gates. Even when they buried his body, she had still refused to accept it.

But those days had passed, and he was really gone. There was no holding it back anymore. She put a hand to her face and bent toward the floor, her left hand still clutching the necklace. *I've lost him,* she thought. *No . . . he was taken.*

When she had wept her eyes dry, Arinay steadied herself and strode downstairs. As she passed her soldiers, she let the necklace show around her neck. But the ring she kept hidden in her garments. It was for her and her alone.

She continued down the stairs until she reached a basement underneath her small palace. Clusters of soldiers stood around a group of Dividers. They were on their knees, chains holding their hands behind their backs. The soldiers all held spears pointed toward their prisoners, swords resting at their hips. Torchlight shone into every corner of the large stone room, giving it an orange tint.

Arinay approached one of the many Dividers, and he raised his head toward her. There was no fear in his expression, and she hated him for it.

She leaned in, gazing fiercely into his bright green eyes. "Why did you surrender?" she asked. There was no response. "You came to the Southern Border, begging for us to take you in. You're going to tell me why." Still no answer.

She raised her head and slapped him, nearly leaving her palm numb as his nose broke under the impact. "Answer me!"

The Divider winced at the pain, blood trickling to his upper lip. "We have nothing to say to the likes of you," he responded. "We fought for our cause and failed. There is nothing else to say."

"If you were so dedicated to your cause, then why cower in fear? Do you feel guilty? Shame? Regret for the innocent lives you've taken?"

He grimaced back at her. Blood rolled down from his broken nose and dripped from his chin. "What do you expect us to say?" He scowled. "Do you want an apology? You will get nothing from me. Nothing! We don't regret a single drop of blood spilled from you humans. Not a single drop. Why? Because you deserved it. You all deserve it, and one day we will do exactly what you have done to us for hundreds of years. We will put you under our feet and laugh because you belong there. We will—"

Arinay unsheathed a dagger from her hip and thrust it into his neck, an expression of shock filling the Divider's face as he struggled and failed to find air. She leaned in again. "Always the long speeches with you Dividers," she said. "If you want to die so badly with your pride intact, then allow me to oblige."

She pulled the blade from his throat, and he collapsed on the floor, nothing more than a lifeless body. Pulling a handkerchief from her pocket, she wiped her knife clean and let the cloth fall onto the limp figure. She motioned to the other soldiers as she strolled back up the stairs, and they quickly drove their spears into their targets, finishing the execution in silence.

When Arinay came back up to the main floor, another soldier approached her with a piece of parchment. He bowed and handed her the letter. It was a message from Rorgan. He was preparing to attack Deeria and take the king's throne by force.

She rolled the paper back up and turned to the man before her. "Send a reply to Rorgan of Norvad," she said. "Tell him we will join him in his attack."

He bowed once more, but as he prepared to depart, Arinay grabbed his arm. "Spread the word to our troops. I want every soldier Verish can muster transported to the West Gate. When I give the word, we march for Valia."

Chapter 15

U PON REACHING THE upper level of the palace, Gahlaia and the other Takahrn moved down the corridor at a quickened pace, following Raggorin's lead. As they approached the throne room, the men standing guard opened the doors for them.

The room was almost completely unchanged from when they had left a month or so ago. The square wooden table that was once used for the three rulers and the king remained in its usual place. Further down, near the throne, three figures stood together in deep discussion: King Tirehn, Queen Ahmeras, and Anahka. In Borhiim and Gahlaia's absence, Anahka had been the one to explain all she knew about the Takahrn. She was their voice.

As the small group entered the room, the three broke from their conversation and walked over to meet them. Anahka especially looked relieved to see them. Tirehn smiled at them, and Gahlaia noticed that he had finally decided to wear his father's crown after the incident during the coronation had provoked him otherwise. Its gold exterior glinted as the sun shone through the windows.

When the king came closer, Borhiim and Gahlaia took a knee. The Takahrn behind took notice and followed suit in a rather awkward fashion.

"Please," Tirehn said, "there's no need for that. How was the journey?"

Gahlaia and Borhiim rose, and she shrugged slightly. "A bit

rough, but it could've been much worse."

"We brought a few of the slave traders back with us," said Borhiim. "The guards escorted them to their cells in the lower levels. You can pass judgment on them however you see fit as far as we're concerned."

Tirehn gestured toward the other Takahrn, still on one knee. "Are they from the villages?"

"Yes," Raggorin interjected, taking his place at his lord's side. "What do you wish them to do?"

"That's not for me to decide," the king replied. "They're free to go as they please."

Gahlaia put her hand up. "They came to us with nowhere to go. But more than that, I think there is one you should meet." She turned and looked at the Takahrn, rolling her eyes. "You don't need to keep kneeling."

All fifteen rose together. From the back of the group, a hornless female Takahrn came forward, the Terrkoris mark on her left shin clearly visible. She gave what could have been considered a bow and introduced herself. "My name is Rista," she said. "I have no lineage or fancy titles to give, only my name."

"My name is Tirehn," the king said. "My lineage isn't much to speak of either. At least, not in a positive light."

Rista chuckled, but her expression remained serious. "Quite the understatement," she said with a raised eyebrow. "Was it not your ancestor, the great King Graan, who falsely accused our people of treason?"

"You certainly know your history," the king responded in a calming tone, "but I wouldn't call him great."

"Then tell me, King Tirehn. How is it that after hundreds of years and generations upon generations of kings, only now does one of you wish to make amends for the sins of your fathers?"

Tirehn paused a moment, and Gahlaia could tell he was thinking carefully of what to say next. Raggorin opened his mouth to reply, but the king shook his head. "Cowardice, I suppose," was his response. "Cowardice and fear of loss."

"Loss?"

"Loss of power, loss of authority . . . I know I can't amend what has already been done. I know that. I know my words mean nothing to you. So may my actions in the future give you reason to trust me, even a little."

Rista looked him up and down, gave another glance at his elvish queen, and let out a sigh. "For what it's worth, you have my gratitude. You freed both me and my brethren from that old fool in the east as well as the entire sector, from what I've heard. If you do intend to continue this way, then only time will tell if we can trust you."

She gave a faint smile that appeared to release a burden from Tirehn's shoulders, and he nodded toward her.

Borhiim stepped forward. "What of the other sectors?" he asked. "Have they given any responses?"

It was Tirehn's turn to sigh—a sigh of uncertainty. "Zinnyah of Cleptyn sent word back. She remains neutral. She won't free her slaves, but neither will she move to attack us. Verish and Norvad have kept silent, but Norvad worries me the most. Any messenger falcons we send north never return."

"What's worse," Ahmeras said, "Norvad soldiers have been gathering near their border. There's a good chance they'll attack Deeria before the month is over."

Gahlaia looked confused. "Did we send spies northward?"

Ahmeras grinned. "You could say that. I saw them with my own eyes."

All eyes shot directly to the king, who put his arms up in defense.

"Don't blame me," he said. "I didn't send her. Soon after you left, she vanished without a trace. It doesn't help that she can shapeshift."

Even Raggorin looked surprised, but they quickly moved on.

"What of Verish?" Borhiim asked.

Tirehn shook his head. "I'm not sure. They haven't replied to any of our messages, but at least the falcons come back to us. All the same, I've sent fragments of my army south in case they attack from the West Gate. They'll send word if anything changes."

Gahlaia bit her lower lip. She knew things were looking grim. Deeria's army was the largest of the four by a fair margin. It was the king's army after all. However, if both Norvad and Verish were to attack as a united force, there wasn't much they would be able to do. They would be grossly outnumbered.

"There has to be a way we can bring Cleptyn to our side," she said. "Their forces rival even Deeria's, especially if the Gorrobin tribes join them. Without them, it's only a matter of time before Norvad and Verish take Valia and usurp your authority. The Takahrn we've taken all this time to set free will return to chains, and all of this will have been for nothing."

"That is if Verish does in fact intend on joining with Norvad," Raggorin pointed out. "Our army is split to the north and south. Verish has shown no signs of hostility, at least not yet. If it comes down to it, I can go to Cleptyn myself to bring my people to our cause. If the Gorrobin will listen to anyone, it's one of their own."

Tirehn nodded in agreement and turned back to face Gahlaia and Borhiim. "As Raggorin said, whether Verish will actually attack or not is still up in the air. However, I think we can all agree that Norvad will attack eventually. If this is the case, I cannot leave my forces alone. I will go north. If you two would accompany me, we may yet live through this."

Raggorin put a hand on Tirehn's chest and faced him with concern. "My lord!" he exclaimed. "You must reconsider this. A king has not graced the field of battle for generations. If you fall—"

"I am well aware of the dangers, Raggorin, but we'll all be dead anyway if we don't act now. My army needs to move north, and they'll need me to lead them." He turned to Anahka. "I need you to head south and join with our forces near Verish. If Arinay moves to strike, we need to know."

She nodded.

His gaze fixed on his queen. "You need to remain here. Someone needs to take care of things in my absence. Soon after we leave, send Raggorin east."

"Don't worry about me," Ahmeras said. "Just promise you'll come back."

The king nodded and looked back to the two Takahrn. "Will you join me?" he asked.

"Of course," Borhiim said, giving the elvish salute. Gahlaia followed his example.

"If I may," Rista said, taking a step forward, "I'll come too."

"Have you been in battle before?" Tirehn asked.

She looked almost insulted by the question. "I have a Terrkoris mark. If you plan to split your army in half, you'll need as much strength as you can muster."

"Bold words," Gahlaia said, "but she has a point. Other Takahrn are still taking refuge here in Valia. If we can bring them to our cause before we depart, we'll be all the better for it."

"Alright," the king replied. "We leave in two days. You have until then to gather those who are willing to fight."

THE PALACE WAS a large place to be certain—even larger than

Gahlaia had imagined. Many of the rooms and chambers lay empty, only used for special occasions. When the Takahrn were given the choice to stay in Valia, many of them were allowed to stay within the palace. Anahka had been given first choice since she had stayed behind to voice the Takahrn's concerns. Gahlaia and Borhiim had been gone and only now were assigned rooms.

Ultimately, they chose chambers side by side. The last thing either of them wanted was to be living next to humans. Gahlaia had nothing against any of the people in the palace, but strange or fearful looks were not uncommon. With everyone still getting used to the two races living as one, it made sense.

She spent the remainder of the day with Borhiim, going around the city to speak with any Takahrn who would join them in traveling north to meet with the army near the Norvad border. In the end, it had been a productive effort. Most, if not all, refugees were more than willing to fight to protect their freedom. What's more, their brethren in the other sectors were still in chains. Whatever the reasoning, the incentive was there, and even one hundred Takahrn would increase their chances of survival.

Positive outcome or not, Gahlaia was exhausted. She had spent almost the entire month traveling, and soon they were going to have to start moving again. For tonight at least, she was going to try and relax a bit. She closed her door, entered the empty corridor, and let out a long sigh. She finally felt clean.

Moving southward, she headed for the main balcony. The sun had set hours ago, and a downpour had begun outside. Gahlaia was fascinated by the rain. It hardly ever reached the Dirtlands, and she had grown tired of the dry air that permeated those desert-infested plains. The relatively cold and humid contrast was something she wasn't used to, and she enjoyed it for the change alone.

Arriving at the glass doors, she opened them quietly and stepped out. The roof above stretched out far enough for her to stay dry, but still open enough to watch the rainfall. Resting her arms on the railing, she dipped her head out to let the drops fall lightly on her face. The breeze brushed soothingly on her face, calming her nerves.

"You like the rain too?"

Gahlaia jumped back, startled by the voice. She turned to her right and saw Borhiim standing near the edge of the balcony, his arms hanging over the rail. His dark brown hair looked combed, trimmed, and clean. He wore a green sleeveless shirt and grey pants. The scruff that had started growing under his chin had been shaved, but still he wore no shoes, letting his claw-like toes move around freely.

He gave a half smile, amused at her startled reaction.

"How long have you been there?" she asked, composing herself.

"Longer than you have," he replied, turning his attention back to the growing storm. "I can leave if you want some time alone."

"No, it's fine. I think I'm just tired is all. I didn't even notice you were there."

For the next hour, those were the only words spoken. There weren't many words that needed to pass between them, nor did they desire them. They just wanted to enjoy the storm. It was strangely mesmerizing and almost soothing. Lightning began to flash across the sky, adding to the chaos before them. Borhiim smiled as it flared the sky, but Gahlaia hardly even noticed it. Her mind flooded with thoughts she never believed she would have.

Since she broke out of her cage in Verish, all that had been on her mind was vengeance and freedom. Now that things started to look more positive for her and her people, the anger had started to fade. Things she had put off began to resurface.

Gahlaia put a hand to her left rib. She lifted her shirt slightly and looked at the skin. It was covered with a small patch of scales—grey dragon scales. It was her father's color. At the start of the year, she had noticed them starting to grow, and she feared her whole body might be covered by them. But soon after they started to replace her skin, the spreading stopped, leaving nothing but a round area on her left side. Perhaps her elvish blood kept them at bay. Gahlaia had asked some of the other Takahrn if they had the same thing, and most did.

In the dragon culture, scales were held in incredibly high value. Dragons never shed—the same scales they were born with stayed until their death. As they grew, their bodies merely grew more scales in places where soft skin had stretched out during adolescence. For only one reason would dragons ever shed their scales: mating.

When two dragons mated, they would remove one scale from their massive bodies and trade them. Whether through some form of Terrkoris magic or perhaps something more, the new scale would attach itself to the new bearer. It was meant to signify the unity—a unity to last an eternity. Even when elves and dragons would mate, the dragon would still give the elf one of their scales. The elf in turn would wear it like a necklace, showing their dedication to the pairing.

For Takahrn, however, mating was completely new territory. To her knowledge, none of her kind had ever mated, and if they did it, no offspring had been seen. All of them had been born around the same period of the second age, hence why their numbers were so small compared to any other race. Considering how they had been born of two very different species, it was unclear how Takahrn might mate if they ever did. The elvish tradition was to hold an ancient ceremony that had long been lost to human recollection, while the dragons' way was much simpler.

Gahlaia scrunched her eyebrows in thought and rubbed her thumb over her scales. *Could Takahrn even have children?* Since there had never been any mating among her people, there was no way of knowing at the moment.

She shook her head, and Borhiim took notice. "You sure have a lot on your mind," he said. Once again, having forgotten he was even there, she quickly pulled her hand from under her white shirt. He looked down at where her hand once was and then back up to her. "Are your scales the color of your father's?" he asked.

She nodded. "Are yours?"

Borhiim shook his head and lifted his shirt. Just above his abdomen was a patch of dark red scales. "My mother's were silver, if you remember," he said, letting his shirt drop back in place. "I never noticed them until recently, since the Anamoris spell broke."

Gahlaia put her head down. The rain struck the edges of the balcony with a fury. More thoughts reemerged from her mind. "How . . . how much of your past do you remember?" she asked.

Borhiim leaned forward again and put his arms on the railing, rain pelting across his face. "All of it, I think," he replied, barely speaking over the rising storm. "Though most of it is nothing but wandering in the middle of nowhere. It wasn't until I hit the Dirtlands that I found any form of a life outside of struggling for survival."

"But what about before that? Before the Anamoris spell?"

Borhiim raised his eyebrows. "Yeah . . . I remember it. Though part of me wishes I didn't. Things were so much simpler back then. Tensions were high with the elves, but for us, it was the closest thing to peace we had."

"It really was." Gahlaia sighed and smiled, looking out toward the lightning.

"As I recall, we were pretty close friends," he continued.

"As close as kids could be at that age. Our parents—"

"They were among the few that mated for anything other than

obligation," he interrupted. "They were fairly close as well. Didn't they . . ." Borhiim's voice trailed off as if a new memory had just hit him. "Were we . . . ?"

Gahlaia shifted her weight uncomfortably. "Betrothed?" she said, keeping her gaze on the clouds. "Yes. We were."

Chapter 16

Day thirteen of the fifth month.

G WENDALL SAT IN her usual place in her armchair before her open chamber window, the late evening sun shining through. The cold wind slipped in, leaving her shivering but still comfortable. The chilling temperatures of Norvad were a luxury to her, especially after all those years in the Dirtlands.

She looked down into the Norvad capital like a queen overseeing her people. *Zerah is truly a beautiful place.* But despite all the luxuries she had been given, no smile graced her face. It remained emotionless, unwilling to show any signs of joy or despair. It was all the same to her. Friends, family, war, lies, loss . . . It all blended together in her mind like a grey cluster of weariness. But among all the swirling and confusion, two separate thoughts reached the surface.

First, there was Borhiim. The image of his figure standing on that balcony all those months ago, his hand outstretched, refused to let go of her. He had begged her in the sincerest of ways, and still she had left him there. If it had been less than a month before then, she would have gone to him without a second thought. For the longest time, it was nearly all she could think about. Now, she was haunted by endless dreams of his lone form, standing in the darkness, reaching out to her. Perhaps everything she assumed was wrong. Perhaps Borhiim really was everything she hoped he was. And perhaps . . .

No.

There was a second thought, and it steadily grew stronger than the first. Her dead brother cried out to her in her mind. She could faintly hear his words speaking to her. All day they repeated in her head, pleading for vengeance. They had started after she had been shown his bloodied ax blade back in Valia, and at first, she ignored them until they started to get louder. She had covered her ears and screamed in the night, but still, the voice was ever-present. Now, sitting in the middle of the day, watching the people go about their business, she had grown accustomed to the sound. Her reaction had started as reluctance, then uncertainty, and today it was weariness. The screams had finally dulled into whispers. She sighed in relief.

She turned when a knock came at her door. At last, a smile lifted her mood. She spun back to her original position and sat comfortably in her red armchair. "Come in, Rorgan," she said.

The door opened slowly, and the young man stepped into the room. "You knew it was me?" Rorgan asked.

"Oh, please," she responded with a chuckle, "who else comes to see me?" The whispers in her head faded into nothingness. Her mood had finally lifted, and it felt good.

"Come now, my lady," Rorgan said, striding to her side. "You make yourself feel so unimportant."

"Aren't I?"

Her gaze rose to meet the deep blue eyes staring at her from above. Looking hard enough, she thought she spotted a hint of purple skirting across the edges, and then it was gone.

"Of course, you're important," he replied, walking toward a smaller chair. "May I?"

Gwendall nodded, and he settled in the chair next to her. With a slight sigh, he moved into a comfortable position and joined her in observing the people in the city roads. Gwendall watched as two children ran at each other with long sticks, swinging them as though they held broadswords in their small hands. One pushed harder, and the other fell to his knees. The child on top raised the stick high and thrust it into his friend's left armpit, the felled enemy throwing his arms in the air dramatically and falling to the ground for added effect. She couldn't help but smile at the scene, but when she turned to Rorgan to comment, he was staring at her.

Immediately, shame appeared on his face. "I'm sorry," he said, just barely above a whisper. "I just . . . You've been here for some time, and while it's true we've known each other long . . ."

Gwendall leaned back in her chair, clearly seeing he felt awkward. "If you have a question, Rorgan, feel free to ask. It's alright, I assure you."

Courage evidently restored, he continued, "I wanted to see if you had a mark."

"Mark?" Gwendall questioned. "What do you mean, 'mark'?"

Rorgan readjusted his position, furrowing his brow. "An Anamoris mark."

Gwendall's confusion only increased. She opened her mouth, but Rorgan spoke up before she had the chance.

"I know it sounds strange, but just hear me out. Do you have any birthmarks or darker portions of skin anywhere that you thought strange?"

"I don't know what that has to do with any—"

He shook his head. "Trust me." His voice remained soft and calm, almost soothing.

Reluctantly, she nodded.

For a moment, the hint of a smile flashed on the young man's face, a quiver of nervous air exhaling from his lungs, and then swiftly replaced once again by his calm composure. He leaned in slightly.

"I'm not sure if I would call it strange," she said, "but I do have something . . ."

"May I see it?" he asked.

Another reluctant nod.

Gwendall lifted her silver shirt slightly, revealing her abdomen. Almost in the very center, the skin was a slightly darker color in specific patches. From a glance, they almost appeared to be burn marks or something similar. Rorgan looked completely intoxicated at the sight. His lips moved slightly, but she couldn't quite catch the words.

He lifted his head but kept his gaze on the skin. "I think it is," he said.

"Is what?" Gwendall asked.

"How much about our ancient history do you really understand, Gwendall?" he asked. "About our elvish ancestors, I mean."

Gwendall almost scoffed at the question. "Come on, Rorgan, you know this. I love history."

Rorgan smiled. "That you do. Then perhaps you could refresh my memory?"

"But what about—"

"I know, I know. I'm getting to that. What can you tell me about High Elf Tarkuv?"

Gwendall put a hand to her chin in thought and then gave her response. "Tarkuv was the elvish king of old. He had been there since the creation of their species. He was one of the oldest, wisest, strongest, and among the few in recorded history to have an Anamoris mark, the symbol of the soul. The Righteous Ones were the only other known elves to possess such a mark. He ruled Deerium until the ancient war when the Dragon King Gahlorm struck him down during the Battle of Fate."

"And what of his offspring?" he asked.

She shook her head. "He had none, at least not according to the history books."

Rorgan chuckled. "Yes, that's correct. But what if he did? Could such a thing be possible?"

Gwendall shrugged. "I guess, but what's the point of speculating? There's no . . ." Her sentence slowly faded out as Rorgan pointed a finger toward her. Her heart skipped a beat.

"Your hair," he said. "Have you never wondered about it? It's golden, almost as bright as the material itself. In all my time traveling across Deerium, I have never seen anything like it. As I recall, the High Elf had that same hair."

Gwendall blurted out a loud laugh. "Really, Rorgan? That's your big assumption? All because I have different colored hair and an odd birthmark, you think I'm related to the High Elf? Don't you think that's a bit of a stretch?"

"Maybe it is, but still the possibility exists. It might even explain the voices in your head."

She took a step back. "How do you know about that?"

Rorgan beamed at her in triumph. "I didn't," he said. "You just told me."

He winked before continuing. "Your parents lived in the Dirt-lands all their lives, and their parents did the same." His voice grew softer as if he were the only one in the room. "Perhaps Tarkuv kept his child hidden, smuggled it out somehow. The south would be the perfect place to hide. All the elves were being taken captive in northeastern regions, moved into the mountains of the Claw . . ."

"Rorgan, what is this all about?" Gwendall asked, growing impatient with his ramblings.

He stood and moved toward the door, then turned to face her and reached out his hand.

Gwendall stepped forward, staring at him in concern. Yet another person asking for her trust.

"If you wish to understand, then let me show you," he said.

She hesitated but took his hand all the same.

Rorgan led her down the hallway and into his own dimly lit chambers. The room itself was very large, the walls covered head to toe in oakwood. On one side was a large bed. To the left of it was an empty birdcage, likely used for housing messenger falcons. Several wooden chairs were sprawled across the floor with the largest one pushed under a wide wooden desk inlaid with grey marble and covered with several different maps.

Gwendall looked at them with wonderment. In the center was a hand-drawn map of all of Deerium with smaller places sketched in certain areas. To its left lay a map of Norvad with its villages and forests shown in greater detail. Finally, to the right, and slightly overlapping the center one, a map of a place she had never seen before, but only heard of in ancient tales of grandeur: the Drake, the ancient world of the dragons. Massive mountains, vast islands, and other locations that didn't make sense to her. Gwendall couldn't take her eyes off it. The parchment looked thicker than the rest as if it were made of a tougher material, but the edges still gave way to yellowing signs of age.

"Where did you get this?" she asked excitedly as Rorgan moved to one side of the room.

He faced his sprawling bookshelves that spread across the entire right wall, running a finger over the manuscript titles to find what he searched for. "I came across that map almost a year before I met you," he responded, keeping his main attention on the task before him. "There were several parchments like that one hidden here in the north."

Gwendall's eyebrows raised. "There's more?"

"Of course. Many original texts of history were written by the dragons before or during the war, then copied by human hands. Ah, here it is."

Rorgan pulled a grey book from the end of one of the shelves and walked toward the desk. Pushing aside the old maps, he placed the thick manuscript on the dark surface.

Gwendall stared at the cover. The whole exterior was rough and grey, aside from the two symbols that shared the front: the two primary marks of magic. The Terrkoris was black with shades of green along its boundaries, while the Anamoris was a crisp white.

Rorgan opened the book slowly, audible creaking sounds coming from its spine as he did so. He flipped for several moments, looking briefly through the text to reach his desired place. He continued until at last he halted a little past halfway through, pointing a finger at a passage.

"Here," Rorgan said. "This is where it talks about it. When some elves were born, they struggled to access their abilities for quite some time, their markings barely noticeable on their bare skin."

Gwendall looked over to inspect the words Rorgan had pointed to as he spoke.

"Their true forms hid underneath the surface, like a sort of untapped potential. Until they could access it, they were almost mortal. In fact, I would say they were. That's the difference between our ancestors and us. We can't reach our ancient magic anymore because we've lost our access to the marks the elves had. At least, most of us have."

"Most of us?" Gwendall asked. "All of us have lost it. The elves drew their power from the nature around them. The dragons kept them from doing so, keeping them captive in the mountains."

Rorgan shook his head. "Elves with Terrkoris magic were kept from doing so. Anamoris magic is much more . . . potent. Why do you think it was such a rare gift? The dragons couldn't block something so strong. Yes, any elves who possessed the Anamoris mark were killed during the war. That much is true. But their offspring weren't. You weren't."

"Rorgan, it's just a birthmark. I'm not Tarkuv's descendant. There's no way you can believe otherwise. If I was, wouldn't my brother have had those powers too, or my parents for that matter?"

"They could have, but the magic could have still been dormant. Besides, several generations of unused power . . . Who knows how it could have affected your family line."

Gwendall put up her hands and shook her head, trying to grasp all that was being said. "Hold on, why are you telling me all of this? Why now? I mean, how long have you known about this?"

Rorgan sighed. "I had my suspicions not long after we met, but I wasn't sure until recently. I could . . . feel it."

"Feel it?"

Rorgan paused, then turned. He removed his shirt, revealing his muscular back, and a faded birthmark almost identical to Gwendall's. However, while still viewable, it was even more washed-out than hers.

She stared with her mouth agape. "How long have you—"

"For as long as I can remember. It's an Anamoris mark. At least I think it is."

"Does that mean . . . Are you . . . ?"

Rorgan gave a half smile. "No. I'm not. I've tried doing all I could to awaken it, but nothing ever worked. I can sense a few things that others can't, but it is extremely slight and leaves me more confused than anything. It feels like I'm on the cusp of something, but I can't reach it, like having a word on the tip of your tongue. As I said, generations of unused and untapped potential can affect things like this."

He pulled his shirt back on and turned to face Gwendall. He smiled, but she could see the sadness in his eyes, a deep sense of longing.

She couldn't help but feel sorry for him, always knowing of great power and knowledge and then realizing that same power would always be inches from his reach. It was a side of him Rorgan had never shown her.

"But you," he said. "You're different, I think. After . . . what happened with your brother, I felt something change in you. Something clawing beneath the surface."

Gwendall remained silent, lowering her gaze to the floor.

Rorgan took a step forward. "You're not so different from the elves all those generations back. If you are Tarkuv's descendant, then the Anamoris power you could wield would be greater than anything this mortal world has ever witnessed."

She lifted her head and gazed into his eyes as he smiled down at her. It was a calming smile, one appearing to convey genuine care. She felt it sooth her confused mind, at least for a moment.

"Did my brother know about all of this?" she asked.

"A little. We spoke briefly about your family and his own feelings on the matter."

"Did he have this untapped potential too?"

"No. He didn't even have a mark as I recall. He was human. If he wasn't, then—" Rorgan immediately caught the words before they came out. "I'm sorry, that was wrong. What I meant to say was—"

"It's alright. I know what you meant. If he was more than human, he might have survived all those months ago." She swallowed hard. *If I was stronger, I could have saved him.*

"Gwendall . . ." He paused before responding. "Let me help you. With the knowledge we have, we could find a way to fully reveal your Anamoris mark. With you here, we could end this conflict with the king faster. Fewer people would have to die, and we could set everything back to the way things were."

Gwendall let out a long sigh, her gaze on one of the room's small windows. The howling wind whistled and hummed across its closed exterior, the chill air growing stronger.

"I don't think things will ever go back to the way they were," she replied.

"Perhaps not," he said. "I don't want to force you into making a decision. You can take as much time as you wish."

The voice that had earlier faded behind Rorgan's own now returned to her head. It cried out to her, screaming for vengeance. *That's right*, she thought. *This isn't about me.*

"People have died, Rorgan," she said. "How many of them could have been saved if I had been able to do something? If any of us were able to do something. I don't need time to think about this. I want you to help me. Please."

He smiled at her again and nodded. "Tomorrow then. I have some things to prepare before we can begin. In the morning, we can start."

With those final words, Gwendall left the room, closing the door behind her. She walked through the quiet hallway with confidence in her step, her head held high. For once, she felt as though she were needed. As though she were important. No longer did the voice seem to dominate her mind. Now, it complimented her thoughts. It wanted justice, and she was going to give it what it desired.

For a moment, almost too brief to notice, she felt a tinge of something run through her body. Something sensational. Something powerful.

BEHIND THE CLOSED door, Rorgan was also feeling quite confident. The smile he had given her only grew and with it his physical form.

The candles on his wall snuffed out as his façade melted away to show his true self. The teeth under his lips grew into fangs, and his already tall figure became even taller. His hair changed to a greasy silver that fell in knots down his back, eyes darkening into a deep purple, flashing with hints of red. His arms grew skeletal, ending in hands bearing pointed, talon-like nails. The faded mark he had revealed on his back vanished like mist in wind. She had bought his lies. Every last one of them.

Tarubas cocked his head as he heard a light scratch at his small window. He walked to the glass and opened it, a small messenger falcon flying through. Tarubas closed the window to hold the shivering winds at bay and took the letter. He removed the bindings on the parchment and read it to himself. It was from one of his generals near the border of Deeria. They had spotted troops coming from the south. From Valia. The general was requesting that more soldiers be sent to the border as soon as possible, or they would have little chance of succeeding in their planned invasion.

He snickered. Everything was going as planned. Tomorrow, everything would finally be underway, and then he could make his next move. Reinforcements were not necessary. Not yet. Not if Verish had anything to say about it. But he would have time to think about that later. Now, he would revel in his victories.

He strode across his room, locked his door, and then moved to the bookshelves where he reached up and pulled down a dark green book. He placed another hand on the wood where it had sat, pulling a small lever. The whole shelf clicked as a lock from inside the wall unlatched. He returned the book to its place and pulled the bookcase open like a door. Creaking slightly, it revealed a stairway leading upward.

Tarubas stepped in, pulling the bookshelf back into its original place. Following the spiraling stairs up, he came to another door. He reached out his hand and felt the spiritual energy surge out of his fingertips toward the lock. It clicked inside the handle, and he pushed open the door to a hidden balcony. He closed the entrance behind him and stood at the edge, facing north.

Through his eyes, he could see for miles upon miles. The Horned Bay, the Northern Forests, even the Frigid Pass with its ice-covered mountains. But they were dim, as if seen through a blurred window or foggy spectacles. He looked up into the cloud-covered sky. Snow was coming tonight, that much was certain. It reminded him of another time and another place. A place he had almost completely forgotten. A place he could never return to.

His memory filled with hundreds of unique sights and smells that he wished for so dearly but knew he would never experience again. To him, they were better off forgotten. *Better off forsaken.*

The wind pressed hard on his body, and he closed his eyes as it tore away his troubles. It grew louder and louder in his ears, but to him, it was like a soothing melody.

And as snow began to fall and the storm began to grow, one might have seen the faint etchings of a massive figure standing upon that balcony, flickering in and out of existence like a billowing phantom. The dim illusions, perhaps, of a dragon's old and discarded form.

Chapter 17

Day fifteen of the fifth month.

BORHIIM STARED UP into the dark and cloudy sky, no rays of sunshine to be seen. Hard drops of pouring rain descended onto the grassy plains, turning them muddy under the rows upon rows of soldiers. They waited patiently for the incoming invasion. The Norvad army would have to make the first strike.

He looked to the left and right of his position.

In the front lines was the cavalry, led by King Tirehn himself, fashioned in his gold and silver armor. At his side was the usual sword that he used for dueling, with a tall silver shield in his right hand. Strapped to his back was a two-handed broadsword, a gift from the people of the Gorrobin tribes when Raggorin was first enlisted as an advisor.

Behind were leagues of archers with hands to their quivers, awaiting the command to take aim. Their arrows were tipped in steel, and the feathers on the ends were bright red. They also carried swords at their sides when the enemy inevitably drew closer.

And finally, just in front of the thousands of foot soldiers—the Takahrn. Although their numbers were nowhere near the other parts of the army, they were just as potent and effective. Some brandished weapons of varying types: swords, spears, maces, and axes. Others chose to rely on their strength, their claws at their sides, ready for the oncoming and inevitable battle.

Gahlaia stood at their head, ready to lead a large group of winged

Takahrn into the fray just behind the cavalry. They wore light armor that would keep them fast in the air and agile when the fighting grew closer.

Borhiim himself stood at the front of the wingless with a sword in his right hand and his left claw free to rip through any flesh he could reach. He wore Deeria's usual armor, customized with a hole in the back for his tail, and a shield on his back.

It had been a while since he had wielded any weapon other than his talons, but he didn't want to put his trust in the Devil's Flame. Since the coronation, it had grown completely silent within him. Even when he focused his body and mind as he had before, he still couldn't feel its pull. It wasn't just that it was unresponsive, it was as if it had never existed in the first place. Besides, even if he could bring it to life, who knew how far his control over it would be. On the field of battle, with both friend and foe on every side, humans and Takahrn could be burned to nothing without his realizing it.

Rista stood just behind him without weapons. Like Borhiim, she wore the regular armor but with a few differences. Her short tail was free, and two holes were made at the top of her helmet where her horns shot through. Her Terrkoris mark that lay dormant on her shin had been covered by plating with the symbol scraped roughly into the metal.

Borhiim looked a little to his left and toward the front. Gahlaia had her eyes forward, and even if she were aware of his presence, she wouldn't look at him—not after that night on the balcony. They had hardly spoken at all to each other since then, and their unfinished conversation lay between them, but neither desired to continue it. At least, not at the moment. There were more important things at the moment. Still, Borhiim couldn't help but glance in her direction. There was a good chance neither of them would survive what was to come.

He said one last prayer to the Eternal under his breath for good measure. Whatever happened next, death hung over all of their heads. It was just a matter of time before they would know who would be chosen to leave for the other side.

The downpour turned to hail, clattering and banging its pellets of ice onto the armor and shields of all who stood at the ready. To the north, crossing over the Norvad border, another army came into view through the fog and storm. Their armor was dark grey, almost black. They were led by leagues of cavalry with a tall man at their helm. He rode a jet-black horse, his entire body covered in grey dragon scales for armor, save for his shoulders and knees that were given their own set of plating. In his right hand he held a bronze mace, with a cape made of wolf skin flowing behind him. Etched on the left shoulder armor was the mark of a grand general: an X with a vertical line through it.

He gave a loud war cry, and the rest of the Norvad army followed his example. They clanged their weapons and shields together, booming over the wet terrain like a long clap of thunder.

Borhiim's heart pounded like a drum. Since his journey to Valia, he had seen his fair share of battles, but never had he been in a situation such as this. Deep down, he knew he was afraid. Not afraid just for himself—but for those around him. This could be the last time he ever saw their faces.

He spun around toward Rista. Her face was directed toward the ground in deep concentration. Her eyes were shut tight, and her lips moved ever so slightly.

"How far are they?" Borhiim asked.

Rista's eyes remain closed, but she stopped murmuring. "Not far," she replied. "I just need a little more time."

Borhiim returned to his position only to see Tirehn looking right at him from up at the front, barely over the heads of the others. He shook his head in the king's direction, and Tirehn nodded.

"*Archers!*" he screamed over the hail and war cries of the opposing army.

Upon command, arrows were put to bowstrings and pulled up toward the clouds. The sound of the tug of string traveled across the lines and into Borhiim's ears.

Tirehn raised his sword and held fast, waiting for the right moment.

The Norvad grand general pulled on the reins of his horse, reeling it back, and directed his mace forward. With that one motion, the cavalry charged, the leader and remaining foot soldiers holding their ground.

"*Release!*" Tirehn cried, bringing his sword down.

Instantly, the twang of bows rang out, and hundreds of arrows flew through the air toward their target. They descended upon the mounted troops like fire from the sky, many in the front lines collapsing immediately, rolling and tumbling into the mud with mixtures of fractured bones and bloody wounds. Yet many continued their stride, shields raised to protect themselves from the assault.

Tirehn shouted again, prompting another volley of arrows, but the horses were getting too close. They would be upon them soon.

The king looked to Borhiim once again, and he in turn looked to Rista.

She opened her eyes. "They're here! Whenever you're ready."

Borhiim nodded to the king, and Tirehn in turn barked out his order. Rista's eyes rolled almost completely into the back of her head as she placed her hands on the wet ground. Her left shin, where her Terrkoris mark lay under her armor, began to shake violently.

A low rumble came from deep underneath the muddy plains as the cavalry drew ever closer. When they came almost within striking distance of the king's army, their lines were suddenly broken. Out of the ground came massive roots numbering in the hundreds. They were pointed on their ends like spears and shot diagonally toward Norvad's mounted soldiers. They dug deep into both man and horse, killing them almost instantly.

Tirehn called for another round of arrows, and they found their marks in any straggling survivors.

Rista groaned under the strain until she could hold the spell no longer, and she recoiled onto the ground. The roots descended back into the mud, leaving many bodies in their wake. Borhiim heard Tirehn call out toward his army, and the horse regiment charged northward, followed by Gahlaia's group of winged Takahrn taking to the skies. Borhiim raised his sword, and all those behind him charged into battle. Even Rista, still visibly drained, ran with the army, a slight limp in her stride.

The Norvad grand general, still looking to be in shock and unsure of what had just occurred, lifted his mace to the sky and brought his forces into a stride to meet their enemies.

Time moved in slow motion as the two huge armies rose to meet each other in challenge.

Borhiim inhaled and exhaled at an irregular pace, watching as Gahlaia and the forces in front of him fell upon their prey. Arrows soared into the sky from the north toward him, barely noticeable through the constant barrage of ice and rain. He pulled the metal shield from his back and placed it above his head, keeping pace with the rest of the soldiers. He rolled his tail around one of his legs just in time as an arrow nicked the tip of the hair on its end. His shield dented under the attack, one arrow piercing the cold steel, stopping inches from the top of his head. Around him he watched soldiers fall into puddles of mud, their eyes lifeless and empty. His heart pounded harder, but he kept going, clenching his teeth and baring his fangs. Under his breath came a continuous rattle of low growls.

Arrows were no longer an option. The armies met with a clash of metallic sounds and weapons scraping across plating and flesh. Before long, Borhiim had taken sight of his first opponent and rushed at him with a fury, giving his own war cry. The Norvad soldier, noticing his oncoming attacker, thrust a long dark spear in his direction, an expression of terror rushing across his face.

Borhiim swung his blade to the right and pushed off his heels, knocking the spear tip away from his chest and closing the distance between them. Dropping his shield in the grass, he outstretched his left talons and reached for the man's soft skin below his helmet. The soldier jumped back, the tips of the nails scratching at his neck. He lost his balance and slipped in the mud, falling flat on his back. The soldier quickly dropped his spear and pulled out a shortsword to try and block any attacks his predator might bring down, but it was far too late. Borhiim was already on top of him, slashing his sword down and stabbing the end between the armor plates and into the flesh underneath. The soldier screamed, and Borhiim sliced his head from his shoulders, his weapon covered in Norvad blood.

Without thinking twice, he moved on to his next foe, his body fueled with nothing but adrenaline and anger.

All was chaos. It consumed everything like a spreading poison. Bodies dropped like flies under the strike of a weapon, the slash of a claw, and the trampling feet of horses. Borhiim continued his move forward to where he believed the grand general to be. If the man wasn't already struck down, he was determined to find him and fell him on his own. But in the constant slashing and swinging of his blade, he had lost his sense of direction. At this point, he couldn't move forward without coming into contact with another soldier he needed to cut down.

Deep in his mind, he felt for the magic once again. Nothing else mattered to him. He was being bombarded with soldier after foot soldier, and the bodies were piling up all around him. Nearly all he could think of was survival. He wanted to live through this. There was so much he still needed to do, and so much others depended on him to be. He reached inside himself for some sort of reaction. Anything at all. Still, there was nothing. The Devil's Flame evaded his grasp, most of Borhiim's attention on the battle before him.

Another man ran toward him, screaming. He threw himself on Borhiim, swinging his sword and shield wildly. Borhiim ducked under another swing, the blade whizzing barely above him. He took the opportunity to strike but was taken aback when the soldier hit his head hard with the side of a shield, knocking his helmet into the puddles of mud and blood behind him. He staggered back in a momentary daze but kept his balance.

The man went for one final sideways cut toward his foe's neck. Borhiim, his vision blurred, rushed forward at such a speed that it took the soldier by surprise. Grabbing the man's sword hand with his left, he blocked another strike from the shield with his right elbow. Knocking the shield away, he slid his sword under the man's breastplate and through his spine. Borhiim then slashed his throat with his talon and kicked the body into the mud, metal still in the corpse. He leaned forward, put a foot to the wet and slippery armor, and with a heave pulled the blade from the remains.

Borhiim took a moment to catch his breath. His head ached, heart pounding like a drum. He stared at the grotesque picture around him. Lifeless husks of metal and bleeding carcasses were all around, impossible to ignore with even a single step. Looking into the faces, Borhiim felt his anger and adrenaline slowly began to dissipate, replaced with remorse. These people were sent to their deaths all because their ruler demanded it of them. They could have had families waiting for them back in Norvad, only to be sliced to ribbons on the battlefield. *Honor . . .* he thought. *There's no honor in this.*

Borhiim shuddered, squinting at the disgusting scene. Upon the bloodied ground and muddied plains, on the fields of battle that were sung of in taverns and palaces, there were no heroic deaths. There would be no truthful songs for them because the truth was too repulsive to sing. There would be no cheers of joy. No smiles on the faces of children. No feast deserving of the victors. Only death and sorrow awaited, and such a thing was never meant to be celebrated.

Shaking his head hard, Borhiim took hold of himself and focused. From the corner of his eye, he saw someone. Someone familiar. A Takahrn, down on her knees and fighting for her life. She ducked and spun from side to side to avoid the swing of the blade above her, but her weariness was slowly overtaking her. Borhiim, finally regaining himself, ran back into the fray toward her. He swung his sword into the back of a soldier who moved in his direction and kicked him aside, keeping to a sprint.

The soldier standing over the Takahrn raised his broadsword into the sky to finish the foe at his feet, but as he saw Borhiim descending upon him, he quickly changed the course of the blade, throwing it upward at his enemy's face. Borhiim dug his foot into the mud to slow his run, turning his face to the right. The end of the broadsword dug deep into the left side of his face, leaving a vertical gash up his cheekbone. He fell into a puddle of mud and spun to the right as the large blade came down toward him again at blitzing speed. Using the end of his tail, he grabbed his attacker's foot and tugged, catching the enemy off balance, leaving the soldier slipping and nearly falling down himself.

Taking the chance, Borhiim got to his feet and sized up his opponent. The man was of medium height yet built much stronger than many others his size. He wore the same dark grey armor with a mark on his left shoulder plate. Three long stripes were etched into it, signifying the third sector. It was the insignia of the Norvad generals, those underneath the grand general. Borhiim stared at the broadsword in the man's hand. Under the blood and rain streaks were symbols—ancient elvish words. How the man was able to get his hand on an elvish sword Borhiim wasn't sure, and he wasn't given the time to think it over.

The general charged at him again, gripping the handle of his weapon tightly. He swung diagonally at Borhiim and then brought the sword back again, slicing clean through his opponent's blade. Borhiim could barely keep pace, but he could see the man's face growing weary. Humans could only take the strain of such magic for so long before giving in, and he was reaching his limit. As the next strike came, Borhiim ducked, placing his knees and hands to the ground, and threw his body at the man with full force. All air escaped from the general's lungs in an instant as he fell backward, losing hold of his blade. As he crashed into the mud, the Terrkoris left his body immediately, his physical exterior instantly growing feeble, almost as frail as paper.

Borhiim heard the audible crunch of softened bones, and when he looked into the face of the man, he saw him desperately gasping for breath. His face was one of agonizing pain, and it grew paler by the second. Rising to his feet and reaching for the sword of a dead soldier nearby, Borhiim brought the blade down with a grunt, ending the general's suffering.

Adrenaline left him once again, and a sharp aching rose on his face. He reached up and wiped away the blood that trickled from his gash into the edges of his mouth. He could almost feel his body struggling to heal the wound.

He turned back to the Takahrn he had tried to reach, and seeing her collapsed to the ground, he rushed to her side and lifted her. It was Rista. On her right side was a long wound that cut through the metal of her armor, and her tail had been severed.

"Rista!" Borhiim yelled, trying to shake her awake. "Rista, come on!"

Her eyes opened slightly, and she coughed hard. "Shut . . . up," she whispered. "Leave . . . the dead in peace."

"You're not dead yet. We need to get you out of here."

"There's nowhere . . . to go. Besides, I—" she coughed again. She tried to continue speaking, but her words were too quiet to understand, and soon her lips moved without sound. Her eyes rolled back, and her head drooped, hanging like a rag doll's.

"Rista, wake up! *Rista!*"

There was no time for mourning. Another soldier charged forward, and Borhiim was forced to move on once again. He wasn't sure how Deeria's army was faring, but at that point, it didn't matter to him. He swung the weapon in his hands with blurred vision, tears burning down his cheekbone into his open wound.

Gahlaia, he thought as he cut through another soldier. *I have to find Gahlaia.*

It felt like hours passed by as he slowly made his way across the plains, looking every direction for his comrade. He didn't see her anywhere, not even among the dead. Another soldier came toward him and managed to cut into his right shoulder. Borhiim's hand felt almost numb, and he lost his grip on his sword. He swerved to the side and managed to get close to his foe, cutting him down with his talons. He looked around again, trying to make out the cluster of figures in the increasing amount of hail. He squinted as something came into view.

In the distance, past another group of Deeria and Norvad foot soldiers, he spotted wings. Taking the chance, he limped in that direction. In moments, a mixture of relief and terror rose in his chest.

Gahlaia was in the center of a plethora of bodies, bruised and scratched all over. She moved her powerful claws in quick motions and kept her wings tucked at her sides to protect them from attacks from behind. Directly in front of her was the grand general himself, swinging his mace in fluid motions with his left hand and cutting through the air with a shortsword in his right. His cape was gone.

Gahlaia was on the retreat, showing clear signs of exhaustion. She knocked away the incoming mace with her claws, leaving a gash in the metal where she did so. She pulled her head back to avoid another slice of the shortsword and moved in, grabbing the grand general's left hand and reaching for his throat. He twisted and brought the hilt of his sword to Gahlaia's head, slamming her to the ground.

Borhiim tried to rush in as quickly as he could, but yet another soldier came into his path. He dodged a swing and cut at the man's sword hand, then toward his face, dropping him. He reached inside himself one last time as he pressed further toward Gahlaia. Still, he did not sense the Devil's Flame. *I need you*, he thought. *Please!*

Gahlaia struggled on the muddy ground, dodging two weapons at once. Spreading her wings, she brought them up as if trying to gain some leverage. But the grand general swung down his mace and shortsword in unison toward the wings, smashing them both into the mud and pinning the Takahrn down. Gahlaia shrieked as the spikes of the mace crushed her right wing and the blade thrust deep into her left.

Borhiim cried out as he rushed for his foe, and the man looked up from his prey below in surprise. *I need you!*

The two bodies fell hard, but the general spun his weight around, pinning Borhiim underneath. He grasped the Takahrn's throat and squeezed hard. Borhiim clawed at the man above him, but he couldn't reach his face. *Please! I need you now. Please!*

He looked to his right where Gahlaia still lay. She was teetering on the edge of unconsciousness, the two weapons still stuck in her wings.

He had to survive. He had to.

A burning sensation tinged the ends of Borhiim's soul ever so slightly. He could feel it. It grew until he could no longer contain it. He felt the Devil's Flame turn red in his eyes. He shoved his hands upward and released. The dark fire spewed out like a furnace and licked the grand general's entire body until nothing remained. Borhiim gasped for air, his very breath transformed into murky flames lashing their way into the sky. He tried reeling them back in but to no avail. Every exhale was another blast of the Devil's Flame, and it flowed from his hands uncontrollably. His emotions soon began to shift against his will, and a single feeling replaced them all.

Rage.

Borhiim rose to his feet, the dark flames spinning around him like a tornado of magic and destruction. He charged into a cluster of soldiers as his mind went blank, the echoes of a hundred screams ringing in his brain.

WHEN BORHIIM AWOKE, the rain and hail had ceased, but thin clouds still permeated the skies. He stared up, watching the beams of dim sunlight slip in and out of the moving haze. He lifted himself and looked around, his cheekbone stinging. The mud puddles had completely dried up all around him as if they had never been there at all. In fact, the more he came to, the more he realized what had happened.

He was sitting in a massive crater of scorched ground, at least twenty feet in diameter, with no signs of life in it anywhere.

Slowly, Borhiim rose to his feet and climbed out, the terrain still warm to the touch. Beyond the crater were rough outlines of burned portions of land, jutting out erratically. Pieces of armor from both Deeria and Norvad and what looked like charred remains spread across the ground.

Borhiim put a fist to his mouth in horror. There were even burned pieces of what looked like horns and wings in the blackened areas of the field.

"Borhiim!" came a voice. "Thank the Eternal, you're alive."

He heard Tirehn run to his side, but Borhiim kept his gaze on the scene before him, his eyes wide with shock. All he could remember before passing out was releasing the Devil's Flame . . . and the screams. So many screams.

"Did . . ." he said. "Did I do this?"

Tirehn didn't respond. He didn't need to. Borhiim knew what his answer would be. He staggered back. He could feel his stomach turning. "I killed them. I killed my own people . . ." Realization came over him like a wave. "Gahlaia! Did I—"

"She's fine," Tirehn said, raising his hands, palms out. "You need to calm down and come with me. We have to leave."

The king took a step forward and placed a hand on Borhiim's shoulder, but Borhiim recoiled and almost fell backward.

"Stay away!" Borhiim yelled. He looked around once more at what was left of his dead comrades. It made him sick just looking at it—but still, he couldn't look away. There was nothing he could do. They were gone, and he had been the one to do it. His stomach rumbled and churned uncontrollably. Lurching forward, he leaned down into a patch of trampled grass and vomited.

ANAHKA GASPED FOR breath as if she had just awoken from a nightmare. Her head lurched upward, but she immediately let it fall back to the ground as pain racked her lower body. Her mind was swirling with thoughts she could hardly piece together. The sky above was cloudy, and the air smelled of filth.

Slowly, it all started to come back to her. King Tirehn had sent her to join the army in the south, but upon her arrival, Verish had attacked. She sent a falcon back to Valia as instructed, but by the time word reached them, it would be too late. Arinay led the charge against the army, and they stood no chance.

At that, she felt only more confused. She should be dead.

A headache shook her brain, and upon lifting a hand to her forehead, she felt a large bruise. Raising herself slowly, grunting at the pain, she stared down. She was wounded, a cut running from her right rib to her left hip. It wasn't deep, thank the Eternal, but it left dried blood on what remained of her armor. If she weren't Takahrn, the bleeding would have surely killed her.

Several minutes passed before she felt comfortable enough to stand, and even then her head wouldn't stop spinning. Bodies too numerous to count surrounded her. Some wore the colors of Verish, but most were soldiers of Deeria, with Takahrn spread among them. If she weren't so focused on staying upright, she would have been more shocked. Anahka had hoped that others might have survived, but everywhere she looked there were corpses. If there were survivors, she couldn't see them, and what could she do for them if she did? She was barely alive herself.

The hours passed by as she walked among the dead, kneeling beside her kind to pray over them. There wasn't much else she thought she could do but hope that the Eternal had taken them into His arms. And in those hours, the urgency she once had melted away. Verish was marching toward Valia, but there was nothing she could do about it. When the queen received her letter, she would assume Anahka had perished in the attack. All Anahka could do was hope that those in Valia would survive somehow.

But as her thoughts started to swirl in her head, they were suddenly halted. Across the battlefield, just barely visible, she saw a form. Hoping it was a group of survivors, Anahka hurriedly limped toward it. As she drew nearer, however, her hopes were quickly dashed. The closer she got, the larger the form appeared, until she could make out the massive outline of some kind of creature, hunched over the corpses, its face turned from her. It was ... *eating them!*

Anahka resisted the urge to retch, slowing her pace. Yet even as the form came into view, she felt something emanate from the beast. It felt magical, hints of both Terrkoris and Anamoris within its unseen touch. It was a sensation she had felt long ago, and its distinctness was something she could never forget. The aura was familiar to her, and with it, old memories she had tried so hard to bury had returned.

The creature was enormous—its tail the length of at least twenty full-grown men swishing back and forth across the bloodied ground. It was four-legged, the musculature under its scales bulging with strength beyond measure. It lifted its head upward, and two great wings spread over the dead. They caught the sunlight that pierced through the clouds, and Anahka gaped at the color of the scales. *Purple!*

Anahka instinctively felt for her abdomen, where a patch of her own scales lay. They too were purple, the color of her ...

Her eyes went wide. She wasn't sure if she should scream or run and was left standing motionless before what she could scarcely believe. Her thoughts ran back to the conversation she had with Gahlaia several months prior.

My mother, whoever she was, mated with my father and gave birth to me. When she saw what I was, she left us. Where she went is beyond me, and I doubt even the Dragon King knew.

Anahka shook her head. It wasn't possible, yet here she was. Her heart drummed in her chest and her breath grew rapid. In all her life, never had she felt more conflicted. A part of her was happy, seeing her mother alive and well. The other part, however, was furious. She didn't deserve to be alive and well, feasting on Anahka's fallen comrades.

But before she could say or do anything, the dragon leaped into the sky, flapping her outstretched wings. Anahka watched her fly upward, soaring eastward. Moments later, she was gone.

Although she had vanished from view, Anahka had some semblance of where the dragon was going. The aura she felt was still there. The two of them were bound by blood, even if her mother didn't realize it. For years she thought that spark of connection had vanished, but now Anahka could feel it rekindle. Nothing else mattered. She knew she couldn't help her friends in the war. It would be over before she even arrived. But this ... This was far too important to her.

Limping in the direction the dragon had taken, Anahka followed it eastward.

Chapter 18

Day sixteen of the fifth month.

BORHIIM COCKED HIS head and looked around. Everything was dark. He had been here before, but why his dreams returned him to this place was beyond him. He knew who he was, yet again he was plagued with more mystery.

The light glistened into sight once again, and for a moment, he thought he heard a voice. A soothing voice, perhaps, if it would only grow louder. But it remained low, barely even a whisper, and then vanished.

"Why am I here?" Borhiim shouted into the void. "Why do I keep getting these visions . . . ?"

The light returned one last time, stronger than before. Borhiim made out the shape of a woman within the brightness, her physical appearance still beyond recognition. The calming voice returned, now loud enough for him to hear. It was one he knew all too well.

"The Claw . . . my son. You must know . . . the truth. The Devil's Flame . . . You must find a way . . ."

Borhiim couldn't believe what he was hearing. The vision grew clear as crystal as the beautiful form of a woman stood before him.

A word hung in his mouth. "Mother?"

At that moment, she clutched her chest and winced, as if some unknown pain were too great to bear. She cried out to him, but no sound came from her throat. Then she disappeared before his eyes like a dying flame on a candlestick.

Far within the darkness, six yellow eyes stared back at him, with the dark pupils of a reptile in each. Something was watching him, and strangely, he could almost feel the thing calling to him, beckoning him onward.

It was then that Borhiim heard them again: the screams. The countless shrieks of his men and women in arms, their lives cut short by his uncontrollable magic. He covered his ears, but they only grew louder. Within the spinning tornado of shadowy fire around him, he saw faces. Unrecognizable faces whose cries reached out to him only to be silenced in the ever-consuming storm of the blaze.

Even in the swirl, he could still see the eyes, drawing him forward.

Borhiim could take it no longer. He clenched his eyes shut, but the vision still stuck in his mind, as if it played on the inside of his eyelids. A tear rolled down his face before being burned away in the flames.

I'm sorry, my brothers. I'm sorry, my sisters. I have failed you all . . .

THE MORNING CHILL was still in the air, and the sun brought a soft orange glow into the clouds that twisted above.

Gahlaia watched the wooden wagon with mixed emotions. The army had used several to carry supplies and provisions that the horses could not bear, especially when many of the horses had fallen in battle. This one in particular, however, carried something it normally would not: Borhiim, his legs chained together. He slept on several bags and other assortments, twitching and turning.

Even after the battle near the Norvad border was over, Gahlaia still had so much on her mind. Borhiim had killed hundreds in his rampage, wiping them clean from existence. But not her. He had done so to protect her, and he had achieved that. But there were still so many supposed dead from both their side and the enemy's, most of whom were still unaccounted for. Worst of all, many of their fellow Takahrn had been slain by his hand. She knew he wasn't in control. She understood that better than most. Still, those were their brothers and sisters. The people they had set out to defend . . . now gone.

But she did not blame him for the fallen. Quite the opposite. To her, those deaths were on her shoulders, not his. He had tried to save her, just like always. Perhaps if she had been stronger, it would have never happened. *If only . . . but I wasn't.*

She winced as a tinge of pain struck her wings. They both sagged, dragging on the ground as she moved onward with the remaining company. She could feel them healing rapidly, but that didn't mean there was no discomfort.

Borhiim jerked forward with a start, breathing heavily. He took in the area around him and then relaxed, letting out a sigh. Gahlaia moved closer, noticing what looked like a half-healed scar across his cheekbone, almost reaching up to the edge of his left eye.

"How did you get the scar?"

He put a hand to the wound and felt the crusted blood over the rough skin. "One of the Norvad generals had an elvish blade," he responded. "Grazed the side of my face with it."

"So now Rorgan's giving out elf weapons to his other generals?" She spat into the damp ground. "Despicable. They can't even use them properly."

Borhiim nodded back in return. "So, we're heading back to Valia then?"

"Yes. With the troops we have at our disposal, we barely scraped out a victory, but there could be Norvad reinforcements. We won't survive another attack, at least not in an open field."

Gahlaia looked at the chains on Borhiim's legs. "You don't need to wear those, you know."

He shook his head and ground his teeth. "Yes, I do. You know I do. You saw what I did. Why do you think I told them to chain me to this wagon?"

"Of course I saw. I'm not blind. You lost control, and you have the right to live with that. You have the right to mourn. We all do."

She leaned in and sliced her right talon across the metal bindings on Borhiim's ankles, keeping her eyes on him. "But if you're going to mourn like us, then you can at least walk on your own two feet. People die in war, sometimes in ways we don't expect. Letting you sit in shackles and wallow in self-pity won't bring them back. So be a man and stand up like everyone else." She didn't enjoy speaking those last words. Her frustration was directed more to herself, but she refused to show it.

Borhiim didn't speak. He stood up and jumped out of the wagon, walking with his gaze straight ahead.

"Just tell me one thing," Gahlaia said. "What happened yesterday?"

"I don't know," he answered. "It's always been hard for me to control the Devil's Flame, but it's never done that before. It was like being pushed by a current. If I resisted, it only pushed back harder."

He sighed, putting his fingertips to his temples. "I've been stumbling around, playing with magic that I can barely contain. I've been no better than a child playing with fire. When I try to summon it, it evades me. When I try to wield it, it controls me, now to a dangerous level. People die if I fail to use it, but more if I do."

He stopped walking, and Gahlaia stopped with him, confused and concerned. "I can't do this anymore, Gahlaia," he said. "I can't go with you to Valia."

Borhiim sprinted ahead, moving past Gahlaia in a flash and into the crowds of moving soldiers and Takahrn, many backing away from him with expressions of fear.

"Borhiim, wait!" Gahlaia yelled after him. She ran in his direction as hard as she could, her dragging wings leaving her grunting. She finally caught sight of him, looking around at the groups of people. "What do you mean you can't go to Valia?" she asked.

"I had a dream," he replied, spinning around and striding in another direction. "It was like the ones I had when my memories started coming back to me." He started running again, forcing Gahlaia to follow.

"What are you doing?" she shouted from behind.

"Where's Tirehn? I need to tell him what I saw."

"Saw what? What did you see?"

Borhiim ignored her questioning, spotting his objective near the front of the army, just behind another cluster of soldiers. He ran off again, and Gahlaia sighed.

"Tirehn!" he yelled as he approached.

The soldiers backed away quickly, leaving the king alone in a circle of people as Gahlaia caught up.

"Borhiim?" Tirehn asked, taking a few steps back.

Borhiim took a brief moment to catch his breath. "I had a dream," he repeated, "or a vision perhaps. It told me to go to the Claw, the mountains in the northeast."

"Wait, wait, wait," Tirehn said, putting his hands up. "A vision? How?"

"I used to have them when I lived in the Dirtlands. They came to me for a short while and restored my lost memories."

"But how do you know these are the same?" Gahlaia asked. "You only received those visions because the Anamoris spell that still had a hold on you was beginning to wear thin. How is this at all the same thing? What if Tarubas is trying to lure you away to set a trap or kill you? There's no way of knowing just from a dream."

Borhiim turned around and looked her dead in the eyes, his face stern. "It was Boria. It was my mother. She called out to me as she did before."

"Before?" Tirehn said. "She's been in your visions before?"

Gahlaia's eyes darted back and forth as she put the pieces together. "She showed you the vision of the Battle of Fate, where your parents met."

Borhiim nodded in excitement. "Exactly! And she spoke to me before. At first, I thought it was just some connection to the Terrkoris and Anamoris, showing me the visions of the dead. But it was more than that. Boria showed me what I needed to see, and now she's doing it again."

"You think Boria is alive?" Tirehn asked. "As in Boria, the Elvish Dragon?"

"Yes. Though in the vision, she appeared weaker than before. If she is alive somehow, then she could be dying. What's more," he looked back at Gahlaia, "she spoke of the Devil's Flame. If I go, I think I might find a way to control it."

There was silence among the small council.

Borhiim faced the king. "I have to go. You know I do. Too many people have already died because I couldn't wield the magic properly. If we want to end this conflict with the other sectors and fight against Tarubas, then I need to be able to use the Devil's Flame. As I am now, I'll only bring more death within our ranks."

Tirehn sighed, paused momentarily, and then turned his attention to one of his soldiers. He motioned to the man, who handed the king a rolled-up map along with a sheathed broadsword. "You'll need these," he said, "along with any food you can carry and one of our horses. Just promise me you'll stay wary."

Borhiim stared at the weapon, putting a hand to the wound on his face. "That's the elvish sword the Norvad general wielded."

"We took it while rummaging through the battlefield," the king responded. "I think if you're going to travel alone, you should at least be able to defend yourself."

Borhiim shook his head and put up a hand. "I can't take this from you. You'll need it."

"And who would use it?" Gahlaia asked. "Anyone without magical properties would only be killing themselves by using such a blade. If anyone is going to wield it, it should be you."

Letting out a long sigh, he took the map and buckled the broadsword to his back. "Thank you, my king," Borhiim said, giving the elvish salute. "I'll put these to good use."

"I know you will," the king replied.

As Borhiim turned, Gahlaia ran to his side. "I'll come with you," she said.

"No," he returned. "You're a leader. The Takahrn need you."

"Don't make this an argument, Borhiim. I'm coming whether you like it or not."

He took a step toward Gahlaia, and she saw a confidence and authority in him she had never seen before. She stood her ground but couldn't deny she was impressed.

"Please, Gahlaia," he said. "Our brothers and sisters need you here defending them. You have the power to fight, and Deerium needs that from you. I don't have that. Not yet."

He placed a hand on her shoulder. It was warm even in the chill morning breeze. He opened his mouth as if to speak, but shut it again, giving her a brief smile.

He nodded to Tirehn and strode to the back of the moving army, preparing to head northward.

Gahlaia followed him and watched as he gathered his provisions and placed them within sacks on the saddle of one of the few horses that remained. She still had so much to say, but the words fell flat on her tongue. There were many things they should have spoken of: old forgotten memories, future aspirations, unfinished conversations . . . The last one stung in her throat.

Having finished his preparations, Borhiim tugged one last time on the saddle and prepared to ride off. But before he could jump onto his mount, Gahlaia grabbed his arm.

"I know," she began, "that you think you're responsible for those deaths back near the border. But you did it to save my skin . . . again. I never thanked you for that."

He shook his head. "It's not something you should thank me for. It cost more lives than it saved."

"But you didn't know that would happen. None of us did. Of course, I know you must mourn, as we all should, and I know you have to leave. But it shouldn't be out of some false sense of duty to repay for deaths that you weren't in full control of."

He shrugged. "If I'm not to blame, then who is? Besides, you can't pretend that you aren't angry with me. I know you better than that."

"I'm not. If I hadn't gotten into that situation in the first place, then it wouldn't have happened at all. If I had been stronger—"

"Don't! Don't do that to yourself."

"Just . . . Just think about it, okay?"

He nodded but didn't turn away from her. His mouth hung open as if he were trying to find the right words. "Gahlaia . . ." he said. "About that night on the balcony. What we talked about then . . . We . . ."

Gahlaia could feel her heartbeat in her throat, and she squeezed his arm tighter. She took a step forward.

Borhiim sighed, as if taking another moment to gather his

thoughts. But instead of speaking, he took her hand in his. With his other, he reached under his shirt and winced, inhaling sharply through his fangs. When he removed his hand from under his shirt, he held a dusky red dragon scale, one of his own. It was half the size of his palm, oval-shaped with a few jagged edges. "Whether you still hold to the old ways or not," he said with a smile, "it doesn't matter to me. We've known each other since the second age—hundreds of years at least. And since I have been able to remember, you have always been my betrothed."

He reached out and offered the scale to her. "What you do with it is up to you. But all the same, it's yours and no one else's."

She stared at the scale in front of her, frozen where she stood. It wasn't what she was expecting at all, but it wasn't unwelcome either. Her hand softened under his hold, her fingers interweaving with his. But instead of taking the scale, she reached under her own shirt, grasping at the patch of dragon skin on the surface. Upon finding a scale that felt to be of similar size to Borhiim's own, she clawed at the edges and pulled at it, groaning slightly under the heat of pain that blazed in her left side. It quickly subsided, and she pulled a grey scale from under her garments and presented it to him.

She smiled as his face lit up. "Are you sure you want to do this now?"

Borhiim raised a shoulder. "We may not live through this war. We may not get another chance. The Dragon Ceremony then?"

Gahlaia nodded and raised an eyebrow. "If you remember how to do it."

"I might be a little fuzzy on the details. You lead, and I'll follow."

The Dragon Ceremony was a quick, straightforward form of mating known to the Drake. Unlike the pairing process of the elves, it was less of a ceremony and more of an exchange. The two dragons would each remove one of their scales and transform into their weaker, elvish-like forms, signifying their vulnerability with one another. They would then perform the exchange, giving part of themselves to the other, both body and soul, linking their minds together. Gahlaia knew it well, back from when her father had taught her in the ways of dragon customs.

The two walked back from the army, far enough that no one could interrupt them. Gahlaia raised her left hand, holding her scale in a clenched fist, her right hand behind her back. Borhiim did the same, placing his left hand next to hers, their wrists barely touching, their arms forming an X. They both closed their eyes, imagining a song that their parents used to play all those years ago. They remembered the twang of harp strings, the sound of a dancing flute, the banging of the drums, and the chanting of the dragons. It was an old song, but still, it resonated strongly in their minds.

Gahlaia began to hum to the beat of the drums in her head, and Borhiim followed her cues. Her voice was soft and low, just loud enough for him to hear it. At a change in the tempo, she took a step to her right, and he followed her with the same movement, eyes still shut tight. She then curled her left leg over her right in another step, Borhiim doing an exact copy. Her right foot moved out slowly from behind at the beat of the humming, and the two performed the motion again.

As the song grew faster, they picked up the pace of their movements, dancing in a perfect circle. Their arms holding the scales began to move up and down, flowing like a river, but always remaining together. As they continued to pick up speed, Gahlaia began to feel something. It felt like fingers wrapping softly around her core, deep in her chest. It was magic she had never felt before, Anamoris in nature.

All her life, she had lived without the powers of the two mystic forms. She was not gifted in that way, given instead unparalleled strength rather than a mark of Terrkoris or Anamoris. But now, in the heat of the moment, she understood how it felt. How Borhiim felt. The sensation and deeply rooted magic . . . For the first time in her long life, she could feel it in her bones.

As she continued to hum the song, she could hear fragments of a voice trickle its way in and out of her mind. At first, she thought it was Borhiim humming back, singing the tune along with her, but the sound never reached her ears. It was hardly a sound at all though she heard it all the same. It was Borhiim—but not his voice. His humming thoughts bounced to and fro within her head, and everything became clear.

They reached the final stages of the dance, the tempo speeding up incredibly from where it had started, their feet moving almost at a full run. Then, at the last piece of the tune, Gahlaia's humming stopped, and they both raised their left hands high into the sky diagonally, still touching.

They paused for a brief moment, both of them gasping for air.

They lowered their arms slowly, directing their left hands toward one another's chest. They opened their eyes and looked at each other, still breathing hard. Gahlaia nodded to him, and Borhiim nodded back. Removing their right hands from behind their backs, they lifted one another's shirts just enough to reveal their patches of scales. A small area of pink skin lay in the centers, where they had removed the pieces in their left fists. They opened their closed hands, the dragon plates still resting in their palms. Moving forward in unison, they each pressed their scale onto each other's vulnerable spot in the center of their chests. Immediately, they both winced.

Gahlaia did not look down but instead watched as her dark grey piece moved and shifted in Borhiim's flesh. It changed its shape slightly until it fit perfectly in with the other red scales on his body. But hers remained its same color. The grey plate stood out among the rest of Borhiim's patch, but it was a part of him none the less. She felt the strange voice in her mind no longer dancing in and out, but remaining consistent. It was still faint, like a whisper among a sea of memories, but it was constant.

The two Takahrn backed away from one another for a moment, each looking at their new scale that had latched onto their bodies. Gahlaia still couldn't believe what had happened. She gazed at her rib: an area of hard, greyish skin with one single piece of dark red in the center. She looked up, and Borhiim was staring back at her. *Can you feel it too?* she thought. A moment of silence, and then she heard it. The faintest of thoughts.

I feel it, Borhiim responded.

They stepped toward each other and lost themselves in each other's eyes, unable to turn away. "So stands the mating of the Takahrn," they said together. "May the Eternal be our witness."

The two embraced, refusing to let the other go. Gahlaia lifted her head and they kissed. It was as if the whole world had grown peaceful, if only for a moment. She never wanted to let him go, and when they finally released one another, a part of her stung with sorrow.

"Borhiim," Gahlaia said. "You will come back, right?"

He let a half smile curve his lips. "I will, and when I do, I'll finally have this cursed power under control."

"May the Eternal go with you."

"And may He go with you. Just stay alive, Gahlaia. That's all I ask."

She nodded, feeling the emotions swell up in her throat. She wrapped her arms around him again, taking even herself by surprise. She had always preferred to keep her feelings in check, but for once, she didn't seem to care. They kissed one last time before Borhiim leaped onto his horse. He looked at Gahlaia, nodded, and rode his way toward the northeast.

As he vanished from her sight, she let her thoughts move toward him again. Three simple words that he would carry with him for the rest of the journey. She felt Borhiim return the thought, giving the same response, and deep down, she could feel a smile beaming on his face.

"Stay alive . . ." she whispered to herself, rushing to join the king's army. "Please . . . stay alive."

Chapter 19

Day seventeen of the fifth month.

G WENDALL SAT BY the fire, waiting to be called back into the tent on the east side of the camp. She stared into the flames, watching them dance and flicker, huddled close to it as the night grew cold. Her mind was lost within the tints of orange and red.

She inhaled a deep breath, held it for a moment, and then released. The air felt clear, even with the campfires and smoke. She thought it had felt that way since they had crossed the Norvad border into Deeria, as if a dense fog had released its grip. In fact, the more she thought about it, the more she felt the air of Norvad to be so much . . . thicker than in any other sector. It was undeniable in her mind, but only perceptible after they had left. She had originally thought to ask the other soldiers or even Rorgan about it, but quickly gave up on that front. Everyone else didn't seem to notice the difference—perhaps she was the only one able to grasp it. After all, she wasn't entirely normal. Not anymore.

The voice had quieted in her head as she commanded it to. For all the failed attempts to bring out her true abilities, they had found minimal success at least. She could control her thoughts again and feel the Anamoris pulsate from below. Reaching into the depths of her core, there was a response. A sensation, still small, its source still unknown.

Gwendall closed her eyes, the orange glow of the fire still seeping through her eyelids. She pictured her hand reaching down within, fingers outstretched toward something in the distance. The black-ness gave a cool, luminous reply, but it was still faint. She reached farther inside, and the light grew brighter. She squinted as she tried to focus over the crackling of the blaze in front of her. The fingers in her mind were so close now, inches from the glow. But as she drew near, it instantly slunk away, keeping a distance until it went black again.

Opening her eyes, Gwendall realized the campfire had flared into a roaring blaze, and she shrank back. But as she stared, it diminished to its original size. She gasped, realizing she had not taken a breath since she had first closed her eyes. Coughing and holding her throat, she grunted behind her teeth. *Another failure,* she thought. *Six attempts and still I can't hold it for more than a couple of minutes.* It was frustrating that the Anamoris was so fickle with her. Magic always was.

She lifted her shirt and looked at the faded mark on her abdo-men. It appeared slightly clearer than before, but only for a moment. Soon, it clouded itself once again, returning to its original dim form. Lowering the garment, she grabbed at a lock of golden hair that streamed over her face and pulled at it in frustration. *How much longer is it going to take?* The pain shot through her forehead, but it only added to her anger. She was stuck, and she couldn't afford to be. So much was riding on her gaining control. With an elf on the side of Norvad and Verish, the king would finally give up his throne, and fewer lives would be lost. But none of it would matter if her Awakening continued to fail.

"My lady?"

Gwendall turned to see one of Rorgan's personal guards, dressed in dark purple armor laced with tints of silver. He bowed toward her, one of his arms gesturing to his left. "Lord Rorgan is ready to see you," he said. "He's in his tent."

She nodded. "Tell him I'll be there soon."

RORGAN FLIPPED ANOTHER page of the mysterious book, trying to seize all the knowledge he could from it. Was there anything he had missed? He ran a finger quickly over the rough paper. His memory served him well. Every piece, every word, every sentence was firmly ingrained in his memory. He knew what he was doing, yet still, Gwendall's Anamoris mark remained faded along with any elvish features that might cue him on what to do next.

Rorgan ran a hand through his hair. Perhaps it was time to move to someone else. Maybe she wasn't what he thought she was. Or perhaps . . . He froze. He knew there was one other option, but due to its potential repercussions, he had put it off. *What choice do I have?*

He cocked his head toward a black bag at the edge of the tent. He walked over, pulled several other manuscripts out, and placed them to the side, revealing the thin book at the bottom. Its front cover was gold, and the back was stark black. Opening the book and turning the pages near its end, Rorgan found what he sought. The dialect was ancient, with words that he had not read for hundreds of years at least. But still, he knew them and knew them well. It was an old draconic language, used before the Great Dragon War.

He squinted and found the words: the Calling Words. The edges of his mouth curled upward. This would be his last attempted Awakening with Gwendall. If this failed to work, there would be nothing left for him to do, and her usefulness to him would vanish. But it wouldn't fail. It never did. His smile widened.

The Shade never fails to impress.

GWENDALL LOOKED UP at the moon as she strode toward Rorgan's tent. It was bright tonight but not completely full. She shivered. The night breeze hit her hard away from the campfires. As she approached the tent, two soldiers with long spears nodded to her and lifted the entrance flap. She nodded back with a flicker of a smile and entered Rorgan's makeshift abode.

Inside, the first thing that caught her eye was the flattened and trampled grass. It shot up and down in patches. Whatever he had been doing, it involved a lot of pacing. At the very center of the rectangular area, the grass looked like it had been pulled from its roots, revealing the damp ground underneath. It formed an almost perfect circle, just large enough for someone to sit in with their legs crossed.

On the left side of the tent, just where the cloth wall met the ground, his black bag lay closed, with his large book of the Terrkoris and Anamoris sitting atop it. From the exterior, she could tell the bag held at least three or four other manuscripts. It didn't surprise her. If Rorgan wasn't helping her with an Awakening, then he was usually reading. Such a thing was necessary to keep the mind fresh and active.

Rorgan stood in the middle of the circle, holding a sheet of paper with elvish scribblings inked onto it. He smiled as he noticed her come in and then turned his gaze downward, eyes darting back and forth between the paper and the ground. She stepped forward and leaned over, looking at the dark etchings on the page. To her amusement, she managed to understand the writing. It formed a circle, matching the uprooted ground in the tent, and roughly translated as "Awaken, O sleeping child of the Light."

Understanding the elvish language was a struggle for her. Many of the manuscripts given to her by Rorgan in years past were copies of older writings translated into the current dialect. Any original versions she did come across were challenging to read in full. However, spending time with Rorgan and his boundless collection of originals had given her a new appreciation for the older tongue, not to mention some hands-on experience with it. Understanding the language was difficult at first, but it soon came to her. Unlike the current language used among humans, the elvish one, or Orratong as it was called, was not comprised of letters. Instead, each word was represented by a specific symbol, with every sentence indicating its end when the last character gave a downward curve on the right side. There were often similarities in appearance between words that had similar definitions, which helped in memorizing each meaning they individually held.

Rorgan placed the piece of yellowed paper down and looked up at her. "Are you ready for another Awakening?"

Awakening. That was a word Gwendall had grown very accustomed to in the past few days. It was, at least according to the many textbooks in the Norvad library, a form of ritual the elves would perform for their young. When an elf child was born, their mark, whether Terrkoris or Anamoris, would be faded and sometimes barely visible. Their physical features were very similar to a human's at this stage, and they would remain this way until their call into adulthood. Once the time came, usually at twelve to fourteen years, the child would perform an Awakening. If successful, they would join the elves as one of their own. Even if not, they were still welcomed by most... for a time, but they needed to continue attempting the ritual.

As years passed and the elves turned from the Eternal, their tradition changed. If a child failed too many times, then their faded mark was burned off, and they were cast out into the Great Sea to be devoured by Sirens, the ancient predators of the waters. If only the elves of old could see how times had changed. *The disgrace of one age*, she thought, *is the future of the next.*

Gwendall blinked as she noticed Rorgan awaiting a response. She sighed. "We might as well try."

He nodded, gesturing toward the grassless circle on the ground. "Have you been doing the mental practices I told you about?" he asked.

"As much as I can manage," she replied, stepping into the ring and sitting with her legs folded under. "They haven't done much good though. Every time I try to pull at the Anamoris, the harder it gets."

"Well, for what it's worth, I expected as much. They aren't meant to bring the magic to the surface, just help you to gain some stamina for the actual ritual."

Gwendall shook her head. "That's what I'm afraid of, Rorgan. I'm not gaining stamina. Every time we perform an Awakening, I don't last any longer than the one before. I think I might even be getting worse."

"This time it'll work."

"And what makes you so sure?" she asked, worried. "What is so different about this one?"

Rorgan leaned down to put a hand on her shoulder. "It has to work, Gwendall. It has to. We'll reach Valia soon, and at that point, we'll be in the arms of open war. If we want Tirehn to give up his throne without a massacre, we'll need you."

That last statement did little to relieve her. She looked down and ran her eyes across blades of grass.

Rorgan squatted next to her. "I know you think yourself weak. I know you think you don't live up to expectations."

"Is that supposed to make me feel better?" she said.

"But that's just it, Gwendall. You aren't weak. You never were. You've gone through so much, and it has all led up to where you are now. This is not going to work because we demand it of you, but because you're strong enough to bear it."

His expression looked so sincere that she couldn't help but relax her frustrations. She lifted her head and stared into his eyes. There was desperation and care in them. A care that reminded her of her brother.

"Don't do this for the war," Rorgan said. "Don't even do it for me. You have a strength that none of us hold, and it is only you who can bring it to the exterior."

He leaned in, his face only inches away from hers. His voice was just under a mutter. "I just need you to trust me. Can you do that?"

At that moment, Gwendall's perspective changed. All these years, even when her brother had been around, it had been Rorgan who had cared for her. It was Rorgan who recommended Doryan to Arinay. It was Rorgan who sent her letters in times of stress. It was Rorgan who had taken her in after everyone else had betrayed her.

It was always Rorgan.

A knot swelled in her throat. She had never thanked him for what he had done. When she needed a friend, he was there. And now, in the dire times of their current situation, he was so much more, and she barely took notice.

She swallowed hard. "Of course, I trust you, Rorgan," she whispered. "I will always trust you."

I HAVE HER. I have her!

Rorgan smiled back at Gwendall as she gave her gentle response.

Despite the lies that ran through his teeth, his smile was genuine. He held her in so much value—or at least the power that hid inside her. It was the closest thing to hope he had been given in the thousands of weary years he had spent in seclusion.

It worked. It actually worked.

He tried desperately to hold in his excitement. Her soul was growing more willing. It was opening its doors to him like the gates of the afterlife, preparing to offer him the fruit of his labors. And yet . . . *No*, he thought. *She isn't ready.* Her soul had given way, that much was true, but only partly. That still wasn't enough. Her core was too strong for him to take control. She still needed to go the extra mile. She needed to care for him above all else. She needed to want to be with him more than anything. She needed . . .

Gwendall needed to love him. He knew it would come to that. It was the final stage.

But there was still time. He could stall long enough for her to give way to him. The war would see to that. Besides, he needed to reveal the Anamoris magic within her first. They needed to fully complete an Awakening.

He smiled again as he began to draw the symbols on the ground around her, matching the example shown on his little slip of paper. He wasn't worried. Not in the least bit. Even if she couldn't handle the strain of the ritual, it wouldn't make much of a difference. The Shade would sustain her, even if she didn't know it.

Gwendall watched in silence as he pressed his fingers into the wet ground, digging as deep as he could to make the symbols as clear as possible. She breathed in and out quietly. Rorgan let out a small grunt as he completed the last curve of the final mark, completing the intricate ring. Seven symbols in total, each about the size of someone's hand, spun around Gwendall in a perfect circle.

He stood up and turned toward the opening of the tent. "Let no one inside," he said to one of the soldiers standing out front. "We need absolute silence at all times."

"Of course, my lord," the man replied, clanking his armored feet together.

Satisfied, Rorgan closed the tent flap, then turned back toward Gwendall. "Are you ready?"

She gave a long sigh, her breath trembling in preparation. "Let's just get this done."

With those final words, she lowered her head and closed her eyes. Her breathing began to slow until it grew almost nonexistent. Unbeknownst to her, the elvish markings surrounding her began to glow a bright white, the color of the Anamoris. It had begun.

Rorgan stepped around the circle slowly and quietly until he stood behind her. He watched as sweat began to bead on her neck and arms, her limbs starting to shake ever so slightly. She was struggling, it was obvious to him. Before long, she would likely fail again. He would have to intervene. Lifting an open palm over her, he felt his own Anamoris flit between his fingers and stretch down into Gwendall's head. He would have to be careful. She was powerful. If she sensed his presence, it was all over. All of it would be for nothing. But he couldn't let it end like this. He wouldn't be left alone. Left forsaken. Not again.

His magic crept its way into her thoughts at a snail's pace, remaining as silent as it could. Soon, Rorgan could picture images in his mind—her images. She was doing exactly what he had told her to do. She had pictured her hand outstretching toward a light, but she couldn't reach it. At any moment, it would vanish as it did before. He could feel it. She was going to fail.

Time for the Shade . . .

He remembered the ancient draconic words he had read just moments before Gwendall had entered his tent, and with them, memories of repressed hatred. He imagined an old cell, hidden deep inside a mountain of the south. He imagined himself, stripped and chained to that filthy stone wall. In the room with him were those accursed elves, the Righteous Ones. He remembered their words to him and their sickening enchantments. They had taken everything from him. Everything.

But remember, he thought, *they weren't the first.* No. They weren't. They were just the final straw that broke his back. The nail in the coffin. The Righteous Ones merely represented everything else that was wrong. They had looked upon his true form and hated him for it. For that, they had torn away all he held close to him. He was a shadow of his former self, all because of what the Twin Worlds had done to him. They would suffer. All of them.

He bared his teeth, and he felt them sharpen into fanged points under his lips. He winced as he felt his face contort back and forth between his fake and true features. Tarubas held in the urge to verbally release his emotions, holding back for all he was worth. The images, the memories—they all enraged him. *Good.* He was ready to do what must be done.

He began to utter words under his breath. Dark words that were never meant to be spoken. They were unfamiliar to the human tongue, coming out as strange slurs and sharp exhales. Tarubas could feel his emotions transform into physical form, a billowing black fog. He felt it stretch out and reach for the shaking body under his hand. Soon, the Shade began to merge with the invisible tendrils of his Anamoris, entering Gwendall's mind and crawling down into her core. He could feel it slither its way through until it found her soul, and upon seeing the emanating glow, the darkness squeezed it with a shadowy grip, feeding it with a sinister power.

Tarubas' head started to grow hazy as his rage enveloped him, but he remained in control. Gwendall, however, he could feel was not faring well. Her mind shifted in and out of focus, her image of the light flickering. He could see her trembling in agony. Then she reached for the Anamoris power once more, and this time it did not retreat from her. Her imaginary hands grasped the luminous energy, and her mind instantly flooded with magic.

Tarubas released his hold on the Anamoris and the Shade, the picture of Gwendall's inner struggle vanishing from him instantly. However, the Shade clung to him like a disease. With Gwendall's soul pulled from its grasp, it turned itself toward him and struck hard. He retreated, gasping, and fought back with all he had. But the more he rose to meet it, the stronger it grew until he finally relented and allowed it to spread within him. He froze for a few seconds until the darkness had its fill, and in those moments, he thought he saw something. It appeared in the form of a man, but it was completely wreathed in darkness that billowed around him like fire. It leaned back its head, and a terrifying laugh echoed in Tarubas' mind. Even he, the Faded Dragon, shuddered at its sound.

But before he could interpret its meaning, the Shade released him, disappearing into the wind. As it did, the vision vanished, and he scarcely remembered it was ever there. Just a fractured thought that he had perhaps conjured from his imagination.

His mind felt dazed and twisted. Breathing deeply to calm himself, he reasserted his human appearance and prepared for Gwendall to finish her Awakening. Looking down at her, he watched as her upper body shook violently. The elvish markings shimmered brighter than ever before, dazzling him. Veins protruded from her forehead as she lifted her face, her eyes finally opening wide. But the pupils were an empty white, completely blank and looking almost lifeless. She let out a gut-wrenching shriek. It hung in the air until her throat could give no more.

With a growing smile, Rorgan observed her features begin to

change. The soul took hold of the mind, the mind took hold of the body, and in that moment the lines between Anamoris and Terrkoris were blurred. Her body grew a few inches taller, her muscles expanding and tightening her shirt sleeves. But strangest of all were her ears. They began to point at their tops, giving her the signature feature of the ancient race. Underneath her shirt, something was glowing brightly—brighter even than the symbols on the ground. It shone through the cloth, and as Rorgan stepped around to look at it, he saw the clear outline of an Anamoris mark.

Then all the lights went out, and Gwendall collapsed into unconsciousness.

Victory flooded through his body. Before his very eyes, an Awakening had been completed, and an elf had been reborn.

HOURS LATER, RORGAN stood outside his tent and faced the northeast, gazing back toward the Norvad border. The moon shone a cool light upon the world. All soldiers were either on the outskirts of the camp for night watch or sleeping soundly around their dead campfires.

Was there anything he had missed? Any inaccuracy? He reviewed the pawns of his game over in his head.

King Tirehn was on the retreat back to Valia, no doubt trying to save what remained of his broken kingdom. Rorgan was worried at first, but with Draag keeping a watchful eye, nothing the king did would ever be unpredictable.

That sick spawn of the old Dragon King was with him, and her actions were all but unreadable. Even with all her strength and abilities, however, her army of Takahrn was too small to be any threat at the moment. Perhaps later down the line it would pose a problem, but by then it would be too late for Gahlaia to make a move against him.

Ahmeras, the ever-loyal queen, was stuck between two forces. Norvad reinforcements were coming from the north, and Verish was attacking from the south. She would be caught in a pincer attack, and behind the capital walls, there was nowhere to run.

Arinay was in Rorgan's pocket. She was blinded, like all foolish humans, by tragedy—the death of a loved one. From the messenger falcons he had received, she was attacking from the West Gate with every soldier and piece of weaponry Verish could muster. With Deeria's army split in two, they would be swept away like sand in a windstorm.

Zinnyah was an odd one. Although she claimed that Cleptyn was neutral in the conflict, there was no doubt in his mind that she would eventually join sides with Deeria. He was counting on it. Ahmeras would likely send Raggorin to try and persuade her, along with those abominations from the Gorrobin Mountains. He might have left already, and that much was out of his control. Cleptyn would intervene later down the line, but as with the Takahrn, it would be too late.

Only one thing bothered him. One person who could disrupt his plans altogether.

Borhiim.

Since the coronation, it had become very clear that he could summon the Devil's Flame, and that had been a problem . . . at first. Before Rorgan had set off to lead the Norvad reinforcements to Valia, he had seen it. The dark red light that shot up to the sky. Even from such a great distance, it was still visible by all, and the soldiers grew restless. But for him, it was a sign of relief. It proved that Borhiim had not yet gained control of the magic. He was toying with things he didn't yet understand, and that boded well for what was to come.

However, Borhiim was still an uncertainty, and Rorgan didn't much care for uncertainty. Borhiim was out of his depth, but that didn't mean he wasn't powerful. If he could harness the Devil's Flame, he could rival even a dragon in power. But to learn its secrets, he would have to make a journey . . . to the Drake. And if he were to make the trek, that would mean he was heading northeast to the Claw. To the doorway. Rorgan could have commanded Draag to follow him, but he wasn't sure if even an assassin of his caliber could survive an encounter with dragon fire. It was far too risky.

He crossed his arms and gave it a moment's thought. *Borhiim can't pass through Cleptyn territory*, he thought. *Not if he hopes to stay out of chains. And if he does go through Norvad, it will have to be . . .*

He let out a breath, feeling more settled than before. Turning, Rorgan prepared to go back into his tent. He had a letter to write and a falcon to send. Gwendall would be waking up soon anyway.

If he is traveling to the Claw, he will have to pass through the Forest of Shadows.

Chapter 20

Day nineteen of the fifth month.

T HE SUN HUNG high in the sky, but the cold remained thick in the muddied and frozen lands on Norvad's edge. Borhiim looked up as the pale orb peeked its way through thick clouds, as if trying to bring some semblance of warmth amid the steadily declining temperature.

It was spring only in name. In the north, there was only winter. There was magic in those lands, no doubt of that. The soil remained fertile from the Terrkoris the elves had left behind, no matter the weather. However, in hopes of staving off the Devil's Flame of the dragons, they had kept Norvad cold, and though their attempts had failed, the result was evident even now. So it had been since the end of the old war, and so it would be for many more generations.

Borhiim sniffed the air and felt a snowflake lightly touch his nose. He wiped it away and let out a sigh, his breath drifting like a mist as more snow started to come down. The air itself was thickening. Thicker than he remembered it being, and it felt unnatural in his lungs. He would need shelter soon. He would need to reach the forest before sundown for the sake of his steed. Not that he was worried for his own safety. For all the trouble the Devil's Flame had brought him, it kept him warm.

He walked over to his horse and brushed a hand across her mane. The valiant creature kept her head down, satisfied as she drank the cold water from the small pool before them. Letting the beast rest, Borhiim pondered his intentions. At first, he had planned to move east through the edges of Cleptyn. But the borders of the sector were barred with barbed wire fencing and armed to the teeth with soldiers of incredible strength and skill. They may not have had a wall as Verish did, but they held fast and strong. Perhaps they didn't have the numbers of Deeria, but Cleptyn soldiers were warriors through and through. Yes, they were neutral in the war, but that didn't mean they wouldn't protect their lands from invaders, especially if a Takahrn were seen traveling freely in their lands.

The only way to get to the Claw without being attacked on sight was through the Forest of Shadows. Borhiim knew this, and it worried him. The place was sick. Some would even say cursed. Over the years, some even tried to burn it down, but when the flames cleared, not a single oak tree was burned. Not a leaf fell, and not a blade of grass withered. It was undying, and none knew why.

Borhiim was not one to believe in myths and stories told in bars. Not often. Many said the forest had always been the way it was, but he knew better. It was once a proud dwelling of the elves. Along with the Green Hills of Cleptyn, it was the home of many of the ancient race long before it became the source of folktales. That was before the old war. Before the dragons. Soon after the Battle of Fate, the beasts of fire drove the survivors from their leisurely living, and the forest was abandoned. It was during the Age of Dragons that it fell to ruin, but none knew why. Not even the elves. Some said it was the Eternal, showing His wrath to the elves for leaving such a sacred place by the wayside. Others thought it to be something much darker. Much fouler.

The Shade.

Whatever had enchanted the forest, Borhiim would have to live with it and find a way to pass through. If Norvad soldiers were afraid of it, then it would be wise for him to take advantage of their fear.

The horse lifted her head and let out a loud neigh, shaking her mane. Done with her drink, she seemed unsettled by the silence.

"Easy, girl," Borhiim said, patting her on the side.

She neighed again, and Borhiim heard it: the thud of approaching hooves. He turned and saw a large group of men riding toward them, somewhere between twenty and thirty. They wore the dark purple of Norvad soldiers, and they had him in their sights.

Borhiim growled under his breath as he jumped onto his horse and rode northeast. *How did they know where I was?*

In the distance, he spotted a large, vague patch of blackness. "Superstition or not," he mumbled under the thudding of his sprinting steed, "we need to reach it."

He slapped the reins and gave a loud cry. The horse blasted onward. Glancing over his shoulder, Borhiim could see the soldiers catching up. Their mounts were fast, but it was more than that. The thickness of the air. These horses had lived in it for years, while his choked on it. Her pace was steady, but their pursuers were gaining on him. *Eternal's wrath indeed*, he thought.

The dark shape in the distance grew clearer. Row upon twisted row of gnarled oak trees and roots shot up from the snow-filled edges of the mass. The Forest of Shadows was close, along with whatever horrors lay beneath its branches. He couldn't look away from it, despite how much it disgusted him, but he couldn't look for long.

Wind shrieked in his ears as an arrow whizzed past his head, grazing the ends of his hair. He looked back and watched as one of the Norvad soldiers placed another shaft to his bowstring, getting ready to fire once more. It released, but he was ready. He grabbed the reins and his horse swayed to the left, the arrow shooting to their right.

The forest was even closer now, only minutes away.

Borhiim felt a burning sensation swell up inside of him. It licked at his veins, calling out to him. *No!* He would not risk another massacre. He swallowed hard, trying to stomach the magic that grew within, but it would not stay silent.

Another arrow sped through the air, nicking his right shoulder, but he paid it no mind. They were just moments from their goal.

The scorching power hit him hard, and he struggled with all his might to hold it in. Fear racked his brain, swiftly overcome by an increasing rage. He held in the urge to scream, but the pain in his body soon grew too much. He twisted toward his pursuers with an outstretched hand, and the Devil's Flame sprang to life. The dark fire reached out for its enemies like a lion pouncing upon its prey, and the soldiers were thrown into chaos. They scattered immediately, some darting left and right while others jumped from their steeds. When the flames were close enough, they blasted their way between the split group, searing only the sides of a few abandoned horses.

Borhiim held his breath, afraid it would combust, trying to lift his burning hand toward the clouds. It swung to his front, spraying a little into the forest before it turned upward. But the trees remained unharmed—not even the Devil's Flame holding sway in its territory.

The fire went out, and he was able to breathe again.

He had reached his destination, but his mount would not enter. She lifted her front hooves, but Borhiim urged her on. They had to go in, or they would die. With one last kick, she relented, trotting cautiously into the woodlands. All sound of the outside world instantly grew quiet. Uncomfortably quiet. Not even the chirp of a bird relieved the silence. Borhiim looked back to see if the soldiers were still trying to track him among the trees, but he couldn't see them. He couldn't see anything past the edges of trees, as if a dark fog had covered everything beyond his view, emanating from the bark of the vegetation.

There was no turning back. Not now.

Only one thing gave him relief: the sweet voice in his mind. The dim thoughts of his mate. They were weaker than they normally were, but still present. Gahlaia was still alive somewhere, and that was all he needed to keep pushing onward.

As they rode on at a slower pace, Borhiim observed his surroundings. Everything was covered with brush and dark green moss, spreading across the ground to the roots of plants like a massive, overcast shadow. It was the only living thing to be seen in the forest save for the trees. The trees themselves were the only thing not bent by the will of the moss. Though tall, they hunched, their deep brown bark tainted with shades of blood red. Gazing upward, he saw that their leaves were pitch black, huddled in clumps along their branches. Not a single ray of sunshine broke through, but whether that was due to the trees or the fog, Borhiim could not tell. Inside the forest, it might as well have been night.

The smell of the place was not entirely foreign to him, but only because he had recently been on the fields of battle. It reeked like a rotting corpse. He let out a long cough, his vision blurring. There was something more to it than the stench. It was the air. As elsewhere in Norvad, the air was thick, only ten times worse than what it had been before. The aching in his throat was even stronger. If he wasn't sure of it then, he was now. This wasn't the work of the Eternal. It was the Shade. More powerful than he had ever thought possible. But he knew how the darkness worked. He knew the ancient scriptures.

Using the powers of the Light, the Eternal brought low the influence of the Shade, cleansing reality of its hold. But pieces of the dark survived, taking form within the hatred of the living, while others took physical shape, hoping to one day return to the skies.

"The hatred of the living . . ." Borhiim pondered the words. He had never been to the Forest of Shadows before, and he doubted any other Takahrn had chosen of free will to go either. Anyone who spoke of it fearfully was scoffed at for being superstitious. Most thought it to be the work of the dragons that had changed the landscape. Now this place was a mystery to him. How had such dark powers come to take hold of such a place? It was a question he did not think he would ever get the answer to, and he was given little time to ponder it.

A series of yells came from behind. Four soldiers had chosen to follow him into the forest, all sprinting on foot. Weapons drawn, they charged at him with reckless abandon. Borhiim gave them no second glance. Snapping his reins and kicking, he urged his mount on. However, she now swayed and wobbled awkwardly, wheezing. Feeling her stagger, he jumped from her just as she began to fall to her left side, collapsing onto clumps of moss. Rolling across the uneven ground, he turned to see what had brought the beast low. Her eyes were white, and her breathing was slackening to a halt. No wounds were visible on her skin, but black veins slowly traced her hide like a spreading poison.

Within seconds, she was dead.

Panicked and confused, Borhiim grabbed at the satchel of supplies hooked on the saddle and heaved it off. The soldiers were close, and he would need food and provisions if he was going to live. But he wasn't going to die like this, running scared from other men. He stepped over the body of his fallen mount, laid the satchel aside, and pulled the elvish broadsword from his back. He squeezed the handle, and the Terrkoris of the weapon met with his own, fusing into a single swell of magic. It did not reject him. It fueled him.

Stopping only feet away, three of the soldiers pointed spears in his direction while the fourth held a strange-looking longsword in his right hand, standing with his body turned to one side. Borhiim had never seen such a blade. It was certainly not of traditional Deerium forge, nor was it elvish.

"Listen to me," Borhiim said, steadying his weapon with two hands. "This forest is cursed. If you wish to live, go back the way you came."

The man holding the sword spoke up. "You're in no position to bargain, Divider," he said. "We make the demands, and you will make your choice. Surrender, or we drag your corpse back to Zerah."

Borhiim tightened his grip on his broadsword, increasing the flow of magic. He could sustain it. His unique abilities guaranteed it. He was confident he could take the first three handily on speed and power alone, but the fourth posed a potential problem. The man's stance gave it away. He had been trained—and trained well. Borhiim, on the other hand, had spent too little time handling a weapon. He was capable with a sword, but his only advantage was the Terrkoris enhancement this one would provide. All the same, he had little choice. He needed to reach the Claw, and he was running out of time.

"Very well," he said. "May the Eternal grant you peace in death."

The first three charged, holding their spears out in front of them to keep a good distance away. The fourth soldier hung back, waiting just behind the others without getting in the way. Borhiim swung his blade horizontally and darted to the right, brushing the metal spear tips aside. Pushing off the ball of his foot, he moved away from the end of the closest spear and slashed again, this time toward flesh. The soldiers could hardly follow the Takahrn's movements. Grasping the hilt, he sliced at a nearby foe. Before they knew it, a man was down, covering a large gash in his side with both palms, letting out his final cries.

The fourth man didn't hesitate. When Borhiim appeared in a flash to his left, the soldier leaped forward, keeping both arms out, thrusting his longsword, then quickly pulling it back in defense. Borhiim blocked another stab to the chest and dragged his blade across his foe's to close the distance. The man anticipated this, pulling the weapon back before the Takahrn started his movement, giving Borhiim time to react to the unnatural speed. The man tried to push away the broadsword as the tip turned downward into a point, but the blunt end of the weapon pressed hard on his sword, crashing into his chest. Instantly his body gave way to the force inflicted, throwing him backward into a heap of moss at the root of a tree.

Borhiim moved to finish his opponent, but movement caught his eye. Spotting the other soldiers from the edge of his still dim vision, he swung wildly to give himself some space, but it wasn't enough. A spear jabbed into the bone of his right shoulder, pain running fast. But when he jumped away and the metal emerged from the flesh, the new wound healed itself in a matter of seconds. The Terrkoris served him well, and externally, his body had never felt better.

Internally, however, he did not fare well. Something was very wrong, and the more he strained himself, the worse it felt. Breathing grew harder with every inhale, turning into shards of glass in his throat. His mind turned fuzzy, and it felt harder to focus.

This feeling . . .

It reminded him of the feeling that overcame him at the Lake of Ice. It felt like Anamoris magic, only twisted somehow. Its nature was tampered with, if such a thing were truly possible. He could feel invisible fingers reaching out for his throat, slowly tightening their grip. From the expressions on the faces of the Norvad men, Borhiim could tell it was affecting them too. In truth, it appeared that it might have been draining them more than it did him. They hunched their backs, their weapons drooping to the ground in their weariness. On their necks, veins of purple and black started to trickle their way into view.

They were all going to die if things continued this way. Borhiim needed to act quickly. He would need to end things now or run. But as he prepared to rush at the soldiers again, he paused. The man he had killed moments ago was gone. The body had vanished—ruffled vegetation and dark blotches of blood serving as the only proof that it had been there at all. Even his spear was missing. The three soldiers noticed this as well, looking around in a state of panic.

"Wait," said the man with the sword, raising a hand. "Something's not right."

Borhiim turned around, and to his confusion, his horse's carcass was also gone. The only remnants were pieces of torn skin on the trampled ground. The body of a man was one thing, but a horse? That was one thousand pounds at minimum, now disappearing without a trace of drag or struggle.

"What have you done?" one of the men shouted at the Takahrn, his voice scratching harshly in his windpipe.

"This isn't me," he whispered back, twitching his head toward his left and right.

All froze. There were sounds, very faint in the distance. One second it came from the east, then the west, with only moments of pause between rustles. The slight snap of a twig, the low grumble of a branch, the scratch of something sharp on oaken bark . . . Then, for a brief second, Borhiim felt it: the presence of another soul, faded but there all the same.

At that moment, one of the spear-holding soldiers let out a shriek before being pulled into a clump of trees behind him. All turned, but by the then, whatever had attacked had successfully pulled its prey deep into the woodlands, leaving no footprints in the overgrown moss. The screaming from the terrified man continued farther and farther into the forest only to be silenced by a loud crack, like the snapping of a twig.

Silence proceeded once again, and Borhiim lost his sense of the unknown presence. For that brief time, though, pictures had flashed in his mind. This thing was no bigger than a man, but it moved too fast to give its true features away. Borhiim placed a hand to the vegetation, trying to get a read on the creature's whereabouts, but he was left with nothing. His head was only growing fuzzier, and his magic felt less available to him.

The remote sounds returned, bouncing through the trees at an even faster pace.

"We need to leave," he said. "If we move as a group, we may yet survive this."

"You think we would trust you?" the soldier with a spear asked, looking around in a panicked state.

"If you value your lives, you'll do exactly what I say!"

The man with the blade stepped forward, clenching the handle until his knuckles turned white. "Do as he says," he replied. "We're dead anyway if we do nothing."

The other soldier opened his mouth to protest but quickly shut it in terror. The forest echoed with a screeching roar, jumping bizarrely between low and high pitches. The three huddled together, weapons at the ready, staring into the foggy darkness of the gnarled branches and black leaves. It was dizzying to look at, almost drowning them in the seemingly endless sea of shadowy, murky green.

The screech ended abruptly, and they were left with a deathly quiet. No wind. No chirping or any sign of the outside world. Only the sharp inhales and exhales of breath.

Borhiim turned his head toward the soldier with the sword. "Tell me your names, mortals," he muttered.

The other man evidently didn't like being called "mortal." He gave a quick, sarcastic chuckle and clenched his spear tighter. "Why does it matter, Divider?" he retorted. "What do you want from us? Is all of this your doing then?"

"Shut your mouth, Kaash," the swordsman said sternly. "Don't say anything if you're not going to think it through first."

Kaash grunted and mumbled but kept his thoughts to himself.

Whoever this sword-bearing soldier was, he was of higher rank to be sure. He bore no three-striped mark, so he was no general. Nevertheless, his armor was slightly different from that of Kaash and the other soldiers. Purple was still its primary color, the signature Norvad tint, but the silver that normally only outlined the edges of the regular armor appeared more prominent. It glazed his shoulder plating, between his arm joints and the area that covered his stomach, fastened under the breastplate. And that sword—it was the most unusual thing of all. No, this man was in some form of command.

"Would you prefer I just call you soldiers?" Borhiim asked. "Or just men?"

"No need," the man said, keeping his gaze drifting between trees, his longsword at the ready. "My name is Jerin."

He made no introduction of lineage, as was customary. He wasn't surprised. Only moments ago, they were at each other's throats. "Jerin, Kaash," he said, "you may call me Borhiim if you wish."

"I will call you nothing!" Kaash exclaimed. "We are at war. You will—"

"I thought I told you to shut up," Jerin responded.

Borhiim turned his head toward the swordsman. He had thick,

short brown hair. A dark beard, barely longer than stubble, spread across his jawbone and chin.

"Keep your voice quiet," Borhiim said. "The moment before this . . . *thing* strikes, I can hear where it comes from. It's fast and only for a brief moment, so when I shout a direction, attack without hesitation. Do this, and we may yet live."

Kaash raised his head to make another remark, but Jerin jabbed him in the side, nodding toward the Takahrn. With those final words, it grew silent again. All cocked their heads, and Borhiim tried to get a read on what would eventually return to attack them. There was no indication of anything.

Then sound returned, bounding from ear to ear, jumping in several directions at a startling rate. A snapped twig, a slight rustle, the scratch of talons—the sounds kept going. For a moment, he even thought he saw something dart above their heads in the blackness, leaping from his left to the right, tree to tree.

Then the presence of the soul appeared again in his mind, and for those waning seconds, he had a direction.

"*In front, Jerin!*" he shouted, and just as the words left his mouth, the thing emerged from the dark, reaching for the soldier.

Jerin did not falter. Upon hearing the command, he thrust his blade forward, and it plunged deep into whatever now stood before him.

It had the body shape of a man, but its skin was pale, drained like a skeleton. At the tips of its fingers and toes were long fingernails, jagged and bent. Grey rags were barely holding onto the creature's frail-looking body. The face was distorted, and its hair was oily and long, falling to its hips.

The thing grabbed the hilt of the blade, still embedded in its stomach, and held it in place, staring at its enemy with glowing purple eyes. With the other hand, it grabbed at the back of the man's skull and leaned closer, revealing fangs underneath its dry lips.

Jerin tried to pull away, but the hand was firmly gripping his, holding the longsword in place. Whatever the being was, it was much stronger than it looked. It wasn't daunted by any attempts he made to get out of its reach.

Kaash turned and attacked, thrusting his spear deep through its upper left side.

The being still appeared unperturbed, leaning closer to Jerin, whispering in a raspy voice. "Hungry..." it croaked. "So... hungry."

The tips of its fangs pierced the skin of its victim just as Borhiim made his move. With all his might, he slid his elvish broadsword toward the thing's middle and cut sideways, throwing it back and releasing Jerin from the deathly grip. The strike would have sliced any other creature clean in half, but not this beast. It gave an ear-piercing scream when Borhiim moved forward again to strike, and they all covered their ears.

Clutching its deep wounds in its front and side, it ran out of sight, limping and whining to itself as it ran. "So...hungry!"

The sounds all died out, and the three were alone again, dark blood covering their weapons.

Jerin wiped his sword on the mossy ground, then touched his neck where the sharp teeth had left their mark, wincing. Borhiim looked at himself. The purple veins of Shade were starting to grow steadily, and the other two weren't faring much better. They needed to leave. He needed to leave. After strapping the broadsword to his back, he placed his hands on the ground, feeling for the Terrkoris. He needed to know which direction to go. It was dim, but he could feel it all the same: the other side of the forest. His way out. "I will say this only once," he said. "I'm heading northeast. If you wish to live, follow along."

Kaash shook his head. "We're not friends, Divider. You don't get to tell us where we go."

"We would be dead without him," Jerin replied. "It's clear that he won't kill us if he isn't provoked."

The soldier threw his hands up. "And you trust him over your own comrade? He's the enemy, Jerin! Our job was to bring him back to Zerah. Those orders came from Rorgan. If we don't follow them, it would be better if we were dead."

Borhiim shifted his stance in interest. *Rorgan knows where I am?* It shouldn't have been possible. The Norvad ruler would be weeks away from his location. By all accounts, there was no way Rorgan would be aware of where he was going. Unless . . .

"Tell that to the other soldiers who refused to enter this place at all!" Jerin said. "They left only four of us to take him down, and we failed. With just the two of us, do you really think we can do it?"

Kaash said nothing.

"Thought so. Right now the only thing we can do is try to survive however we can. If that means following this Divider, then so be it."

The soldier shook his head again. "You're a fool, Jerin. I'm going back. If we cross paths again, I won't waver in cutting you down like the traitor you are."

Kaash turned away and began to walk southwest.

"If you go alone," Borhiim shouted after him, "you'll lose your way. The Shade won't let you leave."

The only response that came from the man was the loud cry of an old elvish curse, and then he was gone. He pressed back the way they had come, pushing branches out of his way and leaving mossy footprints in his wake.

Jerin looked to the Takahrn in expectation, and Borhiim turned in the opposite direction. "Follow me then."

As the two paced onward for what seemed like hours, Borhiim started to grow weak. His legs felt like they might collapse and tumble like a pile of rocks. His vision flickered from blurry to clear and back every few seconds, and the farther they walked, the harder it was to tell if they were still going straight. He stopped momentarily to place a hand on the trunk of a nearby tree to sense for the direction again. They were veering a little off course but still gaining some distance. The Shade wouldn't easily loosen its grip on them— the constant headaches and blurred vision were proof of its influence.

Beside him, Jerin sheathed his blade. Then, reaching inside his breastplate, he revealed a silver necklace hanging from his neck, with a single copper piece attached to the end.

"What's that for?" Borhiim asked.

No answer came. The man just kept staring at the old coin, turning it over between his fingers, as if unaware of anything else in the world.

Borhiim quickly decided to change the subject. "That sword," he said, trying to keep his mind off the pulsating pain in his head. "I've never seen anything like it. Where did you get it?"

Jerin faced him, his face serious. "I made it," he responded before turning his attention back to the woodlands ahead.

"Made it? You're a blacksmith?"

He sighed, resting a hand on the hilt of his weapon. "I was. Forging a blade and learning how to swing it are more closely related than most people think. My father taught me everything I know. He was . . . varied in the talents he could pass down."

"Varied? What's that supposed to mean?"

"Doesn't matter."

The silence grew awkward as Borhiim studied the man's behavior. It wasn't easy to determine. One minute he was trying to cut him down, the next he was standing by Borhiim's side but giving him the cold shoulder. He understood the hatred the soldier might feel, but why come with him at all then?

"Tell me, Jerin," he probed. "Why follow me?"

"As I said already," he answered, "if it wasn't for you, I would already be dead. I'm in your debt, which I intend to repay. Besides, I can't go back with Kaash. The other men probably think I'm a traitor now, and even if they let me go with them, I have no desire to be in their company. They were cowards not to follow us into the forest. I don't stand with cowards."

Borhiim raised his eyebrows. "How blunt of you."

"Blunt or not, it's the truth. To lead with fear is to lead to death, and I don't intend on dying anytime soon."

His gaze drifted toward the soldier. "What's so important that you refuse to die?"

"Isn't it enough for me to be afraid of death?"

"Perhaps, but you just said that to be afraid is to die. There has to be another reason."

"Maybe there is, but it wouldn't mean anything to you."

Jerin stopped walking, and Borhiim turned to face him. He looked dreary and pale. The skin on his neck where the monster had bitten him had grown purple and black, as if diseased.

"I'm not here to chat with you like old war friends," Jerin said. "Just lead us out of this place, and we can go our separate—"

Before Jerin could finish his statement, his head recoiled, and his right eyelid twitched uncontrollably. He winced, putting a hand to his neck. Then he dropped to his knees, his eyes fogging up like breath on a windows, and fell backward.

Borhiim rushed forward and shook him, the man's body almost completely limp. "Jerin? Jerin!"

No response.

Chapter 21

Day twenty of the fifth month.

FAR TO THE east, atop a peak of the Gorrobin Mountains, Raggorin was escorted toward the prime village of his tribe. Goirah it was called, the centerpiece that united all the tribes. It had been over a week since Queen Ahmeras had sent him into Cleptyn territory to negotiate, and now he was closer than they ever had been before. He knew that if he swayed the Gorrobin tribes, Zinnyah would follow. He was prepared to do what was necessary, perhaps more than anyone could have thought. For his king, and for his people, he would do it.

Two Cleptyn soldiers, fashioned in silver and green armor, walked behind him, escorting him forward. Despite being a Cleptyn citizen himself, Raggorin was not welcome in Gorrobin territory or anywhere in the sector, for that matter. Not since the coronation. He looked around, breathing in the sweet mountain air of what had once been his home. Even with the specially made metals that the Cleptyn soldiers wore, they shivered in their boots, but the cold meant nothing to him. These mountains were his solitude. He was bred on them, the small amounts of magic that remained in his people keeping him warm even through the harshest blizzards. The whole mountain peak was covered in thick snow, with wooden huts jutting out of white mounds. The tribes of the Gorrobin always preferred simple living over the fanciful palaces of the sector capitals, and it suited them well.

As Raggorin and the two figures behind him walked on in the deep slush, doors began to open, and people started trailing behind in large numbers. They all knew who he was, and a few even looked at him with momentary excitement before their faces turned grave. None of them spoke, eager to see what was about to happen. Only the harsh winds and constant crunch of feet digging into the snow filled the stillness.

The two soldiers stopped, and Raggorin looked up at a stone mansion three times the size of all the other buildings. Unlike the wooden houses of the village, it was carved in ancient times, continually increasing in size as subsequent tenants added to it. The mansion was as he remembered it when he had left, only larger and grander. Before the door, a long slab of stone paved the way for several hundred feet. It expanded into a space that was big enough for at least a hundred people. Etched into its middle was a twenty-foot circle, the symbol of two deer antlers at the center. It was the sign of the Lord Gorrobin, leader of all tribes in the mountains.

The men led him up the narrow steps and onto the porch. Just under the portico, standing in front of the big door to the manor, two figures watched him with blank expressions. To the left was Zinnyah, ruler of Cleptyn. She was dressed in her usual battle armor, leaning on a tall battle-ax. The greens of the dragon scales shone under her silver breastplate, serving as her protection if the situation were to get out of hand. However, she wore no helmet, allowing her red hair to flow behind her. Seeing her was relief enough. It meant she had received his letter and was at least willing to hear him speak.

To the right was someone he was all too familiar with: Yaruk, the Lord Gorrobin. His attire was almost identical to Raggorin's and the rest of the villagers': a long piece of cloth slung over his right shoulder and down under the armpit of the other. He wore only one sleeve, leaving his left arm bare, showing the clear indents of his musculature. A golden band circled his wrist, the symbol of the antlers marked in black. His long hair and beard were light grey, the only indication of his old age. Yaruk was a big man, stronger than even Zinnyah. She may have had the upper hand with weaponry, but in sheer might, no one was his equal. He had been the Lord Gorrobin for many decades, even longer than King Hyrehn's rule, and made it clear he intended to stay as such for many years more.

Not if Raggorin had anything to say about it.

He had always hated Yaruk, and he suspected the man hated him too. Being a leader in the mountains gave him far too much power. He may not have been Zinnyah's advisor, but he held a lot of sway in her decisions, and his view of things was . . . twisted, to say the least. The Cleptyn ruler was still young, youngest of all three sector rulers, and many of Yaruk's ideas influenced her too easily. Raggorin had disagreed with Yaruk at almost every turn, on many occasions coming close to blows. He suspected Yaruk had sent him specifically to be an advisor in Deeria just to get him out of the way, and it had worked. *But not today*, he thought. *Not anymore.*

The two soldiers stopped, and Ragorrin stepped forward into the circle of stone. "Ruler Zinnyah!" he shouted for the whole crowd to hear. "I come to you on behalf of King Tirehn and Queen Ahmeras to negotiate an alliance."

"There is nothing to negotiate, Raggorin," she replied, lifting her ax over her shoulder. "I have already given you my terms. I won't risk the lives of my sector on a foolish war."

"And what of the Takahrn? Are you not putting them at risk?"

Yaruk stepped forward, his expression the same hard sneer Raggorin had come to know. "What do the Dividers have to do with this war? We are talking about human lives."

"They have everything to do with it!" he exclaimed, but catching the anger in his mouth, Raggorin swallowed, breathed deeply, then continued. "The Takahrn are still enslaved here within your borders. That is the very reason this war was started in the first place."

Zinnyah opened her mouth to respond, but Yaruk beat her to it. "And why should that matter? They have done nothing but plunder and attack us at every turn. That is why they were enslaved in the first place. Deerium would be running with our blood if we set them free."

"You know that's not true," Raggorin said, directing his gaze to Zinnyah. "You were there when we read the old writings of King Graan. You know what he did. The Takahrn were falsely accused."

Yaruk took a step forward. "And what proof do you have that those were indeed Graan's words?"

"King Tirehn found the scroll in his father's coffin, with Graan's seal. Why would he take them to his grave if he wasn't trying to hide—"

"As I recall, Hyrehn's coffin was never to be opened. Why is it that a prince was allowed passage into a place that was treasonous to enter?"

"He is your king, Yaruk!" Raggorin said, pointing a finger in disgust. "That prince is now your king, and you all betrayed him when he sought the truth of the Takahrn's abuse."

"Betrayed? That king you speak of has fabricated evidence for his own gain. He seeks nothing more than to take power from the other sectors and lead without supervision."

At that, Ragorrin snapped. He wouldn't take insults from a snake like Yaruk. "Don't talk to me about taking power! I've been around long enough to know where your allegiance lies, Lord Gorrobin. You aren't defending your people from the Takahrn. You're afraid of losing your rank, of being taken down from that throne you've built for yourself, just like King Graan once was!"

Yaruk took another step forward. "I stand for Cleptyn! For

Deerium! I have built no throne. I live only to serve our people as I always have!"

"Have you? Look around! The Gorrobin have always been about living on the bare minimum. That has always been our way. Yet here you stand, living in a mansion like you rule the world!"

"How dare you speak to me in such a way!"

"*Silence!*" Zinnyah boomed, pressing her hand to Yaruk's chest.

He flashed a glare of momentary anger in her direction, and when she met it, he bowed his head and regained his composure.

"I'm afraid your long journey has been in vain," she said, facing Raggorin. "I stand with the Lord Gorrobin on this. I cannot go to war without the full support of the Gorrobin, and I cannot release the Takahrn."

He shook his head. "You must understand, my lady. If the Takahrn are not released, then Tirehn has already lost. It is impossible to remain neutral in this situation. If they are not set free, then you take your side with Norvad and Verish."

At this, she hesitated. "My statement still stands. Cleptyn will not align with Deeria."

Raggorin let out a sigh. He had a feeling it would come to this. The only people at this point with a swaying voice were Zinnyah's advisor and the Lord Gorrobin. If he was going to try to reason with her . . . *There's no other way.*

He walked back outside the circle and held up a hand. "Very well, Ruler Zinnyah. If you stand with the Lord Gorrobin, then allow me to invoke an old tradition of my people."

He paused, and the crowds around them began to murmur in confusion, Yaruk's face immediately turned red as the words slipped from Raggorin's lips.

"I call for a Rebranding."

At this, the people went into a frenzy, shouting their views in a deafening and abrupt uproar of voices, Zinnyah and Yaruk looking taken aback by the demand.

A Rebranding was both a form of ceremony and a hand-to-hand battle to the death. To invoke one was to insult the current leadership of the Gorrobin in every way and lay their life on the line in the circle. For the people of the mountains, strength led above all else, and such was how the ceremony would decide the victor. Yaruk had challenged the previous Lord Gorrobin when he was barely a man, at least fifty years ago. Few Rebrandings had taken place at all in their history before then. It was not a custom that everyone looked well upon. But Raggorin needed to convince Cleptyn to align with Deeria, or all would be lost. Everything they had worked for, snuffed out in an instant.

"You are no longer of the Gorrobin!" Yaruk yelled, silencing the masses with his commanding tone. "Your allegiance is not with the people. You cannot call for a Rebranding."

Many in the crowd nodded and mumbled in agreement with the rebuttal.

"I have just as much right as any of you."

"No! You are the king's advisor. You cannot hold such a position and claim leadership of these mountains."

In response, Raggorin unsheathed the knife strapped to his right leg and held it up in the air. Pressing the cold metal to his left palm, he slid it quickly across the skin. He spun around slowly, showing the bloodied hand to all who could see him. "May you all bear witness," he said firmly. "I hereby renounce my title as an advisor and voice of the king. Any actions I now take are my own."

He faced Yaruk once more and closed his fingers into a fist, letting the red liquid drop to the stone floor. "My blood is of the tribes. So it has always been. By the right of my lineage, I declare you inadequate to lead our people. To deny my demand is to willingly forfeit your title as the Lord Gorrobin."

Silence. All eyes had turned to Yaruk, and he nearly buckled under the weight of their burning stares. Grunting, he turned Zinnyah. "Permit me, my lady."

"Very well," she replied. "If this is your way of resolving this conflict once and for all, then so be it."

A smile cracked on his face as he moved forward to the edge of the large circle. He unsheathed his own knife and slit the flesh of his left hand, holding it up high. "I accept your demand, Raggorin," he said. "May the Eternal make known His will."

The crowds made no cheer in reply. Instead, they started to slowly clap their hands and stamp their feet, the sound steadily growing in unison and volume. Even the wind seemed to slow to the beat of the sound.

Raggorin and Yaruk both placed their left hands on the edge of the circle, leaving handprints of blood, signifying their dedication to the task. The Rebranding was about to begin.

The sound grew louder. *Boom . . . Boom . . . Boom.*

They laid their knives aside, pulled off the blades strapped to their backs, and placed them outside the circle.

Boom! Boom! Boom!

They stepped into the ring, free of any weapons, and stood over the bloody prints they had made.

BOOM! BOOM! BOOM!

Yaruk held up a hand, and everyone went quiet. He was breathing hard, his features twisted into a fit of rage. "This is your last chance!" he barked. "If you submit to me now, I will make your death quick and painless."

Raggorin took a ready stance. "Death comes for us all. Mine won't be at your hand. Not now. Not ever."

"Always one for the bold words. Why am I not surprised."

Ragorrin raised his fists, smirking. "I learned that from you. You're a viper, Yaruk. You poison the minds of those you get close to and bite off the heads of any who stand in your way."

Yaruk had heard enough. He clenched his hands into fists and inhaled. "*Begin!*" he cried.

BOOM!

With that last sound from the crowds, the two began to circle each other slowly, each waiting for the other to make a move.

Raggorin knew he was at a disadvantage. Among regular men, he was much stronger than most, towering over them. But Yaruk was not like most men. He was almost seven feet tall, with a body larger and stronger than any he had ever seen. It was almost inhuman. One solid blow in the right place, and it could be over for Ragorrin in mere moments.

However, Yaruk still had a skull like everyone else, and breakable bones. Strong, yes, but still breakable. If Raggorin were to succeed, he would need to outspeed him and strike only when he needed to. He would have to trust in his stamina and his skills with his feet. But such a thing had always come naturally to him. He had trained Tirehn in the sword, along with many others. He knew how to move swiftly.

Yaruk steadily approached. Making his first move, he threw a fist toward the left side of Raggorin's head at blitzing speed. Raggorin shuffled his feet and brushed the strike away with the back of his wrist, moving to the right. He was quick, but not quick enough. Another fist dug into his left side, causing an audible crack as it shattered one of his ribs. All air escaped from his lungs as he grimaced at the instant pain that struck him, but he kept moving. Twisting his feet and bringing his right arm up, he crashed a blow hard into Yaruk's jaw, giving himself a moment to regain his breath. His hand ached from the attack, but it did its job all the same.

His opponent didn't give him much time, reaching out to take another swing, but Ragorrin kept stepping back and avoiding them as they came. Yaruk roared, rushing at Raggorin with a fury and kicking wildly as the enemy moved continuously out of reach. Soon, Raggorin was once again at the edge of the circle with nowhere to run. Another kick came toward him, landing on the side of his knee. He felt the leg twist as pain shot up his body and he collapsed.

Yaruk stood over him, radiating confidence, looming above his bent enemy as if he had already won. His lips curled up behind his grey beard, and he reached to grab his weakened opponent by the throat to end it. He never got the chance.

With his good leg, Raggorin swiftly pressed up to his feet. He reached and pulled the ends of the beard above, yanking Yaruk's face directly into his own forehead. The large man staggered back for a moment, his nose broken and bloodied, leaving him in a momentary daze.

Raggorin shook himself, trying to kill the headache now permeating his thoughts and focus. He charged toward his foe, preparing to meet him head-on, limping and jumping on one foot. Now was his chance, possibly his only chance. A punch brushed across his cheek, staggering him a bit, yet he still moved forward. Yaruk was more out of it than he was, and that was all he needed. A second fist blasted toward his face, and Raggorin moved just barely away from its range, sliding himself close enough to avoid any powerful blows. He was inches from his opponent.

Yaruk grunted, throwing a knee into Raggorin's groin. The agony was excruciating, almost enough to bring him to his knees, but it fueled his anger enough to press him on. His enemy was in close range now. Close enough to reach. Grabbing a handful of grey hair from the back of Yaruk's head in front of him, pressing his left hand on his enemy's chest, and placing his good leg behind himself, he pulled as hard as he could.

The crowd gasped as Yaruk's massive body smashed into the ground, the back of his skull slamming into the stone floor. He shrieked, but Raggorin was already on top of him, silencing his outbursts with strike after strike from his fists. He kept swinging until Yaruk's face was bloodied and purple with bruises and broken bones. His hands cried out for him to stop, but he didn't care. The adrenaline left him thinking about only one thing and nothing else.

The wind grew quiet. Not a single soul watching the scene playing out before them made a sound. There were no words for what they now beheld. At least half of them had never witnessed a Rebranding ceremony before, and it had truly lived up to its reputation. It was a battle of strength and skill, using whatever means necessary.

Raggorin had borne all Yaruk had to offer, and still, he was the one on top. He gave another punch to the pulped features that had once resembled a face and then hesitated. He stared at his defeated foe and recoiled. This was the moment. The final moment. He drank it in.

Yaruk spat up blood and laughed. "Do it ..." he said, choking and coughing, his voice rough and scratchy. "The people ... must bear witness."

Raggorin still held his fist high, frozen in the air.

Both men and women shouted among the masses, calling out for him to end it. There was no other way it was done. A Rebranding was always a battle to the death. Always.

"You see?" Yaruk continued. "You must kill me ... or die yourself. Only—" he coughed again. "Only one of us may leave this circle alive. It is ... our law. You knew that."

Raggorin still waited. This man had turned his people against him. Against the world. He knew even then he should feel remorse for what would follow, but none came. *This is* my *home.*

He growled under his breath and placed a hand beneath Yaruk's chin, lifting his other fist higher up.

"For my king. For my people. *For my home!*"

He brought his fist was down hard, then again, and again. He clasped both hands together and smashed them into the skull of his prey like an iron hammer. Bones cracked and shattered, and some looked away as the sound broke the quiet of the mountain peak.

Yaruk was no more.

Raggorin breathed unevenly as he heaved himself up over the corpse. The adrenaline began to leave him, replaced with the unbearable aches all over his body. His head, legs, face, hands, groin—they all screamed pain. Reaching down, he unlatched the golden band that clung to the left wrist of the corpse and placed it on his own. It was his by right as was the title that came with it.

Zinnyah's face was white with shock, but she kept her composure. Before her stood the new leader of the mountains, the Lord Gorrobin.

"Now," Raggorin said, limping forward, "may I speak with you in private, my lady?"

Chapter 22

Day twenty-one of the fifth month.

BORHIIM AWOKE, A cold sweat across his brow. *Another nightmare.* Since the battle at the border, it was all that came to him whenever he closed his eyes, and it was always the same one. Piles of dead bodies, with blurred and unclear faces, all thrown on top of each other in a hill of corpses, with him standing above them, watching as more fell at his feet . . . by his hand. Every time he drifted into sleep, the pile would grow until there was no one left for him to strike down.

And those eyes. Those six reptilian eyes always stared back at him.

Taking a deep breath, he wiped the sweat away and prepared for them to move on once more. His head was starting to hurt again, but he didn't mind it as much anymore. It was better than reliving his dreams. Right now, the reality in front of him felt less savage. Looking around, Borhiim squinted to try and regain his vision. It cleared slightly, and his memory of the hours prior came back to him.

Among the endless trees and identical scenery, he had stumbled upon a cluster of stone ruins. Perhaps it was even a temple in a time long past. Rows of twisted and jagged pillars made what could have been an entrance once, with two crumbling statues standing in the center of a large room that had lost its roof years ago to war or wear, black and red branches creeping in from above. That was all he had seen before drifting off to sleep. When survival was at the forefront, not much else mattered at the moment.

He leaned forward and felt Jerin's neck. It still looked veiny and grotesque, but there was a pulse underneath. He was alive, after all that had happened, but not by much. While Borhiim had carried him, Jerin had slumped motionless over his shoulder. For a while, he thought the man was dead. He hadn't moved or emerged from his unconsciousness since his collapse earlier. If they didn't get out of the forest within the hour, it was likely that Jerin wouldn't make it, and his own strength was already waning.

Borhiim stood up with a grunt, his legs cracking and aching under his weight, and reached for his broadsword. Clenching the hilt, he felt the Terrkoris surge into his body, giving him strength once more. His muscles tightened and clenched back into position, returning his stamina. His head and eyelids still ached, but at least he could make the journey a little less painful for himself.

Borhiim reached into his satchel, pulled out a slice of hardened bread, and nibbled on the crust. It tasted like salt and ash in his mouth. Everything did since they had come to this place, but it did its job. After strapping his blade onto his back again, he wrapped his satchel tight across his chest. He shoved the bread down his throat and wiped the crumbs from his lips. It would be time to get moving again soon, but first, he wanted to take a closer look at where they were.

He was rather lucky to have found an empty dwelling within a dark and cursed forest that appeared to go on forever. It was almost odd. The ruins themselves felt out of place, but he wasn't about to complain. Feeling his way farther inside to what appeared to be the main room, he came face to face with two sculptures. They were tall, over ten feet high. Both were made of slick marble, one white and the other black. They were both human in shape, but their ears were pointed like an elf's. The one on the left looked female from what was left of it, white and dazzling. Her hair stretched down to her feet, braided back behind her head. She bore no expression, looking straight toward the entrance to greet anyone who entered. In her left hand she clasped a long grapevine, and a sickle in her right.

The statue on the right side was a male, dark and brooding, his face bent down. He wore a thick cloak with the hood pulled back, revealing his bald, scarred head. In his right hand he also held a sickle, his left index finger pointed straight down.

Borhiim had seen these statues elsewhere, in some older temples in the Green Hills of Cleptyn and on the howling cliffs at the World's Edge. They were named Viiroram and Mortoram by the Righteous Ones thousands of years ago, long before the Takahrn's time. They represented Life and Death, Light and Dark, working together in harmony.

Instead of gods that watched over the people, the Righteous Ones said that the souls of the pure formed both beings, beginning life in the physical world, moving to the afterlife, and then returning as new creations, purged of all sins of their past lives. The Righteous Ones themselves claimed to be the first elves to complete the cycle of death and reincarnation. It was a clever and well thought-out religion . . . but a lie all the same. That is all it had ever been: a ploy to put them on top.

Borhiim stumbled through the rubble past the statues, turning his attention to a small stone that stood knee-high. Carved on the cracked surface were words written in elvish: "To sow righteousness is to reap purity. To sow purity is to be purged into perfection." An old, forgotten saying from an old, forgotten cult. Still, he recoiled at the saying. They sounded a lot like the words of the Wrath Reaper, keeper of the Shade. Ironic that the beliefs of a religion seeking purity would parallel a false god from ages past.

As he put a hand to the words, the fractured face crumbled away and fell to the floor. Underneath were more carved phrases and symbols, but much older, hardly visible in the darkness. They read, "May the Light of the Eternal shine upon us. In the presence of our Maker, the Shade will hold no sway." This one Borhiim recognized immediately. It was a proverb that his father used to say in prayer. *But the words had been covered up*, he thought. *Covered by the sayings of the Righteous Ones.* He shook his head. "Why am I not surprised?" he said aloud.

He turned on his heels to head back to Jerin but something to his left caught his eye. Despite the darkness surrounding him, he could make out a wooden door. It hung open, barely attached to its hinges, the entrance even darker than everything else. Borhiim stared in bewilderment, for the longer he gazed, the more his head began to spin with something peculiar: faint whispers, words he had never heard before. The hairs on the back of his neck stood up as the strange sound continued to swirl in his eardrums, scratching at his skull. He had half a mind to leave the room and move on, but his curiosity got the better of him.

He stepped toward the opening.

As he walked into the room, the shadows steadily faded away, revealing the interior. To Borhiim's disappointment, the room was empty save for markings on the stone floor. They were not carvings like the words outside, but instead painted on the ground in black ink. *No.* Not ink. Dried blood. As he leaned over them, the whispers in his mind grew louder. The markings were not in a language he had ever seen, but they looked draconic. Unlike the symbols of the elf tongue, they were letters strung into words and sentences he couldn't translate. They were far too old, perhaps dating back from even before the war of the first age. Reaching out, he held a hand over one of the words and felt the groove of the letter.

Instantly, his sight flashed black and white. Borhiim recoiled, shaking his index finger as if he had burned it, and for a moment, he thought he saw a figure standing on the other side of the room. The being was dark, flickering out of existence like a shadow and then coming back into view. It stood behind the written sentences with its arms stretched upward, speaking in an unknown tongue, its voice matching the whispers in Borhiim's head word for word.

He didn't need to clearly see the being to know who it was. Tarubas: the Faded Dragon himself.

At his feet, just to the left of the bloodied phrases, another figure flared quickly into view. It was the body of a man, who was groaning his dying pleas. Borhiim looked upon the face. *Rorgan.*

The individual standing above finished its words, now more of a shout than a whisper, and Rorgan grew skeletal and deformed. His nails grew jagged, and his teeth turned to fangs in his mouth. The creature rose to its feet, no longer begging for its life, but instead mumbling to itself. "Hungry . . ." it said as it ran out of view. "So . . . hungry."

Borhiim stood petrified as Tarubas, lowering his arms to his sides, stepped closer, only inches away. His face was thin, with long, silver hair that fell down his back, unkempt and greasy. Then slowly, his features began to change, until he was a completely different person: a human male. Borhiim's eyes widened as the realization smacked him across the face. It was Rorgan, the ruler of Norvad—at least that is what he appeared to be. Tarubas had taken on the identity of Rorgan. A false identity.

At that moment, as swiftly as it had appeared, the scene vanished, and Borhiim was alone in the dark room. He tried to process all that had happened, but his head wouldn't stop aching. And the whispers . . . They wouldn't stop repeating over and over.

Borhiim now understood. The creature that was chasing

them . . . *that* was the real Rorgan. The person ruling Norvad had been the Faded Dragon all this time. That's why the forest had become so sick. He had been playing with the Shade. Harnessing it. Using it. If the Faded Dragon had truly been working behind the scenes for centuries as Tirehn had said, Borhiim could only imagine the numerous forms he had taken and the people he had toyed with in order to take their place. And the forest was guarded by the very people he had replaced, left in their tortured state.

A voice screamed from outside, somewhere on the outskirts of the ruins.

Borhiim sprinted out the way he came. Another scream pierced the air. It was Jerin, awake and in a panicked state. Any skin visible beyond his armor was covered with black and purple lines. He was standing, spinning to look all around, but whatever he perceived only scared him more.

Borhiim grabbed the screaming man by the shoulders and shook him. Jerin's eyes were completely glazed over, as they had been since he had gone unconscious, but now the dark veins that swelled in the wound at his neck had spread to his face.

"Jerin!" Borhiim cried. "*Jerin!*"

The soldier quieted at the sound of another voice. "Borhiim?" he asked. "Is that you?"

"Of course it's me. Listen, we need to leave. Right now. You're getting worse, and I don't know how much longer you've got."

He grunted under his breath. He had been a fool. Why did he wait so long to leave? Why did he spend so much time in the temple? Now, because of his carelessness, another person's life was in danger.

Leaning down, Borhiim hauled the man over his shoulder like a sack of potatoes. He stepped out of the ruins and placed a hand to the trunk of a nearby tree, feeling for his sense of direction. The Terrkoris was even fainter than last time, but it gave him a direction.

Turning, he ran northeast.

"I can't see," Jerin said, bouncing up and down on his shoulder. "Borhiim . . . I'm blind!"

Hours flew by as Borhiim sprinted in his dedicated direction. He stopped only to make sure he was going the right way or to grasp the hilt of his elvish blade and rejuvenate himself. The noises in his head wouldn't stop. The whispers from the ruins, the screams of the dead, the vision in the dark room—they constantly fought inside him until they blended into chaos. Even the sweet, faint voice of Gahlaia, his newly rediscovered mate, faded into the background of his mind under the immense pressure. *Please make it end. I just want it all to end.*

He stopped again. The air was getting harder to breathe once more, making his throat swell. Jerin had grown silent on his back, but he didn't have time to check for a heartbeat. He needed to save him. He needed to save all of them. His palm touched the gnarled bark, and his course appeared for him. They weren't far from the edge of the trees. They were almost out. The thought made his heart race with excitement. He had grown very tired of the forest and the pain it brought with it.

He pressed onward, but from behind Borhiim heard a dim rustling. A snap of a twig maybe. *No. Not now.*

The sound grew louder behind him, like something bounding from tree to tree, and it was gaining on them. *No, no, no, no!*

Borhiim could almost taste freedom in the distance. He could feel it. They were so close, but so was the creature bounding closer through the woodlands. It all came down to which he would meet first. He felt the dusky fire swell in his core. It burned with his frustration. *Maybe . . . maybe just this once.* The Devil's Flame surged to his fingertips as he pointed them behind himself, but as it prepared to come forth, Borhiim pulled it back. He told himself he wouldn't use it. It wouldn't do him much good now, only make things worse. It always did.

He composed himself as best he could, keeping at a running pace, and he felt the fire dim within him. It was contained—at least for now. Turning his head to one side, he glimpsed the thing coming toward them. It was the creature that had attacked them earlier. He was almost certain of it. It came into view yet again, crouching on a branch, pausing in preparation. Then suddenly, at the edge of his vision, he saw it pounce forward, claws outstretched and mouth opened wide.

Borhiim leaped straight ahead as fast as he possibly could, Jerin's motionless body flying from his shoulder. As they both passed a final row of trees, the tips of the beast's outstretched hands fell just out of reach.

Light flashed and stung Borhiim's eyes as they landed on wet ground. He covered his eyes, trying to allow them to adjust to the brightness that shone all around him. Then, lowering his hands slowly, he blinked. They were surrounded by grassy plains covered in melting ice and snow. In the far north, he could see the Frigid Pass. They had made it out.

His headache began to clear, and his eyesight sharpened again as if a storm cloud had been lifted from his gaze. But the whispers were still there, groping at the edges of his mind, clinging for all they were worth.

Borhiim stood up and attended to Jerin, who was starting to groan and roll around in the damp grass. The dark tints on his neck, face, and body began to dissipate, and when he lifted his lids, his eyes could be clearly seen. They were green. Bright green. Borhiim hadn't noticed in the darkness of the forest.

"What . . ." the man said. "What happened? Where am I?"

"It's okay," said Borhiim. "We made it out. Thank the Eternal, we made it out."

Borhiim had never been so happy to see the sun in his life, and even with the chill temperature and cloudy skies, he still found himself basking in the rays that burst through. He would never take the daylight for granted ever again.

A low-pitched screech broke his daze, and he spun around. From the edges of the forest, just past the roots of the trees, the creature that had chased them to the edge had found its way out, dragging itself in the mud by its arms.

Jerin stood up and unsheathed his longsword at the sight of it, moving much more easily than he had previously.

Scars covered the creature's whole body, including one at its side and two on its front where Borhiim and Jerin had struck it earlier. Its eyes were bright purple, darting back and forth, never focusing long on any one thing. Borhiim couldn't tell if this thing was Rorgan or one of the others Tarubas had taken the place of over the years. It was sad and disturbing to behold, as it crawled its way toward them, mumbling the same words repeatedly. "Hungry. Always . . . hungry. So . . . hungry."

"What is it?" Jerin asked, pointing his blade toward its head.

"It's a man," Borhiim answered. "Or at least it once was."

"Well, what's it doing in a place like this?"

"I think . . ." He considered his reply. The vision he had seen in the ruins sped to the forefront of his mind. "I think it was put here. Something like this doesn't happen by accident. This . . . thing was put on guard. To protect this place."

Borhiim pulled the broadsword from his back. Stepping up to the abomination groping at his feet, he raised his blade and brought it down swiftly, releasing its head from its shoulders. The raspy mumblings ceased midsentence. There was nothing else to be done except to put it out of its misery.

"Jerin," he said, turning his attention to the soldier, "how did you and your men know I was here? How did they know where to look?"

He shrugged. "We received orders from Rorgan that a rogue Takahrn had been tracked to the eastern side of the border. I was tasked to lead one of the five parties sent to search for you. The others are probably still out there."

Borhiim shook his head. "But isn't Rorgan moving south with reinforcements?"

"I believe so."

That was all the confirmation he needed. "Tarubas."

"What?" Jerin asked.

"Tirehn said that Tarubas was getting his information from the inside, but if he was already in the king's council, then he could get his information directly. We know that Tarubas escaped the Waters of the Righteous using Anamoris magic, and to change a mortal into a creature like that . . . To do what he did . . . The Shade. He's using the Shade."

Jerin put his hands to his temples, looking only more confused by the reply. "I'm sorry, what? What are you talking about?"

"Doesn't matter," Borhiim responded. "You're free now. Go back to wherever you came from. I trust you can find your way back to a village from here?"

"Perhaps, but then what? If I left without you, I would be banned a traitor, and my—" he stopped himself, feeling for something inside his breastplate. "I can't go back. Not now. Besides, you've saved my life at least twice now. I'm further in your debt, and I never leave anything unpaid."

Borhiim raised his arms. "Right now, your debts mean very little. You can't come with me. Where I'm going, you'll only slow me down, and for all I know, you could go behind my back and get me into more trouble than I already am."

"Didn't you hear me? Why would I betray you if it would get me thrown into prison, or worse? Plus, if you want to avoid going through the Frigid Pass, you'll need someone to escort you. Someone dressed in Norvad armor so as not to draw attention."

Borhiim sighed harshly. The last thing he wanted was a straggler, but he was being given little choice. Jerin knew a faster route, which was something he sorely needed after the delay the Forest of Shadows had presented.

"What you think matters little," Jerin said. "I'll still follow you even if you won't let me travel with you. I have nowhere else to go. You either kill me right here, or you let me come along."

"Fine," Borhiim replied grudgingly.

"Good. Where are we headed?"

"The Claw. Lead the way."

GAHLAIA CONTINUED AT the pace of the rest of the army, squinting in deep contemplation. Borhiim's thoughts had grown faint in her head over the last few days and then suddenly spiked back up again. It concerned her not knowing what was happening.

"Where is he?" Tirehn asked, tapping her on the shoulder. "Has he made it through the forest?"

"I think so," she said. "His voice just got much clearer. I can almost understand his words."

"What's he saying?"

Gahlaia raised a firm hand. She swore that sometimes Tirehn acted like a king and other times a child. But that wasn't much of a surprise. He was still very young. Several minutes passed between the two in silence. Then she lifted her head and faced the king.

"I don't believe it."

"What is it?" he asked. "Is he alright?"

"He's fine, but . . ."

Tirehn stared at her expectantly, waiting for her to give her reply.

"It's Rorgan," she whispered.

Part Three
For Truth

Chapter 23

Day twenty-two of the fifth month.

DAWN HAD ONLY just broken over the far eastern mountains, and yet, despite the quiet that still spread over most of Deerium, Valia was wide awake. Its walls were under siege.

Ahmeras strode swiftly across the battlements protecting the capital city. She ducked low as another volley of arrows soared over her and into the streets within. "Curse you, Arinay," she groaned to herself.

The Verish army had shown up at the front gates the day prior and had been slamming their battering ram and firing showers of arrows into the city all through the night. It had been a nightmare, to say the least, but that wasn't what scared Ahmeras the most. The main portion of Deeria's army had been split between the north and south, and while the northern portion had succeeded temporarily, she had been told that they were on the retreat. The southern portion was even worse. Verish had completely decimated their militia, and without it, Valia had little hope of fighting back.

For now, the city held. The front gates were massive and thickly overlaid with steel. No battering rams would break through, not even if they rammed it for weeks on end. It was true that Valia couldn't strike back with its current numbers, but they weren't in too much danger either. The walls were almost as impenetrable as the Southern Border. Almost.

Even with all this in mind, Ahmeras couldn't help but be unsure of their situation. She knew the Verish army's capabilities. It had protected their borders for generations, and for the level of regard they were given, the force shown here didn't match up. Something was not right.

She looked out over the wall and into the open field that sprawled southward. The groups of soldiers stood in rows and lines that formed massive rectangles of metal and weaponry. The front was led by a group of cavalries, with the archers stationed behind. At the back lay carts and small wagons, filled to the brim with provisions and supplies. Any stragglers at the head were sent to the front gate to hammer at the door with a large ram made of both wood and steel, ducking as Valia struck down with rocks and arrows from above. So far, they had little success at even budging the iron bolts holding the doors together on the inside.

Still, Anahka's letter had said that the force that had taken them down had been enormous, beyond count. That was the strength that Verish held: they had numbers in spades. What made them weaker was that it was normally spread across their long borders. But if the letter was correct, Arinay had united her militia under one attack, and while the army before them looked impressive, it wasn't as big as she had expected. Ahmeras had been to Verish long ago. She had seen what they could do with her own eyes. This was only the first wave. She was sure of it, and whatever was coming next would decide the fate of the entire kingdom.

At last, she reached the front portion of the wall. Keeping herself hunched low, she addressed one of the officers. "Commander Teriul."

The soldier faced her with his whole body, clicking his heels together as a form of salute. "Queen Ahmeras!" he replied in a booming voice. "Apologies. I wasn't aware of your arrival."

"It's fine. Update me on the situation."

His face turned grave at her request. "Things remain mostly unchanged, my lady. At this rate, we can hold the gates, but with Verish at the entrance, all provisions outside the city have been completely cut off. Boxed in like this, we could starve if this goes on for too long."

"At this point, that concerns me the least. We're months away from getting there, and Verish is running on limited supplies as well."

"Of course. But . . ." His expression remained concerned as he turned to look at the armies outside.

Ahmeras leaned in closer. "You see it, don't you?" she asked.

He nodded grimly. "Their numbers are too small. There must be more coming. For them to launch a full-scale attack with their current forces . . . It would be suicide. Our southern troops wouldn't have been defeated so handily by this amount."

Another bang from below rang out, but the gates stood sturdy.

Slowly lifting herself to ensure no more volleys were being fired, Ahmeras peeked over the wall. There were at least thirty men down below, pulling the battering ram back and steadily slamming it into the doors.

She grunted. "Commander," she said, keeping her gaze on the scene, "Arinay leads their army, is that correct?"

"Of course, my lady," Teriul responded. "She heads up the cavalry."

Ahmeras looked out toward the front lines of horses. In the dead center, difficult for anyone other than an elf to see, a woman was heading up the masses. Arinay wore white armor with a spike on her left shoulder. Her helmet was slick, curving down and pointing in the back. It wasn't too different from the design of the elvish armor of old. Her curly blonde hair had been cut, barely visible beneath her helmet. At her side was a sword with a white hilt to match the rest of her attire.

Ahmeras watched her with great interest and a hint of disgust. Arinay held her head up high, her eyes directed to the walls before her. It made the queen sick. Not but a few months ago, this ruler had sworn fealty to the king, and now she carried herself as if she ruled everything in her line of vision. From the distance, Ahmeras even thought she caught a smirk. The Verish ruler had something more up her sleeve, but so did she.

"Do we have men on the ground?" she asked, stepping away from the edge.

"We do, my lady. Our mounted troops are at your command. However, to strike with our current forces would do very little."

The queen ignored his words and ran back the way she came. "I will be joining them soon. When I give the signal, open the gates."

He stared in disbelief. "Open them? But, Queen Ahmeras, if we open them—"

"Just trust me, Teriul. Keep your gaze northward. The king will be returning soon with his militia. When he does, notify me immediately. Then, when I give the order, open the gates."

The officer gave no more argument. He clicked his feet again and responded with a thundering, "As you command!"

TIREHN HELD THE reins of his steed in a tight grip. He prayed to the Eternal that Ahmeras was safe, but there was no way of knowing. He had received a letter not a day ago about the status of the southern section of the army. They had not survived. Just as Gahlaia had predicted, Verish had attacked, and it was unlikely any had lived through the encounter.

He shook his head harshly. He couldn't worry about that now. It didn't do him any good. He needed to focus on the task at hand. The Verish army had likely reached Valia by now, and he would need to somehow scatter their forces. If his troops could reach Arinay, then maybe they could disrupt the Verish chain of command. It was a gamble, but what else was there? For all he knew, the capital was already under siege and taken over. *No!* he told himself. Ahmeras was smart. Smarter than anyone he knew. She would find a way to survive. She always found a way.

He swung his head around. Gahlaia walked behind him, leading her small band of winged Takahrn. They only numbered in the fifties now as opposed to the over one hundred they had before the battle up north.

"Do it now," he said.

She nodded and turned to the Takahrn next to her. He was darker skinned, with short black hair. He bore thick horns on the top of his head and a longer tail than most. She nudged him lightly, and he nodded back, spreading his dark wings wide and taking to the skies. He flew past the horses that led their army forward and soon disappeared from view, swooping higher and higher into the clouds.

"What do you have in mind?" Gahlaia asked over the trampling of feet and hooves.

He shrugged. "Right now, very little. It all depends on where Valia stands, or if they stand at all."

"And if they don't?"

"They will." They had to, or they had already lost.

ARINAY HEARD ANOTHER bang reverberate from the wall. She knew it was futile, but it served its purpose. For all its advantages, Valia had only one way in or out, and as long as they stood at the forefront, they had them trapped. She needed to stall for time. Time that was quickly running out for her enemies.

She smiled, directing her stare southward. In the far distance, she could make out a speck of darkness. She only needed a few more hours at most. Then she would have her revenge. The sweet, savory taste of vengeance. It was all she desired now, and it wouldn't be long before it was given to her. The Deeria capital may have been a fortress when it came to direct attack, but once the battlements were brought low and the gates struck down, there would be nothing to stand against her. Their soldiers were too few.

Deep down, she didn't wish to proceed. A tinge of pity for her victims still clung to her soul. All this death, all her hatred, had been for a single life that she had lost. Was it truly worth everything they had gone through? *Would Doryan have wanted this?*

She squeezed her fist around the reins of her horse, trying to snuff out the very thought of remorse. This was for so much more than that one loss. Doryan was just the spark. This wasn't just for him anymore. It was for all her people who had been beaten, robbed, and slaughtered by the Dividers. The zealous groups that had spawned the Grey Wings, the slaves that had murdered their masters—her sector had seen more hardship on that front than any of the others. She deserved her revenge. She deserved justice.

Arinay refocused her attention as another crash from the gates sounded. "Release!" she cried, swinging her left arm forward.

On cue with her command, hundreds of arrows caught the wind behind her, arching upward and falling upon unknown targets beyond the city walls. She didn't need to see the enemy fall in front of her. She just needed to keep Ahmeras and her soldiers tense.

An hour passed with continual shouts and commands. The constant clanging of the battering ram was starting to rack her skull with a headache. It had been a long while since she had led an attack herself, and her mind was still getting used to the ongoing clutter of sounds. She lifted a hand to rub her thumb over her forehead but stopped in midair. To the right of the city borders, something flew onto the battlements. It was there only for a moment before it disappeared into the capital. *Just a bird*, she thought. There were lots of birds that had flown up and down the large ramparts. Still, something about that one in particular set her on edge.

AHMERAS NODDED TO her soldiers, all ready and mounted, holding their positions before the front gates. She had dressed herself in the gold and silver armor that was customary for the Deeria militia, not a shade different from her subordinates. As she mounted her horse, she saw a winged Takahrn land on the battlements above.

"Where is Queen Ahmeras?" he asked, addressing Commander Teriul. "King Tirehn is on his way."

Before the officer could respond, Ahmeras cried out from down below. "I'm here! What is it Tirehn needs?"

The man turned toward her and leaped from the wall, slowing his descent with the flap of his massive wings. He straightened and gave the elvish salute. It had been so long since she had been given such an honor that even in their current predicament, it lifted her spirits a little.

"I speak for Lady Gahlaia and King Tirehn," he said. "I was sent to oversee the current situation. Does Ruler Arinay lead the enemy forces?"

She let a smile cross her face. As usual, Tirehn was thinking the same thing she was. "She does," Ahmeras replied. "She heads up the cavalry. If we can hit her as a group, I think I can reach her."

The Takahrn looked confused. "But even if she does separate

from her army, how will you—"

She put a hand up. "Just tell Tirehn what I've told you. He'll understand what I'm talking about."

He didn't hesitate. At her words, he saluted again, bowed low to the ground, and flew off to the north. She watched as the Takahrn flew out of her line of sight, high into the cloudy sky. Arinay may have had them cornered at present, but if they could just get this right, they might be able to turn things in their favor.

Ahmeras lifted her head. The commander stared back, awaiting her orders. "On my signal, Teriul. Just tell me when the king comes into view."

And as her subordinate left, she bowed her head and prayed, as Tirehn likely was doing. Perhaps if more than one voice were raised to the heavens, they might be heard over the chaos.

"Eternal, giver of Light, breaker of Shade . . . Save us. Save us all."

THE SUN HAD started to lift high into the sky, blocked by the endless clouds, painting the world a dim orange. Gahlaia watched the Takahrn land between her and Tirehn's mount. He was heaving, his hands to his knees, wings sagging to the ground.

The king raised a clenched fist, and the entire army ground to a halt. "How is the city faring?" he asked.

The man took a moment to gather himself and then gave his response. "Valia still stands. Arinay heads up the Verish army, numbering in a couple thousand. She stands at the head of her mounted soldiers, sending men to bring the front gates down."

Gahlaia saw Tirehn sigh in relief at the news. Dire as it was, it meant that Ahmeras was still alive. She, however, thought the report grimmer than first assumed. She put a claw to her chin, and her tail whizzed back and forth in reflection.

"My lord," the Takahrn continued, "Queen Ahmeras plans to open the gates and join you in a frontal attack."

Tirehn recoiled. "What? Why? There's no way she can survive . . ." He stopped, eyes narrowed. "Does she plan to move toward Arinay?"

"Yes, my lord. She said if you both hit Verish together, she could reach her."

It was then that Gahlaia saw realization cross the king's face. Whatever Ahmeras planned to do, he understood. "Very well. Let's move!"

With that, the army began to march again.

Gahlaia kept at pace, but the first statement still bothered her. She knew quite a bit about the Verish militia, including its size. They may not have had the strongest of soldiers, but their numbers were nothing to scoff at. But with only a couple thousand . . .

She placed a hand on the messenger's shoulder. "Are you sure about your estimation of their forces? Was it only a couple thousand?"

The Takahrn gave her a puzzled look. "Only? Compared to our numbers, that's a sizable difference."

"I know, I know! But are you certain that's their numbers?"

"Yes. I saw it with my own eyes."

The words had barely left his mouth before Gahlaia spread her wings and caught up to the front lines, landing to the right of Tirehn's steed. "Surely you know that's not all they have at their disposal," she said.

"I'm aware," the king replied. "Right now, it doesn't change our current position. Arinay is at the head. If we take her down, we can infiltrate the front gate. So long as we can break through to the city, we have a stronger chance of defending it."

Gahlaia slowed her pace, pulling herself back with the rest of the Takahrn. She wasn't convinced. It was all too easy. All the same, there was nothing else to be done. Verish was at their head, and Norvad reinforcements were at their back. They had to strike one, and better to gain control of a fortified capital then be hit in the open field. She swallowed and scrunched her brow. There seemed to be no end to their uneasiness. Such was the way of war, after all. There would be no rest until one side won over the other or trampled them under their feet.

Gahlaia placed a hand to her ribs, covered with armored plating. She felt a warmth underneath. It stretched up her spine into her mind, soothing her anxious thoughts. It was Borhiim. She wasn't always certain what he was thinking, but just knowing he was still there was enough for now.

So she marched, preparing to rush headfirst into death's arms once again, and this time, there was no one to save her. She scoffed at the thought, rebuking her wandering fear. She was stronger than that. No one needed to save her. No one was going to die because of her mistakes. *Never again.*

AMONG THE FAST-MOVING army, led by the king himself, there lay a shadow: Tirehn's shadow. It stretched in the same direction as the other black trails, hiding from the sunlight, streaming westward. Yet Draag knew that not a single eye noticed him crouching in the center of the umbra. He knew no one could see him, disguised within the darkness cast by the king and the horse.

Draag kept his black hood up, covering his long, dark, unkempt hair. It curled back behind his pointed ears, stiff and filthy. In both hands, he held his long scythe low to the ground, preparing for the inevitable. The very thought of it all amused him. His mind crashed in multiple directions like several river currents fighting for supremacy. But it retained one simple goal. In the depths of that chaos, a voice rose above the rest. The voice of command, at least for now. It spoke darkly, in a deep, roaring tone, like the booming of thunder.

Not yet. I need him in position. Wait for my signal.

Draag nodded to himself and strapped the scythe onto his back, sighing deeply. "My will is yours to command, my liege," he whispered, and in the murkiness of the king's shadow, he felt a faint glow shine out from inside his hood: the Terrkoris mark, releasing its strange magic. This body was very strong. It never ceased to impress him.

He didn't enjoy taking orders from Tarubas, but he would bear it for now. Like the Faded Dragon, he was willing to bide his time. He would soon have what he desired. The wait would be worth it.

His disappointment quickly shifted back to enjoyment, and a smile plastered his face. He moved quickly, keeping step within his hiding place. *It won't be long now.*

THE DAY DRAGGED by, continuously punctuated by the crashes before them. Arinay was growing impatient. She turned and looked behind one last time. She was not disappointed. The dark blotches in the distance had grown larger, coming into view as masses of soldiers and weapons, not half an hour away. Large siege towers, ladders, ballista, and catapults, all fashioned with steel and hardened wood. They moved slowly, but the waiting was nearly over. She beamed. It was finally time.

"Lady Arinay!"

She turned at the shout. On the east side of the wall, at Valia's edge, an army rose over a small hill. At its front, King Tirehn himself rode in, head held high and sword drawn. Soon, the whole band of soldiers and Dividers came into sight, and Arinay stared in disbelief. Their numbers looked barely under two thousand. Greatly depleted from what it could have been, but all the same, they were headed up by a massive group of cavalry, with winged Dividers just behind.

She cursed. "Rorgan was supposed to take care of them."

But she had little time to think about it, for as the army came to a halt beside the fortifications of the capital, a loud creak came from the front gates. To her shock, the huge Valia doors began to open.

AT THE FAR rear of the Verish army, the king had seen it. The reinforcements, thousands more infantrymen, bringing with them metallic weapons built solely for the goal of overtaking their city. Their way of life. If Arinay's army reached the walls, it would be a massacre. They had to act now.

Tirehn spun his horse around to face the soldiers behind him. On their faces, he could see it—a fear so palpable that he could almost feel it squeeze its tendrils around his chest. It was undeniable, yet understandable. Here they stood, following a king barely old enough to be called a man, confronting an army that dwarfed theirs. How could they face such a thing without fear? It would be uncanny if they didn't.

He gulped down his own emotions, cleared his throat, and met his army with the most confident face he could muster.

"People of Deeria!" he cried. "For generations, you have lived under my father's rule and his father's before him. All that time, you lived by their lies and deceit for the sake of their greed and fear. They led you with a false notion of peace. A false notion of truth! They split us apart from each other and left us to wallow in their false-hoods... all to spread their agenda: that it was all folly. That morality was all that they willed it to be."

He pointed his blade at them and ran it across the front lines. "Only because you decided to fight against my father's system have we made it this far. Not because of me, but you! And now they wish to take that from you. They wish for things to return to the way they were. To go back to turning a blind eye to injustice. To tear down the lives you have built!"

Tirehn yanked the reins of his steed, facing the Verish army in front of them. "People of Deeria! Stand with me now! If we are to face our end, let it be here, under the Eternal's gaze, on the fields of our families and all we hold dear!"

For the first time in Deerium's history, human and Takahrn alike shouted together. On the plains of the green battlefield, soon to run red with their blood, they stood as one body, a momentary bliss among the horrors of war.

As the king readied himself, the ear-piercing cry of a horn rang from the city. It was Ahmeras. He was sure of it.

At its sound, Tirehn led his full might into the fray. Winged Takahrn took to the sky, and horses at the back led the foot soldiers forward. He watched as Gahlaia and her band of comrades flew just above him, shouting their battle cries at the top of their lungs. He saw movement at the now opened gates, and what soldiers Arinay had posted there were struck down by trampling hooves, dropping their battering ram to the ground. Out of the city rode a group of armed cavalrymen, running straight for the Verish troops.

Two Deeria hordes, charging toward the same objective.

ARINAY STEADIED HERSELF as best she could, grasping the reins with her left hand and drawing her sword with her right. "Archers!" she called out.

Arrows stopped horses and soldiers dead in their tracks, causing them to roll and tumble under the feet of the rushing army. They kept moving forward. She would need to head them off.

She raised her blade upward and pointed at the incoming forces. "Cavalry! *To me!*"

And that was it. No speech. No declaration of inspiration. Just three screamed words, and the numbing pounding of her heart.

The two groups of Deeria soldiers met halfway and merged into one seamless unit, directed like an arrow toward its target.

Arinay's head felt empty. She had rehearsed this moment in her mind countless times, imagining herself charging into the field of battle. But it was nothing like she had expected nor like anything she had hoped. There was one instinct that pushed all others aside: *survive.* Kill or be killed without mercy. Barbaric perhaps, but the reaction of anyone when death stared back at them.

She held her breath a split second before the collision, and then . . . it had begun.

Horses collided, blade struck blade, and claws slashed at the throats of their victims. All turned to chaos in an instant, the noises blurring together in loud clangs and cracks.

Arinay's blade met with her first attacker, and as she swung out in fury, she felt her mount hit another in front of her, and she was flung into the air. She rolled across the trampled grass and thrust herself up, feeling a sharp pain in her side. She ignored it as best she could, swinging her sword at a soldier who thrust himself toward her. Stooping under an ax blade, she dug her blade between the sections of his breastplate. The soldier fell limp, and putting her foot to the man's chest, she pulled the steel from his flesh and moved on.

She heard a cluster of shrieks overhead and ducked as the winged Dividers swooped down at the masses. Talons drooped down low, just above her, and she heard her soldiers let out their final screams as their heads loosed from their shoulders. Arinay sprang back to her feet and charged at a wingless Divider to her left. He noticed her just as she fell upon him, and he swung a mace toward her shoulder. She could tell he wasn't used to wielding a weapon at all, like many of his kind. She parried the attack with a two-handed blow, bringing her sword back toward him. The Divider dropped the mace and swung his left hand at her face with clawed fingers, but it did little for him. Arinay's blade came across his arm, and it fell shorn before a final strike dropped him to the ground, a gash cut from his left side.

She spun around, looking for her next target. There was one person she wanted more than all others. Only one.

She didn't need to look long. Beyond the group of soldiers that she had swiftly cut down, Arinay spotted the king, clashing blades with her Verish forces, dismounted yet strong. He twisted his blade with skill and precision, not allowing a single strike upon his gold and silver armor. She edged closer, slicing away another nameless infantryman in front of her, slowly closing the distance between herself and the king. But as she inched closer, thrusting her blade into another man's stomach, she heard wings clap down toward her in a low rumble.

Arinay turned, and before her stood a Divider, plated in armor, with two holes at the top of the helmet for the horns. Her hair was blonde, darker than her own, and her eyes were murky red. Arinay had seen her face before. At the coronation.

It was Gahlaia, one of the slaves from the Dirtlands.

Arinay pointed the tip of her sword toward the Divider. "You!" she fumed. "You killed him! You killed Doryan!"

Gahlaia shrugged with weariness and stood at the ready. "Yes, I did."

Arinay half-expected her to try and explain herself, as she had all those months ago. But there was no remorse. No guilt. It was as if she had been drained of it all, and it only made Arinay's anger swell more. Gahlaia didn't have the right to be tired of answering for her crimes. They were just that, crimes.

Her focus had been redirected. Arinay now had a target for her vengeance. There was no need for words after that. Gripping her blade tightly, she rushed the Divider in a fury. She was completely outmatched, but she thought little of it. All technique with the weapon was gone, and she slashed wildly at her foe, just hoping, praying, that the metal would connect.

Gahlaia tucked her wings to her back and ducked, twisting her body away from slice after reckless slice that came at her. She kept her claws at her sides but made no move in retaliation.

"Strike back, you coward!" Arinay yelled as she threw another cut her way. It was useless. She no longer acted out of focus or even desperation to live, but rage.

Jumping aside, Gahlaia evaded a thrust from the dirtied sword. Grabbing the ruler's wrist with her left hand, she slashed across Arinay's forearm with her right, her claws digging through the metal coating like a knife through parchment. Arinay dropped her sword as the pain racked her, and Gahlaia brought a leg hard into her gut, sending her reeling back into a pile of bodies behind her. Dazed, the Verish ruler stumbled to her feet. She hunched over as she held in the urge to vomit, her stomach churning. She stared at the Divider, who watched as she struggled to contain herself.

Arinay reached for the right side of her hip and unsheathed a long dagger. She would end this here or die trying. That was all that flooded her thoughts. But before she could charge again, she froze.

The cold steel of a blade kissed her throat. Arinay stood in confusion, and Gahlaia looked just as bewildered. Holding the blade to the ruler's neck was a soldier wearing the white of Verish mail.

"Traitor . . ." she muttered.

The man's left cheek glowed with a strange symbol: a Terrkoris mark. "I'm not the traitor here," came the response, in a female voice. A familiar voice.

The man's features and armor began to shift and transform before Arinay's eyes, and soon a Deeria-clad woman stood in the place of what was once a Verish infantryman. She removed her helmet, revealing her pointed ears and letting her dark hair flow freely.

Gahlaia's face turned white with shock. "Queen Ahmeras!" she said. "What are you doing here?"

"Saving my city," the queen responded. "Why else would I be here? Find Tirehn. We can't hold off an attack like this forever. Not outside the walls of the city."

With those final words, Ahmeras lifted her weapon from Arinay's neck and brought the hilt cracking into her skull. Arinay's mind went instantly black.

GAHLAIA SWOOPED UPWARD over the clashing forces, letting the harsh winds smack across her face. Looking ahead, she saw what she feared. The Verish reinforcements had massive siege towers, five in total, and tall enough to scale the Valia walls. They moved slowly, but still, she was surprised they moved at the speed they did. No humans could keep them going at that pace.

Fixing her gaze on the bases of the metal monstrosities, she understood. Pushing them forward were Takahrn, their horns and tails severed, chained firmly to the very things they were being forced to push. Their skin was covered with scars and bruises that even their quickened healing had trouble keeping up with.

Gahlaia burned with anger, guiding her descending body toward the towers, but she was soon met with a volley of arrows shot from the back of the army. She kept her distance, but only just. There was nothing she could do. The army needed to retreat, and soon she would be alone in the sky, ripe for the picking. Relenting, she swung away. *I'll come back for you*, she swore to herself.

Below, she spotted Tirehn among the hordes. "Tirehn!" she shouted. "We have Arinay! Pull everyone back!"

He ripped his blade from another soldier and nodded up to her, commanding anyone who could hear him to withdraw.

Gahlaia called out to the Deeria soldiers, and soon the other winged Takahrn joined the chorus. "*Back to the city! Retreat! Back to Valia!*"

Masses upon masses of infantry moved northward to the front gates of the capital, and as they inched closer, the doors began to open.

Gahlaia spread her wings wide and let them pull her higher up. She directed the others into the city, but as she moved to enter as well, she spotted something far to the north. A large shadow, covering the plains past the city walls.

She needed no second look. She knew they would come eventually, and sure enough, they had.

It was the Norvad army, bringing what might they had left across the mud and green of Deeria. They would be upon the walls by the day's end.

Chapter 24

Day twenty-six of the fifth month.

F AR TO THE north, on the eastern edge of the border between Norvad and Cleptyn, Borhiim came upon a small village. Hardly a village at that. It rambled across the freezing snow, no more than twelve houses in total, bringing in stray travelers from all over. It was likely the last sign of human life before one crossed into Cleptyn territory, heading toward the mountain ranges of the Claw.

Borhiim strode into the village, keeping his head down, letting the darkness do its job. At first, he thought his arrival might cause alarm, but none was raised. People gave him no more than a single glance before continuing on their way. In a damp place such as this, they had perhaps grown used to many a mysterious wanderer. He was no different.

Jerin, walking at his side, pulled back his hood and looked around. "This is it," he said. "We might as well rest up here. It'll only get rougher as we go."

Borhiim lifted his head and took in the odors of the new location. Smoke and alcohol, with the moisture in the air sticking to his face. It wasn't pleasant, but it would do. "Then let's hope they have a tavern," he responded with a nod.

Sure enough, on the far side, sitting nearly shoulder-to-shoulder with another house, there was a tavern. It was twice as large compared to the other buildings, with a wooden sign hanging by a metal bar over the front door. Carved into its front were the words "The

Burning Ale."

Charming name, Borhiim thought.

Jerin pushed open the door, and the Takahrn followed him in. The main room was dimly lit, with candles spread across the few square tables in the center and a fireplace to the right. At the far side was a long counter, chairs tightly pulled up, save for a couple that housed what were likely the usual customers. To the left was a small entrance to a hallway, probably leading to the bedrooms.

They walked to the counter and took their seats, Jerin waving to grab the barkeep's attention. "We need two rooms," he said to the grubby old man at the other end. "Just for tonight."

"Very well, sirs," he replied in a tired voice. "That'll be two silver pieces."

Borhiim pulled the satchel from his back, reached a hand into it, and pulled out two silver coins and one copper. He placed the tips of his fingers to the metal and dragged them on the wood toward their new owner.

The barkeep looked at the pieces in confusion. "I'm sorry, sir, but I don't take tips. Never took a coin in my life that I didn't earn. But if you wish, I can get you some ale."

Jerin nodded. "I'll take one."

"Just some water, please," Borhiim said with a raised hand.

"Thank you, sirs. The two rooms at the far end of the hall are yours." He leaned in slightly. "Apologies that I can't give you any of the larger ones. Them soldiers have taken nearly all the space I have."

Both turned in the direction the man had pointed. Near the fireplace, a group of seven Norvad soldiers had pulled two of the tables from the middle closer to the wall. They laughed and mumbled among themselves, watching a young boy playing the bagpipes.

Borhiim grunted, placing his arms on the counter. "That's the last thing we need."

Jerin shrugged. "They seem distracted. Besides, they're not exactly sober."

The barkeep returned, placing a medium-sized mug and large glass of water in front of them. Jerin grabbed his by the handle, thanked the old man, and took his first swig. Borhiim sipped sparingly, trying to keep the ends of his cloak sleeves up to hide his talons.

When Jerin at last slammed the beaker down on the counter, he turned to the Takahrn questioningly. "I know you haven't been in much of a talking mood these past few days, and to be fair, neither have I. All the same, might I ask you something?"

Borhiim shrugged. "I don't see the harm. But if I give you an answer, then you have to respond to one of mine."

"Fair enough, I suppose." He paused, gathering his words together. "A few weeks back, a large portion of the Norvad army was stationed at the border to the south, and they met the Deeria forces in battle. I've heard rumors that those who looked into the sky that day saw something miles upon miles away. They say a stream of light shot into the clouds. A pillar of dark fire, unlike anything they had ever seen."

"And you believed them?"

Jerin took another sip of his ale. "Of course I didn't. Not at first. But then I met you. I saw how you scattered my soldiers near the Forest of Shadows. Remember?"

"I'm not hearing a question."

He moved closer and whispered his next words. "Was it you, all those weeks ago?"

Borhiim leaned back in his chair, and it creaked slightly. He let out a sigh, keeping his eyes ahead. "Yes," he answered. "I wasn't in complete control of myself. I don't remember much of it."

"Well, what do you remember?"

Borhiim closed his eyes, trying to picture the moment. He saw the flames lick around him as he jumped into a fray of soldiers, and then darkness. All that followed was the piercing ... "Screams. I remember the screams. Not much else."

Now it was Jerin's turn to lean back. His face looked more bewildered than satisfied by the response, but he posed no further questions. He merely continued to drink his ale.

"My turn," Borhiim said, taking a bigger gulp of water, and letting the refreshing coolness slide down his throat. He pointed to Jerin's chest. "What's with the necklace?"

The man reached into his cloak and pulled out the silver chain with the single copper piece hanging from it. Gripping the coin between two fingers, he gave his reply. "Three years ago, I met a woman in Zerah. A couple of the other soldiers dared me to try and charm her, so I went over to her and did just that. I said she was as beautiful as the radiant sun. Not the most original saying, I'll admit, but she seemed to get a kick out of it. She smirked at me, flicked this copper piece at my feet, and told me to take poetry lessons."

Borhiim chuckled, rolling his eyes. "You've kept the coin all because you lost a dare?"

Jerin shook his head. "I kept it because she's my wife," he said. "That was where we first met. We built a house in the northwest, just over the Horned Bay."

"How long has it been since you've seen her?"

"A couple of months at least. Since Rorgan declared war on the king, he's called every soldier to arms. I didn't have much of a choice in the end."

Borhiim nodded. "And here I thought all the other sectors fought for slavery, though I shouldn't be surprised. The causes of war are usually broader than first assumed."

Jerin shrugged. "Everyone fights for a cause. Just because you're on the same side doesn't mean you have the same reasons for being there."

Borhiim pondered the words. They were loaded but not untrue. He had seen it happen throughout history, even before the humans had taken hold of the world.

"What about you?" Jerin asked. "You have someone waiting for you?"

He turned in his chair, keeping a close eye on the laughing soldiers at the end of the tavern. "I guess you could say that."

"Where is she?"

"Fighting."

"WHAT ARE WE waiting for?" the commander shouted. "Why aren't we moving the siege towers into position? It's been days, Lord Rorgan! The walls are still holding. We could have ended this—"

Rorgan held his hands up. "I've already told you, Commander Brogtan. They have Arinay, your ruler, in their custody. Also, if we move the towers, we would have little chance of holding them in position. With Tirehn's forces within the walls, the battlements are too fortified."

Brogtan looked like he was trying to come up with a reply, but nothing came out.

The Norvad ruler shook his head in disgust. This was one of Verish's highest-ranking officers, and he was nothing more than a dimwitted fool. "I only ask that you think before you open your mouth," he said, turning his back.

The commander mumbled an old elvish curse. "Who put a coward from the north in charge of our ranks?" he murmured.

Rorgan immediately turned back toward the large man, staring him down inches from his face. "Do not test me, Commander. I have grown tired of your incessant grumblings. Stay quiet and stay loyal to your betters. That way we all get what we want."

As the ruler towered over him, the commander dropped his gaze and slunk away. Satisfied, Rorgan continued his stride through the clumps of Verish and Norvad infantry, making his way to a small tent set up a day ago. The commander and other men may not have known it, but in truth, he cared little for the safety of the Verish ruler. She was of little use now in her captivity. But all the same, he needed to stall if they were to get the time they needed. He glanced back toward the front lines, watching as they fell to streams of arrows fired from the Valia walls, and then entered the shelter.

Nothing lay inside save for a single woman. An elf.

Gwendall knelt in the very center, her eyes closed. She didn't move when he walked in. Rorgan could tell her mind, or rather her soul, was elsewhere. For the past few days, she had been building the magic deep within her, growing familiar with its pulse. Rorgan could sense the spiritual energy flowing from her like a river that had just broken through a dam. He felt it more than even she could know. It fueled him with a familiar feeling. A feeling that he had never witnessed in another living thing. Not for an age. She was finally ready.

He cleared his throat and spoke quietly to her. "The Verish army is growing restless. I don't mean to rush, but—"

"It's alright, Rorgan," she replied, opening her eyes. "I'm sure they are. I wouldn't blame them."

He looked down and watched as the glowing Anamoris symbol under her shirt slowly faded away. He smiled. "It's been just over a week, and yet you've already grown so much stronger."

She said nothing, nodding slightly.

Rorgan knelt. "You know what it is I'm going to ask of you. You are the descendant of the High Elf after all."

He paused. This was all that was left. She needed to trust him. Only then could he make the final switch. She needed to follow him, and he needed to follow her. It needed to feel genuine. He let the next words slip out slowly.

"When Tirehn falls, you must take his throne. If you do this, I will serve you to the end, as will all of Deerium."

Gwendall did not shrink from his gaze. She did not falter. Not even a little. No longer was she the frail, fearful person she had once been. There was confidence in her eyes. *Good.*

"I know you will," she answered with a smile. "You've done so much for me, and I plan on doing the same. I won't fail you. I won't fail anyone."

Rorgan held back his joy and excitement. *Just a little more. Just one more step!* "Alright then," he said. "Shall we go?"

Tirehn and Ahmeras stood side by side on the battlements. For once, the queen appeared confident in their current predicament. Arinay was locked deep in the prison cells below the palace, and the army was secured within the walls.

"What is it?" Ahmeras asked, concern in her tone.

He shook his head. "What are they doing? Why are they waiting? They haven't moved in days."

"What can they do? I mean, even with their siege towers, I feel good about our chances should they attack."

"So—what? They just retreat? No. They're planning something, and we need to act. Rorgan's down there. He knows what he's doing."

Tirehn spun around and looked into the city. At the base of where they stood, Gahlaia sat alongside a couple of other Takahrn, tending to their wounds. He could send them out, but they were too few in number. They would be shot out of the sky before they could do any damage. Deeria couldn't do any substantial harm outside of raining arrows on the front lines. Like it or not, they were at the mercy of their enemies, waiting for them to strike first. The Norvad force had to come to them.

He groaned, looking around at the fortifications. Every soldier was ready for the inevitable battle. They just weren't sure when that battle would come.

"So, do you think it's true?" Ahmeras asked, snapping Tirehn from his trance. "What Gahlaia said about Rorgan?"

"I do," he said without hesitation. "Gahlorm the Dragon King was her father, and Tarubas is his older brother. He's her uncle. If I believed anyone on this, it would be her."

"But if that's true, and he is . . . what did they call him? The Faded Dragon? If he is the Faded Dragon, then why hasn't he just burned everything to the ground? Why work in secrecy?"

"I don't know. He uses only Anamoris magic. In all the history books I've read, never have I seen a dragon use magic outside of the Devil's Flame, at least not on the scale Tarubas has."

"Nor have I. But then—"

Ahmeras was silenced by the sudden screeching of metal coming from beyond the wall. The creaking of wheels, the chants of soldiers—it all began to grow in volume. The Norvad and Verish armies had started moving, their towers filled with armed infantry, steadily pushed by the Takahrn slaves down below.

"*Gahlaia!*" the king shouted.

At his call, she stood up and gave a loud war cry that echoed through the city streets. When she took flight to the battlements, the other Takahrn prepared to join her, either by wing or alongside the other soldiers.

Tirehn drew his sword, and the queen and the rest of their men followed suit. The unsheathing of blades from scabbards reverberated across the walls while soldiers standing behind placed shafts to their bowstrings.

The metal contraptions scraped across the plains, sliding ever closer.

"*Archers!*" The bowstrings pulled back; steel tips pointed toward the moving forces below. "*Fire!*"

Men raised their shields as the arrows descended upon them. Even still, bodies fell to the ground, trampled by those behind. Arms and legs were pierced, and soldiers screamed into the night, drowned out by the war cries and squealing of metallic wheels rolling through the grass. Armed forces reached the wall, lifting ladders to the stone, only to be shot down at the first sight of anything crawling up. They were too exposed, unable to make the climb.

"We need to stop those towers," Ahmeras said as another torrent of arrows flew down in front of them.

"Gahlaia!" Tirehn shouted. "You're up."

"About time," she answered. Spreading their wings, the other winged Takahrn followed her over the battlements and into the fray.

Spears sailed toward them erratically. Gahlaia spun out of the way, narrowly escaping a steel-tipped end. She grabbed the wooden handle as it passed over her and threw it back, pinning a soldier to the ground. As she moved closer to the towers, she spotted the chained Takahrn below. They stopped their pushing momentarily as the winged beings swooped overhead. Not even the cracks of the whips behind them could make them continue their press toward the wall. They stood there, strapped to the metal, frozen in disbelief.

Gahlaia could see faint flickers of hope in their eyes. The slaves were all held fast in thick shackles, three long metal strips that wrapped from one end of the tower to the other, nailed tightly into the left and right sides. No blade was going to break them, but her claws could. Only hers.

She turned to her comrades and nodded to them. "Take as many as you can back to the city! I'll deal with the chains!"

They gave the elvish salute and split into groups, descending onto the five towers with a vengeance. There were six Takahrn on each one, making thirty in all. It would be a struggle to take them all in a single trip.

Gahlaia did not stop her descent but instead waited overhead for the first group of whip-cracking soldiers around the towers to be cleared. When one looked barren enough, only then did she fall upon it. Outstretching her claws and dodging another spear, she scraped her talons over the metal strips. With a loud screech they broke free, and the Takahrn were quickly retrieved by the others, a few carrying two at a time, one under each arm.

Satisfied, she took to the skies again, moving to the next fortification. Memories flashed through her mind of a time long gone, of her own years as a slave. It was a fate no one deserved, least of all her people. It all culminated in one singular thought that stayed with her through the battle.

She needed to save them.

BORHIIM SQUIRMED IN his seat. His abdomen was bothering him, a slight tinge steadily growing more painful. His mind flooded with a rush of phrases. *Save them. We have to save them. I have to save them.*

He shook his head, trying to understand their meaning. They were not his thoughts. They were Gahlaia's. But now, as loud as they were, they were hard to differentiate from his own.

"You alright?" Jerin said, finishing off the final swigs of his ale and slamming the mug to the counter.

Borhiim shook himself one last time before settling down. He placed his hands back on the wood and breathed hard. "Yeah," he replied. "Something's happening . . . elsewhere."

"Elsewhere? That's not vague at all."

"It's a bit hard to explain."

"If you say so."

With that final push, the thoughts dimmed. They left Borhiim more than a little concerned, but like usual, there wasn't much he could do about it. She was in Valia, and far from his reach. He was stuck where he was, listening and hoping that nothing would happen. *She'll be fine*, he told himself. *She's always been the strong*er *one. Eternal save her.*

He turned to Jerin, who had just handed both the empty mug and glass back to the barkeep with a mumbled "Thank you."

"Well," Borhiim said, "if you're done, I say we get some sleep. We have a long day ahead of us."

Jerin opened but then quickly shut his mouth, staring at something behind him. Borhiim felt a wobbly hand grasp his left shoulder. He faced the person standing behind him and groaned.

One of the many Norvad soldiers had approached him, looking hardly in his right mind. He wore the armor of their sector, with smears of liquid on his breastplate. His helmet was gone, likely dropped and forgotten after his hours of drinking. "Would you look at this!" he said quite dramatically. "We have a mystery man in our midst!"

The other soldiers at the table laughed at his comment, taking their attention away from the boy with the bagpipes. They all spoke at the same time, and Borhiim could barely understand a single one of them.

"We don't want any trouble," Jerin said, putting his left hand up but slipping his right toward the hilt of his longsword.

The drunken man raised his arms in return. "Hey, I mean no harm. Don't you mind me. I'm just curious about this young fellow here."

He leaned closer. Too close for Borhiim's liking. He could smell the alcohol on his breath, and it made him want to gag. He had never been a fan of ale, even before his memories returned. Something about it made him a little uncomfortable, and this situation was only solidifying that feeling.

"You're the only one here looking to hide his face under a hood, mystery man," the soldier said. "What's the matter? Afraid to show that scar of yours?"

Borhiim pulled his face away from the man and felt his left cheek. The gash he had received in the battle at the border hadn't healed as his other wounds had. Instead, it had twisted into a long scar. He hadn't even noticed it was still there until it was pointed out to him. He had heard of the power of elvish blades, leaving permanent wounds on even the strongest of creatures, but only now did he believe such a thing was possible. Ironic that the very sword on his back would be the weapon to leave a mark on him.

"Let's go, Jerin," he said, standing and nearly knocking the unbalanced soldier over. "I'm tired."

Jerin nodded and they headed for the hallway. The soldier behind him continued to ramble on angrily, but they ignored him. Deep inside, Borhiim could feel a fire settle back down in his chest, and a whisper slowly faded from his mind. A whisper that had once addressed him back in the Forest of Shadows. Those dark words spoken by the Faded Dragon.

"WHAT DO YOU feel?" Rorgan asked.

Gwendall reached out a hand toward the wall as another shower of arrows fell on the front lines. Every single soul upon those battlements, hundreds at least, were visible within her mind. They lit the darkness behind her eyelids like candles brightening up a room, all ready to be snuffed out. Others, however, appeared stronger than the rest. The king, the queen, and many of the Dividers. She was strong, but her abilities were still new to her.

"I can feel all of them," she said. "But some of them I'm not sure of. I don't know if I can kill the king."

"Don't worry about him for now," Rorgan responded. "Just focus on everyone else. Can you do that?"

"Yes. I have them."

"Then you may begin, my lady."

Reaching out with both hands, she felt for the souls, and their energy flocked to her in an instant. Her Anamoris symbol began to glow brightly under her newly fashioned armor, the white light shining through the plating.

They were all under her control.

GAHLAIA REACHED THE city borders, dropping two freed slaves within the walls before flying back up to the battlements. She watched as Tirehn and Ahmeras called out another strike of arrows before approaching. "That's all of them," she said. "The towers won't be moving anytime soon."

"Good," the king replied. "We may yet live through this."

"Wait," Ahmeras said. She squinted, and Gahlaia followed her gaze. She had spotted two figures approaching the front lines. They bore no helmets, their faces revealed. "It's Rorgan! I see—"

Before she could finish her sentence, they were taken aback by the sudden silence. The continuous twanging of bowstrings had come to a halt, and all war cries from the walls had reached a dead stop.

Gahlaia turned in horror, watching in bewilderment and panic as every single soldier standing at their sides lost their voices, clutching plated chests before falling to the ground in a united thud. She stopped one of the soldiers from falling off the wall, and looking into his eyes, she saw no life in them. They were blank, held within nothing more than a soulless husk. His skin had turned grey and hard like stone. She had seen this only once before—the day her mother was taken from her. And the nagging pain in her brain . . . It reminded her of something.

The Waters of the Righteous!

She immediately faced Tirehn and Ahmeras. Their faces had paled with shock as they watched soldier after soldier collapse like puppets without strings. They had no words. Without hesitation, Gahlaia grabbed them both, thrusting them over each of her shoulders, and leaped from the walls. They didn't protest nor shout nor cry in surprise. All forms of shock had been trumped by the sight of their army falling to pieces under an unseen force. Gahlaia's wings strained under the weight of the king and queen. They had to get to the palace, or at the very least farther away. There was no surviving what was coming for them if they stayed. Not if it was what she thought it was.

She had known that Rorgan, or Tarubas, had Anamoris magic, but nothing on this scale. Not even the Righteous Ones had such strength. Not since High Elf Tarkuv had there been anything like this. Not since before she was born. Now here they were, in an age when magic was thought to be dead or dying, watching as masses of people had their souls smothered out of existence. All because of a refusal to change. A refusal to accept the truth and do what was right.

Something she had heard Ahmeras and Tirehn say came to Gahlaia's mind. *Sometimes making the right choice means walking the hardest path.* They had been right in the end, perhaps to an extent they had never dreamed of. She had to wonder, with this kind of hardship, was doing the right thing even worth it? Was saving some lives worth the death of others? Not long ago, she would've traded the humans for her people in a heartbeat, but now, that line had skewed. Flying over a city of innocent humans and Takahrn, she was no longer sure which was worth giving up, if any.

Landing in front of the palace gates, she took a moment to take in a couple gulps of air before departing again. "Stay here," she said between breaths. "Evacuate the city if you can."

"Evacuate?" Ahmeras said. "The front gates are the only way to move large amounts of people. The people have nowhere to go."

"It doesn't matter. No matter how small a number, get people out, even if it's little by little."

"You speak as if we've already lost."

"Did you not see what just happened? If we haven't lost already, then we're on our way there."

"Wait," Tirehn said, grabbing her by the shoulder. "Where are you going?"

"Isn't it obvious? I'm going to find that filthy scum who's done this and rip his head from his body."

Before the king could protest, she was already gone, leaving them alone and helpless.

DRAAG WAS HALFWAY down the city walls, his scythe firmly piercing the stone. When Tirehn had been taken by the Divider, he had momentarily lost his target, to the dismay and frustration of the voice in his head. It scolded him furiously, but he assured his master that he still had eyes on Tirehn, and with his vision, he was correct. He could see the king standing with his queen in front of the palace, unsure of what to do next.

But as he watched, he also saw movement in the darkened sky. Someone speeding back toward the top of the wall. There was a fire in her gaze. It was the leader of the winged Dividers. Gahlaia, as Tirehn had called her. "Lord Tarubas," he mumbled, "a Divider, their leader. She's coming for you."

Does she know?

"Yes."

A couple of seconds passed, a distinct pause.

Change of plans. Follow her to the wall. Stay hidden, and when you're clear, kill her.

With a flourish, Draag scaled back up the stone, whispering the same words he always did. "My will is yours to command, my liege."

A HARD BANG came at the door of his chambers, and Borhiim jumped from his bed, a dream of six yellow eyes fading from his mind. He had no idea how long he had been asleep, but it didn't feel very long. He looked out of his foggy window, wiping some of the mist away to clear up the image. It was still very dark, far from dawn.

Another crack came at his door, harder this time, several voices coming from the other side. "Come on out, mystery man," said one. "We never had a chance to finish our little chat."

He groaned, pulling at his cramped tail. "Stupid drunks," he muttered. Standing, he grabbed his cloak and threw it over his tired body, letting his tail wrap around his right leg for cover. This whole journey was starting to exhaust him, and he was feeling more irritable by the second. Whatever optimistic side of him he was known for was slowly dying away with the cold and snow.

He groggily opened the door, and before he could utter a single word, the bony knuckles of a fist met his scarred cheek, cracking him to the ground in surprise. The punch was unbalanced and weaker than a fair share of hits he had taken before, but it staggered him all the same. As he raised his upper body, he saw a man standing over him—that same man who had approached him earlier. Behind him were the six other Norvad soldiers, sneering from the frame of the doorway.

"You disrespected me," the man said, grabbing the collar of Borhiim's cloak. "No one disrespects me in front of my men."

The combination of grogginess and the new pain in his cheek left Borhiim feeling increasingly angry. "You command these men?" he asked. "In that case, what a poor job you're doing." He didn't mean to be clever with the drunkard hanging above him, but at the same time, he couldn't care less. He just wanted some sleep.

In the back of his mind, the whispers were growing louder again.

Another fist struck the side of his face, even weaker than the last one. But as the man raised his arm to strike a third time, he froze, staring at something untangling from Borhiim's right leg. His expression instantly shifted from rage to sinister interest, a smile creeping onto his lips.

Unfortunately for him, before he could speak his mind, Borhiim grabbed both his arms and threw him to the other side of the room.

As the man stumbled back, he tripped over his own feet and fell to the wooden floor. When Borhiim stood up, so did the soldier, wobbling as he did so. They faced each other, glaring, and the man pulled a sword from his side.

However, as each prepared to rush the other, the grating of a blade across wood came from outside the room. The other six men backed away from the doorway, and Jerin walked into view, his longsword dragging over the floorboards.

"Now, that's enough of that," he said in a calm yet threatening tone. "I already told you we don't want any trouble."

The soldier shakily pointed his weapon at Borhiim. "You with him?" he asked. "Don't you know what he is? He's one of them. The Dividers!"

The tip of the longsword struck harder into the wood, splintering the boards, giving the men behind all the more reason to creep farther away.

"Put the sword down. You wouldn't want the barkeep to have to clean up your mess in the morning, now would you?"

"You *are* with him." He now pointed the sword at Jerin. "To harbor a Divider is treason. You're a traitor."

Jerin took another step, lifting his weapon in a readying stance, but they never clashed.

A thud rang out in the room.

Both faced Borhiim. He had fallen to his knees, clutching his stomach and gritting his teeth. His scales burned with an unnatural fury, and a scream filled his thoughts. The sound of someone familiar. "Gahlaia . . ."

The croaking whispers increased as the scream shook him harder.

GAHLAIA REACHED THE edge of the wall and flapped her wings as hard as she could, pulling herself upward. Inches from the stone, she flew higher and higher up the fortifications. To her right, more soldiers fell from the wall, their bodies turned to the hard substance like the others, cracking like old sculptures when they hit the ground below. She needed to hurry. Now was their only chance.

As she reached the top, she hovered above the battlements, looking over them to find her target. The other winged Takahrn had descended upon the Verish and Norvad forces but were being struck down one by one, either by spears or arrows or the unseen force attacking them all. The tides of the battle had quickly shifted, and she could see it on everyone's face. She let her feet hit the top of the wall and sprinted to the end of the battlements, ready to jump off once more. However, just before she leaped, from the corner of her eye she spotted a blade slicing through the air toward her.

Gahlaia folded her wings and ducked, the cold metal cutting through strands of her hair. She rolled away, leaped up, and took to the skies, trying to see her attacker. There was none. No one at all. Only the shadows cast by dead bodies and the stone fronts of the battlements.

Then, coming into shape in the air, a dark, hooded figure came at her, swinging a black scythe.

As she swept through the air to gain some distance, the tip of the blade cut into her left leg. Gahlaia tried her best to ignore the pain, flying east across the wall, frantically trying to escape her pursuer. Glancing back, she saw no sign of her enemy. Not even a flicker. She went even higher, powered by panic, and looked back one more time. The figure reappeared, plunging his weapon into a group of confused soldiers before vanishing again.

Pain racked her leg, blood dripping down her foot. Her thoughts were on one thing and one thing only: Borhiim. He had promised to stay alive, and now she was the one at death's door, fleeing for her life.

No! she thought. This wasn't how it was going to end. Not for her. She still had so much to do. If this unknown opponent was going to come at her, she would face it head on. No fear.

She twisted herself around midair to face her foe, but almost immediately, a long weapon spun its way toward her, the blade piercing her left wing. In agony, she fell back down onto the eastern edge of the wall, only a couple of feet from tumbling over the side. Even as strong as she was, she felt her bones crack and shatter as she hit the stone, the scythe still lodged in her wing. She crawled toward the edge, but it was no use. She could barely move without pain spreading through her entire body, and her right arm had gone completely numb.

The cloaked figure stood over her, leaning a hand on the end of his weapon's handle, pushing it farther into the muscle. She screamed, and he appeared to take a sick pleasure from it, drinking it in like some kind of drug.

Pulling out the scythe, he raised it over his head like a sledge-hammer.

I can't die here!

With a last burst of strength, she pushed herself upright with her right wing, bringing a claw across the dark being's face. He cried out, slicing the air wildly with long streaks of his blade. She turned to the right to avoid them, but her body gave way to the pain. She was far too slow. The sharp metal of the scythe cleaved her already wounded wing, carving clean through, leaving only a stub of muscle and skin attached to her back. The dismembered portion fell to the ground, and with another loud shriek, Gahlaia felt her feet slip from the edge of the battlements. Her aching body flipped backward, and she fell toward the open plains of Deeria.

"*GAHLAIA!*"

The scales burned even harder on his skin. Borhiim couldn't hear her screaming anymore. Her thoughts had grown completely silent. He shook his head violently, trying to convince himself it wasn't real. *I can't hear her. I can't hear her!*

The Devil's Flame began to rise and with it, the whispers in his head now became shouts, squealing their draconic words into his skull, calling out to him with their enticing sounds. He felt his eyes burn, and billows of smoke rose as he breathed out his nostrils. *I can't hear her!*

The drunken man went from confused to terrified, pushing Jerin aside and crying out for help. The other men followed him, running down the hallway.

"Borhiim?" Jerin asked, his voice shaking.

Borhiim's hands had clenched into fists, murky flames licking out between his fingers. "Run . . ."

Jerin sheathed his sword and did as he was told. "Everyone out!" he shouted. "Everyone out of the tavern!"

Borhiim clutched his face with his scorching hands. The fire did not singe him but rather grew around his body, not burning his clothes or anything attached to him. Only everything else. Tears ran down his cheeks before they dried from the intense heat, and he clenched his teeth so hard they almost cracked under the pressure. *I . . . can't . . . hear . . . her!*

With those final thoughts, the magic erupted, blasting in every direction. His only reward was the sound of screams. Screams of the dead. Screams that had clung to his dreams for days on end, only now, there was one more added to their chorus. A female voice.

JERIN LOOKED AT the clearing smoke. The tavern was destroyed, and anyone who didn't get out before the explosion was likely already dead. There was no way anyone could have survived something like that. He and a few others had only barely gotten out of range of the vicious flames. Flames like he had never seen.

He stepped closer. The smoke was almost completely gone. It was unnatural. All of it.

Other men and women looked on in terror. There was no sign of where the tavern once stood, only a massive crater with a single spot of wooden flooring at the center of it. It was small, a few feet in diameter, untouched and unburned. It was where Jerin imagined Borhiim's chambers had once been, but Borhiim was gone.

Faintly visible in the deep snow, a lone set of footprints stretched away from the village. Tracks too deep for the wind to blow away completely, for now at least.

Pulling his hood over his head, Jerin followed them, disappearing into the night.

Chapter 25

Day twenty-seven of the fifth month.

DAWN BROKE OVER the horizon, and yet so few were left to see it rise.

Commander Teriul ran down the steps, farther into the fortifications of the wall. The scene outside had become a complete massacre. Soldiers dropped left and right, with no sign of an attack coming from anywhere. All that was left were their empty and lifeless bodies turned rigid as stone. But as far as he was aware, he remained untouched by whatever kind of sorcery was moving into their city, and from where he was standing, he and the rest of the survivors were all that kept the front gates closed to the armies outside.

Once he reached the end of the stairwell, he stood silently at what he beheld. In the cramped area lay the bodies of the four soldiers who had been stationed by the large lever and metal cogs leading to a rusted arm of iron that opened the gates. All those brave men lay on the floor around the contraption, their bodies just as husked as those above. The magic had spread, and now even those inside the walls were falling prey to it.

Teriul stepped over one of the corpses and examined the lever. It had not been moved. The gates were still closed. He let himself sigh. Of all the insanity around him, there was at least one thing still in place.

He cocked his head. Footsteps echoed down the stairs he had just taken. Several pairs.

Drawing his sword, he prepared for the worst, only to feel a sense of relief. Three Deeria soldiers, men under his command, stopped at the bottom of the steps.

Teriul lowered his blade. "How many survivors are left?" he asked.

"Not many, Commander," the man in the middle said, "and more are being taken by . . . whatever this is."

"Then what are you fools doing down here?" he barked. "Get back up there and find those who can still stand. We need to rally together." He sounded strong and confident, but deep down, he knew it was worth very little. He was afraid and confused just as much as the rest, but he wouldn't allow himself to show it.

The man on the left stepped forward. "Actually, sir," he said, "we are here to relieve you of your position. King's orders. He wants the front gates as guarded as possible."

Teriul looked at them, perplexed. He tightened his grip on his hilt. "King Tirehn said all this?"

"Yes, Commander."

"When?"

"Just now, sir."

That confirmed it for him. He thought something felt strange. Teriul pointed his sword toward them and took his stance. "Funny you should say that, because King Tirehn is at the palace. I saw him taken away myself, but you wouldn't have known that, would you?"

The three soldiers looked at each other, and their faces began to change drastically. They were empty of all emotion, becoming blank and pale. The men drew their weapons in unison.

"I'm only going to say this once," Teriul growled. "Put down your swords, or this will get—"

But even before he could complete his commands, they all

rushed at him, blades held high over their heads in a very untraditional form of attack. It was without any sense of logic. They charged at him, exposing themselves completely. Hardly the training any soldier would think highly of.

Teriul ducked as a blade swung over his head, bringing his own blade slicing across all three of their stomachs at once. It cut deep. Deep enough to kill any man in seconds. Yet despite their insides spilling from their open wounds, they still pursued him, unfazed by the lethal blow. As his body twisted, he felt the tip of one of the swords dig into his turned back, and he fell to his knees. The commander looked down and saw the same tip protruding through his chest, piercing his breastplate.

Coughing blood, Teriul looked up into the faces of his killers. Their eyes had turned completely white, just like those of the four dead soldiers lying on the floor. They were not themselves. They were not the men he had trained. They were their bodies, he was certain of that, but their minds were not their own, as if something else had them in a kind of trance. The soldier who had stabbed him released his grip on the sword, leaving it lodged in the commander's back. He limped toward the metal lever across the room, grasped it with both hands, and pulled it down with a loud screech. The other two soldier moved toward the cogs and began to turn them.

As soon as the sound of the gates reverberated outside and the gears spun on their own, all three soldiers collapsed to the ground, their bodies going limp. Just as with the others, their skin hardened like heated clay.

Teriul tried to move as he heard the massive doors creaking above, but it was no use. He toppled over to one side, watching as their final hope was dashed before him.

The gates were open, and their enemies were ready to enter in.

"HOLD YOUR GROUND!" Tirehn cried.

The soldiers stood fast as the gates groaned open, but the king knew that fear had taken them over. It had penetrated them all. Nearly all their men on the walls were either missing or dead, and he could only venture a guess as to why.

Gahlaia had not returned. That above all scared him. She, the strongest of them all, gone. The leader and rightful ruler of the Takahrn, no longer among those on the battlefield. "Eternal, let her still be alive . . ."

The gates slowly opened wider, and he grasped his sword and shield all the tighter. A few winged Takahrn, a little over fifty wingless ones, and a few hundred soldiers, all standing against several thousand waiting outside.

"*People of Deeria!*" he screamed, the words scratching his throat. "Stand with me now! Let us hold fast unafraid! Even when the bells of death ring at our door, may we face it and strike back!"

The gates ground to a halt.

"For your homes! For your families! The Eternal be our witness!"

In charged the Norvad and Verish soldiers. No lines of formation, just hordes of armed infantry running all at once, bringing down their wrath like the fangs of a lion upon its prey. They screamed in unison, drowning out the war cries of those final, daring individuals who were all that remained of the army of Deeria.

Tirehn had never felt a stronger rush adrenaline than he did then, and in those fleeting moments, fear was gone. All sense of pride, home, truth, family—all was pushed aside. There was only the blade in front of him and a hope that he would aim true lest he fall among his lost brethren.

But that was all it was: fleeting moments.

The sheer number of them, even in the confined space between the open city gates, overflowed and trampled over all. One soldier would be cut down only for three more to continue in his place. A never-ending stream compared to the king's forces, and they were quickly taken by its current.

Tirehn knocked a sword away with his golden shield and stuck the end of his blade as deep as it could go, only to be immediately taken by another soldier on his right, then his left. He felt metal cut between the plating on his arm, then his leg. He lost hold of his sword, and his shield was kicked from his hand. Crashing to his knees, he lifted his head to stare death in the face, but it never came. Instead, he was dragged to his feet, fists cracking over his jaw. The armor was stripped from his body, and the hilt of a sword struck his gut. Even being held up by his arm, he sagged to the ground as the blows grew in harsh succession. Only when he heard someone cry out in the distance did they cease their onslaught. The screaming and war cries came to a full stop, as if they were controlled by some outside force.

The battle was over almost as soon as it began.

They let go of his arm and shouted for him to get up. Despite the abuse, his legs still worked, albeit only just. His right leg limped. Heaving himself up, he peered through his bruised eyes. He could barely see.

A woman stood in front of him. Tirehn could see pointed ears, with golden hair curled behind them. He squinted, trying to get a clearer picture.

"Gwendall?" he said. "What have they done to you?"

"Done to me?" she asked. "They haven't done anything, save for showing me who I really am. More importantly, what have you done to your kingdom, Tirehn?"

"The Takahrn are innocent. You must understand. We are all being played. Rorgan . . . he's more than he appears. He's planned all of this to go this way. He's—"

Gwendall poked a finger into Tirehn's chest. "I know exactly who he is. He saved me from you!"

"*You know nothing!*"

The outburst took even her by surprise, and everything grew deathly quiet.

"Don't you understand?" he continued. "He's the one who has been using all of us as pawns in his game, and we have all been blind to it. He is Tarubas. He is the Faded Dragon!"

"Am I now?"

Out of the crowds of soldiers, Rorgan stepped into view on Gwendall's left, confidence emanating from him, his chin held high. "How convenient of you to throw such an accusation upon someone you're in conflict with," he said. "But if that were true, then would I not wish to take the throne for myself? Would I not desire to take your title and become king of all the sectors?"

He faced the armies, his arms outstretched. "Let it be known! I am not your king, and I never will be." Rorgan directed a finger toward Gwendall. "Here stands before you . . . an elf. One of the last of our time."

Upon being announced, she lifted a hand toward Tirehn's face. Under her armor, he saw something glow. Instantly, he felt something pull inside his chest. It was a pain he had never felt before. He fought against it, and he saw her strain under his resistance, but slowly, he was dragged to his knees.

The soldiers looked on in amazement and terror.

Rorgan continued. "She is the descendant of High Elf Tarkuv, the great ruler of Deerium from the first age! It is by the right of her lineage that I call for her to take the throne. Is it not her birthright?"

Murmurs of agreement and fear rustled through the crowd, followed by nods and gestures. The Verish and Norvad soldiers did not need convincing. Not much anyway, and they were the majority now. Deeria was theirs.

But among the whispering soldiers, a blade whizzed through the air, and the silence was broken. A Norvad infantryman leaped out of the clumped hordes, swinging his sword toward Rorgan's neck.

Gwendall, reacting with unnatural speed, grabbed the wrist of the soldier's sword hand, halting the blade inches from Rorgan's skin. He didn't even flinch, nor did the smile on his face falter.

Releasing her hold on Tirehn, Gwendall moved her Anamoris to the new attacker, and he also struggled against it. However, unlike the king, this man held his ground against the pull, and she strained harder. The sword fell from his hand, and before the eyes of them all, his form changed. The Norvad colors became those of Deeria, the physical features of a man shifted into those of a woman, and the Terrkoris mark appeared on her left cheek.

Ahmeras grunted as her true form revealed itself, but she still did not fall to her knees. She shook slightly, staring back at her adversary. "You are not my queen," she growled. "You'll never be anyone's queen."

Gwendall pushed harder, but her power failed to penetrate Ahmeras' soul. She was too weak now, and Tirehn could see the magic was slipping from her grasp.

But as Ahmeras resisted, the blunt end of an ax struck the back of her skull, and she collapsed to the ground.

Tirehn shouted in protest as the masses began to close in around her, but his mind went black as something hard smashed him into unconsciousness.

ARINAY GRASPED THE bars of her cell with both hands, listening intently to the noise far in the distance. The clanging of metal on metal had ceased, and the constant shouting of victory shot down into the dungeons. The united voices were so numerous it almost sounded like thunder.

A smile crept its way onto her face. Verish and Norvad had broken into the city, and it was likely they had already taken the king's forces into captivity. Her cell would soon be replaced with her enemies, as she had so strongly hoped.

"Lady Arinay."

The voice took her by complete surprise, and she leaped away from the bars to stumble onto the ground. It sounded close, yet there was no one there to speak.

Then, from the darkness beyond her cell door, a lone figure came into existence as if from nothing. His black hood was pulled back, revealing his pointed ears and dark hair. His grinning face was wounded, four half-healed gashes cutting horizontally. One of them went directly across his eyes and nose, yet the eyes themselves were still intact. In his left hand was a long scythe. In his right was a ring of keys—the keys to the cell doors.

Arinay stared at the elf with a sharp intake of breath, and he stared back at her. Even as his gaze remained in place, his fingers fumbled through the keys until they landed on a single one and placed it in the slot of her door.

"My apologies," he whispered. "I meant no disrespect. I'm only here to deliver a message."

She got to her feet and composed herself. "Well, what is this message?"

The lock clicked and the door squeaked open, the man stepping inside. His smile never wavered, and it only served to make her uncomfortable. He grasped the scythe in both hands, leaving the keys in the slot. "My liege wishes you his best and sincerest gratitude."

"Liege? And who would that be?"

"Do you not know him? No, perhaps not. Not really." He shrugged. "No matter. He sends his thanks for all you have done . . . and his honest farewell."

With that final statement, he flashed the blade of his weapon straight toward her, and before she could so much as scream, it was over. No final words. Any darting thoughts lasted mere seconds before they were silenced forever.

Doryan . . . Where are you? I can't see—

AHMERAS AWOKE SLOWLY, her vision blurred. Her head ached, and she could feel the dried blood in her hair. It was of little consequence compared to everything else. She lay motionless, letting it all sink in. It still didn't feel real.

Her eyes darted around, surveying the surroundings. She lay in the dark and damp dungeon below the palace. A few candles were lit, leaving the cell mostly dark. It smelled foul, and she held back a gag. Tirehn was nowhere to be seen. She prayed he was still alive. There was nothing else she could do but pray and hope. If he was still alive, it would likely not be for long. Not after the speech Rorgan had given.

Heaving herself up, she looked to the cell on her right. To her shock, there lay Arinay, or rather, her body. She was slumped against the wall, throat slit. Her dead eyes gawked up to the ceiling, unmoving. Ahmeras thought she could see a hint of regret in them. Regret, and maybe fear—an emotion that seemed to be infecting everyone today.

Ahmeras almost jumped when she noticed the cloaked man leaning against the wall near the stairs. He toyed with the blade of his scythe, running a finger over the blunt edge of the metal. His gaze remained on his weapon.

"Ah," the man began. "I see you're awake. Good." He let his hood fall back, and he ran a hand through his black hair that streamed down his shoulders. As he did, a pointed ear revealed itself, barely sticking out. "Lord Tarubas sends his regards."

Ahmeras' eyes widened in horror. She would recognize that face anywhere. "Draag?"

The name stung on her tongue. It was one she had not heard or spoken in years, not since she had mentioned it to Tirehn in those long conversations of their childhood. Those were her younger days that only he could know about. A life that she lived beyond the Great Sea. A life that she had longed to leave behind.

The figure appeared entertained by her terror. "You may call me Draag if you wish," he said.

Ahmeras stood and shuffled close to the bars. Her body ached and screamed at her. "Brother?"

Draag chuckled, low and gritty. "So, you know me, do you?"

The queen listened to the sound of his voice very carefully, and then, as quick as the shock had plastered on her face, it was gone. "No," she said. "You're not him. You're not Draag."

"Aren't I?"

"No, you're not. I above all would know a shapeshifter when I see one. You have his body, his features, but not his voice." She shakily lifted a finger. "How dare you take his form."

He chuckled again, shaking his head and sighing. "You see

much, Queen Ahmeras, but perhaps not as deeply as you believe. I am your brother, and yet I am not. This is his body, but not his mind. My mind . . . you might say has long been dormant."

"Cryptic," she replied. She wanted to say more, scream at him for defiling her brother in such a way, press further about his strange statements, but she just didn't have the strength. She felt exhausted, more so than ever before. Instead, she pointed to the cuts covering his features, trying to get out the words.

Seeing her gesture, he answered, waving a hand over his face. "A parting gift from one of your friends."

She pushed back from the bars. "Gahlaia . . ." she whispered.

"Correct."

Her eyes flitted back and forth across the floor, and she felt herself gain strength. "I saw my brother die. I was forced to watch as he was murdered by the Sirens. You have no right! *How dare you!*"

Ahmeras reached out from the bars with one arm, but her other one slipped, and she fell to the ground.

Draag smiled at her. "Ah, so you do remember."

He parted his cloak and lifted his shirt, revealing a large wound on his left side. It looked like a chunk of the muscles, even into the bone, had been completely removed. The scarred skin on its surface bore rows of teeth marks as if he had been attacked by a wild animal. By all definitions, it was a fatal wound, yet he appeared unaffected by the injury.

Ahmeras wasn't sure what to think anymore. It indeed was the bite mark, but she had never seen it healed. "But . . . I buried you. How are you—"

"Believe what you wish," he said abruptly. "I'm not here to reminisce."

"Then why are you here?"

"To ensure that you stay right where you are until preparations are complete."

"What preparations?"

"Why, preparations for your execution, of course."

WHEN TIREHN'S EYES opened, he was in another place entirely. He sat at a round marble table, leaning against the back of a wooden chair. The room was cramped and hardly lit. A lone candle sat on the table, serving as the single point of light. Sitting across the table, Rorgan stared intently at him. He wore the purple robes of Norvad, the same garments he had worn during the coronation ceremony and the wedding several months back. It felt like so long ago now.

"This is where it began," Rorgan said, looking around at the room. "This is where it all started for you and me."

The king refocused his gaze and began to come to grips with where they were. The whole place had a faint, metallic scent, and sure enough, piles of ashes were scattered across the edges of the floor. It was the room where his father had kept all his forbidden books and scrolls—the secret library that had burned before his coronation.

"Comfortable?" Rorgan asked.

Tirehn grunted. "It's hard to be comfortable when you've been beaten to a bloody pulp."

"Maybe so. All the same, I thought we could both benefit from this moment in time before all is said and done."

"If you wanted to be of benefit, then you would show me what you really are." He stared back through his bruised eyes, but he did not slink away. "Surely this is not your real form. You've been far too careful about that."

There was a pause. The air had never been more silent then it was now.

"Show me the Tarubas that I've heard so much about," Tirehn said. "Show me the Faded Dragon."

Rorgan sighed, and as the breath left his lungs, his form became enveloped by shadow, a twisted and murky darkness that billowed like a thick fog. It covered the candle's light until it blackened the whole room.

Tirehn could feel it—the Anamoris grabbing at him as it had with Gwendall. However, there was more to it than that. It may not have felt as strong as the pull from before, but it certainly felt more unnatural. Something about it wasn't right. The magic seemed skewed and pushed further than its limits demanded. He put a hand to his mouth, holding in a gag. A disgusting odor permeated the dark room, the smell of filth. Even the reek of carcasses that he had become acquainted with paled in comparison to this. It was the epitome of foul.

When the shadows cleared and the light of the candle came back into view, a new figure sat at the other side of the table. His clothing had changed to rags, barely fitting on his skeletal body. His cheeks were drained and thin like the rest of him, and two glowing, purple eyes gazed back at the king, flashes of red skimming their rims. His hair was silver and knotted in places, nearly reaching the ground.

When the being spoke, pointed teeth and sharp fangs glinted in the orange hue of the candlelight. They were pure white, a stark contrast to his exterior. "Satisfied?" Tarubas said in a dark tone. "Now then, I'm sure you have questions. Ask, and I will answer them to the best of my ability."

Tirehn continued. "Why? Why give me this opportunity? What do you have to gain?"

Tarubas lifted his slender arms and placed his hands on the table. His fingers curled into claws, not much different from a Takahrn's.

"As I said, we both benefit from this moment. If you wish, you may try to tell someone about our meeting, but who would believe you? If this morning's events told you anything, it's that none of them have any faith left in your views on anything, let alone anyone who could make a difference."

"But why do this at all? Why take this risk?"

A half smile curled on his left cheek. "It's no risk. Besides, I'm not completely heartless. I know of all the trouble you've gone to in uncovering my plans. It means everything to you, and I know the pain of not getting what you desire most. This will be your last day alive, Tirehn, and I wish you to leave knowing what it is you sought to find."

"And you? What do you get?"

Tarubas leaned closer in his chair. "No one knows who I am. Not really. Not yet. So much has happened that I wish for others to know. Perhaps I'm being childish, but at this point, that means very little. I want someone I can let it out to, and as a person on the verge of death, you make the perfect candidate. You are the only one who has ever come this far. To meet you face to face, that's an opportunity I wouldn't dare pass up."

"That's it?"

"That's it. Now ask your questions. We don't have as much time as I would have liked."

Another pause.

"Alright," Tirehn replied. "If you recall, there was a book that the Cleptyn advisor mentioned but forgot about a day later. He said the book mentioned you by the name the Forsaken. Why?"

"Ah. A loaded question, to be sure." Tarubas scratched his chin with the tip of a nail, as if gathering his thoughts for a response. "As dragons, we receive our titles based on our efforts, usually in battle. My title, the Faded Dragon, was given to me after the Great Dragon

War. My brother, Gahlorm, stole what was rightfully mine and left me to rot until I was needed again. Thus my name was bestowed on me: the warrior who had lost his relevance. When the war with the elves led to my defeat in battle, the Right—"

He stopped momentarily, almost choking on the words before continuing. "The Righteous Ones took me into captivity and did what they wanted with me, casting their spells, trying to learn how to contain our race. They brandished the name the Forsaken as if to mock me. And the dragons? They left me there. No one came looking for me. I was forced to use . . . unpleasant methods to free myself."

"So, you did kill the Righteous Ones."

"Of course I did. Those filthy wretches embodied everything wrong with the world. People think they're able to remove the blemishes from their souls, or maybe they cling to some savior who will wash it for them, but from my experience, nothing could be further from the truth. No actions, no god, and no magic can save you from the darkness. It is our nature to fall victim to the Shade. An inevitability, really."

Tirehn had heard those words before: the Shade. It was spoken of in old history books and writings from before even the elves walked the world. It was uttered only in hushed tones, especially among the Takahrn. Devils, monsters, and even the hatred of the soul—history ascribed them all to the Shade and its keeper, the Wrath Reaper.

"You use the Shade?" Tirehn asked.

Tarubas gestured to himself. "How do you think I became . . . this? Surely the question has crossed your mind as to why I haven't used my true form, burning everything down with the Devil's Flame."

He sighed, and the king thought he heard a tinge of sadness in his tone. The edges of red in his purple eyes grew until they consumed all of his gaze. Tirehn jumped in his chair as an image flashed in front of him. It looked translucent, like a thin mist that couldn't quite grasp hold of reality. It appeared as a face—the massive head of a beast of some kind. But in moments, the picture faded away completely, and the redness turned back to purple in Tarubas' eyes.

"You see?" he said. "It's because I can't. Everything has its price, and that is the toll the Shade required of me. For generations, I've worked in the shadows, forced to stay at the human level. It's been maddening, to say the least. The Devil's Flame requires Terrkoris and Anamoris, and the Shade took one of those from me."

"Terrkoris."

"Yes. The Shade enhanced my strength in one aspect but weakened it in another."

"And Gwendall? How does she play into all of this?"

Tarubas smiled at the mention of her name. "She is my last hope. She is everything to me. For too many years to count I have searched for one such as her, for the descendant of the High Elf. And when I finally found her, I soon found my life had its purpose returned. Everything hinged on her existence."

"Care to elaborate further?"

He leaned back. "You'll see soon enough. I think that's enough questions. The rest will fall into place for you before long."

"So, that's it then?" Tirehn said, frustrated. "You want everyone to live by your agenda or die by it? That's insane."

Tarubas stood up, the chair falling to the floor behind him. "You don't think I know that? I'm not here to exact revenge or to claim a just cause. There is no just cause! Don't you understand? I'm merely taking what I wish to take. All I ever wanted was to go home, but no one seems to care much for what I want, do they?"

He stopped himself, closing his eyes as if to regain his composure. He then let his previous smile return, his voice shifting from angry to playful in an instant. "Wasn't it your father who said it best? 'Truth is folly. Find an idea to stand upon and the people will follow. Proclaim sins to be acts of holiness, and they will stand by you.'"

Tirehn tried to stand and strangle him for using his father's dying words against him, but his body cried out in agony, and he slumped back in his seat with a grunt. "*Don't you dare speak those words to me!* You're the one who put those words in his head in the first place!"

Tarubas continued, ignoring the insults thrown his way. "I'm merely presenting my view of reality to the people, and they will follow me, Tirehn. They always have, and they always will."

Those words slipped into the king's ears, his mind starting to grow black. The candlelight flickered out, a final statement hanging at the edge of his consciousness.

"Hear my name in your dreams and know that this is my world. Hear my name and know that your fathers knew it all along. Hear my name, Tirehn, and hear it clearly."

Tarubas.

ELSEWHERE, DEEP WITHIN the farthest mountain of the Claw, farther north than the rest, a woman stared blankly at the wall of green mineral before her. It was made of pure emerald, glowing faintly in the darkness of the cave. Upon its surface, climbing hundreds of feet high, were symbols carved in a darker shade of green. The elvish words, every last one of them, covered the whole slab.

The Anamoris swirled around her like a parting sea, flowing into the surface of the wall, and directing itself into a single symbol. The moment the unseen force reached the specific word, the Terrkoris in the emerald reacted, and the two merged in a luminous dance. The symbol grew brighter than the rest, and the woman reached out and touched it with her index finger. Immediately, she withdrew her hand. An image flashed to her mind, following a stream of the Terrkoris racing down the mountain at lightning speed. It passed range after range through the snow until it left the Claw altogether, focusing on a single figure traveling along silently. His hands were firmly at his sides, and his hood was blown back in the wind. Under his cloak, she spotted a tail swishing back and forth at his heels, with sharp claws at the ends of the fingers sticking out of his sleeves. *Borhiim*, she thought.

Behind him, another man was desperately trying to keep pace with the Takahrn. A human from the looks of him. He kept his hood up, clutching his chest with one hand as if grasping at something. She couldn't tell what.

The magic released its grip on her, and the vision faded.

She stared at the symbol she had touched only seconds prior, reading it aloud to herself. "Devil's Flame." It had been a sign, and there was no mistaking its meaning. The Emerald Emblems were never wrong. The Seer had spoken, and in that moment, her spirits were lifted.

He's close, said a voice that was not her own, and as it rang out, six eyes flickered in her thoughts. *He needs a trail to follow.*

Tapping into the Anamoris as she had done before, she felt it grab at her soul. The magic hurt beyond measure, like a muscle too strained to function correctly. She held back the tears that hung in her eyelids. She needed it only briefly, then it could do the rest by itself. Outstretching a hand, she let the spiritual energy flow from her arm toward her target. It ran out of the cave and darted away. "Find him," she said aloud. "Find him and bring him to me."

Now all she could do was wait.

Chapter 26

Day thirty of the fifth month.

RAGGORIN LIFTED HIS hooded face to the sky. The sunset spread its orange glow over the clouds above. It had been just a few days since Norvad and Verish had taken Valia, and already the gates had been opened again to the public as if nothing had happened. Masses rumbled in from villages all over. He knew their numbers well enough to know it was no coincidence. They had been called for something: the crowning of a new king, or rather, a new queen.

Rorgan had been very clear in his open invitation to Cleptyn, and now they would join the people in celebration of the new peace. He scoffed. This wasn't peace. Not as it should be. Before long, the Takahrn would be put back under restraint, and all the sectors would conform once again to a false view of the world.

As he passed through the massive gates into the city, it became even more apparent to him how full the city was. It wasn't quite as bursting as during the coronation several months prior, but on such short notice, it was shocking to see so many. He smirked. It was the perfect cover.

A man hauling an old cart leaned close and whispered gruffly. "Are we the last ones?"

Raggorin nodded. "That we are. Rally anyone you can find and call them into position. When the people gather at the palace, come in a few at a time. We don't want to raise any suspicion. When the signal is given, you have my leave to attack."

"As you command, my Lord Gorrobin."

With that, the man departed into the crowd. Raggorin, however, had his own part to play.

TARUBAS SCROUNGED THROUGH his black bag, dumping a few of his old books on the wooden floor. The final manuscript to drop out, the last of four, looked small in both dimensions and page count compared to the others. It had no fanciful exterior like many other ancient texts, but rather was bound together very loosely. Notes and slips of paper stuck out from its sides like an old journal or notebook that had never been well kept. Its cover was a faded grey save for blotches of grime and dirt.

He snatched at it just as it hit the top of the small pile he had made and began to flip through its pages. It felt like sandpaper under his fingers, an almost nostalgic feeling at this point. On the very first page was the Anamoris symbol sketched into the center, with a familiar phrase written in elvish just below it.

"We rise as the pure. As one we hold to perfection. We stand as the Righteous Ones."

Tarubas grimaced as he sped through its contents, his head aching as he tried to remember where it was. He knew the spell was there, but his memory was growing hazy as of late. *Curse the Shade!* For all its advantages, it was finally starting to catch up to him—the consequences he had been warned of. But it didn't matter to him now. It couldn't. He was so close to finding a way back. An escape. If he could only last a little longer, then all his problems would melt away.

He stopped, his eyes fixed upon the page. There it was. *The unfinished spell.* Running his index finger across each inked symbol, he felt his mind slowly began to draw itself back from the brink. He smiled at the irony. After all their work to control and use the powers of the dragons for their own, after all their experiments, they had still fallen short. The Anamoris, even with the Righteous Ones' combined might, had not been enough, and it never would be. But for him, the very person they sought to consume . . . that was a far different story.

The Shade never fails to impress.

His door clicked open and closed with the slightest hint of a creak. Fuming, Tarubas spun around only for his fury to dissipate when he saw Draag standing before him, head bowed in reverence.

"My liege," he said, "all has gone as you said. I saw Zinnyah and Raggorin with my own eyes. Cleptyn and Gorrobin soldiers have entered the streets, disguised as merchants. If all goes as assumed, they could overwhelm the city by nightfall."

Tarubas grinned. "Excellent," he replied. "Everything is ready then."

"Ready for what exactly?"

"The finale."

ZINNYAH PUSHED OPEN the doors to the throne room with a grunt. When she last walked these long hallways and corridors, a new king had been crowned. Now that king had been overthrown. Time was either passing her by faster than she realized, or the world was changing at a faster rate. The table that used to sit at the center of the room was gone, and there were no guards as there once were. The only things keeping the place from being completely bare were the throne at the other side and the woman sitting in its seat.

Gwendall rose and strode over to meet the Cleptyn ruler. Her golden hair was braided and pulled back, revealing what looked to be elvish ears. She wore a simple dress, yet Zinnyah could not help but notice a very real change in her composure. It was as if the young woman she had seen before was gone, replaced by someone completely different. Physically, she appeared much stronger than months prior, and that seemed to give her a confidence she lacked previously.

"Ruler Zinnyah," Gwendall said, "Rorgan tells me of the letter you sent him. We are honored that you have accepted our invitation."

When Zinnyah bowed her head, she did so with a hint of uncertainty. "Lady Gwendall," she replied, "I have heard much of what has transpired, yet even standing here, I find it all hard to come to grips with. Are you . . . ?" She gestured to her, unsure of how to word her sentence.

Gwendall chuckled, waving a hand over herself. "Yes. These past months have been interesting, to say the least. I've gone through some . . . changes."

"But how?"

The doors behind them creaked open again. Rorgan stepped into the throne room, dressed in a dark purple robe, with a sword at his left hip. "She underwent an Awakening," he interjected. "We uncovered an Anamoris symbol that had not been completely wiped from her bloodline."

Zinnyah faced him as he strode to Gwendall's side. "So, she really is High Elf Tarkuv's descendant?"

"She is indeed. Without a doubt."

"Rorgan," Gwendall said, "is everything ready for tonight?"

"It is, my lady."

She turned back toward the Cleptyn ruler and bowed. "Apologies, Ruler Zinnyah. I wish we had more time to explain the details of what has ensued, but I must get ready."

"It's alright. I'll see you at the execution and your coronation, of course."

Their final words given, all three of them exited the room, Zinnyah pacing her way down to the first level of the palace. She then moved into another long, empty corridor, narrower than the last. It was lit by only a couple of torches hanging from the wall, leaving patches of blackness between their reach.

At the hallway's end, staring out of a lone window, was a cloaked man, dressed in dark grey. His hood covered most of his face, but she didn't need to see him to know his identity. At his hip was a sheathed broadsword, a large elvish blade resting in the corner.

"Raggorin," Zinnyah whispered, "is everyone in?"

He nodded, leaving his eyes fixed on the streets beyond the glass. "All is as you instructed, Ruler Zinnyah."

"Perfect. How're the dungeons?"

"Filled to the brim with Deeria soldiers, all ready to fight when they get the okay. However, Tirehn and Ahmeras are not in the same prisons. They were both moved into separate holdings, guarded without any possible access. We won't be able to contact them until the execution. Not unless we want to reveal ourselves."

"That poses a problem. We'll need to bribe the executioner."

He gestured to the sword in the corner and flashed a half smile. "I can do you one better, my lady. As of an hour ago, I am the executioner."

She returned his smile and nodded. "Well done. The Lord Gorrobin title suits you well."

THE DAY WAS quickly coming to its end. The sun had finally dropped under the horizon, and the sky in turn began to shade itself into darkness. On a normal day, the clouds would be the only things blocking the stars from illuminating the world, but not tonight. Torches were lit in the darkness, obscuring the starlight, and whispers began to stir as soldiers and townsfolk gathered at the palace.

Tirehn blinked hard as the blindfold was removed from his face, the light of the nearby flames overwhelming his pupils. Screams and shouts rang in his ears as everything came into view.

He was standing on the main balcony of his palace above crowds of people just like when he was crowned king. It was almost poetic, being praised and adored one moment only to be ridiculed now. Masses upon masses flooded the city streets below, many of them recognizable as Verish and Norvad soldiers. Others, however, appeared as simple folk of Deeria. The very people he had sought to protect and aid, now turning their backs on him. But he could see fear in some of their eyes. They were desperate and afraid, and he could hardly blame them. With swords at their backs, few would act differently.

Just below, staring up at him with a stern expression, he spotted Zinnyah among the people. She was dressed in her green and silver armor. Rarely was she ever seen without it, and tonight was no exception.

To his right, Ahmeras also had her blindfold removed. "Thank the Eternal, you're alive, Tirehn," she said, her words nearly drowned out by the noise.

"Did they hurt you?" he asked.

"Of course they did, but it's nothing I haven't borne before." She turned her head. "Tirehn . . . My brother. I saw him."

The king's mouth hung open for a moment before he could reply. "You mean Draag? How? You said he was dead."

"He was . . . or is. I don't know how, but I saw him. It was his body, that much was clear, but someone else is controlling him. He said . . . He says he killed Gahlaia."

Tirehn's heart dropped. The realization of their situation hit him like a sprinting horse. There really was no way out. There really was no way of saving the Takahrn, at least not for him. Looking down over the railing, he watched as his fears came to pass. He had always wondered if the people would grow to hate him, and now he had his answer. They were blind, and only now could he see that he would never be the one to free them.

Behind him, Gwendall entered through the glass door onto the balcony, Rorgan just behind her. She wore a golden dress with etchings of white on the sleeves and strokes of green and purple along the skirt's edge. As she lifted her hand in a fist, the people fell silent. All hushed murmurs died out, and she raised her voice to speak.

"People of Deerium!" she said, stretching her arms toward Tirehn and Ahmeras. "Before you stand your king and queen. The very same people who have led you to where you are now. Their crimes are many, but most of all, they have spread lies about your rulers to cover up their alliance with those who would destroy us all: the Dividers."

The shouts of anger and protest grew until they were near deafening.

Gwendall waited for the noise to die down before continuing. "Are these the ones you wish to rule? These murderers? These liars?"

More outcries.

"Then, by the will of the people, may we end this insanity here and now."

Tirehn was the first to be dragged to his knees. A large soldier cloaked and hooded in dark grey walked into his view, unsheathing a large broadsword. The blade was lowered to rest lightly on the back of his neck, and his gaze turned to Ahmeras. Her eyes met his. He had never seen such stark terror plastered on her so firmly. She jumped toward the armed man, but three soldiers grabbed her from behind, holding her in place. She scrambled and struggled with all her might, the men's feet dragging across the floor, but it was to little avail. She could only watch.

"I'm sorry..." Tirehn whispered. He wished to say so much more, but the words stuck in his throat as the blade overhead sent shivers down his spine. He felt the sword lift, and the king looked up into the face of the executioner in shock and bewilderment.

Standing over him, holding the broadsword high in the air, Raggorin smiled down at him. He nodded to the king, and with a flashing movement, directed his swing sideways, striking down one of the three soldiers standing next to him. He let the blade rest in the body of his victim and cast aside his cloak, pulling another broadsword from his back, an elvish one, and then rushing at the oncoming soldiers.

Screams echoed from the crowds below, and everyone was thrown into a state of panic. Norvad and Verish soldiers fell into ranks, and civilians spread out in all directions. Tirehn watched in disbelief as groups of citizens and merchants pulled off clothing, revealing Cleptyn armor. They unsheathed swords, plunging them into the unsuspecting enemy.

The two men holding Ahmeras immediately released their grips on her, joining Raggorin in his attack. Both she and the king turned, watching as the scene unfolded before them.

Gwendall and Rorgan appeared taken aback by all that transpired, inching closer to the glass door behind them. She stretched out her hands as if to reach with the Anamoris, but their opponents did not slow down.

"What's wrong?" Rorgan said, putting an arm in front of her.

"They're too strong," she replied, teeth gritted. "Their souls feel . . . stronger than most, and their numbers are too large."

Tirehn looked at the men plowing through the soldiers. They had removed their garments, showing their clothing underneath. It matched Raggorin's, most of their bare chests being shown. They were Gorrobin warriors.

"Then we need to leave," Rorgan said, pushing Gwendall through the door and following her.

Two soldiers rushed out from the palace, joining the battle taking place on the balcony. Ahmeras grabbed two blades from the corpses of some Norvad men and tossed one to Tirehn. Without hesitation, they joined the clash, cutting down any enemy in their path. Before long, the balcony was clear, and Raggorin directed his men through the door in pursuit of Rorgan and Gwendall.

"Raggorin," Tirehn said, "I've never been so happy to see you."

He turned and grasped the king's hand in his. "The feeling is mutual, my lord. I'm glad you're still among the living, but I'm afraid we don't have much time. Zinnyah has joined our cause. We need to take Gwendall and Rorgan into custody, or this was all for nothing."

But before Raggorin could leave to join his men, Tirehn grabbed his arm. "Not Rorgan. He can't be allowed to live. Raggorin, Rorgan is the Faded Dragon. He's Tarubas."

Ragorrin stared at him with his eyes squinted and mouth agape, cocking his head. "Rorgan . . . Are you certain of this?"

"He revealed as much to me. I've seen it with my own eyes. If we don't kill him, then everything that we've gone through could just repeat itself."

But as Raggorin turned to run into the palace, Tirehn pulled him back. "Wait," he said. "There's something I need you to do. Take

Ahmeras and get her out of here."

"What?" Ahmeras exclaimed. "I'm not going anywhere!"

Tirehn ignored her. "You remember the passageway under the palace? The tunnel?"

Raggorin nodded.

"Take her. Please, Raggorin. She must live. I beg you."

"*I won't leave you!*" Ahmeras screamed.

"What will you do?" Raggorin asked Tirehn, worry crossing his face.

"I'll meet with Zinnyah, and we'll take Tarubas down for good. Join us when you're done. Please . . . Will you do this?"

Raggorin paused only for a second, then slowly nodded. He stepped toward Ahmeras, and though she struggled, she was too weak to put up much resistance.

"Tirehn," she said through her tears, "don't do this. You can't make me leave you!"

The king put a hand to his queen's cheek. "Listen to me. If what you said about your brother is true, you need to go back there. Go west. Find the Siren Isles. You have to."

He leaned in and kissed her. "I love you, Ahmeras," he whispered. "Don't ever forget that."

Then he strode away, her screams echoing in his head.

Rorgan directed Gwendall farther into the palace, escorted by several soldiers. He drew a sword from his side, darting his gaze back and forth as they passed through the corridors.

A Norvad commander met them, giving a quick bow. "My lord," he said, "our forces were taken by complete surprise. The streets have been overrun, and many in the chain of command have been captured or killed on sight. The Deeria soldiers have been freed, and we risk an ambush from below. I fear the palace will be taken within the hour."

"Bar the gates," Rorgan demanded. "No one leaves the palace, and no one comes in. Send any remaining men you have down the corridors. The enemy is just behind us."

"As you command!"

With that, Rorgan pulled Gwendall down the hall until they reached the throne room. The soldiers moved in front, opened the doors, and shut them in. Rorgan fished into his pocket and pulled out a key, locking the entryway and then barring it with a beam that had been resting in a corner.

Gwendall shook her head. He could feel her emotions emanating from her like a terrible stench. The uncertainty and fear that she had worked so hard to cover with her newfound confidence were now returning to the surface, but it was too late for that. The time had come. Her arms started to shake at her sides, and she cursed under her breath, squeezing her fists until her knuckles turned pale.

"Rorgan . . ." she said, her voice choked. "I'm so sorry. I couldn't do it. I know I could before, but these people aren't like the rest. They're—" She stopped, the tears swelling in her eyes.

He spun away from the doors and faced her. *This is it*, he thought. *This is the final step.* His heart pounded in his chest faster and faster. This was the moment. His moment.

Rorgan stared into her eyes and grabbed her shaking arms, his touch soft and warm. "Don't be sorry," he said with a comforting smile. "You have nothing to be sorry for. None of this is your fault. I was the one who allowed the front gates to be opened to the public, and I'm the one who trusted Zinnyah. You are not at fault here."

A small tear slid down her cheek, and Rorgan reached up to wipe it with his thumb. "No matter what happens, know that you are my queen. You are everything to me. You always have been."

He placed his palm to her cheek, and her head tilted toward it. She raised her hand and placed it over his. She was reciprocating. His heart pounded harder.

There was a loud bang on the doors behind them. *Not yet. I'm so close!*

"How long have we known each other?" he continued. "Surely you know how much I care for you."

"I know," she murmured.

Another bang on the door, this time louder. The wooden boards cracked under the pressure. They ignored it, keeping their gazes on each other.

"Gwendall," he muttered, taking a long pause. *This is it. This is it!* "I . . . I love you."

Time seemed to freeze as the moment of truth came to its climax. *This is it!*

Gwendall lowered her head, closing her eyes. A smile came across her face as if all the chaos surrounding them had vanished. Then steadily, she gave her reply.

"I love you too."

Rorgan let a sinister grin stretch across his face, and just seconds after the answer had passed her lips, he pulled away from her. He muttered the draconic words under his breath and felt the Anamoris swirl around him like a tornado. The Shade overwhelmed his body, and as he opened both hands toward Gwendall, the twisted magic directed itself toward her. He could feel her struggling against the unnatural pain, but it was no use. He gripped her chest with the magic so firmly that she could barely breathe. Her arms spread to her sides, and her body slowly began to lift from the ground. Her face looked both confused and heartbroken as her body twitched with visible agony.

The wooden bar finally gave way, snapping in two. The doors swung open with a screech, groups of Gorrobin soldiers standing in the frame. Rorgan ignored them. The spell had already begun, and there was nothing they could do to stop it. She had finally given herself fully to him. He could take complete advantage of her soul and the incredible power that lay within it.

Tirehn and Zinnyah ran into the room, along with several Gorrobin warriors. They stopped as they saw what was taking place, the Anamoris quickly spreading through the throne room. The air spun around Rorgan and Gwendall like a tornado. Under her dress, her Anamoris mark began to glow, and a thick mist appeared before it, feeding off its spiritual energy.

Rorgan closed his eyes as the mist pulled the glow from her, passing it to him. He absorbed the energy, feeling its power meld with his own. It was working. The unfinished spell was now complete, thanks to the Shade's added strength. He could feel everything in the room, as if he had eyes everywhere.

One of the Gorrobin soldiers ran past Tirehn to attack, but it was like pressing against a wall. The tornado of air and magic kept them apart, the soldier unable to get anywhere near Rorgan or Gwendall.

"What is this?" Tirehn exclaimed. "What's happening?"

Rorgan smiled at hearing the king's voice, but his focus remained on Gwendall and the spell that held her in place. Soon, the glow from her mark faded, and he could feel the Anamoris had completely drained from her. His form began to change as the swirl of magic and Shade reached its pinnacle. His hair shifted into its long silver form, and even his purple robe faded away, replaced by an old and filthy garb. He grew taller, and his nails lengthened into long claws on his hands. He smiled, and the teeth underneath his lips became pointed like a beast's. He felt his eyes turn a glowing purple, red running to and fro near their rims.

He still couldn't change into his draconic form, but that didn't stop the rush of exhilaration that flowed through him. This was who he was—Tarubas, The Faded Dragon, and now all those before him knew it.

Gwendall, her body still frozen in the air, looked down at him. "Rorgan?" she uttered through a scratchy throat. "What are you—"

"I'm sorry, my dear," he said in a completely different voice, "but this is beyond you. Take heart. You will live on within me, or rather, your spirit will."

Her head bent backward, and she screamed as the pain became too much. Shifting into a stone-like material, her exterior began to crack. Her shrieks died out as her body crumbled to a fine powder. Her clothes fell to the ground—nothing left but a pile of dust.

Tarubas turned to face Tirehn, Zinnyah, and the Gorrobin soldiers. The tornado wall finally dissipated, and despite his skeletal appearance, he had never felt so alive. Never had he felt a surge of magic as he did now, and it was growing by the second. Combined with his own Anamoris abilities, he began to sense every soul in the vicinity, stretching down the corridors.

"What have you done?" Zinnyah said, grasping her blade all the tighter, taking a ready position.

"What I must," he replied, the grin never leaving his face. "I suppose I should be grateful. Without you, perhaps Gwendall would have never been as willing as she was. As vulnerable. As exploitable." He snickered. "Ah, but I think that's enough of that for now. I would ask you to surrender, but I know it would fall on deaf ears. Besides, you're far too dangerous to leave alive."

Tirehn and Zinnyah both lurched as if to charge at him, but their bodies remained fastened where they were. He had them in his grip, and now that he had what he wanted, he was going to enjoy it.

EVERYTHING AROUND TIREHN seemed to shake, save for Tarubas. He cocked his head in a discomforting fashion, and everything vibrated around him. Images flickered to life. Images of a dragon, slithering around the room like smoke. They flared in and out, fueling the king's dazed vision. He turned his head and saw that Zinnyah was also stuck fast, but the Gorrobin soldiers were not.

Before Zinnyah could raise her voice, a blade dug into her chest. The warriors' faces were completely emotionless, one of them holding the sword that had pierced her. The soldier pulled the weapon from her, and the men moved to Tarubas' side.

"You see," he said grimly, "everything is mine now. Everything and everyone."

Zinnyah fell to her knees, dropping her sword. She clutched the wound with both hands, choking as she tried to speak her last words. They never came. Tirehn tried to cry out, but the words never left his lungs. He could do nothing. He could only watch as everything was slowly and painfully stripped away from him.

Tarubas stared as she fell to the ground dead, blood dripping to the floor. "Clean that up," he said, and without question, the men obeyed.

His eyes finally set on Tirehn, and the king felt his head pulsate. He could feel his limbs start to move again, and he staggered back as if he were being pushed out of the room. He clasped his blade as tight as he could, but no matter how hard he tried to move forward, he could only go backward.

Tarubas opened his mouth as if to speak, but the words did not reach Tirehn's ears. The voice was in his head, booming and drowning out everything else.

WHO AM I, TIREHN? WHO AM I? I AM YOUR GOD! YOU ARE MINE! ONLY MINE!

Before he knew it, Tirehn had backed himself down the corridor and out the glass doors, inching closer to the balcony railing. Tarubas followed him.

No! the king cried in his mind. *This is not how I die! I won't!*

The heel of his left foot hit the bottom of the railing, and he finally felt himself pushing back against the force that held him. He lifted his arms, pointing his sword toward the enemy before him. This was how he would end it: fighting for what believed. For what he called home. For the Eternal, Ahmeras . . . everyone.

Tarubas halted momentarily, looking genuinely impressed. *Very well, King Tirehn*, came his response. *Die on your feet then.*

But just as Tirehn prepared to come to blows, he felt a sharp pain blaze in his innards. He dropped his weapon, and looking down, saw that a blade had pierced his back, protruding through his stomach. It was a scythe blade.

His eyes turned to his right. A hooded man was standing behind him, his face peeking over the king's shoulder. His hair was black, and four scars crossed his face.

"Don't you see?" he muttered in Tirehn's ear. "You die on our terms. You will fall, just as Gahlaia did."

Gahlaia! All became clear to him. This was Draag, or whoever was controlling his corpse. But even as that thought came to him, it started to wither. His breaths grew erratic, and he could feel the blood in his throat as a hand pressed his body deeper into the scythe's edge. His life was fading. As Tirehn's vision dimmed, he could see Tarubas laughing, the sound ringing in his skull. This truly was his end. He had lost. He had failed them all.

But as he shut his eyelids, one last surge, one final lingering bit of strength, rushed forth. He clasped the hand that lay on him in an iron grip and succumbed to the force that had previously been pushing him back.

With a heave, both he and Draag fell from the railing toward the ground below.

Through it all, Tirehn's eyes remained closed. He wasn't sure how he felt at that moment, and it only lasted a few seconds. Tarubas' voice was gone, and his head was clear. A prayer came into his mind, but the words played so fast in his head that he scarcely understood them. But they were for him and his Maker alone. And as a searing agony crushed his body, his thoughts drifted away.

All went dark.

AHMERAS WAS BARELY conscious, slumped on the horse with Raggorin just behind her, driving the mount eastward. The walls of Valia were steadily vanishing from sight, and soon they were in green pastures. Slowly, she turned her head to look up at Raggorin and was surprised to see tears streaming down his face.

"You should have left me," she said.

He wiped the tears from his face with his forearm. "I couldn't . . . King Tirehn wanted you safe. No one else could get you to safety. Not in the chaos of battle."

"But your men. You left them."

Raggorin kept his gaze straight ahead and more tears replaced the ones that he had wiped away. "You meant more to him than any of us, Ahmeras. He needed you to be safe."

She shuddered. "You speak as if he's dead." But even as the words left her lips, part of her knew. She knew Raggorin had felt it too—the immense pressure of distorted magic that surrounded the capital. The city was lost.

Now tears flooded her eyes, and they burned. "But... your men."

"*I know, curse everything, I know!*" Raggorin yelled, whipping the reins harder.

Ahmeras was taken aback. She had never heard him shout like that. He was always so composed, which meant that it all cut deeper than he let on. She could see it now. He was struggling with the decision much more than she was. He had left his soldiers to die alone, or worse.

"This is what Tirehn wanted," he said, barely over the sound of galloping hooves.

Ahmeras finally broke. She let it all out, the tears, the cries, all of it. She hardly noticed that Raggorin was there. For all she cared, she could have been floating in a void of darkness, with nothing but her thoughts to keep her company.

But when the world around her became clear again, she no longer felt sorrow. Even the physical pain her body was in paled in comparison to the single thought that drowned the rest.

Revenge. I want revenge.

Groaning with discomfort, Ahmeras pulled herself up on the steed and stared out into the grasslands. "I know where we need to go," she said. "Just follow my directions."

SEVERAL HOURS HAD passed, and below the palace balcony, Draag's eyes regained their focus. He lifted his head, and his broken bones twisted back into position all on their own. There was no blood. All his wounds sealed themselves instantly.

He stood up, staring at the king's body. Tarubas' voice in his head shrieked in command, but he tried his best to ignore it. He stared into the sky and lifted his left arm, stretching his fingers wide. He could feel his power across the vast landscapes of the world, even if only faintly. Deep in the southeast, however, he found what he sought. Anahka's mother, the last true dragon left in Deerium, was soaring through the skies. He could feel her muscles rippling under her wings, the swishing of her tail, and the smoke from her nostrils.

Long had he watched her, and soon, very soon, his observations would pay off. Tarubas may have gotten his finale, but Draag's was still to come. He knew it well and could scarcely wait for that day to come.

The Vessel of Reaping is nearly complete.

Pulling the scythe from Tirehn's limp body, Draag turned back toward the palace.

FAR TO THE northeast, the storm swirled through the night, completely ignorant of the events in Deeria. Borhiim trudged on through the deepening snow. He had discarded his cloak long ago and given it to Jerin. He had no need for it. The flame within him gave him all the warmth he needed.

He wasn't entirely sure where in the Claw he was, but he knew he was getting close, very close, to where he needed to be. Just as his dreams had drawn him to take the journey before him, he felt something tow him toward his destination. Like a rope tied to a tree, he was grabbing the other end, following its trail. It was Anamoris in its nature and pull.

Under his feet, he could feel the Terrkoris in the area. Before, he could lightly survey a landscape with the touch of his hand, but now it felt skewed. Not due to lack of the physical magic. Quite the opposite. It was overflowing from the land, multiple streams crisscrossing one another. When he would get the sense of one direction, he would be drawn into another, and all led to more confusion than it was worth.

He was left with only the spiritual element, trusting that its path led him true.

At his side, Jerin tramped on. He was wrapped in both cloaks but still shivering in the cold.

"You shouldn't have come!" Borhiim shouted over the howling wind. "You should have gone back!"

"T-too late . . . now," came the reply.

Another blast of wind and snow blinded Borhiim, but he pushed himself forward as best he could. However, when he could see again, Jerin was not at his side. "*Jerin?*"

No answer.

Without giving it a second thought, he turned around and went back. Sure enough, face first in the snow, Jerin had reached his limit. The cold had won its small victory, just as it did with any unsuspecting travelers.

Borhiim knelt and heaved him over his shoulder. He was ice cold, pale, and barely breathing. He didn't have long, and there was nothing the Takahrn could do for him. He was no healer, and was far from anything warm. All he could do was watch as yet another life flitted away.

Am I cursed? Is this how my life is always going to be?

He lifted his gaze and looked back the way he had come. He felt a tug. The slightest strain of the Anamoris. Whatever was drawing him in, it was moving. Or perhaps it had begun its movement earlier, and he only now realized it. Borhiim wasn't sure.

Out of the fog, stepping clearly into view, a woman approached them. She was tall. Very tall. Her face and limbs were incredibly slender, drained of nourishment and life. Her hair was of a peculiar style. It was cut short and curled on the right side, while the left was long and straight.

That was what gave it away over everything else. The face looked familiar, but it was lacking the strong features it once had. She looked weak, which was not a word he would have ever used to describe her before. Even in the visions, she had appeared as she did all those years ago as if nothing had changed. Now, Borhiim could see that time had not been kind. Not to her.

As their eyes met, he tried to utter something. Any sentence or phrase appropriate for such a shocking reunion. But there was only one word that graced his lips, turning itself into a question.

"Mother?"

Epilogue

"**B**ACK IN YOUR cells!" one of the slave traders shouted, pointing a spear.

The group of Takahrn inched slowly into the barred area, and two armed men shut the metal door before them, latching it shut.

The Takharn couldn't remember what day it was, and frankly, it mattered very little. Every day was the same. Wake up, impress the buyers, eat, sleep, repeat. For years it had been that way. Such was the life of a Takahrn in this day and age. Rumors of the king abolishing slavery had spread fast, but they turned out to be just that—rumors. No one was going to save them. Not now. Not ever. It was best to just accept the way things were, lest they fall into the madness that had already clung to so many of them.

They listened as the two men murmured and joked with each other.

"It's nights like these that I wish we could find better jobs," one said.

"Perhaps," said the other, "but what can you do? Sellswords is what we are, and outside of the slave trade, there's not much sellswording to be done."

"I know that, but still, why did they have to put us on the night watch? I'm not much of a night person myself, and I just wish that—"

"Quiet," the second one said, gripping his spear with both hands. "I thought I heard something."

They both froze, listening for anything that would cause alarm.

Nothing came.

The first man relaxed, slapping the other on the shoulder. "Don't scare me like that! It's not funny, you know."

"I wasn't joking around! I swear, I thought I heard something."

"Yeah, like the rustling of a bird, or the scampering of a rabbit. Ooh, or maybe the shrill outcries of a ghost."

The second man punched the first in the side, growling. "Don't you make fun of me! I was being serious!"

But just as the first prepared to make another sarcastic reply, a twig snapped in the clump of trees to their left. It was loud and quick, startling them both.

They clasped their weapons once again, going silent. "Who's there?" one of them called.

They were answered by yet another snap, closer this time. Pointing their spears toward the vegetation, they began to shake with fear.

The Takahrn looked on from their cage, watching with piqued curiosity.

A figure bolted out of the trees, outstretching claws toward them. It was too fast for anyone to get a good look at it, especially in the darkness of the night. The men thrust their spears forward to meet it, but the creature leaped over the attack, its whole body slamming them to the ground. They both looked up into the face of a woman, her long hair falling to the ground as she bent down toward her prey.

"Please," one of them begged. "We don't mean any harm."

"Of course you do," she responded. "You mean to harm everything and everyone around you. Ridding the world of people like you would be a blessing."

They raised their voices to plead with her, but even as the words left their mouths, she moved her claws to their neck and slit their throats.

She stood up, leaving them to gurgle and choke their final moments out.

The Takahrn backed away from the cage door as she moved toward it and gripped the latch with her claws. With a screech, her talons ripped through the metal as if it were made of paper, and the door swung open.

Even in the darkness, they could see horns sticking out from the top of her head and a tail flitting between her legs. She was winged, but her left one was severed at the root, leaving nothing but a stub of muscle and skin.

She gave the elvish salute to them and spoke in a firm voice. "My name is Gahlaia, daughter of Gahlorm, Dragon King of the Drake, and Meriss, Queen of the New World. If you wish to live, then come with me."

To be continued . . .

Acknowledgements

Firstly, I would like to thank my family for sticking by me this entire time. I have been "writing books" since I was little (though many of those were mostly pictures with two words on each page), and my attempts at writing something seriously in the past have been . . . interesting to say the least. I am sure many of you doubted that I would ever finish this work and publish it. But you guys have continued to support me in my endeavors, and for that, I am extremely grateful. Thanks, Dad, for being an avid reader while also providing honest feedback. Thanks, Mom, for all the sweet things you've said in support and in reading this book. Thank you, Mema Peggy, for introducing me to my consultant, Jenne, as well as drilling so much literature into me growing up (so . . . so much literature). Thank you, Papa Bob, for reading my book and being supportive and giving great feedback through all the drafts, even though you don't typically read fantasy. Thanks, of course, to my three siblings who have, even while waiting to read this until it was published, still expressed much excitement. That really gave me confidence to push through.

I huge thank you to my consultant, Jenne Acevedo, who also set me up with my incredible editor and proofreader: Robin Larin and Valerie (I never got your last name, but you did an excellent job regardless). Thanks to Felix Ortiz for the awesome cover design. I couldn't have thought of a better look for my debut. I also want to thank the people who read my book or portions of it while giving me honest feedback. It was well needed. I especially want to give a shout out to Ashley Hayes. From one writer to another, it means a lot that you enjoyed my work.

Lastly, I want to thank God for giving me this opportunity. Without Him, this would have fallen apart years ago. I owe everything to Him, including my life.

About the Author

Cameron Michaels is an epic fantasy author, currently residing in Mesa, Arizona. Homeschooled and growing up reading the Chronicles of Narnia, Cameron has always dreamed of other worlds that he desperately wanted to put to page

When he's not writing, Cameron enjoys watching people play Dungeons and Dragons, anime, podcasting, and, of course, reading fantasy. He loves his native state, but deep down, he is always dreaming of the next time he can visit the cabin his family has in the New Mexico mountains, where he can read and feel close to nature in peace.

For more on Cameron Michaels, visit his website, Instagram account, or YouTube channel to stay up to date:

www.cameronigmichaels.com
instagram.com/cameronigmichaels